EARTH UNAWARE

By Orson Scott Card from Tom Doherty Associates

Empire
The Folk of the Fringe
Future on Fire (editor)
Future on Ice (editor)
Invasive Procedures (with
    Aaron Johnston)
Keeper of Dreams
Lovelock (with Kathryn Kidd)
*Maps in a Mirror: The Short
    Fiction of Orson Scott Card*
*Orson Scott Card's InterGalactic
    Medicine Show*
*Pastwatch: The Redemption of
    Christopher Columbus*
Saints
Songmaster
Treason
A War of Gifts
The Worthing Saga
Wyrms

THE TALES OF ALVIN MAKER

Seventh Son
Red Prophet
Prentice Alvin
Alvin Journeyman
Heartfire
The Crystal City

ENDER

Ender's Game
Ender's Shadow
Shadows in Flight
Shadow of the Hegemon
Shadow Puppets
Shadow of the Giant
Speaker for the Dead
Xenocide
Children of the Mind
First Meetings
Ender in Exile

HOMECOMING

The Memory of Earth
The Call of Earth
The Ships of Earth
Earthfall
Earthborn

WOMEN OF GENESIS

Sarah
Rebekah
Rachel & Leah

From Other Publishers

Enchantment
Homebody
Lost Boys
Magic Street
Stone Father

Stone Tables
Treasure Box
*How to Write Science Fiction and
    Fantasy*
Characters and Viewpoint

EARTH UNAWARE

THE FIRST FORMIC WAR
Volume One of the Formic Wars

Orson Scott Card
and Aaron Johnston

TOR®

A TOM DOHERTY ASSOCIATES BOOK
NEW YORK

EARTH UNAWARE

A Tor Book
Published by Tom Doherty Associates, LLC
175 Fifth Avenue
New York, NY 10010

www.tor-forge.com

Tor® is a registered trademark of Tom Doherty Associates, LLC.

ISBN 978-0-7653-2904-2 (hardcover)
ISBN 978-1-4299-4656-8 (e-book)

First Edition: July 2012

Printed in the United States of America

0 9 8 7 6 5 4 3 2 1

To Eric Smith,
for silly accents, grisly deaths, and spontaneous musicals.
On stage you are a thousand characters,
but off it, the most constant of friends.

CONTENTS

EARTH UNAWARE

CHAPTER 1

Victor

Victor didn't go to the airlock to see Alejandra leave the family forever, to marry into the Italian clan. He didn't trust himself to say good-bye to his best friend, not without revealing how close he had come to disgracing the family by falling in love with someone in his own asteroid-mining ship.

The Italians were a four-ship operation, and their lead ship, a behemoth of a digger named Vesuvio, had been attached to El Cavador for a week, as the families traded goods and information. Victor liked the Italians. The men sang; the women laughed often; and the food was like nothing he had ever eaten, with colorful spices and creamy sauces and oddly shaped pasta noodles. Victor's own invention, an HVAC booster that could increase the central heating temperature on the Italians' ships by as much as eleven degrees, had been an immediate hit with the Italians. "Now we will all wear one sweater instead of three!" one of the Italian miners had said, to huge laughter and thunderous applause. The Italians had been so smitten with Victor's booster, in fact, that it had brought in more trade goods and prestige than anything else the family had offered. So when Concepción called Victor in to talk to him just before the Italians decoupled, he assumed she was going to commend him.

"Close the door, Victor," said Concepción.

Victor did so.

The captain's office was a small space adjacent to the helm. Concepción rarely closed herself in here, preferring instead to be out with the crew, matching or surpassing them in the amount of labor they put in each day. She was in her early seventies, but she had the energy and command of someone half her age.

"Alejandra is going with the Italians, Victor."

Victor blinked, sure that he had misheard.

"She's leaving from the airlock in ten minutes. We debated whether it was wise to even tell you beforehand and allow you two to say good-bye to each other, thinking perhaps that it might be easier for you to find out afterward. But I don't think I could ever forgive myself for that, and I doubt you'd forgive me either."

Victor's first thought was that Concepción was telling him this because Alejandra, whom he called Janda for short, was his dearest friend. They were close. He would obviously be devastated by her departure. But a half second later he understood what was really happening. Janda was sixteen, two years too young to marry. The Italians couldn't be zogging her. The family was sending her away. And the captain of the ship was telling Victor *in private* mere minutes before it happened. They were accusing him. They were sending her off because of him.

"But we haven't done anything wrong," said Victor.

"You two are second cousins, Victor. We would never be able to trade with the other families if we suddenly developed a reputation for dogging."

Dogging, from "endogamy": marrying inside the clan, inbreeding. The word was like a slap. "Dogging? But I would never in a million years marry Alejandra. How could you even suggest that we would do such a thing?" It was vile to even think it; to the belter families, it was on the wrong side of the incest taboo.

Concepción said, "You and Alejandra have been the closest of friends since your nursery years, Victor. Inseparable. I've watched you. We've all watched you. In large gatherings, you always seek each other out. You talk to each other constantly. Sometimes you don't even *need* to talk. It's as if you know precisely what the other is thinking and you need share only a passing glance between you to communicate it all."

"She's my friend. You're going to exile her because we communicate well with each other?"

"Your friendship isn't unique, Victor. I know of several dozen such friendships on this ship. And they are all between a husband and his wife."

"You're sending Alejandra away on the basis that she and I have a ro-
mantic relationship. When we don't."

"It is an innocent relationship, Victor. Everyone knows that."

" 'Everyone'? Who do you mean exactly? Has there been a Family Meeting about us?"

"Only a Council. I would never make this decision on my own, Victor."

Not much of a relief. The Council consisted of all the adults over forty.
"So my parents agree to this?"

"And Alejandra's parents as well. This was a difficult decision for all of
us, Victor. But it was unanimous."

Victor pictured the scene: All of the adults gathered together, aunts and
uncles and grandparents, people he knew and loved and respected, people
whose opinion he valued, people who had always looked upon him fondly
and whose respect he had always hoped to maintain. All of them had sat
together and discussed him and Janda, discussed a sex life that Victor
didn't even have! It was revolting. And Mother and Father had been there.
How embarrassing for them. How could Victor ever face these people
again? They would never be able to look at him without thinking of that
meeting, without remembering the accusation and shame.

"No one is suggesting that you two have done anything improper, Victor. But that's why we're acting now, before your feelings further blossom
and you realize you're in love."

Another slap. "Love?"

"I know this is difficult, Victor."

Difficult? No, unfair would be a better word. Completely unfair and
unfounded. Not to mention humiliating. They were sending away his closest friend, perhaps his only true friend, all because they *thought* something would happen between them? As if he and Janda were animals in
heat driven by unbridled carnal impulses. Was it too much to imagine that
a teenage boy and a teenage girl could simply be friends? Did adults think
so little of adolescents that they assumed that any relationship between
sixteen- and seventeen-year-olds of the opposite sex had to be motivated
by sex? It was infuriating and insulting. Here he was making an adult-sized
contribution in the trade with the Italians, bringing in the largest share
of income for the family, and they didn't think him mature enough to act

properly with his second cousin. Janda wasn't in love with him, and he wasn't in love with her. Why would anyone think otherwise? What had initiated this? Had someone on the Council seen something between them and misinterpreted it as a sign of love?

And then Victor remembered. There was that time when Janda had looked at him strangely, and he had dismissed it as pure imagination. And she had touched his arm a little longer than normal once. It wasn't sexual at all, but he had liked the physical contact between them. That connection hadn't repulsed him. He had enjoyed it.

They were right, he realized.

He hadn't seen it, and they had. He really was on the brink of falling in love with Janda. And she had fallen in love with him, or at least her feelings were moving in that direction.

Everything swelled up inside him at once: anger at being accused; shame at learning that all the older adults on the ship had talked about him behind his back, believing he was moving toward disgraceful behavior; disgust with himself at realizing that perhaps they may have been right; grief at losing the person who meant the most to him in his life. Why couldn't Concepción simply have told him her suspicions before now? Why couldn't she and the Council have said, "Victor, you really need to watch yourself. It looks like you and Alejandra are getting a little close." They didn't have to send Janda away. Didn't they know that he and Janda were mature enough to act appropriately once the family's fears were voiced? Of course they would comply. Of course he and Janda wanted to adhere to the exogamous code. Victor would never want to do anything to dishonor her or the family. He and Janda hadn't even realized that their relationship might be headed toward perilous waters. Now that they knew, things would be different.

But arguing would only make him look like a child. And besides, he would be arguing to keep Janda here, close to him. Wasn't that proof that the family was right? No, Alejandra had to go. It was cruel, yes, but not as cruel as keeping her here in front of him every day. That would be torture. Now that their love—or pre-love or whatever it was—had been so flagrantly pointed out to them, how could he and Janda think of anything else whenever they saw each other? And they *would* see each other. All the time,

every day. At meals, passing in the hall, at exercise. It would be unavoid-
able. And out of their duty to honor one another and the family, they would
become distant and cold to each another. They would overcompensate.
They would refrain from any look, any conversation, any touch between
them. Yet even as they tried in vain to avoid each other, they would be
thinking about the need to avoid each other. They would consume each
other's thoughts, even more so than before. It would be dreadful.

Victor immediately knew that Alejandra would understand this as well.
She would be devastated to learn that she was leaving her family, but
she would see the wisdom of it as well, just as Victor did. It was one of the
many reasons why he respected her so much. Janda could always see the
big picture. If a decision had to be made, she would consider every ramifi-
cation: Who would be affected and when and for how long? And if the
decision affected her, she would always consider it dispassionately, with
an almost scientific eye, never letting her emotions override any wisdom,
always putting the needs of the family above her own. Now, standing here
in Concepción's office, Victor realized that perhaps it wasn't respect that
he felt for her. It was something else. Something greater.

He looked at Concepción. "I would suggest that I go with the Italians
instead of Alejandra, but that wouldn't work. The Italians would wonder
why we were giving up our best mechanic." He knew it sounded vain, but
they both knew it was true.

Concepción didn't argue. "Alejandra is bright and talented and hardworking, but she has yet to choose a specialty. They can adapt her to what
they need. You, however, are already specialized. What would they do
with their own mechanic? It would put you in competition at once. No,
they would not accept the situation, and we could not do without you. But
it was generous, if pointless, for you to consider it."

Victor nodded. It was now a matter of clearing up a few questions.
"Alejandra is only sixteen, two years too young to marry. I'm assuming
the Italians agree to wait until the appropriate time to formally introduce
her to potential suitors from their family. They understand that they can't
possibly be zogging her now."

"Our arrangement with the Italians is very clear. Alejandra will be bunk-
ing with a family with a daughter her age and no sons. I have met the

daughter myself and found her most agreeable and kind. I suspect that she and Alejandra will get along very well. And yes, the Italians understand that Alejandra is not to be considered a prospect for marriage until she comes of age. When that time comes, she is not to be coerced into a relationship or choice. She will move at her own pace. The decision of who and when to marry is entirely her own. Knowing Alejandra, I suspect she will have her pick of bachelors."

Of course Janda would have her pick, Victor thought. Any suitor with an eye for beauty—both physical and in every other respect—would immediately see the life of happiness that awaited him with Janda at his side. Victor had known that for years. Anyone who spent five minutes with Janda would know she would one day make an attractive bride. Everything that men hoped for in a companion was there: a brilliant mind, a kind disposition, an unbreakable devotion to family. And until this moment, Victor hadn't considered this opinion of her anything other than intelligent observation. Now, however, he could detect another sentiment buried within it. Envy. Envy for the man lucky enough to have her. It was funny, really. The feelings he had harbored all along for Alejandra were like emotions filed away in a mismarked folder. They had always been there. He had just given them a different name. Now the truth of them was glaringly obvious. A long friendship had slowly evolved into something else. It hadn't fully developed and resulted in any action, but its course was set. It was as if the boundary between friendship and love was so thin and imperceptible that one could cross it without even knowing it was there.

"The Italians can never know the real reason why Alejandra is leaving," said Victor. "They can't know that she was moving toward an unacceptable relationship. That would forever taint her and drive off potential suitors. You must have told them some invented reason. Families don't just send off their sixteen-year-old daughters."

"The Italians believe that Alejandra is going early so that she may have time to adapt to being away from her family and thus avoid the homesickness that plagues so many zogged brides," said Concepción. "Such emotions, however natural, can put a strain on a young marriage, and we have explained to the Italians our desire to avoid it."

It was a smart cover story. Homesickness happened. Victor had seen it.

Sooman, a bride that had come to El Cavador a few years ago to marry Victor's uncle Lonzo, had spent the first weeks of their marriage crying her eyes out in her room, bemoaning the loss of her Korean family. She had come willingly—no zogging is a forced marriage—but homesickness had crept in, and her constant weeping had really gotten to Victor. It made him feel like an accomplice in a kidnapping or rape. But what could be done? There could be no divorce or annulment. Her family was already millions of klicks away. Eventually she had come around, but the whole experience had been a burden for everyone.

"What assurance do we have that the Italians will abide by these conditions?" Victor asked.

"Alejandra isn't going alone. Faron is going with her."

Again, this was wise. Faron had come to the family late in his teens, when the family rescued him and his mother from a derelict mining ship after pirates had stripped it and left them to die. The mother did not live long, and Faron, though he was hardworking and grateful, had never fully become part of the family.

"Faron is a good miner, Victor. He's been waiting for an opportunity to get on with a bigger clan. He wants to be piloting his own digger someday. He won't accomplish that here. This is Faron's choice. He'll watch over Alejandra and see to it that her needs are met, not as a guardian, but as a protector and counselor. If any suitor tries to approach Alejandra too soon, Faron will remind him of his place."

Victor had no doubt of that. Faron was big and well muscled. He would defend Janda as his own sister should the occasion ever require it, which it probably never would. The Italians weren't stupid enough to threaten their own reputation and alienate themselves from other families. Zogging was crucial to mixing up the gene pool. Every family upheld the practice as sacrosanct. To marry well was to preserve the family and build the clan. True, there were belters who dogged and married only within their own clan, but these were considered the lowliest of low class and were alienated from everyone else, rarely able to find families willing to trade goods with them. No, in all likelihood, Janda would be given all the luxury and protection the Italians could afford. Faron was only a formality.

"It's an ideal situation," said Concepción. "It works out well for everyone.

Now if you hurry, you can catch her at the airlock. I'm sure she would like to say good-bye."

Victor was surprised. "But I can't possibly see her off."

"But you are the person she will most want to say good-bye to."

"Which is exactly why I can't go," said Victor. "The Italians will be there. They might catch some sign of special emotion at our parting. Alejandra and I never noticed that we were conveying any emotions to each other at all, yet apparently we were or you never would have felt the need to hold a Council. So we might reveal something that *we* don't detect but that everyone else does. And the Italians are sharp and suspicious. They made me take the HVAC booster apart three times before they would believe that it works. No, as much as I would love to say good-bye to Alejandra, it would only put her at risk. They can never suspect that there was ever anything between us. I appreciate you coming to me beforehand and trusting me enough to give me the opportunity, but you must understand why I respectfully decline."

Concepción smiled sadly. "Your reasoning is clear, Victor, but I also know the pain behind it. And the pain your decision will bring to Alejandra." She sighed, crossed her arms, and examined him a moment. "You don't disappoint me, Victor. You're the man I always hoped you would grow to be. Now I just hope that you will forgive us for what we have done to you and your dear friend."

"There is nothing to forgive, Concepción. I'm the one who needs forgiveness. I have lost us Alejandra two years early. I've taken her from her parents and family. That wasn't my intent, but that doesn't change the fact that it's happened."

What he didn't say were his others reasons for not going to the airlock. He simply couldn't face Janda, for one. Not because of his shame, though he felt plenty of that. It was more the finality of the event. He couldn't look at her knowing that it would likely be the last time he would ever see her again. He couldn't bear that; he didn't trust his emotions enough. He might do something foolish, like cry or stammer or turn red as a beacon light. And he didn't want the weak side of him to be her final impression of him. Nor was he willing to steel his jaw and square his shoulders and see her off with a cold, stately handshake, as the Council would expect. That would be an affront to their friendship. It would imply—to him, at least—that their relationship had meant nothing to him after all, that it could be ended as dispassionately as two acquaintances parting ways. He couldn't allow that. He wouldn't let their final moment be an exercise in pretense and awkwardness.

Besides, not seeing Janda off was best for her. If she did love him, then his abandoning her at her departure would only make it easier for her to forget him. He would be doing her a favor. Then again, Janda knew Victor. She might suspect that he hadn't come for that very reason, and therefore the plan would backfire. Instead of stamping out their love, it would only endear him more to her.

Or, she might jump to the wrong conclusion entirely. She might think that he had not come because now that true feelings were laid bare, he found her revolting. She might think: He hates me now. He despises me. I'm the one who looked at him with love in my eyes. I'm the one who touched his arm. And now that he knows what my feelings were, he thinks me vile and repulsive.

This thought nearly sent Victor flying from the room and rushing to the airlock to tell Janda that no, he didn't think any less of her. He never could.

But he did no such thing. He remained exactly where he was.

Concepción said, "The members of the Council will be perfectly discreet on this matter. Not a hint of gossip will escape any of our lips. As far as we are concerned, we didn't even meet on the subject."

She was trying to reassure him, but hearing her stress the confidentiality of the situation only stoked Victor's shame. It meant that they were so disgusted by him and Janda, so repulsed by it all, that they were going to pretend that nothing had ever happened. They were going to go about their business as if the memory had been wiped from their minds. Which of course was impossible. No one could forget this. They could *pretend* to have forgotten, yes. They could smile at him and go on as if nothing had ever happened, but their faces would only be masks.

There was nothing else to say. Victor thanked Concepción and excused himself from her office. The hall that led to the airlock was just ahead, but Victor turned his back to it. He needed to work. He needed to occupy his mind, build something, fix something, disassemble something. He took his handheld from his hip and checked the day's repair docket. There was a long list of minor repairs that needed his attention, but none of them were a screaming emergency. He could get to them soon enough. A better use of his time might be installing the drill stabilizer he had built recently. He would need permission from the miners before touching the drill, but he might get that if he asked today. The Italians hadn't pulled out yet, so the miners wouldn't be ready for the drill for another hour at least. Victor switched screens on his handheld and pulled up the locator. It showed that Mono was down in the workshop.

Victor hit the call button. "Mono, it's Victor."

A young boy's voice answered. "Épale, pana cambur. What's shaking, Vico?"

"Can you meet me in the cargo bay with the pieces for the drill stabilizer?"

Mono sounded excited. "Are we going outside to install it?"

"If the miners let us. I'm heading there now."

Mono whistled and hooted.

Victor clicked off, smiling. He could always count on Mono's enthusiasm to lift his spirits.

At nine years old, Mono was the youngest apprentice on the ship, though he had been following Victor around and watching him make repairs for several years now. Six months ago the Council had agreed that an interest as keen as Mono's should be encouraged not ignored, and they had made his apprenticeship official. Mono had called it the happiest day of his life.

Mono's real name was José Manuel like his father, Victor's uncle. But when Mono was a toddler, he had learned to climb up the furniture and cabinets in the nursery before he had learned to walk, and his mother had called him her little mono—"monkey" in Spanish. The name had stuck.

Victor flew down the various corridors and shafts to the cargo bay, launching himself straight as an arrow down every passageway, moving quickly in zero gravity. He passed lots of people. Now that the Italians were pulling out, and the trading and festivities were over, it was back to life as usual, with everyone taking up his or her assigned responsibility. Miners, cooks, laundry workers, machine operators, navigators, all the duties that kept the family operation running smoothly in the Kuiper Belt.

Victor reached the entrance to the cargo bay and found Mono waiting for him, a large satchel floating in the air behind him.

"You got everything?" asked Victor. "All three pieces?"

"Check, check, and check," said Mono, giving a thumbs-up.

They floated through the hatch into the cargo bay and then over to the equipment lockers, where the miners were busy gathering and preparing their gear for the day's dig. The ship was currently anchored to an asteroid, but drilling had stopped ever since the Italians had arrived. Now the miners looked eager to get back to work.

Victor scanned the crowd and noticed that many of the men were over forty, which meant they were members of the Council and therefore knew the real reason why Janda was leaving. Victor wondered if they would avert their eyes when they saw him, but none of them did. They were all so busy making their preparations that no one even seemed to notice that he and Mono were there.

Victor found his uncle Marco, the dig-team leader, over by the air compressor, checking the lifeline hoses for any leaks. Miners were extremely protective of their gear, but no piece of equipment was given more care and inspection than the lifeline. The long tube connected into the back of every miner's spacesuit and served two purposes: It was the miner's anchor to the ship—operating like a safety cable. And it was the miner's source of fresh air, power, and heat. As the sign above the lockers read: CUIDA TU MANGUERA. TU MANGUERA ES TU VIDA. "Take care of your line. Your line is your life."

"Épale, Marco," said Victor.

"Épa, Vico," said Marco, looking up from his work and smiling.

He was a member of the Council, but he showed no sign of hiding anything. He appeared to be his normal, happy self. Victor pushed the thought away. He couldn't live like this, constantly questioning the thoughts of every person over forty on the ship.

"Nice work with that heater doodad you made for the Italians," said Marco. "We got some good equipment out of that trade." He gestured to a large metal cage anchored to the floor, filled with slightly used pressure suits, helmets, mineral readers, and other essential equipment. Most of it looked newer than anything miners on El Cavador had ever used, which might work to Victor's favor—he was about to ask permission to access the drill, and it would help to be in the miners' good graces.

"What time are you going out this morning?" asked Victor.

Marco raised an eyebrow. "Why do you ask?"

"I've been working on something," said Victor, "an enhancement for one of the drills. It's still a prototype, but I'd like to test it. And since you can't fire up the drill until the Italians pull out, I thought maybe I could install it before your guys get out there and start digging."

Marco eyed the satchel.

"It's a stabilizer for the drill," said Victor, "for whenever we hit ice pockets. It's a way to keep the ship from pitching forward and the drill steady."

Victor could see Marco's curiosity nibbling at the bait. "Ice pockets, huh?"

Nothing was more annoying to a miner in the Kuiper Belt than ice pockets. Asteroids this far from the sun were dirty snowballs, masses of rock laced with an occasional pocket of frozen water, methane, or ammonia. The laser drill could bore through it all, but it produced a rocketlike reaction. Unless the ship was moored to the rock with the retrorockets firing as a counterforce, the laser would simply knock the asteroid away from the ship.

So as long as the laser was digging through rock—for which all of the retrorockets had been calibrated—the ship held steady and the dig went smoothly. But the moment the laser hit a pocket of ice, the laser would burn right through it, losing the ship's upward force. The retrorockets were still firing, however, so the whole ship would pitch forward, causing chaos inside for the crew. People fell over, babies couldn't sleep.

Then, after the laser had seared through the ice and hit rock again, the upward force would return, the two forces would then equalize, and the ship would pitch back again. Everyone called it the ice pocket rodeo.

"I know what you're thinking," said Victor. "The drill is working. What if my 'improvement' damages the drill?"

"The thought crossed my mind," said Marco. "I don't like anyone touching the drills unless absolutely necessary."

"You can watch everything I do," said Victor. "Step by step. But in truth, the installation isn't that invasive. The main sensor goes up by the retro-rockets. Another piece is wireless and goes down by the blast site on the asteroid. All I'm doing with the drill is installing this third piece, the stabilizer. It makes minor adjustments in the drill's aim when the ship moves because of an ice dip. It's designed to keep the laser pointed straight down into the blast site, instead of wavering or shifting mid-drill." Victor pulled the device from the satchel and handed it to Marco. It was small and intricate, and Marco clearly had no idea what he was looking at—though this was to be expected since nothing like it existed. Victor had built it from junked parts, scrap metal, and polycarbonate plastic.

Marco handed back the stabilizer. "So this will take care of ice dips?"

"Not completely," said Victor. "But it should minimize them, yes. Assuming it works."

Victor could see Marco's mind working. He was considering it. Finally, Marco pointed a finger and said, "If you damage the drill, I'll have you sucked back into the ship through your lifeline."

Victor smiled.

Marco looked at his watch. "You got forty-five minutes. We'll be checking equipment until then."

"Not a problem," said Victor.

"And that's including however long it takes for you to suit up," said Marco. "Forty-five minutes total, from this moment."

"Got it," said Victor.

"And work on the *old* drill," said Marco. "Not the new one."

Victor thanked him, and he and Mono hurried to the lockers. As they changed into their pressure suits, Mono peppered Victor with questions, as Mono was always prone to do. Most of them were mechanical in nature, so Victor was able to answer them without much thought. The rest of his mind was at the airlock. How had Janda looked when she left? Had she acknowledged Victor's absence or pretended not to notice it? Probably the latter. Janda was too smart to risk revealing her feelings now.

"Hola," said Mono, waving a hand in front of Victor's face. "Earth to Vico. We've got a green light, and the clock is ticking."

Victor blinked, snapping out of his reverie. They were in the airlock, sealed and ready to go. The light over the airlock hatch had turned green indicating that they were clear to exit.

Victor entered the command in the keypad. There was a hiss of air, and the exterior hatch slid open. Mono didn't waste any time. He pulled himself through and pushed hard off the hull, launching himself into space, whooping and hollering as he flew. Victor launched after him, his lifeline unspooling like a single strand of spider's web behind him. Victor's thumb found the trigger on his suit, and the gas propulsion kicked in, gradually slowing his forward motion. He rotated his body back toward El Cavador and saw the Italian ship Vesuvio as it was maneuvering away.

Janda was leaving.

The other three ships of the Italian clan—also named after volcanoes in Italy: Stròmbuli, Mongibello, and Vulture—were a short distance away, waiting for Vesuvio. Soon they would accelerate and disappear.

Victor refused to watch them leave. Better to stay busy. "Let's go, Mono. No time for flying."

Victor hit the propulsion trigger and shot forward back to the ship, heading toward the side facing the asteroid, back where the old laser drill was housed. Several thick mooring cables extended from the ship down to their anchors on the asteroid. Victor moved past them, being careful not to entangle his lifeline. When he reached the drill, he stopped, brought up his feet, and turned on his boot magnets. The soles of his boots snapped to the surface, and Victor stood upright.

He and Mono got to work removing the panels on the drill and exposing its inner components. The stabilizer was a quick install. It was just a matter of bolting it in and plugging it in to one of the drill's mod outlets. Most big machines allotted a certain number of modifications and had built-in power outlets and boards to accommodate them. Victor would have to reboot the drill before it recognized the stabilizer, but his lifeline carried hardware lines to the ship, and he could do it from here using his heads-up display. He blinked and called up the display. The helmet tracked his eyes, and Victor gave the necessary blink commands to reboot the drill. When it came back online, he saw on the display that it recognized the stabilizer. "We're in business, Mono. Now for the retros."

They replaced the drill paneling and flew up to the retrorockets. Victor looked to his left as he went. The Italians were gone. A small dot of white in the distance might have been their thrusters, but it could just as easily have been a star. Victor looked away. Back to work.

The installation on the retros was more difficult since their mod inputs were so dated, and Victor had to make an adapter from parts in his tool belt. Mono asked questions every step of the way. Why was Victor doing this or that? Why wouldn't he try this instead?

"That's how we do it, Mono. We make do with what we have. Corporate miners have stores of spare parts and resources on their ships. We have nothing. If something needs fixing, we pull out the junked parts and use our imagination. Now let me ask *you* a few questions."

It was then that the instruction began. Victor passed the tools and pieces to Mono and asked him questions that didn't explicitly tell Mono how to finish the installation but that pointed him in the right direction. That way, Mono was discovering the steps himself and seeing the logic behind everything. It was how Father had trained Victor, not only letting him get his hands on the repair, but getting his mind in it as well, teaching Victor how to think his way through a fix.

As Mono worked, Victor allowed himself another look out to space. There wasn't a trace of thrusters now. Just blackness and stars and silence. Victor wasn't a navigator, but he knew the big asteroids that were currently in this general vicinity, and he wondered where the Italians might be going. It wouldn't be anywhere close, of course. In the Kuiper Belt it took several months to travel between asteroids. But even so, maybe Victor could guess.

He closed his eyes. It was pointless. There were thousands of objects in the Kuiper Belt. They could be heading anywhere. And what good did it do to know their destination anyway? That wouldn't change anything. That wouldn't bring Janda back. And yes, he wanted her back. He realized that now. He had never been physically affectionate with her in any way that wasn't innocent. And yet now, when he couldn't have her, he suddenly longed for her to be close to him.

He loved his cousin. Why hadn't he seen that before? I'm exactly what the Council feared. Whatever they think of me now, I deserve it.

Mono was asking him a question. Victor returned to the task at hand. They finished the installation and then made their way down to the blast site on the asteroid.

In mining terms, the asteroid was a "lumpy," or a rock rich in iron, cobalt, nickel, and other ferromagnetic minerals. Miners used scanners to look for concentrations of metal in the stone, which they called "lumps." The more lumps or seams of metal they found, the higher the metal-to-stone ratio. No lumps meant the rock was a "slagger" or a "dumpy," a worthless chunk of nothing.

Victor and Mono touched down on the asteroid. Their boot magnets were set to the highest setting, and the minerals in the rock were just enough to hold their feet to the surface. They walked to the lip of the mineshaft and looked down. The laser drill had burned a nice circle into the asteroid, though not with a continuous cutting motion. It actually fired a series of close, single bursts that perforated the rock to a predetermined depth, creating a tight ring of holes. Miners then broke the narrow walls between the holes with the shake-hammers, then pulled out the rock in chunks, building the shaft.

But this shaft wasn't deep enough. The miners hadn't yet reached the lump. When they did, they'd bring in the cooker tubes and refine and smelt the metal on-site, shaping it into cylinders that could be floated back up to the ship. It was tedious, hard labor, but if the lump was big enough, it was well worth the effort.

Victor found a spot on the inner wall of the shaft where the steam sensor could be installed, and then called up Marco. "We're nearly ready to test this thing. Do you have a moment to come help us out?"

"On my way," said Marco.

Victor thought it best if Marco was the one who installed the steam sensor. It was a simple procedure, and it would allow Marco to feel some ownership for the device. Besides, the miners would be the ones moving the steam sensor every time they moved the drill, so they needed to know how to install it at the blast site. It made sense for Marco, as team leader, to have the first go.

Marco didn't come alone. Word had spread, and every miner in the family now gathered around the mineshaft, ready to watch.

"When ice melts it produces steam," said Victor. "This sensor goes down in the shaft and detects steam. The moment the level of steam in the detritus goes up a certain amount, it tells the retros to ease off. Then, when the rock particulate goes up again and steam diminishes, the retros accelerate. Meanwhile, it's sending adjustments to the drill, to keep it from waffling as the ship moves. So the beam always stays dead center on the blast site."

"Won't the heat from the laser burn the steam sensor?" asked Marco.

"That's what the casing is for," said Victor. "It's pretty tough stuff. I'm thinking it will hold."

"So no more ice dips?" asked one of the miners.

"It won't rid the ship of all movement entirely," said Victor. "There would still be some slight shifting since it will take a moment for the sensor to detect the steam, but the movement will be far more gentle, like slight waves instead of sudden, jarring jolts."

Marco flew down into the hole and drilled the steam sensor into the inner rock wall as Victor suggested. When he returned, he ushered everyone back to a safe distance and had them lower their blast shields over their visors.

"It's still a prototype," Victor reminded them. "I can't guarantee the beam won't go off center. It's bound to need some serious adjustments."

"Shut up and drill," said Marco.

Victor blinked the commands into his heads-up display, and the laser blasted down into the rock. Within seconds the laser hit ice, and the ship began to dip. The retros adjusted and the drill countered. It wasn't perfect; the beam still wavered a bit.

"Needs tweaking," said Victor. He called up the commands on his display. His eyes moved quickly, and he gave the appropriate blink commands, making the needed adjustments. Twenty seconds later the laser hit another pocket of ice. Steam issued from the hole, but the retros responded quickly and smoothly this time. The drill responded perfectly as well, without the slightest waver from side to side.

Everyone cheered. Mono was punching the sky, whistling.

Marco was smiling. "She handles light. Sweet."

"So I'm on the right track," said Victor. "Now I can get to work on the *real* version."

"Does Concepción know about this?" asked Marco

"We didn't want to tell anyone until we knew it worked. Now that it shows some promise, I'll get my dad involved. He may have some improvements in mind."

"I'll take two," said Marco, smiling. "One for the new drill as well." He gave Victor an affectionate knuckle tap on the helmet.

When Victor and Mono finally returned to the ship, Mono was on an emotional high. "You'd be rich on Earth, Vico. Stinking rich. All these ideas of yours. They'd pay you millions of credits."

"I'm seventeen, Mono. I'd be lucky to get an assembly-line job. No one would take me seriously. Out here we can do whatever we want. On Earth it's different. Besides, you and I did this together. The stabilizer was both of us."

"I helped with mindless welding and soldering in the workshop. The ideas were yours."

"Your hands are way steadier than mine. You do the micro work far better than I do. Even Father can't solder like you."

Mono beamed.

When they floated out of the decompression chamber and back into the cargo bay, Isabella was waiting for him. She was Chilean, zogged by the family when Victor was just a kid and married to Mother's second cousin. More importantly, she was very close with Janda.

"I need to speak with Vico in private, Mono," said Isabella. "Would you give us a moment?"

Mono shrugged. "I got circuits to rebuild in the workshop. See you around, Vico."

Isabella waited until Mono was gone, then turned to Victor. "I know you're upset. And I don't blame you."

Victor kept his face a blank. Isabella wasn't quite old enough to be on the Council, so she might not be speaking of Janda.

Isabella rolled her eyes. "Don't play dumb, Vico. I'm not an idiot. I know what just happened here. They sent Jandita away. And you hid out with the machinery instead of telling her good-bye."

"Yes, I was a coward," said Victor.

"No, you weren't," said Isabella. "You were trying to make sure nobody on Vesuvio ever accused Jandita of being in love with a cousin. And don't look surprised. Just because I figured it out doesn't mean anyone else did. Jandita was a model of composure at the airlock. I don't think anyone suspected a thing. She actually made the Italians believe she was excited about going."

"How did you figure it out?"

"Jandita is my niece, Vico. I am her favorite aunt. I know her thoughts better than her own mother perhaps. Plus, I'm observant. I see and hear all." She gave Victor a wink, and he furrowed his brow. "Relax," she said. "I never saw anything improper between you two. What I mean is that I know the signs. Jandita is not the first girl to have fallen in love with her cousin, you know."

Victor read the rueful expression on her face. "You're confessing?"

"I was eighteen. He was my second cousin as well. I doubt he even knew that I loved him. The year I realized it, I came to this ship and married your uncle Selmo."

Technically Selmo wasn't Victor's uncle. He was his second cousin once removed, but all men on the ship were uncles, more or less.

"Does Selmo know?" asked Victor.

Isabella laughed. "Of course he knows. We laugh about it now. I was young and starry-eyed. I barely knew what I wanted in a husband then."

"So Alejandra is starry-eyed and naïve."

"Not at all. I suspect she will think of you for the rest of her life. She's far more mature at sixteen than I was at eighteen. My point is you're not a villain, Vico. I know you. You'll beat yourself up over this, and you shouldn't. She's your second cousin. Any place on Earth, you could have married, and no one would have batted an eye."

"Maybe that's because there are more sick and twisted dirtbags on Earth."

Isabella laughed. "They're human, Vico. Just like us. We can't help it if we hold ourselves to a higher standard." She put a hand on his shoulder. "Promise me you won't torture yourself over this."

What did she expect of him? That he could shrug this off and chalk it up as one of those life experiences that everyone has? Isabella meant well. That was clear. She loved him like she loved Janda. But words of comfort couldn't bring the comfort she wanted to give. He wasn't going to wake up tomorrow and think: What a valuable life lesson that was. He wasn't going to move on. Not here, at least. He realized that now. Everywhere he turned he would see Alejandra. Everything would spark a memory of her. She would haunt him here. How could he take a bride onto this ship? Even if the family zogged someone for him in the next year or so, how could he parade a wife through halls that reminded him of someone else? Of course zogging had worked for Isabella. Of course *she* could move on. She had left that previous life behind her. She had closed that door. Nothing in her new life would remind her of her old one. Victor wouldn't have that luxury. Not if he stayed here.

I need to get out, he realized. Go to Luna perhaps. Or Earth or Mars. He didn't know how to make it happen, but he knew in that instant that it must.

He looked at Isabella and gave her the smile she expected. "I will do my best."

She looked content. "Good. I'll be watching you. If I sense any self-loathing, I will beat you senseless."

"I'm sure you could. But honestly, I'll be fine."

"No you won't. But I'm glad you'll try."

They parted then. Victor went to the lockers and changed out of his spacesuit. He would have to tell his parents that he was leaving. Mother would argue with him, but Father would see the sense in it. As much as Father would hate to admit it, he would agree with Victor. He couldn't leave immediately, of course. He didn't have the means. It would be months before they found another family willing to give Victor a ride in that direction. But he could prepare himself now. He could start today. Luna, Earth, and Mars all had gravities, and Victor's legs weren't strong enough to take on the Gs. He needed strength training. He needed the fuge.

The centrifuge was at the heart of the ship. It only stopped spinning twice an hour, to let people in or out, so Victor had to wait a few minutes after he arrived for the hatch to open. Inside there were a dozen people scattered throughout the room, most of them standing on the wall or floor, waiting for the fuge to get back up to speed so they could continue with

their exercise. A few of them like Victor had just entered, and these made
their way to the wall where all the magnetic greaves were hung. Victor
followed them, already feeling the centripetal force pull him to the floor.

He found a pair of greaves that looked to be his size and strapped them
around his shins. Soon he was standing upright, the magnets holding his
feet firmly to the floor. Greaves weren't like real gravity. More like one-
sixth of a G, or what someone might experience on the surface of Luna.
The trick with greaves was you had to work hard to keep your legs under
you, constantly pulling your feet forward as you stepped, dragging against
the pull of the greaves.

But greaves weren't enough to condition his legs, especially if he was
thinking of Earth or Mars. He needed time on the treadmills as well. He
walked toward the center of the room to the hatch that led down to the fuge
within a fuge: the track, the room where the treads were kept. He could
feel himself getting heavier as the fuge picked up speed. When it got going
full tilt, the pull of the magnets combined with the spin would be about
half a G.

To his right was the nursery, a long row of glass-paneled rooms where
the children under two years old lived. In one room, a toddler was taking
a few unsteady steps from the arms of one adult and into the waiting arms
of another. Without the simulated gravity of the fuge, toddlers would never
develop the muscles necessary for walking, or learn how.

There were some free-miner families who didn't have fuges or magnetic
greaves and who preferred instead to always fly in zero gravity. But bats,
as they were called, were completely useless planet-side. Their children
couldn't walk or even stand, their legs thin and atrophied.

Concepción wouldn't hear of it. Everyone was required to spend at least
two hours a day down here to keep leg muscles from atrophying and bones
from becoming brittle. Some people stayed vertical wherever they were
on the ship, electing to wear greaves while they worked. It was a matter of
leverage and efficiency. Most of the labor on the ship required sure foot-
ing. It was far easier to push and pull and lift if your feet were locked down.

Victor reached the hatch and lowered himself into the track. There
were fewer people down here than in the main fuge, and all of them were
younger than Victor, walking, running, listening to earphones, wearing

movie goggles, reading. Yet all of them were vertical. Victor strapped himself into a treadmill and raised the setting to three-quarters of a G. He walked slowly at first, then gradually worked his way up to a light run. After twenty minutes his calves were twitching and his thighs burned. As he lowered the G level and started to cool down, he wondered how much more he would have to train each day to prepare himself to leave.

His handheld began flashing.

Victor stopped the treadmill. The message was from Edimar, Janda's fourteen-year-old sister. She was an apprentice spotter and watched for movement in space: comets, asteroids, anything that might pose a collision threat to the ship. The message read: COME TO THE CROW'S NEST. URGENT!!

Victor didn't hesitate. He left the fuge as soon as it stopped spinning, then moved through the ship quickly, his legs still burning, his shirt damp with sweat.

The crow's nest was a glass dome atop the upper deck, well above the main body of the ship. Victor flew up the long, narrow tube that led to the room and then pulled himself up through the hole in the floor. The room was dark, and the billions of stars beyond the glass dome shined so clearly and distinctly that Victor felt as if he were outside the ship.

Edimar was floating weightless across the room, wearing her data goggles. The computers were extremely sensitive to light, so spotters wore skintight goggles with interior displays instead of using bright computer monitors.

"Épa, Mar. What's the emergency?" asked Victor.

Edimar removed her goggles. "You've always taken me seriously, Vico. Even when nobody else did. You've always treated me like I'm smart."

"You are smart, Edimar. What's this about?"

"And Jandita said that if I ever needed help with something I could come to you. She said you'd treat me fair, help me out."

"Of course, Mar. What is it?"

"I want to show you something. And I want you to be honest with me and tell me what you think it is."

"Okay."

She found another pair of goggles and handed them to him. "The Eye saw something that doesn't make any sense. And I don't want a bunch of people laughing at me if it's nothing."

The Eye was the computer system that kept up a constant scan of the sky in every direction, watching for any incoming objects that might collide with the ship. In terms of safety, it was one of the most important pieces of equipment on board. Even small rocks, if they were moving fast enough, could cripple the ship and prove fatal.

"Have you shown your father?" asked Victor

She looked aghast. "Of course not."

"Why not? He's the spotter. He'll be more of a help interpreting what the Eye sees than I would."

"My father doesn't think I can do this job, Vico. He has zero confidence in me. He wanted sons, and he got three girls. The only reason *I'm* his apprentice and not some *boy* is because Concepción made him take me on. I can't go to him with something that's a mistake. I'd never hear the end of it. He might go to Concepción with it as proof that I'm not fit for this job."

Victor knew Janda's and Edimar's father well, and it sounded like a pretty accurate description. Victor knew he shouldn't ask, but he did anyway. "Why work with your father then, Mar? If it's so difficult, maybe you'd like doing something else, being around other people."

She looked angry. "Because I like what I do, Vico. I like working the Eye. And because he's my father. Why don't you go work in the laundry or the kitchen, if it's so easy to switch?"

He held up his hands in a show of surrender. "Sorry. Forget I asked. What did the Eye see?"

She looked irritated and said nothing for a moment, as if considering whether she wanted to involve him after all. Then her face softened, and she relaxed. "Goggles," she said, sliding on her own.

Victor put on the goggles and stared at the blank screen. "Am I supposed to see something?"

"Not yet. First let me explain. I've set the Eye to notify me of any motion outside the ecliptic, even if it doesn't yet look like a collision. Motion there is more rare, but I've got a thing for cold comets. Before the sun heats them up and gives them a tail, I think they're pretty cool. I figure if I'm the first one to spot a new one, I can get it named after me. It's silly, I know."

"Not at all," said Victor. "Getting a comet named after you sounds pretty chévere."

He could hear the smile in her voice. "I think so, too." Then she was back to business. "So the Eye was looking outside the ecliptic, taking in some really clean data."

Clean data meant there had been relatively little space dust or other particles floating in the Eye's field of view. It meant the Eye could see way far out.

"Then the Eye detected motion and alerted me," said Edimar. "I called up a visual and got this."

An image of space appeared in Victor's goggles. It looked no different from any other view of space. "Am I supposed to see anything unusual?" he asked.

"The motion was here." Edimar drew on her tablet with her stylus, and a tiny circle appeared on the image of space. Then Edimar zoomed in until the tiny circle filled the display. Victor strained his eyes. "I still don't see anything."

"Neither did I. Which means whatever the Eye saw is in deep space. If it were close, we would be getting better visual resolution. And if it's way out there and the Eye detected its motion, then it must be moving insanely fast. The problem is, the Eye doesn't give me enough data to determine the object's trajectory. All I know is that there's fast motion. But the velocity decreases over time. It means the object is either changing velocity or direction, one or the other. Either it's slowing, or it's turning toward or away from us, making it appear to be slowing relative to us. Only neither one is very likely. I've run analyses based on a dozen different distances and possible directions of movement and the only thing that explains the data the Eye is giving me is deceleration."

"It's slowing down?" said Victor. "Natural objects in space don't slow down on their own, Mar."

"No, they don't. And when I say it's moving fast, Vico, I mean *fast*. Fifty percent of lightspeed fast. And that's its speed now, after continuing to decelerate. Interstellar objects don't go that fast, they don't bend without a gravity well, and they don't decelerate. So tell me, am I going to get teased for this?"

"I don't think so," said Victor.

"I should forget about it?"

"Edimar, I think we're looking at a spacecraft."

"Nothing goes that fast."

"Nothing made by humans."

At his words, Edimar visibly relaxed and a silly grin came to her face. "So I'm not crazy to think we've got us an alien starship? A near-lightspeed ship coming into our system and slowing down?"

"Either it's a lightspeed ship or somebody repealed a whole bunch of laws of physics. And either it's alien or some corporation or government is experimenting with a technology so advanced it will make them masters of the universe."

"So I should call a grown-up."

"You should call the Council. Or I will. This isn't just important, it's so important that they've got to make decisions about it right away."

"What's the hurry?"

"Because it might very well be headed for Earth."

CHAPTER 2

Lem

The Makarhu wasn't built to be a science vessel, and it certainly wasn't built for war. It was a mining ship, property of Juke Limited, the largest space-mining corporation in the solar system. But Lem Jukes—mercifully short for Lemminkainen Joukahainen, heir to the Juke Limited fortune and captain of the ship—was prepared to use the Makarhu for any purpose if it meant turning a failing mission into what the Board of Directors would consider a success.

It was an hour after sleep-shift had ended, and Lem was floating weightless in the observation room, waiting for an asteroid to explode. The asteroid was a small thing, a "pebble" no bigger than Lem himself, lazily moving through space half a kilometer from the ship. If not for the ship's laser lights dotting the asteroid's surface and illuminating it, it would have been completely invisible against the backdrop of space, even with the help of the special scope glasses Lem was wearing.

Lem lowered the glasses and looked out the window to his right. The cargo bay doors were open, and the gravity laser was in position, pointing out into space at the pebble in the sky. Lem couldn't see the engineers from his position, but he knew they were down in the lab adjacent to the cargo bay, prepping the laser for the test.

According to the Juke research team that developed it, the gravity laser—or glaser as they had come to call it—was supposed to be the future of the space-mining industry, a revolutionary way to break surface rock and dig deep through the toughest asteroids. It was designed to shape gravity in much the same way a laser shaped light, though since gravity was not reflective, it worked on very different principles; understanding them was way below Lem's pay grade. The company had spent billions of credits to build this prototype, and quite a bit more to keep it a secret. Lem's job was simply to oversee the field tests. A cakewalk of a mission.

That is, if the gravity laser would ever turn on. It was the first deep-space trial, so Lem expected the delays born of extreme caution. But it was beginning to seem as if something was actually seriously wrong with the device and everyone was afraid to tell him.

"I'm waiting, Dr. Dublin," Lem said, keeping his voice pleasant.

A man's voice sounded in Lem's earpiece. "Just a few moments, Mr. Jukes. We're nearly ready to begin."

"You were nearly ready to begin ten minutes ago," said Lem. "Didn't anyone print the word 'on' beside the right button?"

"Yes, Mr. Jukes. Sorry for the delay. It shouldn't be long now."

Lem rubbed his forehead just above his eyes, fighting back the beginnings of a migraine. The ship had been in the Kuiper Belt for six weeks now, where failure would have no witnesses and there would be no massive object to be torn apart if the reaction got out of hand. But the engineers, who were supposedly ready before this flight even launched, had produced nothing but delays. Their explanations might have been completely legitimate, or they might have been sesquipedalian bushwa. Because of the huge time lag in sending and receiving messages to the Board of Directors back on Luna, Lem had no idea what the Board—or his father—were thinking, though he was fairly certain it wasn't unbridled joy. If Lem wanted to preserve his reputation and return to Luna with any sense of dignity, he needed to shake things up and produce results fast. The longer the wait, the greater the suspense, and the bigger the disappointment if the glaser failed.

Lem sighed. Dublin was the problem. He was a brilliant engineer but a terrible *chief* engineer. He couldn't stand the idea of being blamed for any mistake, so he aborted tests at the slightest sign of malfunction. Dublin was so worried about damaging an expensive prototype or pushing it beyond its capacity—and therefore costing the company its investment—that the man was paralyzed with fear.

No, Dublin had to go. He was too cautious, too slow to take risks. At some point you had to make the leap, and Dublin didn't know how to detect that moment. Lem needed to send positive results to the Board now. Today, if possible. It didn't have to be much. Just some data that suggested the gravity laser did something like what it was designed to do. That's all the Board wanted to hear. If it needed further development before it could be used commercially, fine. At least that gave the impression that Lem and the crew were doing something. That isn't asking too much, Dr. Dublin. Just give me one semisuccessful test. The gravity laser worked in the lab back on Luna, for crying out loud. We didn't come all the way out here without testing it first. The damn thing worked before we left!

Lem tapped a command into his wrist pad and ordered the drink dispenser to mix him something. He needed a boost, a fruit concoction laced with something to drive off the headache and get his energy up.

He sipped the drink and considered Dublin. Lem couldn't fire the man. They were in space. You can't send a man packing when he has nowhere to go—though the idea of jettisoning Dublin *into* space did put a smile on Lem's face. No, Lem needed to take less drastic measures. Get a little creative.

Lem tapped his wrist pad again, and the wall to his right lit up. Icons and folders appeared on the wall-screen, and Lem blinked his way through a series of folders, diving deeper into the ship's files until he found the documents he was looking for. A photo of a Nigerian woman in her late fifties appeared, along with a lengthy dossier. Dr. Noloa Benyawe was one of the engineers on board and had been with Juke Limited for thirty years, or as long as Lem had been alive, which meant she had endured Lem's father Ukko Jukes, president and CEO, for as long as Lem had. It was like meeting someone who had survived the same grueling military campaign, a sister in suffering.

No, that was too harsh perhaps. Lem didn't despise his father. Father had done great things, achieved great wealth and power by relentlessly pushing those around him to innovate, excel, and squash any obstacle in their way. Unfortunately, Father had run his family in much the same way.

Is this another of your tests, Father? Did you give me an engineering team led by a butterfly-hearted ditherer to see if I could handle the situation and get a more deserving and reliable person in place? It was just the kind of thing Father would do, laying snares along Lem's path, creating obstacles for him to overcome. Father had always worked that way, even when Lem was a boy. Not to be cruel, Father would say. "But to teach you, Lem. To toughen, you. To remind you that as a child of privilege, no one is your friend. They will claim to be your friend, they will laugh at your jokes and invite you to their parties, but they do not like you. They like your power, they like what you will become someday." That was child rearing to Father. Parents shouldn't coddle their children when bullies pester them at school, for example. *Real* parents like Father *pay* a bully to torment their child. That teaches a child the harsh truth of life. That teaches a child how to use subterfuge, how to build allies, how to strike back at those stronger than themselves, not with violence necessarily, but with all the other weapons at a child's disposal: public humiliation, fear, the scorn of one's peers, social isolation, everything that cracks a bully and pushes him to tears.

Lem wiped the thought away. Father wasn't testing him. There was too much at stake for that. No, Lem wasn't so conceited as to believe that Father would risk the development of the gravity laser simply to teach Lem one of his "life lessons." This was purely Lem's problem. And he would deal with it.

"Dr. Dublin," Lem said into his microphone, "when you said that the test would begin in a few moments, I assumed that you defined a few moments the same way I do, mere minutes at most. But by my clock, nearly fifteen additional minutes have passed. I recognize that the glaser is of utmost importance to this ship, but there are other matters on this vessel that require a captain's attention. As much as I enjoy staring out into space and pondering the meaning of the universe, frankly I don't have the time. Are we conducting a test or aren't we?"

Dr. Dublin's voice was small and hesitant. "Well, sir, it appears that we may have run into a snag."

Lem closed his eyes. "And when were you going to inform me of this snag?"

"We were hoping that we could fix it quickly, sir. But that doesn't seem likely now. We were about to call you."

I'm sure you were, thought Lem. He pushed his cup into the receptacle. "I'm coming down."

Lem made his way to the push tube, one of the many narrow shafts that ran through the ship. He pulled himself inside and folded his arms across his chest. The walls, like the floor and sidewalls of the ship, produced an undulating magnetic field. The magnets either attracted or repelled the vambraces Lem wore on his forearms and the greaves he wore on his shins. Lem said, "Fourteen." At once he was sucked downward. When he arrived, the lab was in such a state that no one noticed him float into the room. Most of the engineers were hovering weightless around the wall-screen that stretched the length of the room. It held countless windows of data, diagrams, blueprints, messages, scribbles, and equations. It hurt Lem's eyes just to look at it. The engineers were politely arguing over some technical matter Lem didn't understand. Dr. Dublin and a few assistants were standing on the wall to Lem's left, looking down on a hologram of the gravity laser that was about one-fifth the size of the real thing. It annoyed Lem when people in a room didn't maintain the same vertical orientation. Being perpendicular to everyone else was indecorous.

"I do love watching engineers at play," said Lem, just loud enough for everyone to hear.

The room fell silent. The engineers turned to him. Without looking, Lem tapped his wrist pad, and the eye assault that was the wall-screen dimmed to half-light.

Dublin stepped off the wall to the left and stood upright on Lem's floor, bending awkwardly as he adjusted his vambraces. Such a brilliant mind, and yet as graceful as a turnip.

"Mr. Jukes," said Dublin, "thank you for coming. I apologize yet again for this delay. It appears that the source of the problem—"

"I am not an engineer," said Lem with a cheerful smile. "Explaining the problem won't hasten its repair. I don't want to distract you any more than necessary from *solving* the problem. That would be a much better use of your time, wouldn't you agree?"

Dublin swallowed and attempted a smile. "Oh, well, yes, that's very kind. Thank you." He took a step backward.

Lem looked at their faces. "I want to thank all of you for your tireless efforts," he said. "I know that many of you are functioning on a few hours of sleep, and I recognize that the glitches and delays we've experienced are more frustrating to you than anyone else. So I appreciate your patience and perseverance. My father assured me that he had assembled the best team possible, and I know that he was right." Lem smiled to show them that he meant it. "So let's pause for a moment and take a deep breath. I know it's still morning, but except for the people physically working on the fix, let's take a two-hour break. A nap, for many of you. A meal for others. Then we'll come back and tear that asteroid apart like a sneeze in a wet tissue."

Lem made a point of not looking at Dublin, though he noticed that a few of the engineers did. If the laser wouldn't be ready within the next two hours, this was Dublin's chance to have a spine and speak up.

Silence in the room.

"Wonderful," said Lem. "Two hours."

Lem launched off the floor and headed toward the push tube. He caught himself at the entrance and turned back, as if struck by an unrelated thought. "Oh, and Dr. Benyawe, would you see me in my office, please?"

Dr. Benyawe nodded. "Yes, Mr. Jukes."

Five minutes later Dr. Benyawe was standing opposite Lem in his office, anchored to the floor with her greaves.

"You have put me in a delicate situation, Mr. Jukes," she said.

"Have I?" said Lem.

"Calling me to your office. The other engineers will assume that I'm meeting with you to give you an account of the test's failure. They'll think I've come here to point fingers and pass blame."

"I was the one who called this meeting."

"They'll assume that I've been speaking with you for some time without their knowledge, giving you information behind their backs."

"So they're bureaucrats, then, and not engineers at all, is that what you're saying, Dr. Benyawe?"

"They're human beings first, Mr. Jukes. Engineers second. They're worried about their livelihoods."

"If we don't return to Luna with anything short of absolute success, Doctor, I think all of our careers are over."

"That is a fair assumption, yes," said Benyawe. "But that's true all the time, isn't it? Fail, and you're looking for a job."

"Just one question, Dr. Benyawe. If you had been in charge, would you have already conducted the test?"

"You want to know if I blame Dr. Dublin for the delay."

"I want to know if you're willing to proceed despite some degree of uncertainty. I want to know if you've reached the point where you think we'll learn more from failure or partial success than from further dithering about possibilities."

"Dr. Dublin found some of the pretest readings unsettling," said Benyawe. "I appreciate his caution. Had I been in his position, however, I would have continued with the test. The glaser is built to accommodate a margin of error within the readings we found."

"So if you were in charge of this team, we'd already have our results."

"The gravity laser, Mr. Jukes, is not a device to be taken lightly. Gravity is the most powerful force in the universe."

"I thought love was."

Benyawe smiled. "You're very different from your father."

"You've worked with my father for a long time."

"He's given me a chance to be part of great things. He also turned my hair white by the time I was fifty."

"So why didn't my father put you in charge of this team, Doctor? You have far more experience than Dublin. And every bit as much knowledge of the gravity laser."

"Why aren't you running your own corporation? You've certainly had plenty of opportunities to do so. You helped launch four IPOs before your twentieth birthday, you took nine different divisions and companies from the brink of bankruptcy into the black, and the rumor is that you've built a private investment empire that knows few equals. And yet here you are, heading up a testing expedition in the Kuiper Belt. Your father doesn't always make decisions based on résumés."

"I took this job, Dr. Benyawe, because I believe in the gravity laser."

"But this test *is* dangerous. If it works wrong on a massy object like an asteroid, this ship could simply disappear."

"I'm willing to take risks. Is Dublin?"

"Maybe Dublin was given strict instructions by your father to make sure you came home alive."

Suddenly Dublin's dithering and delays took on an entirely different meaning. "So Father put me in charge but gave instructions for Dublin to take care of me?"

"Your father loves you."

"But not enough to let me make my own decisions."

Lem knew he sounded petulant, but he also knew he was right. Father didn't trust him. *After all these years, after everything I've done outside of Father's shadow, all of my achievements, all of the ways I've exceeded his expectations, he still thinks me incapable of making decisions, he still thinks me weak.* And he won't ever think otherwise until I take this company. That was the solution. Lem had known that for a long time. Taking Father's throne was the only achievement that Father couldn't argue with or question. It was the only way to get Father to see Lem as an equal. That was why Lem wasn't running his own corporation elsewhere as Benyawe suggested. He could have easily done so. There had been several offers. But Lem had turned them down. Any other corporation wasn't enough. Father would always look down on it.

No, Lem was going to take Father's greatest achievement and make it his own, and he was going to do it so convincingly that the whole world and even Father himself would realize that Lem deserved it. No coup. No trickery. What would be the point of that? Father needed to be a willing participant. He needed to know that Lem had earned it without a scrap of help from Father. Otherwise Father would always believe that it was *his* achievement and not Lem's. No, taking the company was the only way to end it all. Only then would Father realize that there were no more snares to lay, no more games to play or lessons to teach. School was over.

But what if what Benyawe had said was true? What if Father's only motivation was love? It was possible, of course, though it felt like such an alien idea to Lem that he couldn't quite take hold of it. Father was never that transparent. There were always motivations behind motivations, and the deepest ones were usually selfish. Lem didn't doubt his Father's love. He doubted the pure, distilled form of it. That was something Lem had never seen.

Lem smiled to himself. See what you do to me, Father? You always keep me guessing. Just when I think I have you figured out, you make me question you all over again.

Lem needed to confront Dublin. If Father *had* given Dublin instructions regarding Lem, then the delays weren't Dublin's fault at all. Lem excused Benyawe and made his way to the lab. He found Dublin in the control room adjacent to the cargo bay. Dublin was moving his stylus through a holo of the glaser. Bots in the cargo bay followed Dublin's commands and performed tiny adjustments to the glaser. Lem watched from a distance, not wanting to interrupt. It was obviously a delicate procedure. Yet despite the sensitivity of it, Dublin's hands danced through the holo and the touch commands like a concert pianist. Lem watched in fascination, feeling a new sense of wonder for Dublin. The glaser was second nature to him; every component, every circuit, were as known to him as his own hands. Father hadn't stuck Dublin here to test Lem. Dublin had the job because he deserved it.

Dublin put aside his stylus, stretched, and noticed Lem. "Mr. Jukes. I didn't see you come in. I hope I didn't keep you waiting."

"I admire what you've accomplished with the glaser, Dr. Dublin."

Dublin shrugged sheepishly. "Six years of my life."

They were alone. Lem felt comfortable proceeding. "My father placed a lot of trust in you when he asked you to lead this project."

Dublin smiled. "Your father has been good to me."

"You don't have to speak well of him just because I'm his son. I know as well as anyone that he can be a little rough around the edges."

Dublin laughed. "Oh, he's not as bad as some say. A tough exterior perhaps, but below the surface a sweet man."

Lem had to work hard to keep a straight face. Sweet? He had heard all kinds of colorful words to describe father; "sweet" had never been one of them. Yet Dublin seemed sincere. "Did my father ever mention me in relation to this mission before we set out?"

"He told me you were going to be the captain of the ship," said Dublin. "He called you 'most capable.'"

A compliment from Father? A sign of the apocalypse. Of course Father was probably just trying to put Dublin at ease about the crew.

"Did he advise you to take any precautions on my account?" asked Lem. "Did he in any way suggest that you were to take care of me? Look out for me? Keep an eye on me?"

Dublin looked confused. "Your father cares for your well-being, Mr. Jukes. You can't fault him for that."

"A yes or no, Dr. Dublin. Did he did give you special instructions regarding me?"

Dublin was taken aback. He fumbled, searching for the right words, trying to remember. "He said I was to make sure nothing happened to you."

So there it was. Undercut by Father again. Didn't Father realize that this would add another layer of anxiety to Dublin's decisions? Whether Dublin's conscious mind realized it or not, it dangled the threat of "something happening to Lem" every time Dublin went to fire the glaser. Of course he would be cautious. Everything he did carried the possibility of inciting the fury and disappointment of the CEO. But more importantly: Didn't Father realize that instructions like this made Lem seem like a child? "Make sure nothing happens to my boy, Dr. Dublin." How could Dublin fully respect Lem as the captain of the ship if Dublin had been led to believe that Lem needed a caretaker, that he needed watching? It suggested that Lem couldn't take care of himself. And yes, Father knew what he was doing. He knew how this would diminish Lem in Dublin's eyes. That was how Father worked. He makes himself seem like a doting, loving parent with concern only for his son, and yet what he was really doing was chipping away at whatever confidence people had placed in Lem. It was infuriating because no one else saw it. No one knew Father like Lem did. No doubt if Lem revealed his frustration to Dublin or Benyawe, they would tell him he was overreacting and that his father had his best interests in mind. Hell, Father probably believed it himself. But Lem knew better. You're eight billion klicks away, Father, and you're still pulling the strings.

Lem shook his head. And here I allowed myself to believe just for a few moments that Father might have love as his only motivation.

Dublin had to go. Or at least be stripped of his decision-making powers. Not his fault, but Lem needed to send a clear message to Father: I don't need a caregiver.

"I'm promoting Dr. Benyawe," said Lem. "She'll be our new director of

Special Operations. You will maintain your position as chief engineer, but you will report to her. She will decide whether we proceed with tests or not. Please don't think of this as a demotion, Dr. Dublin. Your service has been impeccable. But our delays force me to make some change. The Board will expect it."

Dublin no doubt understood that he was being stripped of ultimate decision-making authority, but he also was prudent enough to understand that he was a temporary casualty of a power struggle between father and son. Either that or he was even more docile than Lem had supposed. Whatever the reason, he offered no argument.

Lem next found Benyawe in the lab, took her aside, and told her of her promotion. She was surprised. "Director of Special Operations?" she said. "I'm not familiar with that title."

"I just made it up," said Lem.

"You're promoting me because I told you I would have moved forward with the test," said Benyawe. "But how do you know that my decision to conduct a test when another engineer chooses to refrain from doing so is not brazen recklessness? Dr. Dublin's caution could very well have saved our lives for all we know. It is a very powerful machine."

"I've read your papers, Dr. Benyawe, or at least all of those that have been made available internally, which is no small number. Were you an academic and allowed to make your findings public, I suspect you would be one of the most revered researchers in your field."

"Dr. Dublin is equally respected, Lem."

"Are you turning down the promotion?"

"Not at all. I'm honored. I just want to make sure you understand my qualifications don't exceed his."

"You take risks when he doesn't." And more importantly, your actions haven't been influenced by Father. "Now, prove to me I've made the right decision."

The test was over as soon as it began. One second the asteroid was moving through space. The next second it tore itself to smithereens. The largest surviving rock fragment spun away from the blast toward the ship, but the collision-avoidance system sprang into action and blasted the rock fragment to dust long before it reached the ship.

Lem and Benyawe were watching from the observation room. Lem lowered the scope glasses. "Well that was rather theatrical. Would we call that a success, Dr. Benyawe?"

Benyawe was already tapping on her data pad, calling up the video of the asteroid implosion and watching the footage again at a slower speed. "We clearly don't yet know how to control the glaser to the degree we would like," said Benyawe. "The gravity field was obviously too wide and too powerful. We still have adjustments to make." She looked at Lem. "Dublin's hesitations were not without reason, Lem. The glaser creates a field of centrifugal gravity, a field where gravity stops holding mass together because it all aligns with the glaser. It creates a field through the continuity of mass. The field spreads with the explosion of the mass, then it keeps destroying until the mass is so dispersed that it no longer works as a unit of mass. The question we have to answer is, How far does the field persist in relation to the mass? Do bigger asteroids generate a wider field? And would that field stretch far enough to reach the ship? We better hope not, because if it did, the same thing that happened to that pebble would happen to us."

"The field seemed contained to me," said Lem.

"On a rock this size, yes," said Benyawe. "But what about a bigger mass? That's why we need to continue testing, choosing targets that are incrementally larger than the previous test subjects."

Lem didn't want to wait. He wanted to send a very clear message to Father now. One that showed Father how free and clear Lem was from Father's manipulations. If Father thought he could control Lem with the pebbles, then Lem would go to the opposite extreme. Right to the big leagues.

"In an ideal world," Lem said, "yes, we would inch our way up to bigger asteroids. But this test just proved that Dublin was unnecessarily cautious. I say we move directly to a rock a hundred times the size of that pebble."

"Your Father wouldn't agree with that."

Which is precisely why we're going to do it, Lem wanted to say but didn't. "My father's assignment to me was to prove that the glaser could be a safe and effective mining tool. He wants to operationalize this as soon as possible. Juke ships will be mining big rocks, not pebbles."

Benyawe shrugged. "As long as you know the risks."

"You've been very clear. I'll find our next target while you and Dublin prepare a brief yet thorough report for my father and the Board. Text only. Send the video in a subsequent message. I want them to receive the good news as soon as possible." Lem knew that laserline messages with a lot of memory moved slowly through the company's data receivers. If he wanted to get a message to Father fast, a brief text message was best.

Lem climbed into the push tube, adjusted his vambraces, and gave the command for the magnets to propel him to the helm. Of all the rooms on Makarhu, the helm had been the most difficult for Lem to get used to. Shaped like a cylinder, with the flight crew positioned all along the inner circular wall, the helm could be a little dizzying. As you entered the room at one end, there were crewmen all around you—above, below, left and right, all standing at their workstations with their feet held securely to the wall with greaves. In the center of the room was a spherical system chart, a large hologram surrounded by projectors. A small hologram of the ship was at the sphere's center, and as the ship moved, so did the celestial objects in space around it, keeping the holo of the ship forever in the center. Lem launched himself to the system chart and came to rest beside his chief officer, an American named Chubs.

"Nice shooting," said Chubs. "We can officially erase that pebble from the system chart."

"We need a new target," said Lem. "A hundred times the size of that pebble. Preferably close and rich in minerals."

Chubs took his stylus from the front pocket of his body suit. "That's easy." He selected an asteroid on the system chart down near the ship and enlarged it so it filled the chart. "It's called 2002GJ166. It's not Asteroid Belt big, but it's big for out here."

"How far away?" asked Lem.

"Four days," said Chubs.

Considering that this was the Kuiper Belt and that most big objects were usually months apart from each other, that was ridiculously close. "Sounds perfect," said Lem.

Chubs looked hesitant. "Actually, not perfect. Not if you want to blow it up with the glaser."

"Why?"

"We keep a constant watch of movement around us," said Chubs. "Our boys here know where all the other mining ships are in the vicinity. Your father was very particular about us conducting these field tests far from the snooping eyes of WU-HU or MineTek or any other competitor. So if somebody is nearby, we make it our business to know about it. And this asteroid, 2002GJ166, is currently occupied."

"Someone's mining it?"

Chubs made a few movements with his stylus. The asteroid minimized, and a holo of a mining ship appeared. "A free-miner family. Not a big clan. Just a single ship. It's called El Cavador. According to the files we have from the Lunar Trade Department, they're a Venezuelan family. Their captain is a seventy-four-year-old woman named Concepción Querales. And the ship isn't any younger. It's probably been patched up so many times over it looks like space junk at this point. It comfortably holds sixty people, but knowing free miners, they probably have closer to eighty or ninety people on board."

"We can't conduct the test if they're there," said Lem.

"I'm sure they would appreciate not being blown to smithereens," said Chubs. "But don't expect them to pack up and leave any time soon. They've been at the rock for a few weeks now building mineshafts. They have a lot of time and money invested in this dig site. And it's paying off for them. They've already sent two loads in quickships back to Luna."

Quickships weren't really ships at all. They were rocket-propelled projectiles that carried a mining family's processed metals all the way to Luna. The rockets were for maneuvering, and built-in sponders constantly broadcast the quickship's location, trajectory, destination, and the name of the family. The family ID was always embedded deep within the quickship so it couldn't be pirated. But pirates had little chance of catching quickships anyway. They moved incredibly fast, far faster than any manned vessel could match. Once the quickships got close to Luna, they turned themselves over to Lunar Guidance, or LUG, where they got "lugged" into Lunar orbit for pickup and delivery.

"If we *did* wait for them to leave," said Lem, "about how long are we talking? A week? A year?"

"Impossible to say," said Chubs. "Juke hasn't done a lot of scans of rocks out this far. We typically stick to the Asteroid Belt. I have no idea how much metal they're sitting on. Could be a month. Could be eight months."

"What's the next closest asteroid?" asked Lem.

Chubs turned back to the chart and began digging around again. "If you're in a hurry, you won't like the answer. The next nearest rock is four months, sixteen days away. And that's four months in the wrong direction, farther out into deep space. So it would be four months out and four months back, just to return to this spot."

"Eight months. Way too long."

Chubs shrugged. "That's the Kuiper Belt, Lem. Space and more space."

Lem stared at the chart. They needed to take the closer asteroid. And the sooner the better. Lem didn't want the miners taking all the metals. The point was to show the Board the economic viability of the glaser. Lem didn't intend to obliterate the rock. He was going to break it up, collect whatever metals he could, sell the haul, and slap the asset statement onto the center of the boardroom table back on Luna.

But how do you vacate free miners from a profitable mine? He couldn't pay them, which, as a man of wealth, had always been his default strategy for anything. The free miners were sitting on their source of income, possibly a long-standing source of income. They wouldn't want to give it up. Which meant the only real option was to take it by force.

"What if we bump them?" asked Lem.

Lem had never witnessed the practice himself, but he knew that it existed. "Bumping" was a corporate technique, though not one you would find documented by any corporation. It was the asteroid version of claim jumping. Corporate ships snuck in on dig sites operated by free miners and chased the free miners away. They were coordinated attacks that required a lot of tech, but they worked. Free miners were rarely strong enough to defend themselves, and if you timed the attack right, the mineshafts would already be dug. So the free miners did most of the work, but the corporates reaped all of the benefits. It was devious, yes, and Lem didn't relish the thought of doing it, but an eight-month trip to the second-closest asteroid was simply not an option. Besides, if rumors were true, Father had done a good bit of bumping in his early days, which would suggest that he could hardly object if Lem did it, too—as long as it didn't become public.

Chubs raised an eyebrow. "You serious, Lem? You want to bump them?"

"If you see another option, I'd be thrilled to hear it. I don't like the idea either, but we can't ask them to leave. They wouldn't. And the Makarhu can clearly take them. My concern is the glaser. I don't want to endanger it in a scuffle. Could we bump them without jarring the glaser?"

"Depends on how you do it," said Chubs. "They're moored to the asteroid. If we catch them unawares, cut their moorings, and cripple their power, we can push them away as gentle as a kitten. They'd be completely defenseless at that point. The real danger is their pebble-killers."

Pebble-killers, slang for "collision-avoidance lasers."

"We wouldn't move on them until we took out their power," said Chubs. "Otherwise they could hit us with their lasers."

"Wouldn't that kill them?" asked Lem. "If we cut their power we'd cut their life support."

"They'll have auxiliary power for life support," said Chubs. "That's not a concern. The real issue is getting close enough to strike them. They might already know we're here. They've got a sky scanner. If we move toward them now, even four days out, they'll know it. Especially if we rush them. They'll pick that movement up immediately and still have plenty of time to build a possible defense."

"You've done this before, Chubs. Surely there are tactics for sneaking up on an asteroid."

Chubs sighed. "There is one approach that usually works if done right. We call it 'Red Light Green Light.' You're familiar with the playground game?"

Lem knew the one, and he could guess at what the name implied. "We sneak up on them when they're not looking."

"When they *can't* look," said Chubs. "Remember, they're moored to the asteroid. So they're rotating with it. We only advance toward them when they're on the opposite side of the asteroid from our position. When they rotate toward us, we become still as a statue before we get in their line of sight, with all of our lights off. A dead stop. Totally invisible. Then, as soon as they rotate around the asteroid, as soon as their back is to us, so to speak, we punch it and shoot forward. It takes a lot of stopping and starting with the thrusters and retros, and uses up way too much fuel, but it's doable. Though it will take a lot longer to get there."

"Set the course," said Lem. "And prepare everything we need for the bump. If they detect us sooner than we would like, I want to be ready to surge forward and take them."

Chubs smiled, shaking his head, already tapping commands into his wrist pad. "You surprise me, Lem. I took you for someone who held the moral high ground. Going to war doesn't seem your style."

"We're businessmen, Chubs. The moral high ground is wherever we set it."

CHAPTER 3

Wit

Captain Wit O'Toole rode up to the front gate at Papakura Military Camp in South Auckland, New Zealand, and presented his American passport to the soldier at the gatehouse. Papakura was home to the New Zealand Special Air Service, or the NZSAS, the kiwi version of the Special Forces. Wit had come to recruit some of the men. As an officer of the Mobile Operations Police—or MOPs, a small, elite international peacekeeping force—Wit was always on the lookout for qualified soldiers to add to his team. If the prospects he had identified here at Papakura were as smart and as skilled as he hoped they were, if they could pass Wit's unique little test, he would gladly welcome them aboard.

A light rain was falling, misting the windshield. The soldier examining Wit's passport stood in the rain, tapping at the sheets, clicking through all the data. He found the photo of Wit and compared it to Wit's likeness. Wit gave the man his friendliest smile. A second soldier with a leashed German shepherd did a loop around the vehicle, letting the dog sniff the vehicle's trunk and underside.

The men were stalling. Wit had noticed the security cameras mounted above the gatehouse when he had pulled up. The computers were no doubt running their facial-recognition software to determine if Wit was in fact who he said he was. Wit only hoped the cameras had gotten a clear enough shot through the rain-splattered windshield or this could take a while.

The passport showed his full name: DeWitt Clinton O'Toole, named for the governor of New York who was the driving force behind the actual building of the Erie Canal, a distant ancestor of his mother. There were stamps and visas from a dozen countries, though these were by no means a complete record of Wit's travels. Those represented his "official" visits to foreign soil. Far more numerous were his undocumented insertions into countries all over the world as he and his team struck hard and fast at whomever was harming civilians. The Middle East, Indonesia, Micronesia, Africa, Eastern Europe, Central and South America.

The soldier with the passport touched his finger to the communicator in his ear and listened a moment. He then handed Wit back the passport. "You're free to go through, Mr. O'Toole."

Wit thanked the man and sat back as the vehicle drove him into the parking lot and pulled into a slot. Wit picked up the envelope off the seat beside him, exited the vehicle, and walked toward the wall that encircled the inner campus. The regimental sergeant major was waiting at the gate with an extra umbrella. He wore fatigues and a tan beret with the crest of the NZSAS embroidered on it: a winged dagger with the words WHO DARES WINS.

Wit was in his civvies, but he saluted anyway.

"Welcome, Captain O'Toole. I'm Sergeant Major Manaware." He handed Wit the extra umbrella. "Bummer your first visit to Auckland's a wet one."

"Not at all, Sergeant Major. I am a fan of the rain. It convinces the enemy to stay inside and not come out and kill us."

Manaware laughed. "Spoken like a true SEAL. Always happy to avoid a fight."

Wit smiled back. Military trash talk. Our Special Forces can beat up your Special Forces. You guys are bumbling idiots. We're the real hardened warriors. Soldiers had been talking this way to one another ever since cavemen had picked up a club. Yet Manaware was saying something else as well: The kiwis had done their homework. They had studied Wit's military record, and, more to the point, they were letting him know it. They were saying, "We're watching you as closely as you're watching us, mate." Which was fine with Wit. He preferred it that way. He hated conversations in which everyone pretended not to know what the others knew. Yet such was the military, especially as you rose up the ranks. There was nothing more cat and mouse than a conversation between two generals in the same army, both of them withholding intel for personal profit. It drove

Wit insane. And it was the primary reason why he didn't hold a place among them. Wit didn't play that game.

Manaware led Wit into the compound. It was like every other military base Wit had ever seen. Hangars, training facilities, barracks, office buildings. They made their way into a building to the right and shook out their umbrellas in the anteroom. Inside, two SAS soldiers were sweeping the lobby floor with large utility brooms. They snapped to attention when Manaware entered.

"As you were," said the sergeant major, continuing to the stairs.

The men immediately returned to sweeping. It had always impressed Wit that the SAS instilled in their men the idea that no job was beneath them; no chore was too low for a man serving his country. The running joke was that at the graduation ceremony following their nine months of training, SAS graduates received the coveted tan beret in one hand and a broom in the other.

Manaware led Wit to a door and gave a light tap.

A voice inside bid them enter.

Colonel Napatu's office was a small space with few adornments. Napatu greeted Wit with a handshake stronger than Wit had expected for a man of Napatu's age and invited Wit to take a chair beside a coffee table.

"May I offer you any refreshment, Captain O'Toole?" asked Manaware. "Perhaps a fruity tea with lemon?" Manaware smiled. It was one last jab of military trash talk. Isn't that what you Navy women drink? Fruity tea with lemon?

Wit smiled, conceding defeat. "No thank you, Sergeant Major. You've been very kind."

Manaware gave a wink and left.

Colonel Napatu took a chair opposite Wit. "I heard you lost three men in Mauritania."

"Yes, sir," said Wit. "Good men. Our convoy was hit by on IED. The point vehicle took the brunt of it. I was in the second vehicle and thus unharmed."

"The world is a dangerous place, Captain O'Toole."

"Improvised exploding device," said Napatu. "A coward's weapon. I heard you carried one of the wounded four kilometers to the extraction site."

"He was a dear friend, sir. He died later in surgery."

Napatu nodded gravely.

"That is why MOPs exist, sir. War always inflicts its greatest casualties on the innocent. Our job is to put a stop to chaos before more innocent lives are lost."

"That sounds like textbook talk, O'Toole. You recite that for all the commanding officers?"

"No, sir. It's simply who we are."

"At least you're not like the damn United Nations, who send their boys in only after a war has ended."

Wit said nothing. He wasn't here to express political views or criticize other forces. He was here for men.

Napatu got the hint and changed the subject. "You boys must meet a lot of resistance from civil law enforcement."

"Almost always. But where we go, sir, local law enforcement is often part of the problem."

"Corruption?"

"Murder. Drug trafficking. Human trafficking. Local police in these situations are often nothing more than thugs in uniforms. It doesn't take much to swing power in unstable countries, Colonel. If you're a tribal warlord, and you off the chief of police, suddenly every police officer has a choice. He can either swear allegiance to you and keep his weapon and badge, or he can watch as you hack his wife and children to pieces. Or, as happens just as often, the warlord executes all the police anyway and populates the police force with his own loyal men."

Napatu sat back in his chair. "The Chief of Defence Force told me that I'm supposed to give you the liberty to recruit any of my men. Full access to all of our facilities and troops. The highest level of clearance."

"I have the official letter here," said Wit, placing the envelope on the table, "signed by the Chief of Defence Force as well as the Minister of Defence."

Napatu didn't look at the envelope. "You and I both know, Captain, that these signatures don't mean squat. I can come up with all kinds of legitimate excuses why you shouldn't take any of my men, all of which the big boys in suits will agree with. Family issues, health issues, emotional issues. They give you these documents because they have to. It would be political suicide to do otherwise. But they don't mean a damn thing to me. The only way you're taking any of my boys is if I agree to it."

Napatu was right. The signatures were more a formality. Wit was actually relieved to hear that Napatu realized that, too. He preferred that Napatu
gave him men because he wanted to and not because someone had forced
his hand.

"What makes you think any one of my men will want to give up their position here to join you?" asked Napatu. "Do you have any idea, Captain, how
near impossible it is to get into this unit? Do you know what these men
have suffered, the grueling torture we put them through for the chance to
wear the tan beret?"

"I do, sir. I've studied your selection process and training cycle. These
men go through hell and back, and only a small fraction of them make
the cut."

"You've studied?" said Napatu. "With all due respect, Captain, cracking
open a book on our process will hardly give you an accurate perspective
of what it means to become an SAS man."

It can't have been more difficult than my SEAL training, Wit thought.
But he said nothing. No need turning this into a pissing contest.

Colonel Napatu jabbed a finger on the table. "These men take themselves to an inch from death to join us, Captain. We push them until we
think they'll break, then we push twice as far. We cull so many in the
training process that it's a miracle we have any men here at all. But somehow a few make it through. Men who have no quit in them. Men who will
endure any physical suffering, make any sacrifice. You don't become an
SAS soldier to impress single girls at pubs, Captain. Your motivation has
to be rock solid. You have to want it so bad that even the threat of death
won't take it from you. And once they're here, once these men have joined
our ranks, they become part of a brotherhood so strong that nothing can
break it. And you think that you, a total stranger, can waltz in here, and
convince them to leave behind everything they've worked so hard to
achieve just so they can join *you*? I find that incredibly arrogant."

It was the token response Wit got every time. Regardless of what language they spoke or what corner of the world they came from, all commanding officers of Special Forces units had the same reaction. They saw
their troops as their own sons. And the idea that any of their sons would
consider going elsewhere was unthinkable.

But Wit knew soldiers better than Napatu did. He understood the warrior mind. The most elite of soldiers didn't join Special Forces to be part of a brotherhood or for the prestige. Men joined Special Forces because they wanted action. They didn't sign up to *train* for fifty-two weeks a year and sleep in comfortable bunks with downy pillows. They signed up to sleep in the rain with their finger on the trigger.

But Wit had to say this delicately; COs had fragile egos. "Your reservations are warranted, Colonel. Your men are the model of loyalty to their country and their unit. However, MOPs offers these men something more. Action. And lots of it. Since we are so few in numbers, we deploy throughout the world far more often than larger forces like yours, which often requires congressional or parliamentary approval. MOPs is not at the mercy of politicians concerned with self-preservation and what military action will mean for them at the voting booths. We move everywhere, sir."

"We do covert missions as well, Captain. Surely you don't think our operations are only what you read about in the press."

"I am aware of your operations, Colonel. Both your covert actions and the missions that never reach your desk because one of your higher-ups vetoed the operation simply because the operation wasn't his idea. There are careerists in this military, Colonel, as there are in every military. You are not one of them, but there are plenty above you."

Colonel Napatu had no response to that. He no doubt knew there were men above him who fit that description. He had been suffering under their command his entire career. What probably rattled him was learning that Wit knew more about the classified operations circling the upper echelons than he did.

"We also offer something else," said Wit. "You will take this as further arrogance, Colonel, but MOPs is arguably the most elite fighting force in the world. At least on a small scale. We recruit from the best Special Forces groups out there. Russian Alphas, U.S. Delta Force, British SAS, U.S. Navy SEALs, Israel's Shayetet 13, French Green Berets. These units only take the best of their soldiers, sir, what they call the 'one percenters.' But MOPs are the point zero one percenters. We only take the best of *their* best. To be counted among us is an incredible honor. Our soldiers don't forfeit their love of country or patriotism when they join us. I would argue that service in our unit is an even higher demonstration of love of country because you are representing your home nation on a global scale. Ask yourself, Colonel, if you were given the opportunity to represent New Zealand, to be one of the few men deemed by your government as your country's perfect soldier, the ideal warrior, would you not at least be intrigued by the idea?"

"I'll concede that some may jump at the chance for more action," said Napatu, "but why would we forfeit our best soldiers to another army outside our own jurisdiction?"

"Because MOPs allows New Zealand to have a hand in global stability without worrying about political ramifications, sir. Send a brigade of New Zealanders into North Africa, and the political fallout could be catastrophic. Suddenly New Zealand is the bully of the world. But send a few New Zealanders who are a part of an international military unit seeking to preserve human rights, and there is little to no fallout. No one can accuse New Zealand of imperialism. Any action taken by MOPs is clearly an act of global goodwill."

"There are those who say MOPs are the dogs of the West, Captain O'Toole, that you boys are nothing more than grunts for American intelligence. Puppets of the CIA nicely disguised as a mini-international coalition."

Wit shrugged. "There are also those who say we are soulless child murderers carrying out the personal vendettas of the current U.S. administration. It's propaganda, Colonel. You and I both know who we are and what we do."

Napatu was quiet a moment. Wit remained silent, letting the man think it through, though he knew Napatu would come around.

Finally, Napatu said, "Who did you have in mind?"

Wit removed his handheld from his pocket and set the device on the table in front of him. He extended the arms on the sides and the thin bar at the top and turned on the holo. A wall of data with photos and records of five servicemen floated in space above him. Wit turned the device around so it faced Napatu.

"There are five of your men we'd like to screen."

"Screen?"

"A capabilities test, sir. We want the best and most willing candidates. If all five pass our screening and demonstrate an eagerness to serve, then we will gladly take them all. If none pass, we will thank them and you for your time and not bother you further. It's that simple."

Colonel Napatu scanned the names and didn't show any surprise until he reached the last of the five, the youngest and smallest of the group. He was the most unlikely pick simply because of his inexperience. He deserved to be among the SAS like any other man in the unit, but he wasn't battled-tested like the other four. He had only been with the SAS for five months and was as green as they came.

"You can have your pick of any of my men," said Napatu, "some of them proven warriors with flawless service records and the highest marks. And yet you choose this one, a greenie?"

"Yes, sir," said Wit. "We are very interested in Lieutenant Mazer Rackham."

The following morning, just after dawn, Wit stood in a small grassy valley two hours northeast of Papakura. Around him, beyond the valley, was the dense Mataitai Forest with its tall Tanekaha trees and vibrant broadleaf ferns. Five men stood in front of Wit at attention, their eyes forward, their feet at a forty-five-degree angle, heels together. They wore military-issued T-shirts, fatigue pants, and solemn expressions. Wit had left them standing that way, unflinching in the morning chill, for the better part of an hour.

Wit looked at each man in turn. They were all physically strong, but only two of them were the heavily muscled bodybuilding types. Two others were of average height and build, and the last, a Maori, Mazer Rackham, was lean and slightly smaller.

Size mattered little in the Special Forces, however. In fact, thick upper bodies and large arms might give you greater strength, but they also made you an easier target and harder to conceal, not to mention top-heavy and less nimble. Wit, who was larger than any of these men, knew all this from experience. He had suffered enough broken noses in sparring matches with men half his size to know that bigger soldiers weren't necessarily better ones.

The handheld in Wit's pocket vibrated, signaling that his men were in position. Showtime.

Wit faced the five soldiers. "Good morning, gentlemen. You know who I am, and you know why you're here. This morning we will conduct a preliminary exercise. If you pass, you are eligible for a screening. Let me emphasize that whether you pass that screening or not, you can take pride in knowing that you were selected from the entire New Zealand Defence Force to participate in these proceedings. You represent the highest degree of readiness and training, and are a credit to your country."

The men kept their eyes forward, showing no emotion.

"While we've been standing here enjoying the lovely nippy morning," said Wit, "my teammates have been hiding in the forests around us. I have just received a confirmation that they are ready to begin and are eager to embarrass you by making you fail. On the ground in front of you are forty-kilo rucksacks. You will each carry one of these to a safe house five kilometers from here. The coordinates of the safe house as well as a map and compass are in your rucksacks. Also in front of you is your weapon, a small automatic rifle that you likely have never handled. It is unique to MOPs. It goes by many names, the Flatliner, the Angel Maker, or my personal favorite, the Hell Ticket, since it sends so many of our unfortunate enemies on a one-way trip to the devil himself. Its technical name, however, is the P87, and if you join us, gentlemen, it will become your truest and most devoted companion, never leaving your side. You will pee with it, eat oatmeal with it, shower with it, and sleep with it. Don't think of it as your weapon. Think of it as the appendage you never knew you had. In the SAS you are trained on many unconventional weapons, but the P87, once you learn its features, may surprise even you.

"But since this is an exercise and not an actual engagement, your P87 is loaded with twenty spider rounds." Wit held up a red pellet. "Spider rounds are not lethal, but they will incapacitate you. If struck, you will receive an electric shock that is hard to forget. If any of you have a pacemaker or are pregnant, I invite you to withdraw."

A few of the men cracked a smile.

"Ah," said Wit. "You're not zombies, after all." He showed them the pellet again. "My teammates are equipped with these same rounds. If you are struck, and believe me, you will know it, your participation in the exercise is over. Unlike real warfare, you are instructed to leave your wounded team members behind. If one of you drops, keep moving. Your mission is not to get your team to the safe house. Your mission is to get *me* to the safe house. I will be playing the role of a diplomat you have been assigned to protect. Should I be wounded, the exercise is over. Like my men hiding in the forest, I am wearing what is called a dampening suit. If struck it will take the electric shock of a spider round without harming me. Since all of you are so concerned with my personal safety, I thought I'd mention it."

Another grin from the men.

"Please wear your helmets and visors at all times. You have five hours to deliver me to the safe house." Wit donned his own helmet and tightened the chinstrap. "Begin."

The men immediately moved into action, putting on their helmets and forming a perimeter around Wit with their backs to him.

"Please kneel down, sir," said one of the men.

Wit took a knee, hiding himself behind the circle of soldiers.

Mazer had hung back and was now snapping cartridges into the rifles and tossing them to the soldier in the perimeter nearest him. That man passed two rifles to his left and one to his right until every man in the circle was armed.

Wit was impressed. The whole maneuver had taken only a few seconds, and the men had reacted smoothly without speaking to one another, as if this had been a drill they had run hundreds of times.

Shots from the trees to the north pegged into the dirt around them. Intentional misses. Something to get the blood up.

Rough hands lifted Wit to his feet, and the men retreated to the south tree line, maintaining a defensive wall around Wit. One of the New Zealanders laid down cover fire, having set his P87 to three-round bursts. Mazer grabbed three rucksacks and followed. The men set up a defensive position in the trees and emptied one of the rucksacks. Mazer found the coordinates and compass and mapped out a route.

Once their destination was known and they felt safe from enemy fire, the real discussion began. Everything was considered. There was a sniper

to the north. There were two rucksacks still in the field. The three rucksacks they had recovered all had the same equipment, so they weren't
likely to find anything new in the other two sacks. They had limited
ammunition. The forests narrowed at some spots, which were ideal loca-
tions for an ambush. They had water, yes, but no food. And the clock was
ticking.

Wit noted how each of the men spoke calmly and intelligently, pointing
out potential dangers or possible alterations to their route. A few of the
suggestions Wit hadn't considered, and he was pleased to see that the others recognized the wisdom of these comments. No one tried to talk over
anyone else, and each of them was humble enough to recognize an idea
better than their own.

All of them were aware that Wit was watching them, of course. They
knew that this moment was as important as any action they would under-
take along the way. And yet it was clear to Wit that none of them was trying
to impress him. This was how they had been trained to act. Orderly, effi-
ciently, cohesively, and without ego.

Mazer Rackham turned to Wit. "Are you a soldier, sir, as well as a diplomat in this exercise? Meaning, for the purpose of our exercise, do you
know how to fire this weapon?"

"Yes I do."

"And will you use it to defend yourself to the best of your ability?"

"Yes I will."

Mazer immediately surrendered his rifle to Wit.

A second soldier spoke up. "Sir, as a diplomat familiar with this hostile
scenario, do you have any intel about the men seeking to harm you?"

Wit smiled. Normal soldiers would treat Wit as nothing more than a
warm body to pull along. Pumping him for information would be against
the "rules." These men knew better. "I know our enemy well," said Wit.
"Both their skills and their tactics."

The questions came fast. How many men? What are their strengths?
What weapons do they possess? Where might they take positions? How
are they communicating?

Twice the group picked up and moved their location, never staying in
one spot for long. When the questions were exhausted they modified their

route and made preparations to move. The first objective was to retrieve the last two rucksacks.

Rather than venture into the open, three of the men spent half an hour hunting down the sniper, who had hid himself in a tree. The sniper put up little resistance. Once he had been spotted, he allowed himself to be shot, and his dampening suit glowed red.

The New Zealanders retrieved the last two sacks and then, with Wit, moved east toward the safe house. They advanced with two men far out front, sweeping ahead of them. Two others protected Wit in the middle— though one of these, Mazer Rackham, was now unarmed. The last man took up the rear.

The ambush came two kilometers later.

Two of the New Zealanders went down, their bodies twitching, before any of the others had returned fire. The MOPs were all around them, in trees, behind logs, tucked in foxholes.

Wit fired three shots, and three dampening suits glowed red in the trees. Two more shots, and two foxholes became quiet. The remaining New Zealanders took out another three MOPs before pulling Wit away to the south. Mazer Rackham, Wit noticed, had retrieved a weapon from one of the fallen soldiers. Spider rounds pinged into the trees and undergrowth around them.

Seventy meters later, they were clear, hustling toward a ravine.

They moved quickly, taking a circuitous route up the ravine, staying close and moving cautiously. Despite the weight of the rucksacks and the rush of adrenaline from the firefight, no one seemed winded.

"Why did you give me your weapon?" Wit asked Mazer. "By arming me, you put me further into the fight. You drew more fire to me since I was now a threat to our enemy as well as a target."

"They were going to be shooting at you anyway, sir. And after weighing the advantages, after considering all we had to gain by arming you, I took that risk."

"What advantages?"

"You're more familiar with our pursuers. You're a decorated and skilled soldier, so you'll be at least as vigilant as I am. You also know our ammunition better than I do, so you're more familiar with its velocity and other targeting considerations. You also intimately know the weapon and all of its capabilities. I don't. Which means you're probably a better shot than I am. Considering how you performed back there, I see that I was right. Most importantly, you have the capacity to defend yourself. In the chaos of a fight, we may not see all the threats to you. If something escapes our notice, you have the ability to eliminate that threat. Our mission is not to survive, sir. Our mission is to get you to the safe house. If you're armed, you might be able to reach it even if the rest of us are dead."

Wit stopped moving. "Halt."

The three men stopped.

"We should keep moving, sir," said one of the other soldiers. "The safe house is only two kilometers away, and our position has been compromised."

"There is no safe house," said Wit. "It's an empty field. We've gone far enough."

"The exercise is over?"

"Yes, it is. Come with me, gentlemen." Wit entered a command on his handheld.

Five minutes later they were down from the ravine, where a dozen MOPs soldiers were waiting. The two New Zealanders who had been shot in the ambush were there as well, visibly disappointed, certain they had failed.

"Congratulations, gentlemen," said Wit. "All five of you have passed this preliminary exercise. My objective was to witness how you functioned as a team, and you did not disappoint. Your actions were especially impressive considering that each of you were handpicked from different units and had never worked together before. This suggests to me that you could easily be integrated into our team should you pass our screening. I should forewarn you, however. The screening is difficult. If any of you have had second thoughts and would rather not participate, now's the time to say so."

No one spoke.

"Very well," said Wit. "As soon as you wake up, we'll begin."

One of the New Zealander's looked confused. "Wake up, sir?"

Five MOPs raised handguns and shot the five New Zealanders with tranquilizers. The New Zealanders looked surprised. Then their eyes rolled back and they dropped.

Wit sat in the back of a rented semitrailer truck, heading northwest on Route 1 into Auckland. The trailer was long and wide and well ventilated, with more than enough room for the five men sleeping on stretchers.

Wit didn't particularly enjoy shooting men with tranquilizers. Especially skilled and capable soldiers who had served their country well. Yet Wit knew it was a necessity. He needed men who were utterly ruthless in the execution of their duty, and the screening, as ugly as it was, as inhumane as it was, measured exactly what Wit needed to know.

A short Filipino soldier named Calinga walked up the line of stretchers, pausing at each one to check the men's vitals. When he finished he sat beside Wit and gestured to the stretchers. "Who do you think will pass?"

"All of them, I hope. We need a lot more than five."

"My money is on Mazer Rackham. The one who gave you his gun."

"Surrendering your weapon is hardly the trait of a supersoldier, Calinga."

"Under the circumstances I thought it smart."

"Would *you* ever give up your weapon?"

Calinga shrugged. "Depends. If it meant I got a better, more powerful weapon in return, one that was better suited to the task at hand, then absolutely. I'd surrender that puppy in a heartbeat. And that's what Rackham did. By giving you his weapon, he got a bigger, more powerful weapon in return. You. He knew that *you* with his weapon was better than *him* with the same weapon. And it paid off. You took out several men, including me. And I don't go down easily."

"I don't need *me* to take out the enemy. I need men who can take out the enemy without my assistance."

"You need men who can think unconventionally and do things that traditional soldiers would never consider. Him giving you his weapon seems like out-of-box thinking to me."

"It's not enough to think outside the box," said Wit. "We need men to tear the box to shreds and burn it."

"So he should have broken your gun into tiny pieces and set it on fire?"

"I'm not criticizing his decision," said Wit. "Under the circumstances it might have been the smartest course of action. But it would have been better if he had kept the weapon and taken out all those men himself instead of having me do it for him. Besides, knowing *what* and *where* to attack is far more important than knowing *how* to attack."

"But he was humble enough to realize that he wasn't as good as you. That has to count for something. I've read the guy's file. He's young, but he has a head on his shoulders."

"They all have heads on their shoulders," said Wit. "Although a headless army would certainly intimidate the enemy. What would we call ourselves, 'The Sleepy Hollow Squad'?"

" 'The Guillotined Gang,' " said Calinga.

The noise outside the truck increased as they got closer into Auckland and traffic picked up. They exited the highway north of town and moved west toward the shipyards. After a series of stops and starts, the truck parked. Wit heard the driver and passenger doors open, and then the rear door of the trailer slid up. Two MOPs soldiers in civvies were standing outside.

The semi was parked inside an abandoned warehouse on the waterfront. Wit had paid cash to rent it for the month, but he hadn't bothered with any of the utilities. Other than a row of small generators humming quietly in the corner, the warehouse was empty and quiet.

One of the MOPs soldiers spoke with a British accent. "How was it riding in the back with the stiffs, Captain?"

"They're not dead, Deen," said Wit. "They're sleeping."

"When they wake up, they might wish they were dead," said Deen, laughing.

"Anyone who wakes up and sees your face, Deen, will think he *has* died," said Calinga. "And it won't be heaven."

"You're a bucket a laughs today, Cali," said Deen.

Deen hit a button in the rear of the truck. The wheels spread farther apart, and the bed of the truck lowered to the ground. He and the other MOP, an Israeli named Averbach, brought the stretchers out onto the warehouse floor. While Wit checked the candidates' vitals one last time, Deen and Averbach changed into full combat gear. Black body armor, boots, helmet, sidearms, assault rifles. When they were finished, they looked impenetrable.

"We all set?" asked Wit.

"The room's prepped and ready," said Averbach. "You tell us who's first, and we'll get them in position."

Wit pointed. "That one. Mazer Rackham."

Deen and Averbach each took one side of the stretcher and pushed it toward the administrative offices on the far side of the warehouse. Wit followed. Calinga stayed behind with the other stretchers.

They pushed Mazer through a series of doors until they reached the room designated for the screenings. It was roughly ten meters square, probably an old conference room. No windows or furniture. Bare walls. One door. High ceiling. Like a cell, only for white-collar office workers.

Deen and Averbach pushed the stretcher to the middle of the room, pulled the straps free, and then lifted Mazer off the stretcher and gently laid him on the floor.

Wit removed a metallic crown from the bag he was carrying and placed it on Mazer's forehead. The crown had three bands: two that wrapped around the side of Mazer's head, and a third that went up over the top and extended three-fourths of the way to the back. Wit entered a code on the front of the crown and then lifted Mazer's head while the two bands on the sides extended to each other and locked together in the back, securing the crown to Mazer's head. Wit gave the crown a tug to make sure it was tight. Mazer would likely get a migraine from the pressure, but that was the least of his problems. Wit then pulled an injection dot from his bag. The dot was a small coin-sized disc with adhesive on the back. Wit stuck the dot atop the veins in the bend of Mazer's arm, then stood up and turned to Deen and Averbach. "You guys ready?"

The soldiers nodded and took their positions inside the room, guarding the door. Wit placed a flat holopad on the floor and extended two slender vertical posts from the back corners. He then retrieved his bag and pushed the stretcher out into the hall, closing the door behind him. Moving quickly, he went to a small office three doors down, where an identical holopad was up and ready. Wit turned on a monitor, and an image of Mazer Rack-

ham asleep on the floor flickered on-screen. There were Deen and Averbach, rifles slung over their shoulders, on either side of the door, blocking
any escape.

Wit leaned forward and put his face into the holospace above the
holopad. On the monitor, a hologram of Wit's head appeared above the holopad on the floor beside Mazer, as if a ghost one floor down was poking his
head up through the floor for a look around.

Wit entered a command on his handheld, and in the other room, the
injection dot initiated. A tiny needle pierced Mazer's vein and injected the
drug to counter the tranquilizer. Mazer blinked his eyes open. Two seconds later he was up, bent low in a crouched position, with one hand on
the ground in front of him, helping him maintain his balance. It looked
like a weak, defenseless position, but Wit knew better. Mazer was set to
spring upward and attack. For a moment, Wit thought Mazer would strike
then and end the screening. But then Mazer ripped the injection dot from
his arm and tossed it aside, still blinking his eyes and forcing himself to
wake.

Wit's hologram spoke. "Lieutenant Rackham, should you ever be cap-
tured, there is a high probability that you would be tortured for information. The device you're wearing on your head directly stimulates various
brain areas. With it, I can make you experience agonizing pain, see blinding light that you can't shut out, or feel like you need to pee so bad your
gut will explode. It's not pleasant. If you give me the information I want,
however, I will stop the pain. Let's complicate matters further by saying
the information I seek would likely compromise fellow members of your
unit and most certainly lead to their deaths. Now, let's pretend the information I want is the name of your first pet as a child. Tell me that name
now or suffer the consequences."

Mazer smiled. "Seriously? Torture? That's your special screening? I'm
surprised, Captain. I was anticipating something a little more innovative."

A light on the front of Mazer's crown blinked, and Mazer threw back
his head and screamed. His whole body buckled, and he crumpled to the
floor, stunned. He lay there trying to catch his breath.

Wit's holo remained cool and impassive. "On a pain scale of one to ten,
Mazer, with ten being the most painful, the shock I just gave you was a

five. And that was only a two-second burst. I am prepared to go much higher and for much longer should you refuse to cooperate. Now, the name of your pet please."

Mazer got his hands under him and slowly pushed himself up into a sitting position. He shook his head, got to his feet, and began doing jumping jacks.

"Calisthenics will hardly appease me, Mazer. Tell me the animal's name now."

Mazer began singing a marching song as he continued with the jumping jacks, something ribald and silly, no doubt learned in the SAS. Wit allowed him to finish the first verse simply because he found it entertaining, then he hit Mazer with another burst and dropped the man to his knees. Mazer pressed the palms of his hands to his closed eyes, gritting his teeth.

Wit hated doing it. The whole process made him sick. But he needed men resourceful enough to take any situation and immediately see their own way out of it. "Your eyes believe you're staring straight into the sun, Mazer. They're begging you to stop this useless resistance and surrender the information I want. Tell me the name, and I will stop."

Eyes clenched shut, muscles tight, Mazer got back to his feet and continued with the jumping jacks, though with far less fervor and coordination.

"All right," said Wit. "We'll come back to the pet. Let's try another one. Your mother's maiden name. Give me that. Surely you remember your mother's maiden name."

Mazer responded by counting his jumping jacks aloud.

"I am beginning to lose my patience, Mazer. This is not difficult. Surrender the information or I will break you."

Mazer's counting grew louder, almost a shout.

The shout became a scream.

Mazer went down, writhing, every muscle taught, back arched, fingers and hands curled awkwardly, his face twisted in a rictus of agony.

Wit released the pain and paused, giving Mazer a chance to move. Mazer didn't.

Wit said, "Perhaps you're currently telling yourself that since you and I are on the same side, since this is merely a test, I won't inflict any serious, lasting damage. It's only natural to reach this conclusion, Mazer, but you're mistaken. I am not the New Zealand Army, soldier. I am not bound by their codes of ethics. Our army is unique. We do not concern ourselves with oversight. We do what needs to be done, as painful and as gruesome as that may be. That includes torturing men like you to the point of inflicting permanent neurological damage. Should you develop a tick because of my tinkering with your brain or a loss of hearing or a loss of coordination or a paralysis, no one will touch us. If I turn your brain to scrambled eggs, I won't get so much as a slap on the hand. We are above the influence of those who would protect you. So for your own sake and safety, give me your mother's maiden name and the name of your first pet or this little exercise will become painful in the extreme."

None of it was true. MOPs never tortured the enemy. It wasn't necessary. If MOPs took any prisoners, the prisoners were usually so terrified that they poured out intel without being asked. But Mazer wouldn't know that, and Wit wanted to put a deep, gnawing fear in the man.

Mazer said nothing.

Wit hit him again.

Mazer flinched, but then rolled on his stomach and got himself into a sitting position. Wit eased the pain and watched, amazed, as Mazer caught his breath. The man should be on his back, unable to get up, and yet here he was, bullheaded and upright.

"Are you ready to cooperate, Mazer?" Wit asked. "Can we end this exercise now? I would like to. I'm bored. Give me the names, and we'll call it a day."

Mazer sat with his head bowed, still and quiet. His lips began to move, and at first Wit thought that he had broken; that he was surrendering the names but no longer had the strength to speak them aloud. Then slowly Mazer's voice grew in volume. It wasn't English, Wit realized. It was Maori. And the words weren't names. They were a song. A warrior's song. Wit didn't speak the language, but he had seen the traditional singing of Maori warriors before. It was half grunting, half singing, with a stomping dance and exaggerated facial expressions. Mazer's face didn't so much as twitch, but the words spilled forth from him, gaining intensity and strength. Soon his voice was filling the room, harsh and booming.

Wit continued sending sharp bursts of pain. Mazer buckled every time, falling to the floor, his song cut off, his body writhing. But as soon as the pain subsided, Mazer clawed his way back into a sitting position and began to sing again in earnest. Soft at first, as he found his voice, and then louder as his strength returned.

An hour later, Wit stopped. He shut off the holopad, turned off Mazer's crown, and went directly into the screening room. Deen and Averbach removed their helmets.

Mazer was on his hands and knees, his shirt soaked in sweat, his arms and legs trembling.

"We're done, Mazer," said Wit. He typed a command onto the front of Mazer's crown. The device loosened and came free in Wit's hand.

Mazer's voice was weak. "So soon? I was starting to enjoy this."

"We've gone long enough," said Wit.

"I didn't break, O'Toole."

"You didn't break. Very good."

"Could you really have caused permanent neurological damage?" asked Mazer.

"No," said Wit. "That was a bluff. The device doesn't damage tissue. It simply overrides your pain and sensory receptors. I wouldn't do anything to impair you. You're too valuable a soldier for that. I was also bluffing about MOPs not having any oversight and being unscrupulously without ethics. Nothing could be further from the truth. Individual freedom and the preservation of human and civil rights motivate everything we do."

"Yet your bosses let you torture potential candidates? Those are some interesting ethics."

"Our enemies are usually murderers and terrorists, Mazer. They often require a show of strength and brutality equal to their own before they relent. My job is to find the men smart enough to know when brutality is necessary."

Mazer struggled to his feet, wobbling a little but soon upright and straight. "Well?" he asked. "Am I such a man? Did I pass your screening? Am I in your unit?"

"No," said Wit. "Because nobody gets in my unit unless they break out. Submitting to torture means you already lost once. You have to *hate* to lose so badly that you'd rather die trying to escape. And then be good enough to escape without dying. Anyone in my unit would have overpowered these two men guarding the door and escaped from this warehouse in three minutes. You just sat there for an hour."

Mazer looked back up at him, stunned.

"Sorry, soldier," said Wit. "You failed."

CHAPTER 4

Council

The helm on El Cavador was always buzzing with activity, but today the crew seemed especially occupied. Now that the Italians were gone and a week of trading and banqueting was over, the whole ship was in a rushed frenzy to make up for lost time with the dig. There were quickships to prepare, flight paths to program, scans of the rock to take and decipher, machines to operate for the miners below, dozens of plans and decisions and commands all happening at once—with Concepción at the center of it all, taking questions, interpreting data, issuing orders, and flying from station to station with the nimbleness of a woman half her age.

Victor and Edimar were floating at the hatch entrance, taking it all in, waiting for a break in the chaos to approach Concepción about the alien spacecraft Edimar had found. From the look of things, it didn't seem like they were going to get that chance any time soon.

"Maybe we should come back some other time," said Edimar. "She seems busy."

"Nothing is more important than this, Mar," said Victor. "Believe me, she'll be glad we interrupted."

Victor turned on his greaves, allowed his feet to descend to the floor, and crossed the room toward Concepción, who had anchored at the holotable with a group of crewmen.

Dreo, one of the navigators, a big man in his fifties, stepped in front of Victor and lightly put a hand on Victor's chest, stopping him. "Whoa, whoa. Where you headed, Vico?"

Victor sighed inside. Dreo fancied himself second in command, even though that position was officially held by Victor's uncle Selmo. Victor gestured back to Edimar, who hadn't moved from her spot by the hatch. "Edimar and I need to speak with Concepción immediately. It's urgent."

"Concepción is not to be disturbed," said Dreo. "We're almost at the lump."

"This is more important than the lump," said Victor.

Dreo smiled sardonically. "Really? What is it?"

"I'd rather speak to Concepción directly, if you don't mind. It's an emergency." He made a move to go around Dreo, but the man put his hand out again and stopped Victor a second time.

"What kind of emergency? A leak, a fire, a severed limb? Because it better be life-threatening if you're going to bother the captain right now."

"Call it a very unique emergency," said Victor.

"Tell you what," said Dreo. "You and Edimar go wait in Concepción's office while I relay your message to her. She'll come the moment she can." Dreo turned back to the system chart on his screen.

Victor didn't move.

After a moment, Dreo sighed and turned back to him. "You haven't gone to the office yet, Vico."

"And I won't until I see you relay my message or you get out of my way."

Dreo looked annoyed. "You are all kinds of trouble today, aren't you?"

He was referring to Janda, of course. As a member of the Council, Dreo would know everything. Victor remained where he was and said nothing.

Dreo grunted, turned away from his charts, and moved to Concepción. He tapped her on the shoulder, and they spoke in hushed tones. Concepción made eye contact with Victor then looked toward the hatch at Edimar. She gave Dreo brief instructions that Victor couldn't hear then returned her attention to the holotable.

Dreo came back with a triumphant smile. "You're to wait in her office like I told you."

"Did you tell her it was an emergency?"

"Yes." Dreo raised a hand, gesturing to the office. "Now go."

Victor motioned for Edimar, and they both made their way to the office.

It was the second time Victor had been ushered into this room today—though the meeting with Concepción that morning about Janda's departure already felt like a distant memory.

"What if it turns out to be nothing?" said Edimar. "What if it's just a glitch in the system? That's the most likely explanation. That's far more probable than it being an alien spacecraft or a secret, corporate near-light-speed ship."

"You went over the data several times, Edimar. If you're wrong, and it's nothing, which it isn't, then coming to Concepción was still the right thing to do. She'll appreciate you bringing it to her attention. You won't be scolded for doing your job."

"Not by Concepción maybe. But my father will be furious."

"It's not too late to go to your father first, Mar."

She shook her head. "No. This is right. Concepción first."

They had been over this already. Edimar was convinced that if she went first to Toron, her father, he would either sit on the data to review it later or he would dismiss the whole thing outright. Victor seriously doubted that Toron would be dismissive in the face of so much overwhelming evidence, yet Edimar had been adamant. "You don't know him, Vico."

She was wrong on that. Victor *did* know her father. Toron was Janda's father as well. But Victor wasn't going to argue the point.

Going to Concepción now, Edimar believed, would cause the least friction between her and her father in the long run. If Edimar ended up being right, then the immediacy of the situation could excuse her skipping Toron and going directly to Concepción. But if Edimar went to Toron first and got rejected, she would then feel a moral obligation to circumvent her father and go to Concepción anyway. Edimar had talked herself through every scenario until Victor was pink in the face. It was an alien ship, for crying out loud. One that could potentially be headed to Earth. Are we honestly going to worry about hurting Toron's *feelings*?

"Concepción can read the data herself, Mar," said Victor. "Let her look at it and decide what it means."

They waited for ten minutes. Finally Selmo, Victor's uncle and Concepción's true second in command, floated into the room. "Concepción will see you, but she asks that you meet her in the greenhouse."

Victor thought that odd. The greenhouse was humid and cramped and a terrible place to meet. "Why not in her office?"

Selmo shrugged, but Victor could tell from Selmo's expression and by the way he glanced at Edimar that he *did* know, or that at least he suspected. It then dawned on Victor what Selmo must be thinking: Selmo was a member of the Council, and here Victor was with Janda's younger sister asking to meet with Concepción mere hours after Janda's departure. The natural assumption would be that this had something to do with Janda. But what? That Victor and Edimar were demanding her return? That was lunacy. Victor would never reveal his love for Janda to Edimar. That would be unthinkable. He and Edimar could never be allies in that, and Victor would never want to attempt it anyway.

But Selmo didn't know that. He merely saw a brokenhearted boy and the departed girl's feisty little sister and jumped to the wrong conclusion. Apparently Concepción had as well. Meeting in the greenhouse was her way of being cautious. There they would be far from the eyes and ears of everyone else in case this *was* about Janda.

This is what my life will be like if I stay here, Victor realized. No one on the Council will ever look at me without seeing Janda also.

"The Eye detected something," said Victor. "That's why we need to see Concepción."

Selmo seemed momentarily relieved until he understood the full implication. He turned to Edimar, concerned. "What is it?"

"We're not sure," said Victor. "We're hoping Concepción will know. It may be nothing. No cause for alarm. Don't tell anyone. We just want to be sure. Thanks for your help." He launched out of the room and made his way down the corridor toward the greenhouse.

Edimar caught up to him, annoyed. "Why'd you go blabbering to Selmo? Now everyone will know I saw something."

"Selmo will stay quiet. And everyone will know soon enough anyway."

"Not if Concepción says it's nothing! There's a chance I'm wrong, Vico. And if I am, I could have forgotten the whole thing and nobody would have been the wiser. Now my father will definitely find out."

Victor caught himself on a bulkhead and stopped to face her. "First, it *is* something. We've established that. Let's stop questioning it. Second, if you want adults and your father to take you seriously, Mar, you need to put this concern about your father aside and think like an adult. Put the safety of the family above your father's *anticipated* reactions and do what you know is your job." He hadn't meant it to sound like a rebuke, but it had come out that way.

"You're right," said Edimar. "Of course you're right."

Victor felt the tiniest pang of guilt then. He had put an end to Selmo's misconception but by doing so he had made it possible for Toron to find out through the wrong channels. But what could Victor do? The alternative was far worse. Having Selmo or others believe that Edimar was somehow aware of or implicated in Victor and Janda's taboo relationship would be a devastating blow to Edimar's reputation on the Council. Victor couldn't stomach that. He wouldn't let the shame of him and Janda spread to Edimar.

"I won't say another word to anyone," said Victor. "I won't even go to the greenhouse if you'd prefer. This is your discovery, not mine."

Her answer was quick. "No, no. I want you there."

"All right. Let's go."

The greenhouse was a long tube four meters wide, with vegetables growing from pipes running the length of the room. The pipes took up every available space on the wall, creating a thick tunnel of green all around you. Tomatoes, okra, cilantro, sprouts, all with their leaves and bodies floating out from the holes in the pipes like seaweed. It was an aeroponic, soilless system, and although the atomized, nutrient-rich mists were sprayed through the pipes onto the root systems only twice an hour, some of the mist always escaped, and the room was always uncomfortably humid. It was also exceptionally bright, and as Victor and Edimar passed through the anteroom and into the actual greenhouse, it took Victor's eyes a moment to adjust to the vapor lamps. The air was thick with the scent of greenery and cilantro and the nutrient solution.

Concepción was deep in the room with her feet pointed toward them, her body perpendicular to their orientation, waiting. Victor and Edimar changed their orientation to match hers and launched what was now up, deeper into the greenhouse. Now the greenhouse felt like a silo, and Victor could see why Concepción would prefer to meet with their bodies positioned this way. They wouldn't have to stoop to keep their feet and heads out of the plants.

Concepción was floating beside a long section of sprouts. Here the plants were shorter, so the "tunnel" was wider, giving the three of them more room to face each other. Victor caught himself on one of the handholds and stopped in front of Concepción.

"I'm sure I need not tell you both how busy we are with the dig," said Concepción. "But I also know that neither of you would call something an emergency unless it absolutely was one."

Victor looked at Edimar and waited.

"The Eye detected something," said Edimar. "A movement out in deep space. I've been over the data dozens of times, and the only explanation that I can see is that it's some type of spacecraft decelerating from near-lightspeed."

Concepción blinked. "Excuse me?"

"I know it doesn't make any sense," said Edimar. "I hardly believe it myself, but unless I'm wrong, and I absolutely could be, there is something out there that is moving faster than humanly possible. I even showed it to Victor to see what he thought because it all seemed completely ridiculous to me."

Victor nodded. "It looks legit."

"Did you show your father?" asked Concepción.

"Not yet. I've been manning the Eye myself today. Father is helping with the dig. Victor and I thought it best to come straight to you."

Concepción looked at each of them before gesturing to Edimar's goggles. "Is that the data there?"

"Yes, ma'am," said Edimar, handing over the goggles.

Concepción put them on and tightened the straps. As she blinked her way through the data, Victor and Edimar waited. After five minutes, Concepción removed the goggles and held them in her hands. "Who else knows about this?"

"No one," said Edimar.

"I mentioned to Selmo that the Eye had detected something," said Victor. "But I didn't say what."

Concepción nodded, then faced Edimar. "Can you decipher its trajectory?"

"Not yet," said Edimar. "Not at this distance. It's too far out."

"Assuming its trajectory was headed toward us," said Concepción, "could you guess at how long it would take to reach us?"

"Not accurately," said Edimar. "Best guess, at least a few weeks but no more than a few months. The problem is I don't know how far away it is. All I know is that it's moving at near-lightspeed and that we can see the light from it, which is obviously moving *at* lightspeed. So it could be closer than we think. I don't know."

Concepción pulled her handheld from its place on her hip and starting tapping commands into it. "I'm calling an emergency meeting of the Council. We'll meet this evening on the helm. I want both of you there." She pocketed her handheld. "In the meantime, don't speak of this to anyone. The one exception is Toron. I'd like him to look at this as soon as possible. It's not that I doubt your interpretation of the data, Edimar. I would have reached the same conclusion myself. But perhaps Toron will see something we don't. You did the right thing coming to me, but I hope Toron proves us wrong. I don't like anything that I can't understand, and I don't understand this at all."

Victor stayed with Edimar as she went looking for her father. He had suggested that she speak with him alone, but Edimar had insisted that Victor come along. "He won't be as angry with me if someone else is there," she had said.

Victor wasn't eager to see Toron so soon after Janda's departure. How would Toron react? Did he blame Victor for what had happened? Did he believe that Victor should have seen where the relationship was headed and taken greater care to end it? Did he harbor ill will? Victor would rather not find out, especially not today, with the sting of Janda's departure still fresh in Toron's mind. But what could Victor do? He couldn't hide from Toron. Sooner or later their paths would cross; it was a small ship. Nor did he want to hide, really. There was a part of him that wanted to apologize, a part that wanted to assure Toron that nothing improper had happened. Victor hadn't known anything was wrong. It had been an innocent mistake. That wouldn't change the outcome of it all, that wouldn't diminish the pain. But maybe it would bring him and Toron a little peace.

Toron was in the cargo bay, making repairs to the mining gear Victor had won in the trade with the Italians. It was no secret that Toron had always wanted to work alongside the miners, but his proficiency and training with the Eye had kept him assigned to the crow's nest instead. He was so absorbed in his work that he didn't notice Victor and Edimar launch from the hatch and land near him.

"Hello, Father," said Edimar.

Toron looked tired and defeated. When he saw Edimar, his expression turned to one of surprise. "Who's watching the Eye?" he said.

"It's on auto," said Edimar.

"You should never put it on auto unless it's an absolute emergency, Mar." Toron glanced at Victor, noticing him for the first time. His brow furrowed. "What is this, Mar?"

"The Eye detected something, Father, out beyond the ecliptic in deep space."

Toron gestured to Victor. "What does he have to do with it?"

"I showed it to him," said Edimar.

"Why?"

"Because I wanted to make sure I was interpreting the data correctly before I showed an adult."

"He's not a spotter," said Toron. "He can't read the data."

Actually I can, thought Victor. But he said nothing.

"Nor is he your teacher, Mar," said Toron. "I am. If you have a question about the Eye, you call me and nobody else. Victor hasn't been trained with the Eye. Getting his opinion is a waste of time."

Edimar raised her voice slightly, surprising Victor. "Did you even hear what I said, Father? The Eye detected something."

"I heard you perfectly," said Toron. "And if you raise your voice at me again, young lady, you will not like the consequences. Any apprentice on this ship would lose his commission with that attitude, and I will not be any more patient with you simply because you're my daughter."

"It's a spacecraft," said Edimar. "At near-lightspeed."

That gave Toron pause. He studied their faces and could see that they meant it. He motioned with his hand. "Give me the goggles."

Edimar passed them to him, and Toron slid them over his eyes. After a minute, he started asking Edimar questions, most of which Victor didn't understand: What algorithms had Edimar considered? What measurements had the Eye taken? What processing sequences had she used? What coded commands had she entered? After that, Toron's questions began to sound more like a rebuke. "Did you try such and such?" "Did you think to do this or that?" At first Edimar answered yes. She had tried everything. But as Toron continued peppering her with possible actions she could have taken, Edimar's confidence began to wane. No, she hadn't tried that. No, she hadn't thought to do that. No, she hadn't run that scenario. By the end of it, Edimar looked near tears.

Toron removed the goggles. "Go back to the Eye, Edimar, and when I get there, we'll look at this a little more thoroughly. If it proves to be something, I'll go show Concepción."

Edimar looked desperately to Victor, asking for help.

"Actually," said Victor, "we've already gone to Concepción."

"Before you came to me?" asked Toron.

"We thought she needed to see it immediately," said Edimar.

"We?" said Toron. "You mean you and Vico? This doesn't concern him, Mar. He replaces lightbulbs and fixes toilets. What the Eye finds is my specialty, not his, and from the way you've responded to all this, I would add, not yours either. I don't see how this is a difficult concept for you to grasp, Edimar. I'm the spotter. Me. I will school you in how to watch the sky. I will help you decipher the data. And I will decide if and when anything is brought to the captain's attention."

Edimar's cheeks flushed.

"Go to the Eye and wait for me," said Toron. "Do not ask for help along the way. Do not get the opinion of a passerby. You and I will address this alone."

"It's not her fault we went to Concepción," said Victor. "It's mine. I'm the one who suggested it."

"And who gave you that authority?" asked Toron.

"Anyone who sees a potential threat to the ship has an obligation to report it," said Victor, reciting policy.

"You know all about *rules,* don't you, Vico?" said Toron.

He meant dogging. This had started as a conversation about an object in space, but it had suddenly become, for Toron at least, about Janda. Toron blamed Victor. Or he hated Victor so intensely for it that it consumed his thoughts, even now, when something as strange and potentially threatening as an alien starship was brought to his attention.

"It's not Vico's fault, Father," said Edimar. "I asked him to help me."

Toron kept his eyes on Victor. "Go to the Eye, Edimar."

"But—"

"Go to the Eye!" It was nearly a shout, and Edimar recoiled, fearing perhaps that a hand or fist would follow. She launched off the floor toward the hatch. Toron stared at Victor until he heard the hatch door close. They were alone.

"I want to be very clear about something, Vico. I want you to listen to what I'm saying because I am only going to say this once. It's something I should have said to you a long time ago. You stay away from my daughters. Do you understand me? If Edimar asks for your help, you ignore her. If she begs for your opinion, you walk away. If she makes eye contact with you from across the room, you pretend she doesn't exist. She is a ghost to you. Invisible. Am I making myself clear? Because it seems to me that you don't know the boundaries of what's appropriate and what isn't."

It was a ridiculous accusation. The idea that Victor would do anything inappropriate with Janda was infuriating. But to insinuate that his behavior toward Edimar could be anything less than honorable was an egregious insult. It was the vilest and most cruel thing Toron could say, especially considering how pained and guilty he knew Victor must be because of Janda.

But of course Toron knew the accusation was baseless. He knew Victor was only helping, that Victor's intentions were purely supportive and protective of the family. That wasn't his reason for lashing out. He was angry because his eldest daughter was gone and his second daughter had sought counsel with the very person who had lost him the first.

Victor kept his voice calm. "Alejandra leaving has nothing to do with this, Toron."

The shove to the chest happened fast, and since Victor wasn't rooted to the floor with greaves like Toron, the force of it pushed Victor back twenty feet. His back slammed into one of the big air tanks, and the metallic clang of the impact reverberated through the cargo bay. It didn't hurt terribly, but it shocked Victor and immediately got his blood up. He reoriented himself, switched on his greaves, and let his feet lock to the floor. When he lifted his head, he could see that Toron was just as surprised as Victor was. He hadn't meant the shove to be so hard, and he certainly hadn't intended for Victor to fly back as he had. But then Toron's expression darkened and he pointed a finger.

"Never speak the name of my daughter again."

Toron turned off his greaves and launched upward toward the hatch. A moment later he was gone. Victor stood erect and stretched his back. He'd get a bad bruise at the most, but it could have been worse. Had he landed wrong he could have broken something. Edimar was right to fear her father. Victor doubted that Toron had ever been violent toward his family— Janda would have told him if such a thing had ever happened, and it would be impossible to keep it a secret on the ship. Yet Toron clearly had the inclination.

Victor wanted to feel angry. He wanted the kindling fire of rage within him to flare up and spur him to find Toron, to confront him, to grab him by the arms and shake the pride and haughtiness and spite right out of him. The ache in his back demanded it. But whatever flames there were within him were extinguished by sympathy and shame.

The Council met on the helm after the young ones had all been put to bed. Everyone wore greaves, and as they gathered they spoke quietly, trying to garner whatever information they could from the others about the purpose of the meeting. Victor had come early and found a corner in the back of the room where the lighting was dimmer and the shadows more pronounced. He wouldn't be invisible, but he'd go unnoticed by some.

It felt odd to be in attendance, partially because this was a side of the family Victor had never seen before, but also because he couldn't shake the thought that the last time the Council had met they had been discussing him and Janda. It left him feeling awkward. What's more, he had no reason for being here. The near-lightspeed ship was Edimar's find, not his. He had nothing to contribute.

Mother and Father arrived. They saw Victor and came to him. Mother looked concerned. "What's this all about, Vico?"

"The Eye detected something," said Victor. "I only know about it because Edimar showed me. Toron will explain everything, I'm sure."

She put a hand on his arm. "How are you?"

It was her way of asking about how he was dealing with Janda leaving. "Fine, Mother. It's been a long day."

To everyone else, Mother was Rena. Her original clan was from Argentina, and Victor had seen them only once as a child when El Cavador had linked with their ship for a zogging of Victor's cousin. The experience had instilled in him a sense of awe for Mother. She had left a vibrant, loving family behind to join El Cavador and marry Father, and it must have taken incredible courage.

"I heard about the drill stabilizer," said Father, smiling. "When were you going to tell me about that one?"

"I wasn't sure it would work," said Victor. "I'll need your help refining it."

"From the way Marco was gushing about it," said Father, "I don't know that it needs much refining."

Father's given name was Segundo, which meant "second" in Spanish. His parents had given him the name because he was their second child, and Victor had always found the name a little cruel. Who slaps a number on their child? Numbers were for livestock. And what's worse, didn't Father's parents realize that to call him Segundo was like labeling him "runner-up" or "second best," always inferior to the first child? Victor doubted that had been their intent, but it bothered him nonetheless, especially since Father had always been the first to do everything in his family. He deserved a better name.

Concepción, Toron, and Edimar emerged from Concepción's office, and everyone fell silent. The three of them made their way to the holotable, and Concepción faced the crowd. "I've called this meeting because we have some important decisions to make."

Victor was surprised to see how informal the whole affair was, with everyone standing where they were, clustered in small groups of husbands and wives and friends. There was no counter to stand around, no gavel to hit, no ritual or procedure or order to follow. It was simply everyone coming together.

"I'll let Toron and Edimar explain the whole thing," said Concepción.

She stepped aside, and Toron plugged the goggles into the holotable. A holo of the image Victor had seen earlier that day in the crow's nest appeared in the holospace. It wasn't much, mostly dots of light representing stars.

Toron was brief. He merely gave context to the image they were seeing, explaining when the data had been collected and what quadrant of sky they were looking at. Then, to Victor's astonishment, he turned the floor over to Edimar. She was clearly nervous, and one person had to ask her to speak up so everyone in the room could hear, but Edimar immediately raised her voice and projected toward the back of the room. The increased volume seemed to steel her courage, and she dove right in. She spoke for ten minutes, being clear and thorough in her explanation. She went into great detail explaining the procedures she had undertaken to verify the data, including calling in Victor to validate her initial assessment. This caused several people to glance briefly at Victor before Edimar continued. There were a few highly technical details and procedures that were unique to the Eye that Edimar knew no one would understand, but she deftly explained these in layman's terms so that everyone got the gist of it all. She then detailed the cross-checks that she and her father had subsequently performed and how everything had led her and him to believe what by now was obvious to everyone in the room. It was an alien starship decelerating toward the solar system. No, we don't know its trajectory yet. No, we don't know when it will get here. And no, we don't know what its intentions may be.

When she finished there was silence. Mother and Father stared at the holo, their faces a little pale.

Finally Concepción spoke. "The question we have to answer is: What do we do about this information?"

"Have we heard any chatter about this?" asked Father. "Have any of the other families reported anything?"

"Not a word," said Concepción. "There are few clans out this far right now, and it's unlikely that any of them are looking beyond the ecliptic."

"We obviously need to warn everyone," said Mother. "We should send transmissions out as quickly as we can. Everyone needs to know about this."

"As I said to Concepción," said Toron, "I'd advise us to proceed with caution. We don't want to incite a panic. Consider the implications. If this is an alien starship moving at near-lightspeed, it clearly has technological capabilities far beyond our own. If it can move at near the speed of light, what else can it do? Can it detect radio? We don't know. If we send a hundred focused, laserized transmissions out in every direction, we might unintentionally attract its attention. We might bring it down on top of us. It's done nothing to acknowledge that it knows we exist. It's probably best to keep it that way."

"We can't do nothing," said Marco. "This could be an invasion for all we know."

"Or it might be completely peaceful," said Toron. "We don't know. We have some information, yes, but not much. Hardly any, really. Is this a research vessel? Do they even intend to enter the inner solar system? Is it even manned? We have no idea. It could be a drone or a satellite sent to take images of our planetary system. If that's true, it has to be an enormous satellite, bigger than anything humans have every constructed. But that doesn't mean that's not its intent. It might be completely benign."

"Or it might not be," said Marco.

"Yes," said Toron. "Or it might not be. All the more reason not to rush to action and draw attention to ourselves. Edimar and I will watch it closely. We'll be evaluating the data constantly, and we'll make everyone aware of any new developments."

"That's not enough," said Father. "I agree with Marco. This thing may be peaceful, but we shouldn't assume that it is. We should prepare for the worst."

"We should remain calm," said Toron. "I suggest we take cautionary action."

"Like what?" asked Father.

"If we send out a wide transmission that anyone can receive, we will draw unwanted attention to ourselves. We might attract pirates or thieves or worse. But, if we identify a few ships in the vicinity we trust, we can send out very focused laser transmissions only to them."

"We haven't seen pirates in a while," said Selmo.

"That doesn't mean they aren't out there," said Toron. "We can't be too cautious. Particularly not in an unknown situation like this."

"Who's close to us right now?" asked Marco.

Selmo came to the holotable and flipped on the system chart. "The Italians are closest. They only left this morning. But they're moving fast. We might hit them if we sent them a message now, but I doubt it."

Laserized radio transmissions, or laserlines, had to be sent with extreme accuracy. Stationary ships and space stations could receive them fairly easily over short distances since the sender knew their exact position in space. But few ships remained perfectly stationary, especially if they were moored to an asteroid. Even the slightest deviation in position would result in a missed message. Trying to hit a ship in flight was next to impossible. It had been done, but only when the ships were extremely close.

"If the Italians stick with their scheduled flight path," said Selmo, "they'll decelerate in ten days. They gave us a point to target for communications when they stop. If we wanted to send them a laserline at that point, we could."

"So we basically do nothing for ten days?" asked Marco. "If this is an invasion, we could be losing precious time. What if this thing *is* headed to Earth? Ten days could make all the difference."

"There's nobody closer?" asked Father.

"There's a corporate ship a few days from here," said Selmo. "A Juke vessel. They've been sitting there for a while doing nothing as far as we can tell. Assuming they haven't moved since our last scan, we could send them a message."

"What would we tell them?" asked Javier, one of Victor's uncles. " 'Hey, there's an alien ship out there. Keep your eyes peeled.' They wouldn't believe us."

"They wouldn't have to believe us," said Toron. "If we showed them where to look and they had a decent sky scanner, they could see it themselves."

"You said we could send the message to people we trust," said Marco. "Since when do we trust corporates?"

There was a murmur of assent from the crowd.

"They're the closet ship," said Toron. "And therefore, they're the best qualified vessel to see exactly what we've seen. If we want to corroborate our data, they're the most sensible choice."

"I don't like working with corporates," said Marco.

"Nor do I," said Toron. "But if this object is indeed a starship, who better to tell than corporates? Their communication systems are far superior to ours. They have relay satellites across the system. If a warning has to be sent to Earth, they're the people to do it, not us."

The room was quiet a moment.

"Whatever this object is," said Concepción, "it won't be close for at least several weeks and probably not for a few months. I think Toron's recommendation to proceed with caution is wisest at this point. I am as alarmed as all of you, but if and when we send a warning, I want to have some degree of certainty as to what we're dealing with. I suggest we notify this Juke vessel and give the Italians the same message in ten days. With all three of us analyzing this, we have a much better chance of understanding it. In the meantime we maintain our position, we continue with the dig, and we let Toron and Edimar track this thing. Any objections?"

"Yes," said Victor.

Everyone turned to him. Concepción looked surprised. "You have an objection, Victor?"

Victor scanned the room. Everyone stared. Some looked annoyed. It wasn't his place to question Concepción. He shouldn't even be here.

"I mean no one any disrespect," said Victor, "least of all you, Concepción. But I don't think this is our decision to make."

"Of course it's our decision," said Toron. "Who else could make it?"

"Everyone," said Victor. "This affects everyone. This changes everything. This is an alien starship. We have no right choosing when it's revealed to everyone else. It affects the entire human race. We all agree that there are basically two scenarios here. Either it's peaceful or it isn't. If it's peaceful, than we have nothing to lose by detaching from the rock now and sending out a transmission to as many ships and stations as we can hit. If there *are* pirates, they will react to the information, not to the people giving it. We should spread the word. We should inform the world. We get the news to Earth as quickly as possible. We let *them* decide how to proceed for themselves. And if this ship's intentions are *not* peaceful, then we do the exact same thing. We warn as many people as we can and we start building defenses immediately. Toron suggests that by sending out a blanket transmission we might draw the attention of the alien ship and make ourselves its first target. But even if that's true, so what? We're eighty-seven people. There are over twelve billion people on Earth. If we have to sacrifice ourselves to protect millions or billions more, then we would do that."

"It isn't that cut and dried," said Toron. "You're making big assumptions about this ship when we don't know yet if it *is* a ship. We know next to nothing."

"That's my point," said Victor. "What right do we have to assume to be experts on this? Isn't it far more likely that someone else will be better equipped to interpret this thing than we are? And who's to say the Italians or even the Juke ship will be experts either? We should tell them, yes, but we should tell everyone else, as well. That creates the greatest likelihood of us learning as much as we can as quickly as we can."

Toron turned to Concepción. "With all due respect, ma'am, this is precisely why Council meetings are intended for people of a certain age and maturity. Vico's intentions are good. And were this a mechanical problem, I would value his input greatly. But this is not a mechanical problem. He's speaking of matters that he doesn't fully understand. Nor should he be speaking at all since he isn't a member of this Council."

"I'm not a Council member, true," said Victor. "But I am a member of this family. And more importantly, I'm a member of the human race, which could very well be threatened here."

"Are you honestly suggesting that we put the safety of other ships, other families, complete strangers, above our own?" said Toron. "Above the safety of your own mother and father? Your cousins and aunts?"

"I'm suggesting that the preservation of the human race is more important than the preservation of this family."

"You would abandon the family that quickly?" said Toron. "Well, I hope I never have to fight for this family with you at my side."

Dreo nodded. "Everyone appreciates what you do, Vico, but this is an adult conversation."

"What am I missing?" said Victor. "What am I failing to understand because of my age?"

"Do you know what it's like to have a wife?" said Toron. "To have children?"

"Of course not," said Victor.

"Then perhaps you can understand why we'd consider your suggestion a bit naïve. I will emphatically reject any idea that puts my wife and children in danger. I would choose to save one of my own daughters over saving ten strangers. Or a hundred strangers. And so would every other parent in this room. It's easy for you to speak of noble sacrifices when you have nothing to lose."

"Toron's right," said Dreo. "Our first obligation is to ourselves. And let's think about this diplomatically, too. If we cause an alarm and it proves to be nothing, we'll look like fools to the other families. No one would zog with us, no one would trade with us. We'd do ourselves irreparable harm for no reason."

"I'm not suggesting that we scream 'invasion' to the world," said Victor. "I'm merely seconding my mother's original suggestion. We tell everyone exactly what we know and allow them to look into it as much as we are. Why would anyone think less of us for our giving them irrefutable evidence? We don't have to give them gloom and doom predictions. We just give them the facts. If anything, this would *build* our standing among the families. We would earn everyone's gratitude and respect for informing them. Consider the situation in reverse: If we were to learn after an attack by an alien starship that another family knew of the existence of that ship and did nothing to warn us, we would despise that family. We would blame them for our losses."

Toron turned to Concepción. "Victor is your invited guest, Concepción. But he is monopolizing the floor."

"He hasn't spoken any more than you have," said Father.

"Yes," said Toron. "And I am a member of this Council. He is not. He is disrespecting the captain."

"She asked for objections," said Mother. "He politely voiced one."

"Which he had no authority to do," said Toron. "I recognize that your son can do no wrong in your eyes, but by the code of this Council, he is out of line."

"I happen to agree with him," said Marco.

"I agree with him also," said Toron. "Everyone here wants to do the right thing. Of course we will send a warning to everyone if that ever proves necessary. But right now is too soon. We don't know enough. And for Victor to presume to know how pirates would respond is laughably naïve."

"We don't even know if there are pirates this far out," said Father.

"Exactly," said Toron. "We don't know. That's why we should be prudent, not rash. I propose we put it to a general vote."

"I second that," said Father.

Concepción looked at the crowd. "Objections?"

There were none.

"Very well," said Concepción. "All those who agree with sending out a blanket transmission immediately."

A third of the room raised their hand, including Mother, Father, and Marco. Edimar raised her hand as well, but a withering look from her father made her put it down again. Victor kept his hand down since he wasn't a member of the Council. Concepción took a visible count, nodded, and said, "All those who feel we should inform only the Italians and Juke ship at this point."

The remaining hands in the room went up, a much larger portion of people. Toron allowed himself a small, triumphant smile.

They were going to do nothing, Victor realized. Nothing immediate anyway, nothing significant, nothing that would ensure their safety in the coming months. They would send out two messages, and then they would sit and wait and hopefully learn something new.

Victor wasn't going to wait with them. He couldn't control when and how the family warned others, but he could control the mechanical functionality of the ship. He could make improvements to the ship's defenses and weapons. He didn't need Council approval for that.

The meeting was breaking up. People were dispersing.

"You tried, Vico," said Mother. "I'm proud of you for that."

"Thank you, Mother." He turned to Father. "We should focus on the pebble-killers first."

"Agreed," said Father, already tapping a command into his handheld. "I'll wake up Mono."

Victor knew he wouldn't have to explain himself to Father. It was obvious what they needed to do. They had to find a way to make the pebble-
killers more powerful and lethal. With the whole ship helping, the work
would have gone much faster, but now it was going to be just the three of
them. Victor hurried from the room. Toron and others would probably
think that his quick departure was that of a pouting teenager who had lost
an argument, but Victor didn't care. Let them think what they wanted. He
had work to do.

CHAPTER 5

Benyawe

Lem was in his office with the lights out, watching a holo simulation of asteroid 2002GJ166 being hit with the glaser. It was a simple holo sim. Only ten seconds long. But the engineers who had put it together had spent three days building it. Every detail of the asteroid had been meticulously re-created. The engineers had even gone so far as to painstakingly re-create the mineshaft the free miners had cut into the rock. In all aspects it was identical to the real thing, albeit a thousand times smaller. At first, nothing happened. Then, as the glaser hit it, the asteroid exploded, sending thousands of rock fragments shooting outward in every direction like a giant growing sphere of gravel. Soon the pieces of the sphere became so far apart that the sphere lost any semblance of shape and all that was left was empty space. The holo sim winked out. Lem turned to Dr. Dublin and Dr. Benyawe, who were standing beside his desk patiently waiting for his reaction. "It's completely obliterated," said Lem. "How am I supposed to mine an obliterated asteroid?"

The Makarhu was less than a day away from the real asteroid. Chubs's "Red Light Green Light" approach had worked flawlessly for nine days. El Cavador was oblivious. The free miners had shown no sign of knowing another ship was approaching their position. No threatening radio messages, no warning shots, nothing. Either they were exceptionally good at playing dumb, or they were in for the surprise of their life.

Now, however, the engineers were telling Lem through a holo sim that it didn't matter anyway, because the glaser was going to annihilate the asteroid and leave them empty-handed. "This is unacceptable," said Lem. "There's nothing left of the asteroid."

"Our math could be off," said Dublin. "We've never fired the glaser at an object this big before. The simulation only runs the data we give it, and we don't have a lot of data. Much of this is conjecture."

"Then what's the point of building a simulation?" said Lem. "You're showing me what *might* happen? I can do that myself. I have a pretty decent imagination. Forgive me for being blunt, Dr. Dublin, but guesswork doesn't help us here. I need facts. What you're showing me are half facts. And to be perfectly honest, not the half facts I want to see. The glaser is a mining tool. We're in the business of extracting minerals. What you're showing me is skeet shooting. I don't care if you blow up the asteroid, but sending millions of pieces hurtling away in every direction is not going to work. Miners can't chase down rock fragments all day. The glaser is supposed to expedite the mining process, not complicate it. I can tolerate this reaction with pebbles, but not with big rocks. That isn't what the Board had in mind."

"You don't want guesswork, Lem," said Benyawe, "but guesswork is mostly what we have. We haven't done enough field tests to predict with a high degree of accuracy what exactly is going to happen. That is why the mission was designed the way it was, with us conducting many tests using gradually larger asteroids."

Lem shook his head. "The original plan is gone. We're seven weeks behind schedule. We have a new plan now, one we've been following for nine days. I agree that our original plan is the ideal, but circumstances have changed."

"Then all we can show you are possibilities," said Benyawe, "nothing definitive. We won't know that until we blast the real thing. We can try to minimize the gravity field more, and that *might* lessen the explosion, but we cannot predict how far the field will spread."

Lem rubbed his eyes, exhausted. It hadn't been a very pleasant nine days. And another round of "data talk" with the engineers wasn't helping. Part of the problem was the lighting—or rather, the lack thereof. Per Chubs's instructions, Lem had ordered the ship to "go dark" when they had set out for the asteroid. This meant turning off all exterior and most interior lights in order to remain invisible from El Cavador's light-sensitive sky scanner. Lem had expected this to be a challenge. Moving around the ship in near darkness would take some getting used to. What he hadn't anticipated was how the lack of light had put everyone in an irritated, cheerless mood. Normally Lem could move through the halls of the ship and hear laughter and friendly conversation. These days the halls were as silent as they were dark.

Even more annoying was the constant stopping and starting of the ship. To sneak up undetected, the Makarhu remained motionless when they were exposed to El Cavador's side of the asteroid, then the ship rushed forward whenever El Cavador was on the far side. Stopping. Starting. Stopping. Starting. It made sleep next to impossible, and Lem's body felt anxious and fatigued because of it.

"You're right," said Lem. "I'm asking for the impossible. I'm asking you to tell me what will happen without allowing you to gather the data to formulate an answer. That's not fair. I realize that. But we are at the eleventh hour, and we have one shot at this. I'm only asking that we do all we can to make that one shot work."

Dublin began gathering his things. "We'll see what we can do, Mr. Jukes."

"I have full confidence in you," said Lem.

Dublin launched himself toward the exit, but Benyawe stayed behind.

"May I have a word, Lem?" she asked.

"You may have a hundred, Dr. Benyawe. It will keep me awake."

"I have remained silent on this issue since we set out for this asteroid," said Benyawe, "but if I don't say something now, before we get there, I'll be disappointed in myself."

Lem knew where this was going. As he had expected, the decision to bump the free miners was unpopular with the engineers. Their world was black or white. An experiment failed or it didn't. Data was right or it wasn't. The prototype worked or it didn't. The idea of a gray area, wherein it was acceptable under certain circumstances to take a dig site by force, was hard for an engineer to swallow. They all knew that Juke Limited was involved in unsavory business practices, but it was much easier to turn a blind eye to such things from the safe and cozy rooms of one's lab back on Luna. Out here in the deep of space, the hard truth of it stared you in the face.

Lem held up a hand. "If you're going to tell me you think bumping these free miners is morally wrong, save your breath. I feel the same way."

"You do?"

"Absolutely. It's cheating, basically. And bullying. Not to mention extremely dangerous."

"Then why are we doing it?"

"Because the alternative is an eight-month round-trip. If we go that far, we will seriously deplete our fuel supplies. Plus we have no guarantee that the farther asteroid will be any more vacant than this one. Who's to say there isn't a whole fleet of free miners moored to the other asteroid?"

"Those aren't our only options," said Benyawe. "We could proceed with the mission as planned. It's not too late for that. We look for more pebbles of gradually greater size and adjust the glaser as we go along. Free miners don't touch pebbles. This would be a nonissue."

"We have to do a big asteroid anyway," said Lem. "All we're doing is jumping ahead. It's unfortunate that we have to vacate the free miners, but that is the world we're living in now. Chubs assures me that we can do this with minimal structural damage to their ship and without harming any of their crew."

"It's not right. We're taking what's theirs."

"Technically, Doctor, it isn't theirs. They have no deed. No right to ownership. That rock is ours as much as it is theirs. Just ask STASA."

Lem wasn't exactly sure he was right. The Space Trade and Security Authority, the international organization that provided oversight for the space-mining industry, might actually side with Benyawe on this one. But if Lem didn't know the minutiae of such policies, he was fairly confident Benyawe wouldn't, either. If he sounded sure of himself, she wouldn't argue.

"But they got there first," said Benyawe. "That has to account for something."

"It *has* accounted for something. They've mined two quickships of metal. We're not leaving them destitute, Doctor. Considering how much they've pulled out of their mineshaft, they're probably at the end of their dig anyway. We're just sending them off prematurely."

She smiled reproachfully. "We don't know if they're at the end of their dig, Lem. That's baseless speculation just to help us sleep at night."

"You're right," said Lem. "But that doesn't change our situation. Unless another large asteroid pops into existence in the next few hours, we're going through with this."

"Then I'd like it noted in the ship's official records that I object to this action."

That surprised Lem. "You feel that strongly?"

"I do. And I'm not the only one. A lot of the engineers are uneasy about this, not only because it feels like stealing but also because they fear for their lives. What if these free miners are better defended and better equipped than we think? We're scientists, Lem, not soldiers."

"I assure you, Doctor, bumping a bunch of pebble eaters is the safest thing in the world."

"Please don't use that term. I find it offensive. They're human beings."

"Pebble eaters. Rock suckers. Ash trash. Dig dogs. Mine mites. Scavengers. These words exist, Dr. Benyawe, because these kind of people live a less-than-civilized lifestyle. They marry their sisters. They're completely uneducated. Their children never learn to walk. Their legs are just bone and sinew because they never develop them. It's as if they're becoming a different species altogether."

"You're talking about isolated incidents. Not all of them are like that. Most of them are quite innovative."

"Have you watched the exposés, Doctor? Have you seen the documentaries on these people? It's enough to turn your stomach."

"Sensationalism, Lem. You know that. The vast majority of free miners are intelligent, hardworking families who love their children and obey space law. By bumping them we're taking away a family's livelihood."

"And ensuring our own. This is the world we live in now, Doctor. We're not in a lab on Luna anymore. This is the frontier. Out here it's not all squeaky clean. Do we allow ourselves to fail so that a group of free miners can tap an asteroid for everything it's got? No, we don't. We take it. Do I like that option? No, but it's nothing these free miners haven't seen before. This is their world. In all likelihood, they bump ships too. Who's to say they didn't bump somebody off this rock to take it for themselves?"

"More baseless speculation."

"I'm painting a picture here, Benyawe. I'm reminding you that the rules are different out here in the Deep. I don't like it any more than you do. These free miners have an obligation to their family, yes, but we have an obligation as well."

Benyawe frowned. "To the Board, you mean? To our stockholders? Seriously, Lem. You can't compare that to family."

"Just because these people are related to each other doesn't make their cause any nobler than ours. They've got two quickships of metal from this rock. They're going to be fine."

Lem's holodisplay chimed, and a message-acceptance request appeared. Lem waved his hand through the holospace, and Chubs's head appeared.

"We've got an issue, Lem," said Chubs. "Bumping this ship is going to be trickier than we thought. Can you come to the helm?"

Lem left his office immediately. He didn't want Benyawe tagging along, but she either didn't get the cues from his body language or she chose to ignore them completely. Either way, she followed him down the hall to the push tube. Before climbing inside, Lem faced her. "If you write up a formal objection," he said, "I will sign it and put it on record in the ship's computers. Now, if you'll excuse me, I have business on the helm."

"I'd like to come along," she said.

It was a bad idea. Engineers never came to the helm, and this wasn't a good time to start, especially knowing how opposed she was to the bump. "This isn't a matter for the engineers," said Lem.

"I'm not just an engineer, Lem. I'm the director of Special Operations, an appointment you gave me. I'd say bumping a ship clearly qualifies as a special operation."

Lem suddenly understood why Father would put a man like Dublin in charge of engineers. The Dublins of the world never questioned you. If they disagreed with superiors, they zipped their lips and towed the line. That didn't make them better leaders, per se, but it certainly made Lem's and Father's jobs easier. Benyawe was another breed entirely. Staying silent was not in her DNA. But wasn't that why he had promoted her in the first place? He wanted straight counsel.

"You can come," said Lem. "But I can't have you arguing with me at the helm."

"I don't argue," said Benyawe.

"You're arguing with me now."

"I'm strongly disagreeing. There's a difference."

"Fine. Don't strongly disagree with me then. My point is, on the helm I am the commanding officer. You can ask questions. You can make observations. But if you take issue with anything I say, keep it to yourself until we're alone."

"Fair enough."

Chubs was waiting for them at the systems chart. The map had been replaced with a large holo of El Cavador. It was nothing like the original holo Lem had seen of the ship—that had been a 3-D rendering the computer had on file for the specific make and model of ship. This was the real thing. The Makarhu was now close enough to the asteroid to take high-res scans of the free-miner ship, and Lem couldn't believe what he was seeing.

"It looks like a tank," he said.

"We've been running scans through the computers all morning," said Chubs. "I've never seen anything like it, not on a free-miner ship, anyway. They've got armored plates welded all over the surface. Plus I've never seen this much proprietary tech on a single ship. See these protrusions here, here, and here. That's tech."

"What kind of tech?" asked Lem.

"We don't know," said Chubs. "These boxes here could be pebble-killers. Our computers can't make heads or tails of it. Most of it looks like it's built from scrap. The computers keep recognizing individual pieces from machines, but since the pieces are all used together in odd combinations, we have no idea what the tech is really for. Whoever these people are, they're either certifiably insane or genius innovators."

"I'd rather they be insane," said Lem.

"Makes two of us," said Chubs. "I don't like them having machines we can't understand. Makes me nervous. And that's not the worst of it." He glanced uneasily at Benyawe.

"It's okay," said Lem. "She's here at my invitation." Lem smiled to Benyawe, appearing nonchalant, though in truth he felt a little panicked. El Cavador looked tougher than he had anticipated. He shouldn't have brought Benyawe.

Chubs turned to the systems chart and tapped a command. A dozen cables stretching from El Cavador down to the surface of the asteroid suddenly glowed yellow. "Here's the bad news. They have twelve mooring lines anchoring them to the asteroid. That's three times more lines than normal."

"Meaning what?" asked Lem. "They've seen us? They're adding more lines to hunker down?"

"No way," said Chubs. "You don't keep that much cable lying around. This has to be how they anchor all the time."

"Maybe they've been bumped before," said Benyawe. "And now they lay down more lines to discourage anyone from trying again."

"My assumption as well," said Chubs. "From the looks of their ship and the number of anchor lines, I'd say these people have seen their share of pirates and claim jumpers."

"And corporates," said Benyawe.

Lem shot her a look, but she was facing the holo and didn't meet his eye.

"The other thing that bothers me is all the activity we've detected outside their ship," said Chubs.

"What kind of activity?" asked Lem.

"Spacewalks. And lots of them. Some to lay down more hull armor. Some to work on their collision-avoidance system. They've been very, very active. We haven't seen more than three or four guys out at a time. But it's like they know a war is coming."

"They've obviously detected us," said Lem. "They're building defenses for our attack."

"I'm not so sure," said Chubs. "It's only three or four guys out there. If they were in prebattle panic mode, they'd have a whole crew out. They'd put every available man behind an effort like that."

"Maybe that *is* every available man," said Benyawe. "Maybe only three or four people are left. Maybe they had an outbreak or something. It's happened with free miners before."

"But they *do* have other people," said Chubs. "We've seen them. While these three guys are strengthening the ship, they've got thirty guys working the mine. It's basically life as usual."

Lem shrugged. "It's not that strange if you think about it. They've seen us coming, and they're trying to mine as much as they can before we get there. That's what I would do."

"The other possibility," said Benyawe, "is that they don't know we're coming, and strengthening the ship is simply what these three or four guys do. That's their job. They're simply going about their business. You could argue that the state of the ship substantiates that idea. It's well defended. It doesn't get that way overnight. You can see scorch marks and dents all along their armor, which would suggest that the armor has been there a long time."

"Maybe," said Chubs. "It could also mean the armor plates were scorched when they applied them."

"Not likely," said Benyawe. "Some of these dents and marks stretch across multiple plates. This is a ship that's seen action, which brings up another possibility. Maybe they're not preparing for war with us. Maybe they've got a feud with another family, or there's a ship of thieves in the area."

"There's no one else in the area," said Chubs.

Benyawe shrugged. "So maybe they're prepping to set out on a six-month journey at the end of which is their enemy. Who knows?"

"I've had enough guesswork for one day," said Lem. "I want answers. How does this affect the bump? Are we a go or not?"

"The mooring cables are the biggest problem," said Chubs. "That's a lot of lines. We can't bump the ship unless every one of those lines is severed. We could cut them with the lasers, but it would be tedious work. It would take way too long. Bumps need to happen fast. Two minutes at the most. Gives them less of a chance to retaliate. I suggest cutting the cables a different way."

"How?" Lem asked.

Chubs tapped more commands into the system chart, and the holo of El Cavador winked out. A holo of the asteroid took its place, with El Cavador now a small ship moored to the surface. "We'll land over here," said Chubs. "On the blind side."

Lem watched the holo as the Makarhu approached the opposite side of the asteroid and landed at a spot just below what would be El Cavador's horizon line, hiding the Makarhu from view yet keeping it within striking distance.

"They still haven't seen us at this point," said Chubs. "We wait here until four hours into their sleep schedule, when everyone is good and gone to dreamland. Then we send in twelve breakers."

The breaker bots were small, disc-shaped explosive drones. Corporates used them for mining, sending them down narrow mineshafts to break up large chunks of rock for extraction.

"There's a ridgeline here," said Chubs, highlighting the feature on the asteroid. "It runs from our landing site to within a hundred yards of El Cavador. We can take a shuttle out along the ridgeline without them seeing us. The shuttle stops here at the edge of open ground. We throw the breakers from there. Our pilot steers each one to a different mooring line. The bots attach to the lines, then we detonate them all at once. That's when the attack begins. Once the lines are cut, we come forward with the ship and take out their pebble-killers and their power with our lasers. It's over at that point. We can brush them aside easy as anything. Ninety seconds tops."

Lem stared at the holo a moment. "Throwing the breakers? You can send them that far with that much accuracy?"

"The breakers have mini cams. We have a very good pilot. He can steer them pretty much wherever you want them."

"Won't El Cavador detect the movement?" asked Lem. "Won't they see the breakers coming?"

"Their collision-avoidance system doesn't monitor the surface of the asteroid. It can't. They've got miners walking around the surface all day. Believe me, it's the last place they would look for an attack."

Lem didn't like it. This was supposed to be a clean operation. They would swoop in, zap a few devices on the hull, push the ship aside, and be done with it. Simple. Nothing with breakers. No explosions. No creeping up in a shuttle. This was far more variables than Lem had intended.

One of the crewmen launched from his workstation and landed near Lem.

"They're rotating away, sir," said the crewman. "We can accelerate as soon as you're ready."

This would be the last push forward. They were close now. They would land on the rock within a few hours. Lem turned to Benyawe. Her face was a mask. She seemed poised, but he knew she was angry. She'd hate this new development more than he did.

"What's the word, Lem?" said Chubs. "We can cut bait now and scoot away if you'd like. Otherwise we need to punch it. We have a brief window here."

Nine days, thought Lem. They had come nine days. The rock was right there in front of them. What would you do, Father? Go off and shoot some more pebbles? Fly eight months to a different asteroid? Or knock these gravel suckers off the rock? Lem could almost feel Father here beside him, looking over his shoulder, shaking his head in disgust, oozing disappointment. "Why do you even have to think this one through, Lem?" Father would say. "Are you a Jukes or are you a child?"

Lem turned to Chubs. "Put us on the rock."

CHAPTER 6

Marco

Victor was on a spacewalk, outside El Cavador, bolting one of the pebble-killers into place with his hand drill. Mono was beside him, his feet anchored to the hull, holding the PK steady with bracing cables. They had removed the laser a few days ago and taken it into the cargo bay to make modifications. Now, with those completed, they were reinstalling it on the side of the ship.

Victor wasn't sure if their efforts would make much difference. If the alien starship proved to be aggressive, Victor probably couldn't do much to stop it. The starship moved at near-lightspeed, which required an almost inconceivable amount of energy and huge leaps in technology, far beyond anything human tech had ever achieved. And if the starship's builders could do that, there was no telling what their weapons could do.

Victor inserted a bolt into his drill and moved to the next hole, noticing that the hole was slightly off its mark. He looked up and saw that Mono had fallen asleep. The bracing cable drifted lazily away from Mono's open hands, and his arms floated limply beside him. If not for Mono's boot magnets, he probably would have drifted away from the ship.

"Mono," Victor said sharply.

Mono jerked awake, suddenly alert, eyes wide. He grabbed the bracing cable and pulled it taut. "Sorry. I'm awake."

"No you're not. You're exhausted. And I don't blame you. I've pushed you way too hard today."

"No, no. I'm fine. Really. I'm good now." Mono blinked his eyes in an exaggerated manner and shook his head to force himself to stay awake.

"Three more bolts," said Victor. "Then we'll go inside. It's already an hour into sleep-shift. You should be zipped up in your hammock."

"I'm fine," Mono said, though Victor could tell from the look on his face that if given five more seconds of silence, the boy would be asleep again.

A message from Mother appeared on Victor's visor. "It's late, Vico. Bring Mono inside. His mother's worried."

Victor and Mono finished the install, collected their things, and hurried to the airlock. Mother greeted them inside with containers of chili and two hot arepas wrapped in a cloth. Victor wiggled out of his pressure suit and sucked the first taste of chili up through the straw. It was hot and spicy with finely minced peppers the way he liked it.

"Perfect as always," he said.

Mother scowled. "You're not winning me over with compliments, Vico. You're in trouble. Mono should have been in a bed an hour ago."

"I'm not tired," said Mono, though he was barely keeping his eyes open.

Mother smiled. "No, you're as perky as a jackrabbit." She frowned at Victor. "You're not resting and eating like I told you to, Vico. You need eight hours of sleep a night. As does Mono. He's nine years old."

"Nine and three quarters," said Mono. "My birthday's coming up."

"You're right, Patita," said Victor. "I'm sorry.

Mother squinted. She always got that suspicious look in her eyes whenever Victor called her by the nickname he had given her as a child, as if he were concealing something. "Did you even go to bed last night, Vico? You weren't in your hammock this morning."

Victor bit into the arepa. It was hot and buttery. "I slept a few hours in the workshop."

Mother sighed and looked at Mono. "And what about you, Monito? Are you learning anything from my son besides rebellion and disobedience?"

Mono's mouth was full of arepa. He said something, but it was unintelligible.

"He says he sleeps like a baby," said Victor. "Eight hours a night."

Mono smiled and nodded to show Mother that the translation had been correct.

"At least one of you minds," said Mother.

Victor kept quiet. He knew Mother wasn't really angry. She knew the work they were doing needed to be done. She just didn't like it.

"Father should be the one getting the tongue lashing," said Victor. "He's sleeping less than I am."

"Oh don't you worry," said Mother. "He's heard plenty from me today already."

All of them had been working feverishly since the Council meeting, Father more than anyone.

"The Italians should be getting the laserline about now," said Mother.

Victor nodded. "Still no word from the Juke ship?"

Mother shook her head. "We should have gotten a response by now, at least an acknowledgment of message received. But so far, nothing. Selmo thinks they pulled out before they got the message. They're not showing up on our scans anymore."

"Or maybe they got the message and shot back to Luna, fleeing for their lives," said Mono.

"Then at least we got the message to someone," Mother said.

"We should have told everyone," said Victor. "We should have told the whole world ten days ago."

She nodded and put a hand on his arm. "Just promise me you'll sleep more."

"Only if you promise to make this chili more often."

"Yeah," said Mono, smacking his lips. "Sabroso." Delicious.

Victor's handheld beeped, and Father's voice came through. "Marco and I could use your help out here, Vico. If you're done with that pebble-killer, send Mono on to bed and come give us a hand."

When not working in the mine, Marco had been helping Father in recent days, joining him outside to build the ship's defenses.

"I'm here with Mother," said Victor. "She can hear you. She's giving me the skunk eye."

"I don't want to leave this thing half installed overnight," said Father, "and these new parts of yours are being a little finicky. Tell your mother I need you."

"Tell your father he's in big trouble," said Mother.

"She says she loves you dearly," said Victor.

Mother rolled her eyes, and Victor knew then that she wasn't going to argue.

"I'm on my way out," said Victor.

"Can I come?" said Mono.

"Absolutely not," said Mother. "I told your mom I'd have you go straight to your hammock, and that's exactly where you're going."

Mono looked ready to object, but a quick look and stern finger from Mother made Mono think better of it. He let his shoulders sag and launched up toward the hatch. When he was gone, Mother put a hand on Victor's shoulder. "Please be careful, Vico. When we're tired, we make mistakes. And you can't make mistakes outside. Even little ones."

"I'll be careful."

Five minutes later he was outside with Father and Marco, his lifeline stretching out behind him to the cargo bay.

"We rebooted," said Father, gesturing to the newly installed PK. "But it's still not coming online."

Using his heads-up display—or HUD—Victor blinked his way into the ship's computer to pinpoint the problem. He wasn't a coder, but he had learned enough code to manipulate it when he needed to accommodate modifications. By the time he had uncovered the glitch, tweaked the code, and brought the PK to life, another hour had passed. Marco and Father were nearby, bolting one of the new armored plates onto the hull. The metal had come directly from the dig site, where the smelting machines had been modified to make them. There had been a lot of discussion on the ship about using the metal, with some people insisting that they send the metal directly to Luna with the rest of the minerals to build up more income. In the end, however, Concepción had sided with Father, and the smelters had been making additional plates ever since.

Victor joined Father and Marco and began helping them secure plates to the hull. He couldn't hear the drill in his hand, but he knew the vibrations would be making noise inside the ship. Most people were sleeping, so if the sound was loud enough to wake them, Victor was sure he'd get a message in his helmet telling them to stop. After several more hours of work, no message came. Initially, Marco made the time pass quickly by telling old mining stories, some of which were so hilarious that Victor and Father had laughed until their stomachs hurt. It was the first time Victor had felt any sense of normalcy with an adult—other than Mother and Father—since Janda's departure.

Eventually the stories dried up, however, and the three of them fell into a silence as they worked. They could stop at any moment, of course; Father and Marco had only started installing plates to keep busy while Victor worked on the PK. With that done, there was really no reason for them to be out this late. Victor stood up to suggest that they call it a night, when something in the distance, down on the surface of the asteroid, caught his attention. A flicker of movement, a streak of something out of the corner of his eye. Victor squinted into the darkness, straining to see. He blinked up the magnification feature on his helmet and zoomed his view down to where one of the mooring lines was anchored to the asteroid. It was hard to see much detail in the blackness, but it looked as if something was on the line.

"Father?"

"Yeah?"

"I think there's something on the—"

There were twelve simultaneous, blinding flashes of light down near the asteroid. Victor instinctively clenched his eyes shut, feeling the ship shift slightly beneath his feet.

"What was that?" asked Marco.

Victor opened his eyes and saw among the dots of brightness still burned into his vision that all twelve mooring lines had been cut. The ship was adrift. Someone had blown the lines.

"It's an attack!" Father shouted. "Hold on to something!"

The first laser hit the PK not two meters from where Victor was standing, slicing it from its base. A mechanism inside the PK exploded outward, causing the PK to shoot back like a rocket in zero gravity. It struck Marco in the side of the head just as he was bending down, tearing him away from the ship and sending him spinning out into space.

"Victor, get down!" Father cried.

Victor initiated the magnets in his hands and waist belt and quickly lowered himself to the hull on his stomach. The alarm in his HUD was beeping. Father must have initiated it. Everywhere on the ship, the siren would be wailing now, waking everyone.

Two laser blasts hit the hull near where Victor and Father lay, slicing off more sensors and instruments. Another laser cut wide to Victor's left, and Victor turned his head and watched in horror as the laserline transmitter was hit. In one swift slice, the laser cut away the entire mechanism, leaving only the mounting plate and a few scorched circuits. The severed piece floated there in space, drifting slowly away. The ship's primary source of long-range communication was gone.

Victor flinched as three more lasers swept across the surface of the ship to his right, not cutting deep into the hull, but slicing away all protruding instrumentations in their paths. Victor closed his eyes, expecting the inevitable, but the lasers didn't touch him. A moment later his alarm went silent, and his HUD winked out. He had no power. His suit was dead. Had a laser cut his lifeline? No, the surface lights on El Cavador were out as well; the lasers must have hit the main generators. Victor took a breath. He wasn't getting fresh air. He no longer had heat. He tried to move, and the rotation of his body caused him to drift away from the hull. No power meant no magnets. He realized a moment too late that nothing was anchoring him to the ship. He reached out, clawing at the smooth surface, trying to get purchase, desperate to cling to something. He looked at Father, who was screaming, though Victor could hear nothing. Father had one hand outstretched, the other hand gripping a recessed handhold. Victor grabbed for Father's hand, but it was more than a meter beyond his reach.

Another laser hit the hull, slicing away another sensor.

Victor turned his head, frantically scanning the sky around him. Was it the starship?

Then he saw it.

At first it was just a black space in the sky where stars should be. Then the ship came closer, and Victor could make out detail. It wasn't a starship. It was a corporate. A Juke ship.

Floodlights blinded him. Victor raised his arm, shielding his eyes, squinting at the light. The corporate ship had approached in darkness and was now charging in, lights blazing. It wasn't slowing down. It was going to ram El Cavador.

Victor looked back at Father, who was still screaming for him to reach. Victor flailed, reaching out, straining, stretching, extending his fingers.

The ship struck.

Father moved away fast.

Victor's body slammed into something hard, the wind rushing out of him in a violent impact to his chest. He felt a flash of pain. The corporates had hit him. He was flat against their ship, and then he wasn't, spinning away, free again, tumbling, disoriented. He turned his head and saw El Cavador moving away from him, his lifeline stretching out, growing taut. He couldn't breath. His lungs were screaming for air. He looked at his lifeline and knew that a hard jerk might tear it from his back. He reached back and grabbed the line just as it went taut. The line jerked him hard, but it stayed connected. He held on. He was tumbling again, trailing behind El Cavador like a trolled fish line.

Then in a single, painful inhale of breath, his lungs expanded again. He took in air. His chest burned. His arm hurt. His suit was cold. His head was ringing. The air was stale.

"Father!"

There was no reply. He still had no power.

El Cavador was drifting awkwardly ahead of him, moving abnormally to the side, like a boat turned sideways in an unforgiving current. The twelve severed mooring cables hung loosely below the ship. Two more laser blasts hit sensors on the side of the ship, though Victor couldn't see what they were. He was still spinning, flying, dazed, limp. Everything was happening too quickly.

Behind him, he saw the corporate ship fire its retros and slow down, coming to a stop right where El Cavador had been. They wanted the rock, Victor realized. The bastards had bumped them for the rock.

Victor rotated his body, trying to control the spinning. El Cavador was still in a dead float, moving away from him. His lifeline was still taut. He was probably forty meters from the ship. He pulled on the lifeline, using the momentum to stop the spinning. His body steadied. The spinning ceased. He could see Father clinging to the ship.

The siren started beeping in his helmet again. His heads-up display flickered to life. He had power. The auxiliary generators had kicked in.

"Victor!" It was Father's voice.

"I'm here." He was already hitting the propulsion trigger on his thumb, flying forward, hurrying toward the ship.

"Are you hurt?" Father asked.

Victor could see Father getting to his feet and then jumping from the ship, flying out toward him. Victor rotated his arm. It wasn't broken. Or at least he didn't think so. "No. I'm okay."

El Cavador was still drifting. He and Father were coming at each other fast. Victor let up on his propulsion just as Father did. Even still, they collided, clinging to each other. Father scanned Victor's helmet, looking for fractures. "You're not hurt? You're not leaking?"

"No." He had never seen Father this rattled before. "You?"

"Fine. It's Marco. Help me get him inside. He's not responding."

Only then did Victor realize that there was a second lifeline trailing behind the ship, albeit farther down the ship from his position. Marco's line had snagged on one of the mooring braces, and Marco's body was limp and lifeless. Father oriented himself and hit his propulsion trigger, flying straight toward Marco. Victor followed close behind him.

They reached Marco and anchored themselves to the ship. Marco's body was limp and nonresponsive. They turned him over. His eyes were closed. His helmet was cracked, though it didn't appear as if air was leaking.

"I don't think he's breathing," said Father. He looked up, thinking, not sure what to do, then came to a decision. "Go open the hatch to the bay airlock. As soon as Marco and I come through, pull in the slack from our lifelines as fast as you can. Then come in after us and seal the hatch tight. You understand?"

"Yes, sir."

Father got behind Marco and wrapped one arm around his chest and another around his waist. He was going to fly him in. "Go, Victor."

Victor launched, pushing the thumb trigger down as far as it would go, hurtling straight to the airlock hatch that led into the cargo bay. The exterior siren lights were spinning, bathing the whole ship in rays of moving red. The damage was everywhere: scorch marks, stumps where equipment had been. Victor reached the hatch, opened it, then moved to the side. Father was coming up fast, carrying Marco's limp body. Marco's legs thumped against the frame of the hatch as he came through, but Marco showed no response. Victor followed them inside and began reeling in the slack from their lifelines, pulling hand over hand as fast as he could. Father was beside him now, pulling frantically. Finally it was all in. Victor sealed the hatch, and air immediately began pouring into the airlock to fill the vacuum.

"Help me anchor him to the ground," said Father.

The lifeline slack was everywhere, floating all around them. Victor pushed as much of it to the side as he could, getting it out of the way. Then he hit the switch on Marco's waist belt to initiate the magnet. He and Father lowered Marco's body to the floor. Father grabbed two anchor straps and put one across Marco's chest and another across his legs, anchoring him flat against the floor. By then the airlock was almost full of air.

"As soon as we get the all-clear," said Father, "take his helmet off nice and slow. Don't jerk it. We need to be easy with his neck."

Victor nodded, and they both got into position.

Father looked at the time counter on the wall and saw that there were twenty seconds before the room was fully pressurized. "Close enough. Go." Father began taking off his own helmet while Victor delicately unhinged Marco's. When he finally got it off, the all-clear sounded, and the light above the exit to the cargo bay turned green.

Father felt Marco's neck for a pulse while Victor fumbled to get his own helmet off.

"Call Isabella on your handheld," said Father. "Get her here now. Tell her I can't find a pulse and he's not breathing."

Victor's hands were shaking as he dialed the code on his handheld. Marco was dying. Or maybe already dead. Father tilted Marco's head slightly back and began giving him rescue breaths. Isabella didn't respond.

"She's not answering," said Victor.

"She's probably already treating people or moving to the fuge. Find her. Get her here now. Have her bring her kit if she has it with her. Go."

Victor detached his lifeline and was up and out of the airlock in an instant, launching himself across the cargo bay to the hatch on the far side of the room. The siren was loud inside the ship, and only the emergency lights were on, leaving much of the room in darkness. No one was in the cargo bay, but Victor found plenty of people out in the hall, a main thoroughfare on the ship. Everyone was wearing their emergency air masks and moving down the hall toward the fuge in an orderly fashion as they had been trained. Babies and small children were crying behind their masks, but their parents held them close to their chests and spoke words of comfort. Everyone seemed alarmed, but Victor was pleased to see that no one was panicking. Most people were upright, wearing greaves, but a few like Victor were flying, calmly moving with the crowd.

Victor scanned the faces but didn't see Isabella. Knowing her, she would be one of the last people to head for the fuge. As a trained nurse, she would stay behind and help anyone who had been injured in the collision, making sure everyone got to the fuge. She was the closest thing El Cavador had to a doctor, and she had even performed a few surgeries over the years, though only in life-threatening situations and always as a last resort.

Victor spotted a familiar face. "Edimar!"

Edimar saw him and pushed her way through the crowd to reach him. Her air mask covered her entire face. "What happened?" she asked. "Why are you in a pressure suit? Were you outside? Where's your mask?"

"Have you seen Isabella?"

Edimar pointed back up the way she had come. "She was helping Abuelita. Why? Who's hurt? What happened?"

Victor didn't wait to answer. He was already away, pushing his way past people, going against traffic, using the handrail to pull himself forward. Edimar called after him, but he didn't turn back. Several people shouted at him as he brushed past them, but Victor didn't care. Marco was dying. He wasn't breathing. Every second counted.

The deeper he went down the hall, the thinner the crowd became. With more room to move around, Victor began launching himself forward, moving faster, covering more ground. He reached Abuelita, his great-grandmother, who was being helped down the hall by two of his uncles. "Where's Isabella?"

They pointed farther up the hall. Victor shot forward, panicked. There were very few people now. What if Isabella had gone into someone's room to help them and Victor had passed it? Or what if she had taken another passageway down to the fuge and Victor had missed her?

He saw her. She was ahead in the hall, putting Victor's cousin Nanita's arm in a sling.

"Isabella!"

She looked up. Victor grabbed a handhold on the wall, stopped himself, and motioned for her to come. "It's Marco. He's not breathing."

She grabbed her bag and launched toward him. "Where?"

Victor turned his body and launched down the way he had come. "Airlock. Cargo bay."

"He was outside?"

"We were putting on some plates when the corporates attacked."

"Corporates?"

He told her what he could as they flew down the corridor. He had to shout over the wail of the alarm. The crowd was thin now. Most people would be in the fuge. They reached the cargo bay. Isabella went through first. They flew down to the airlock. Maybe Marco is fine now, thought Victor. Maybe Father revived him. We'll get there, and Marco will be up and coughing and sore maybe, but he'll be alive, and he'll thank Father and me for helping him, and then we'll all go down to the fuge together and laugh about what a scare it had been.

But Marco wasn't fine. Father was still giving him rescue breaths. Nothing had changed. Marco was still lifeless. Father saw them and moved aside for Isabella to take over. Father looked exhausted and afraid and out of breath. "He's not responding to anything," he said.

Isabella slid her greaves up to her knees and knelt on the floor beside Marco, opening her bag and moving quickly. "Help me get his suit off so I can get to his chest." She had scissors in her hand and began cutting away his suit. Victor and Father tore the fabric away as Isabella cut through Marco's undershirt. Victor watched the chest, willing it to rise on its own, to move, to show a little life. It didn't.

Isabella slapped sensors onto his chest and slid a tube over Marco's mouth. The machine started giving him breaths, and Marco's chest began to rise and fall. It didn't give Victor any comfort. The machine was doing all the work. Isabella pulled a syringe from her bag, bit off the needle cap, spat it away, and stuck the needle into Marco's arm. She flipped on a second machine, and Victor heard the sustained beep of a flatline. His heart wasn't beating. Isabella pressed a disc to Marco's chest. She squeezed the handle, and Marco's body twitched. Victor thought for half a second that whatever Isabella had done had revived him; that Marco was coming around and jerking awake. But he wasn't. His body became still again. Isabella jolted him three more times. Four. Still the flatline persisted.

Isabella looked lost. She removed the disc from Marco's chest and pushed it away. Her hands went back in her bag. They came out with the bone pad. She placed it on Marco's chest, and the skeletal structure appeared on the screen. Isabella slowly moved the pad up to Marco's neck and held it there for a long time, her face just inches from the pad. Finally, she switched off the pad and looked up, defeated.

"His neck is broken. It severed his spinal column. I'm sorry."

The words felt hollow to Victor, like words from a dream. She was telling them that Marco was dead, that there was nothing more she could do. She was giving up.

No, Marco couldn't be dead. Victor had been with Marco just moments ago. They had been working together, laughing.

Father was speaking quietly into his handheld, calling someone down to the airlock.

"There has to be something we can do," said Victor.

"There isn't, Vico," said Isabella, removing the tube from Marco's mouth.

"So we're just giving up?"

"I can't fix what's broken here. He was dead before you brought him in. I'm sorry."

Victor felt numb. His fingers were tingling. Marco was dead. The word hit him like the Juke ship had. Dead. Why had the corporates attacked them? This wasn't the Asteroid Belt. This was the Kuiper Belt. The family had left the A Belt for this very reason: to get away from the corporates.

How had they gotten so close without us detecting them?

Victor looked down at Marco. He has a family, Victor told himself. A wife, Gabi, and three girls—one of whom, Chencha, was just a year younger than Victor.

Father disconnected the lifeline from the back of his own suit and moved for the door into the cargo bay. "Let's go, Vico."

"We're leaving?"

"You and I have work to do."

He meant the ship. Victor had seen some of the damage. The power generator was fried. Sensors were gone. PKs were gone. And the auxiliary generators wouldn't last forever. If the family was going to survive, Victor and Father needed to make big repairs fast.

Victor nodded to Father and moved toward the hatch.

"Gabi and Lizbét are on their way down now," Father said to Isabella. "I'd stay, but Concepción wants us on the helm immediately."

Lizbét was Marco's mother. She still doted on her son.

"Go," said Isabella. "I'll wait for them here."

Father was up and flying. Victor launched after him. A moment later they were in the hall, which was empty now. Father turned toward the helm, taking a side passageway. Before following, Victor looked down the hall in the opposite direction, back toward the fuge, and saw two women coming, still a distance away, heading for the cargo bay. Gabi and Lizbét. Wife and mother. Even at a distance, he could see the terror and panic on their faces.

"Vico, let's go," said Father.

Victor was moving again, following Father, weaving through the passageways of the ship. They arrived at the helm, and Victor was surprised to see the entire flight crew here, all busily working. Some were running cables and setting up lights. Others were at their workstations, speaking into their headsets or typing in commands. Concepción saw Father and flew to him immediately. Victor could tell from her expression that she knew about Marco. Father must have called her.

"Gabi and Lizbét are with him now," said Father.

Concepción nodded. "Are either of you hurt?"

"The corporate ship hit Victor," said Father.

"I'm fine," said Victor.

Concepción looked concerned. "You sure? I'm going to need you, Victor, like I've never needed you before."

"I'm fine," he repeated, though he felt anything but fine. Marco was dead. The ship was damaged, perhaps irreparably so.

"Come with me," said Concepción, turning and flying back to the holotable.

Selmo was there, looking at a large holo schematic of the ship in the holospace above the table. A dozen blinking red dots on the schematic marked damaged areas. "The electrical generator is out, of course," he said. "We don't yet know how badly it's damaged. That should be our first priority. The backup generators are fine, but they can only output about fifty percent of the power we typically use every day. So we'll need to ration power and turn off a bunch of lights and all nonessential equipment. Most of the power will need to go to the air ventilators and the heaters. I'd rather work in the dark than freeze to death."

"Victor and I will handle the main generator," said Father. "What about the reactors?"

"The reactors are fine," said Selmo. "So the thrusters are good. The corporates knew what they were doing. They beat us up, but they left us with the ability to run away as fast as we can."

"Which is exactly what we are going to do," said Concepción. "Once we get our bearings and pick our course, we are out of here. We're no match for a ship that size or that well defended. I know some of you would like to blow them out of the sky right now, but we are in no position to do so. We don't have the capabilities, and we are not going to endanger anyone else on this ship. That asteroid is not worth dying for. We're running."

"No argument," said Father. "But if we can, we should try to collect as many of the parts and sensors as possible that were cut away from the ship. They're just out there floating in space right now, and we might be able to salvage some of the parts. Especially the lasers. Some of those components are irreplaceable. I don't want to push our luck and aggravate the corporates by sticking around, but we should scoop up as much as we can before we rocket out of here."

"Agreed," said Concepción. "Selmo, as soon as we're done here, work with Segundo and Victor on a plan to quickly collect as much of the severed equipment as we can."

Selmo nodded. "The miners can help with that. I've got thirty men already asking what they can do."

"What else is damaged?" asked Father.

Selmo sighed. "Both laser drills are gone. The corporates severed them from the ship, and then sliced them to pieces. There's no way we can repair them. I've already pulled video of the attack. The drills are irreparable. See for yourself." He entered some commands into the holotable, and surveillance video of the exterior of the ship appeared in the holospace. There was the old laser drill, the one with Victor's stabilizer, illuminated by a pair of the safety lights. Selmo fast-forwarded the video, and Victor and Father watched as lasers sliced the drill the ribbons. The light was so bright and the cuts happened so quickly that Selmo rewound the video and showed it to them again in slow motion. Victor felt sick. All his modifications and improvements to the drill, all of which he had created in his head and rarely written down before building them, were gone. Chopped into worthless scrap. Worse still, the drills were the family's livelihood, the two most important pieces of equipment, the means by which the family earned money and survived.

And now they were gone.

Father said nothing for a moment. He understood the implication. The corporates had crippled more than the ship; they had crippled the family's future. How could they mine now? How could they get money for needed supplies or spare parts? How could they exist in the Deep without good drills?

"What else?" asked Father.

"Four of our PKs are gone as well," said Selmo. "That leaves us with two. Here again, the corporates knew what they were doing. They left us with one PK on either side of the ship, enough for us to fly out of here and defend ourselves against most collision threats, but not enough to retaliate and attack their ship. The only upside here, if there is one, is that they didn't *slice* up the PKs. They just cut them loose. I take that to mean they expect us to recover them and repair them elsewhere."

"How kind of them," said Father. "Remind me to send flowers. What else?"

"Our other big loss is communication. The laserline transmitter's gone. We can't send a distress message even if we wanted to."

"It also means we can't warn anyone about the starship," said Victor.

"True," said Selmo, "but that's the least of our problems right now."

"What about ice?" asked Father. "How are we with air and fuel?"

Selmo smiled. "That's a ray of sunshine. The holding bay is ninety-five percent full of ice. We harvested as much as we could from the asteroid when we first got here. So we're fine for fuel and oxygen for a while. That's more than enough to get us wherever we want to go within, say, five to six months from here."

Victor felt relieved to hear that, at least. Ice was life. The reactors melted it and separated the hydrogen from the oxygen. The hydrogen they used for fuel. The oxygen they breathed.

Selmo moved his stylus in the holospace and rotated the schematic. "If you'd like more good news, it appears as if the other life-support systems are undamaged. Water purifiers are good. Air pumps are fine. Whoever these corporates are they picked their targets carefully."

"Leaks?" asked Father.

"None that we can detect," said Selmo. "We're running another scan just to be certain, but it looks like we got through without a breach. We were lucky. The impact wasn't that hard, and their lasers weren't trying to penetrate. Plus the armor helped."

"Who are they?" Father asked. "Why didn't we see this coming?"

Selmo sighed. "That's my fault. This is the corporate ship we sent the laserline to ten days ago. I should have suspected something when they didn't show up on the scans anymore. I assumed that they had moved on. I never thought that they were creeping up on us."

"No one is at fault," said Concepción. "They knew our scanning capabilities and they exploited them. End of story."

"If they got our message, why would they attack us?" Father asked.

"Selmo and I did the math," said Concepción. "When we sent out the laserline, they were already coming for us. They never got our message. They missed it. This has nothing to do with the laserline. They wanted the asteroid, pure and simple."

Dreo came to the holotable. "I've got their network. Give the word and we're a go."

Father turned to Concepción. "We launched a snifferstick?" he asked.

Sniffersticks were small hacker satellites launched from one ship to spy on another. To work, they had to be within range of a ship's network yet far enough away to avoid triggering the ship's PKs. Fifty meters was about as close as any snifferstick dared. Accessing the ship's network was the tricky part, especially if it was a corporate ship. Corporates had armies of coders and specialists who did nothing but devise defenses against sniffer-sticks. Most families wouldn't dream of even trying to hack a corporate. But most families didn't have Dreo, either, who could wiggle his way into any network.

"We launched it just before you came to the helm," said Concepción. "I want to know who bumped us."

"What if they detect us nosing around their network?" said Father. "That might instigate another attack."

"They won't know," said Dreo. "I've taken every precaution."

"No offense," said Father, "but are you sure? We've been out here for years. Who knows what other sweeper programs they've got running these days? They might have new ways to detect us that we don't know about. Is this a risk we want to take? They're corporates. What else do we want to know?"

"They have no reason coming out to the Kuiper Belt when there are so many asteroids in the A Belt, ready for the taking," said Concepción. "If they're moving out here now, the other families will want to know. This will affect all the clans. We've lived in relative peace for a long time now. If corporates are beginning to invade our space, that's intel we need to spread. Dreo assures me we'll remain invisible."

"Then why don't we upload some malware or venomware and damage their systems while we're in there?" said Victor.

"Because we are not going to attack them at all," said Concepción. "I want information, not revenge."

Victor looked at the faces around the table, and saw that not everyone shared in that opinion.

"Please proceed, Dreo," said Concepción. "And bring up their network on the holotable, if you wouldn't mind."

Dreo returned to his workstation, and the schematic of the ship in the holospace disappeared, replaced with a series of three-dimensional icons spinning in space: flight log, engineering, laserlines, field trials, Lem, Dr. Benyawe, and others.

"Give me the manifest," said Concepción. "Tell me who the captain is."

Photos and a holovideo of a handsome man in his early thirties appeared.

Concepción selected the window of data beside one of the photos and expanded it.

"Lem Jukes," she said, reading the name.

"As in *the* Jukes?" said Father. "Is he related?"

"Ukko's son," said Concepción.

"I'll be damned," said Selmo. "The apple doesn't fall far from the tree."

"Copy as much of this data as we can," said Concepción. "I want to know what their intentions are. Then let's get the severed sensors back in the ship and get out of here before Mr. Lem Jukes decides to take more potshots. I'm going to be with Gabi and Lizbét, and then I'll head to the fuge to address the family." She turned to Father. "Don't waste time and energy working on what we can't fix. Work with Selmo to identify those things we can repair. Power first, communication second."

"What about the starship?" asked Victor.

"What about it?" said Concepción. "Selmo's right. We're not in any position to address that right now. Nor can we relay what we've found. We're silent until we get communication back online."

"We're not going to be able to recover everything," said Father. "We're going to need parts and supplies."

"The nearest weigh station is four months away," said Concepción. "The closest help we have are the Italians. They received our message and are watching the sky. If we hurry, maybe we can reach them before they move on. They'll have plenty of supplies we could use."

Victor looked at Father and could tell that he was thinking the same thing Victor was. Going for the Italians was a risk. There was no way to send the Italians a transmission to tell them to stay put and wait. If El Cavador arrived and the Italians had moved on, the ship would be in serious trouble.

Concepción left the bridge.

Victor turned back to the holospace and looked at Lem Jukes. Some of the photos were ID shots: a straight headshot, a profile shot. But others were more casual photos taken from the ship's archives: Lem standing with his father, Ukko Jukes, in a ceremonial photo at what must have been the ship's departure; a more editorial shot of Lem in action at the helm, leaning forward over some holodisplay, pointing at nothing in particular, clearly a staged shot for the press. And then there was the brief holovideo. It was twelve seconds long at the most, running on a loop, playing over and over again. Lem was at a dinner party, sitting at a table after a meal. Empty wineglasses, fancy cutlery, a slice of half-eaten cake on a plate. There was no audio, but Lem was clearly telling a story, using his hands and his charming smile to emphasize his tale. Two beautiful women sat on either side of him, hanging on his every word. The story reached its end, and everyone burst out laughing, including Lem. Then the video began again.

Victor watched it a second time, and this time Victor imagined the words coming out of Lem's mouth. "So we blow up their mooring cables," Lem was saying. "And there were these three men out on the hull of their ship. The devil only knows what they were doing out there. So I told my pilot to rush them, to hit them hard and knock that PK right where they were standing. And lo and behold, that thing smacked one of those gravel suckers right between the eyes."

Laughter from everyone at the table.

Father was talking with Selmo. Victor stared at the laughter in the video.

That man killed Marco, Victor thought. Lem Jukes, son of Ukko Jukes, heir to the fortune of thieves and murderers, killed Marco.

Concepción wanted them to focus on power and communication. Fine. Victor would do that. But he was also going to rebuild one of the PKs, a special one, strong enough to wipe that stupid grin right off Lem Jukes's face.

CHAPTER 7

India

Captain Wit O'Toole sat up front in the cockpit with the pilot until the plane was an hour away from the drop zone. The eight passengers in the cabin were Wit's newest recruits, soldiers plucked from Special Forces units in New Zealand, South Africa, Spain, Russia, and South Korea. In his most optimistic estimations, Wit had counted on finding six men to join MOPs. Coming home with eight was like Christmas come early.

None of the men had ever met one another before this flight, so Wit had intentionally left them alone immediately after the plane had taken off from a private airport in Mumbai. If he had sat with them, they would have deferred to him as their senior officer and waited for him to initiate conversation. But now, as Wit left the cockpit and made his way back to the cabin, he heard laughter and conversation as if the men were the oldest of friends.

Sociability and friendliness were the first traits Wit looked for in possible recruits. There were thousands of soldiers who could shoot with accuracy and fight with ferocity, but there were few who could quickly earn trust among foreigners and strangers. This was especially important in MOPs, whose soldiers often rushed into violent situations where civilians were being brutalized, often by their own militaries and governments. It meant MOPs had the difficult task of earning the trust of those who distrusted anyone in uniform. These men had what it took.

Wit entered the cabin, and the South Korean, a lieutenant named Yoo Chi-won, sprang to his feet, came to attention, and saluted. The others quickly followed his lead and stood up.

"As you were," said Wit.

The men sat down.

"I appreciate the gesture, gentlemen," said Wit, "but this is not the South Korean Army or the Russian Army or whatever. This is MOPs. We follow a different protocol. You need only salute me in formal settings, and those are rare anyway. You will show me a much greater respect in the field by immediately following orders. You need not even address me formally, if you wish. I answer to Wit, O'Toole, or Captain. And speaking of rank. As all of you have no doubt noticed from your introductions and insignia on your uniforms, I am not the only captain on this plane. We have several captains and lieutenants and NCOs among us. These ranks were all well earned. You are to be commended for them. But they are ranks from a different army. You are no longer a captain or a lieutenant. You are all equal. Should you choose to address each other formally, you will call each other 'soldier.' Soldier Chi-won. Soldier Bogdanovich. Soldier Mabuzza. I hold a rank because I have been doing this for a while and my superiors need someone to blame if something goes wrong."

The men smiled.

"There are other small matters of protocol, but these we will pick up as we go along. At the moment, we have more pressing matters. Beneath your seats you will find masks with one hundred percent oxygen. I advise you to begin breathing that now."

All eight men reached under their seats, found their masks, and put them on. Wit put his on as well, speaking through the transmitter at the base of the mask.

"Since all of you are trained in high-altitude jumps, I need not explain the importance of flushing all the nitrogen from your bloodstream prior to the jump."

The men exchanged glances. Wit had not yet told them where they were going or what they would do when they got there. His instructions had simply been to come to a designated hangar at an airfield in Mumbai with nothing but the uniform they were wearing. A plane would be waiting.

"And yes, we are about to make a high-altitude jump," said Wit. "Your new home for the next few months is a training facility in the Parvati Valley in the foothills of the Himalayan Mountains in northern India. These two cabinets here contain the remainder of your gear. Leave your old uniforms here in a pile. You won't need them. They represent your old life. You are MOPs men now. I suggest you change quickly."

The men got up, opened the cabinets, and began distributing the gear. As Wit had suspected, they worked calmly, passing out the equipment and showing as much concern for one another as they did for themselves. They then removed their uniforms and dropped them where Wit had indicated. Wit could have asked them to come in civvies, but the ritualistic shedding of old affiliations helped remind the men where their new devotion lay.

Wit put on a dampening suit, then a jumpsuit, which was thick and heated and laced with the latest biometric sensors. There was other gear as well. Wit had placed a few exotic items in the bags to see how the men would respond. A Korean altimeter, for instance, was completely foreign to everyone but Chi-won. They were the best altimeters in the world, but they were exclusive to the Korean Army. Wit was pleased to see Chi-won quickly show the others how to strap the device to their wrists and plug it into their suits. The APAD—automatic parachute activation device— was a Russian model, and Bogdanovich kindly instructed the others on how it worked and what to expect in their heads-up display just before it activated.

Wit placed his holopad on a table and asked the men to gather. A holo appeared of a large military complex with barracks and training facilities and other buildings, all surrounded by a well-fortified wall.

"This is one of the training camps of the Indian Para Commandos," said Wit, "one of the most elite Special Forces units in the world. The PCs are tough men, well equipped and expertly trained. At the moment, three hundred and seven of them are stationed here undergoing training. Their commanding officer is Major Khudabadi Ketkar, a good man and skillful soldier. Our assignment is to train with his men for the next seven weeks. To initiate the training, Major Ketkar suggested we make a little wager. A game of Capture the Flag. Thirty MOPs versus three hundred and seven PCs. The loser will clean the latrines and mess hall for the extent of the training. I accepted that wager. Not for the prize—we will clean the latrines and mess hall anyway. I accepted because this is a chance for me to show the other MOPs already on the ground that I have brought them eight men worthy to be counted among them. The nine of us are going to take the flag."

The men were smiling.

"Now, here's what we know," said Wit. "The flag is here in Ketkar's office." He touched the holo and left a blinking red dot on one of the buildings, then waved his hand through the holo and zoomed in on the building. Walls disappeared, and the building became a three-dimensional schematic, showing four floors of offices. Twenty soldiers were patrolling the roof. Ten more were patrolling the halls inside. Forty others surrounded the building outside beside a blockade of assault vehicles.

"This is a live feed," said Wit. "Ketkar has nearly a third of his forces guarding the flag. Each of these men is wearing a dampening suit similar to yours. Their weapons, like yours, are loaded with spider rounds. Hit them, and they freeze up. They're out. However, the status of each suit is broadcast to every other suit. In other words, they will know the instant one of their men goes down. So they'll know when and where we're attacking." He waved his hand through the holo again and it zoomed out to the entire compound. "There are guard towers here, here, and here. Each with snipers. The front gate is here. There is only a single road leading up to the complex. As you can see, that road is well defended. This here to the south is the Parvati River. It is fast moving, especially now in spring. Winter snowmelt and glacial thaw coming off the mountains raise the water a few feet. Our camp is here three miles to the south. It's a wide, open meadow with a few tents. Twenty-one MOPs, the rest of our forces, are defending our flag there. From the air it looks like the most poorly defended piece of land in the area, but our boys have prepared a few surprises. They are counting on us to bring them the enemy flag. I have promised them we would do so." He stood erect and looked at their faces. "Now, we have about twenty-nine minutes before we reach the drop zone. Tell me how we're going to do this."

The men understood. There was no plan. They had twenty-nine minutes to devise one. The ideas came quickly, and Wit liked what he heard.

The back of the airplane opened, and Wit was the first one out. It was night, but even in the darkness, Wit could see curvature of Earth below him in all directions. They were only at 32,000 feet, but it felt as if they were in space, rocketing down to solid ground.

To the southwest Wit could see the lights of Bhuntar and the trail of village lights that extended northeast up the Kullu Valley along the Beas River. To the east were the lights of Manikaran, the small holy town where Hindus believed Manu re-created life after the great flood. The PC compound was between the two, sitting on the north side of the Parvati River.

Wit positioned his body into a steep dive, and the speedometer on his HUD ticked up to 210 miles per hour. The HUD also showed air temperature, heart rate, adrenaline levels, and the position of his eight recruits, all matching his speed behind him. They had agreed to land on the roof of Ketkar's building—they could take out the twenty roof guards easily from the air. The challenge would be to do so without alerting everyone else.

The Spaniard, a computer expert named Lobo, came up beside Wit, getting into position. The plan was to override the Indian's network so that downed Para Commandos appeared healthy and unhurt to everyone else. The MOPs wouldn't be in range of the network until about five thousand feet, however, so Lobo would have only a few seconds to get into their network and do his business before Wit and the others started picking off guards on the roof.

"You ready, Lobo?" Wit asked, as they dropped through some cloud cover.

"My eyes are sore, sir. I've been blinking like a madman. But I'm ready." As soon as everyone had agreed to Lobo's idea back on the plane, Lobo had stepped aside and began blinking out a program with his HUD. "I also whipped up a little feedback for the PCs' radios to mask any noise from our descent."

"Well done."

Wit's HUD beeped, signaling it was time to slow down. He switched position, lying flat and building up wind resistance. Lobo shot ahead. The compound was coming up fast. Spotlights swept the area outside the fence. Wit could see vehicles now and the guard towers. The valley was steep and narrow, and the hillsides were thick with evergreens. The Parvati River was a thin line of white running southwest. They were miles from any village. The HUD beeped again, and Wit extended his breaker wings; the swaths of fabric in his suit slowed his descent even more.

Lobo's chute opened far below him.

Wit descended another three seconds before opening his chute and getting his weapon into position. Now he was beside Lobo and three other chutes. They would be the first wave. The next five would land immediately thereafter. Wit's HUD zoomed in on the roof, and the heat signature of twenty men appeared. Wit's computer selected them all, identifying them as TAFTs, or targets for termination. Wit blinked at the five men he intended to take, selecting them, and watched on his HUD as his teammates selected the others.

"Now, Lobo," said Wit.

Lobo's response was almost immediate. "Clear. Go."

The silencer on Wit's weapon muffled the fire, and his five targets on the roof all took a spider round, their suits going stiff and turning red. Wit touched down and released his chute. No one was firing at him. The other roof sentries were down. He grabbed his chute and stuffed it under one of the red PCs. He could hear the man's muffled complaints behind his visor, and Wit put a finger to his own visor over his lips, telling the man to stay quiet.

The other five MOPs landed on the roof and began tucking their chutes away. Lobo was kneeling beside one of the downed PCs with a wire connected to the man's helmet. It was only a matter of time before the men on the ground and those in the towers did a check-in with the men on the roof. If the PCs found the roof silent, they'd know the roof was compromised. Lobo was downloading all of the chatter the sentry had heard and given that night. Voice manipulation software would do the rest.

"Status, Lobo?" Wit asked.

Lobo's lips moved inside his helmet, and then after a brief delay, Wit heard Lobo's words in his own helmet. Only, it wasn't Lobo's voice. It was deeper, with an Indian accent, no doubt identical to that of the downed PC. "All set, Captain. If they call up for a status, I'll tell them all is hunky dory on the roof."

"Let's move," said Wit, leading the others through the roof entrance. They went down a stairwell, across a short corridor, and onto the third floor, taking down four more sentries along the way. These they dispatched with spider pads, small magnetic discs that were the dampening-suit equivalent to a fatal knife wound. Slap a pad on a suit, and the person goes red. Much quieter than gunfire.

A sandbag barricade with four sentries blocked the entrance to Ketkar's office. The New Zealander, an SAS officer whom Wit had nicknamed Pinetop, took the gear and weapon off the downed sentry at Wit's feet and began walking down the center of the corridor toward the barricade. The lights were off, and only Pinetop's silhouette was visible in the darkness. The sentries mistook him for someone else until he was right on top of them. Four shots later, the hall was clear.

Major Khudabadi Ketkar was sitting behind his desk in a dampening suit with a smile on his face when Wit entered. He stood and extended a hand. "Captain O'Toole. I suppose I should not be surprised to see you. Welcome. And I see you brought seven of your finest men."

"All of my men are my finest, sir. It's a pleasure to see you again. Mrs. Ketkar is well, I hope."

"She is nagging me like a frightened hen, but my ears have grown accustomed. She wants to know when you're coming to dinner again. She calls you 'the handsome American.' I pretend not to be jealous." He looked past Wit, saw the four downed sentries at the barricade, and smiled again. "Those are four of my senior officers. I don't think they'll like you very much after tonight, Captain."

"Few people do, sir. Occupational hazard."

Ketkar smiled. "I hope they put up a good fight at least before you shamed them in front of their commanding officer."

"Yes, sir. They are fine soldiers. It was difficult to overrun their position."

"Funny," said Ketkar, smiling. "I didn't hear so much as a scuffle." He picked up the neatly folded flag on his desk and handed it to Wit. "You must tell me how it was done, though," he said.

"HALO jump, sir."

Ketkar frowned. "Attacking from the air? That's breaking the rules, isn't it?"

"I was not aware that our game had any rules, sir."

Ketkar laughed. "No, I suppose it doesn't. It's a bitter irony, though. The PCs are paratroopers. You would think we would look to the sky." He sighed. "Well, you are to be commended for coming this far, Captain. But surely you must realize that escape is impossible. My men have these facilities surrounded. They will never let you out of here."

"With all due respect, sir, I think they will. They'll open the front gate for us."

Ketkar looked amused. "And why would they do that?"

"Because you will ask them to, sir."

"Forgive me, Captain, but our friendship only goes so far. I will do nothing of the sort."

"No, sir. I will do it for you. We have enough samples of your voice now." Wit clicked over to the private frequency. "You ready, Lobo?"

"You're good to go, sir," said Lobo.

Wit began speaking, but it was Ketkar's voice that came out of the speaker on Ketkar's desk. He was broadcasting to every PC. "Gentlemen, this is Major Ketkar. I have just received a personal call from Captain Wit O'Toole of MOPs congratulating us on our victory. Many of you know, but some of you may not be aware, that I sent a small strike force ahead of our main force and asked them to observe strict radio silence. While our main force engaged the MOPs at their camp, creating a distraction, our strike unit has sneaked through and taken the flag from Captain O'Toole without suffering a single casualty. They are now approaching the base. I will meet them outside the gate, along with my senior officers, to give them a hero's welcome. Once they're inside, I expect you to do the same. Our friends in MOPs fought valiantly, but we have shown these cocky bastards who the real soldiers are."

There was a cry of approval and applause from outside.

Major Ketkar was no longer smiling. "Well, that was unexpected."

"Forgive me, sir," said Wit. "I hope this doesn't damage our future dinner plans." He politely slapped a spider pad dead center on Ketkar's chest.

Lobo had two cars waiting down in the building's garage. Wit and the other MOPs climbed inside. All of them were now wearing the red berets of the Indian Para Commandos. At a distance, in the dark, they might pass for senior officers, but if anyone got a close look, the ruse would be up.

"Make a show if it," said Wit. "Lots of celebratory honking."

Three of them carried small Indian flags on sticks that they had taken from Ketkar's desk. They cracked the windows and stuck the flags outside, waving them ceremoniously. Lobo pulled out of the garage, and Bogdanovich, at the wheel of the second car, followed. As soon as both cars were away from the building, Lobo started blaring the car horn in short beeps. The PCs, who were still a distance away, cheered and raised their weapons over their heads.

"They're opening the gate," said Wit. "Don't gun it, Lobo. Keep a normal speed. You're driving a major."

"Yes, sir."

Soldiers were leaving the safety of the barricade and running toward the cars, cheering and celebrating. Wit settled back in his chair, keeping his face in the shadows. The soldiers were still thirty yards away, but they would be on the cars in seconds. The gate was just ahead. "Normal speed," repeated Wit. "Nice and easy." The sentries at the gatehouse stepped outside and snapped to attention as the large gate doors slid open. Wit's car began pulling through the gate, passing the sentries, just as the cheering soldiers behind them reached the second car and began slapping the trunk in celebration. One of the sentries at attention lowered his gaze to Wit's car and smiled. The smile vanished an instant later. Then the man started yelling and reaching for his weapon, and all went to hell.

"Gun it, Lobo," said Wit.

Lobo floored it. Behind them Bogdanovich did the same. The celebration became a furious mad scramble. Men tried climbing on to the second car, reaching for the door handle. Spider rounds pinged off the glass. Bogdanovich swerved and floored it. Men tumbled off the car.

"Roadblock," said Lobo.

There were two vehicles parked in the road ahead with a half-dozen PCs already leveling their weapons.

Chi-won was sitting in the backseat beside Wit. "Chi-won," said Wit.

"Happy to, sir."

There was no explanation needed. Wit lowered his window just as Chi-won did. Their weapons were out the window an instant later, firing. PC suits flashed red and stiffened.

Lobo gunned it. "I'm going through."

"Don't run over anyone," said Wit.

Lobo struck the first vehicle at just the right angle to push it enough to the side to get the car through. Metal crunched. Glass shattered. Tires spun. Lobo put his foot to the floor, the vehicle rocked to the side, and then they were free, racing away. The second car was right behind them. The shots from their rear were less frequent now, but Wit knew they weren't in the clear yet. Far from it. The cars would be overtaken soon. They still had two hundred men between them and the MOPs camp.

They drove for another hundred yards around two winding curves and stopped. All nine of them were out of the car immediately.

Two MOPs soldiers emerged from the woods. Deen, the Brit, and Averbach, the Israeli.

"Evening, Captain," said Deen. "We thought you might not be coming." He looked at the new recruits. "These the new greenies? Pleased to meet, boys. Name's Deen. Whose crazy idea was this? I love it."

"Introductions later," said Wit. "You're about to have some angry PCs on your tail. Every vehicle on their base will be on top of you in about ten seconds."

Deen shrugged nonchalantly then got behind the wheel of the first car. Averbach jumped into the second.

"Where I am taking this, Captain?" asked Deen.

"All over creation," said Wit. "Have a field day. Just keep them occupied."

Deen brushed some glass shards off the front seat. "I see that we're not concerning ourselves with the paint job."

"Try not to total it," said Wit.

Deen gunned the engine and put a hand to his ear, smiling. "What's that, Captain? I didn't catch that last part." He laughed and peeled away, with Averbach right behind him.

Wit gave them a mile at the most. Then the PCs would be all over them. He'd never do such a thing in a real operation, sacrificing two men like this, but Deen and Averbach said they didn't mind. They'd take a spider round to the chest if it meant they got to trash a few vehicles in the process.

Wit was running down the slope through the forest with the new recruits. They tossed aside their red berets and replaced them with their
helmets. Wit's HUD flickered to life, barraging him with intel: temperature, distance to the river, projected water depth based on the amount of
snow and rainfall in the area that winter. Branches lashed at his suit and
helmet. The flag was in his back pouch. They were through the trees. The
footbridge over the river was old and dilapidated. Much of the railing had
fallen away long ago. The river was twenty feet below. Wit never slowed
down. His HUD told him the water was likely deeper to the right. Wit
leaped from the bridge. He flew through the air, hit water, and went under.
The buoyancy of his dampening suit lifted him to the surface, and the current swept him downstream. His HUD gave him the water temperature
and tracked the location of his men. All eight were in the water with him,
moving quickly, bobbing along. The current was relatively calm in spots
but it raged in others. Twice they saw large groups of PCs heading up the
road adjacent to the river, back toward the base, hoping perhaps to stop
whomever had the flag. No one looked toward the river. Or if they did,
they didn't see anything in the dark.

The last mile was uneventful. The river calmed, and Wit moved to the
opposite shore. The suits were heavy and waterlogged, but they made good
time on foot, reaching camp ten minutes later. Wit was not surprised to see
all of the remaining MOPs and about sixty PCs gathered around a bonfire
in their undergarments. A tall pile of discarded dampening suits stood off
to the side. Most of the suits were stiff and red, but a good number of them
were still operable. The PCs and MOPs were mingling and laughing and
drinking and playing cards. Four of them were singing a ribald drinking
song, much to the delight of those around them. No one noticed Wit and
the new recruits, who watched from behind one of the tents.

Wit's instructions to the MOPs at camp had been clear. Don't let the
PCs get the flag, but don't them let feel like failures either. Show humility.
These men are allies not enemies.

Five men were sitting on crates and cargo boxes nearby playing a hand
of ganjifa. Calinga, the Filipino MOP, laid down a hand of the circular
cards and celebrated. Those playing with him moaned. Calinga's wrist strap
flashed green, and he excused himself. He came to Wit, smiling and keep-

ing his voice down. "Evening, Captain. Things turned out well for you, I assume. These the newbies? Welcome to MOPs, gentlemen."

The eight recruits nodded a greeting.

"How'd we do?" asked Wit.

Calinga shrugged. "After we'd shot them all, we told them it seemed silly for anyone to lie stiff as a board in the grass until it was over. So we stripped our suits first, so they wouldn't think we were mocking them, and then we broke out the ration coolers with the vitamin drinks. I think the PCs were hoping for booze, but they seemed grateful enough."

"Did we lose any men?"

"Toward the end of the last assault I shot Toejack and Kimble when no one was looking. It seemed like we should have at least a few wounded. If we were all still standing in the end, it would have felt like gloating."

"Well done," said Wit. He stepped out of his dampening suit and shot it with his weapon. The suit stiffened and turned red. "Drop your suits and shoot them," he told the others.

The new recruits obeyed immediately.

"Now we put them on the pile with the others," said Wit. "Be exhausted. Don't act, just let your exhaustion be seen."

Wit led the others to the pile. He had a stitch in his side, but instead of suppressing the pain like he normally would, he let it aggravate him and winced at the discomfort of it. He tossed his suit onto the pile. The soldiers around the bonfire saw him, and everyone quieted. The new recruits dropped their suits onto the pile. They looked wet and tired and beaten, when a moment ago they hadn't even seemed winded.

Wit spoke loudly. "Those of you in my unit know that I do not like to fail."

The camp was silent.

"I had assumed that we could easily win this exercise, but tonight I've learned that you PCs are tougher men than I anticipated. All of us took a beating. If we work this hard over the next few weeks, we'll learn from each other and become better soldiers and men because of it."

Headlights cut through the darkness, and a small convoy of vehicles pulled in. Wit fell silent, watching the cars approach. Major Ketkar stepped down from one of the vehicles, now wearing his fatigues and looking none too pleased.

"Atten-tion!" Wit yelled.

Everyone at the campfire snapped to attention, including Wit, who saluted the major, even though technically it wasn't necessary.

Major Ketkar mostly hid his surprise. He looked at the men and the coolers and the sausages and the pile of dampening suits, taking it all in. Then he spoke loudly for everyone to hear. "Captain Wit O'Toole has assured me that the next seven weeks of training will be the most grueling, most painful, and most challenging of your lives. After tonight's exercise I believe him. In the morning, I intend to forget that I saw a hundred men in their underwear, standing around a fire like a pack of cavemen." He paused here and looked pointedly at a few of his own men. "But since this is your last night before our hellish training begins, I will turn a blind eye." He smiled now. "You will forgive me if I keep my uniform on."

The men laughed.

"As you were," said Ketkar.

They went back to their drinks and mingling.

Ketkar turned to Wit. "You owe me two new cars, Captain."

"You'll be reimbursed, sir. Forgive me if we took the game too far."

"And damage to one of my trucks, which proved to be a lousy roadblock."

"We'll cover the damage to that as well, sir."

"You will do no such thing," said Ketkar, waving a hand. "Nor will you pay for the cars. I don't want to have to explain to our vehicle quartermaster how the MOPs made us look like bumbling idiots. I'll file an accident report instead."

"We didn't win, sir," said Wit. He reached down to his red suit, removed the flag from the back pouch, and handed it to Ketkar. "Our suits were hit. We were disqualified."

Ketkar studied him, suspicious. "And if I were to interview all of my men and ask them which one of them took down the famous Wit O'Toole, someone would step forward?"

"Many men shot at us, sir. It was chaotic there at the end."

Ketkar smiled. "Yes. And somehow with inflated suits you managed to get all the way back to camp. Most impressive."

Wit motioned to the flagpole, where a red sheet posing as a flag flapped in the wind. "You have men in your vehicles who are still in the game, sir. If you'd like to take our flag, you won't meet any resistance. All of us are out of the fight."

Ketkar smiled. "I think it best if we call this a draw and leave it at that."

"Good idea, sir."

Ketkar saluted and got back into his vehicle, and the convoy drove away. Deen and Averbach stepped out of the woods once the convoy was out of sight, their dampening suits still operable.

"I figured you two would be riddled with spider rounds by now," said Wit.

Deen looked offended. "A little confidence, Captain. Averbach and I don't give up that easy."

"I don't suppose I want to know what you did with the cars."

Deen patted him on the arm and took a drink from the cooler. "Nothing a good motor sergeant can't fix."

He and Averbach moved over to the pile of suits and added theirs to the heap.

"I have to admit this is not what I expected, sir," a voice said.

Wit turned. It was Lobo, there beside him in his undergarments, staring into the firelight, soaking wet and holding a vitamin drink.

"Will the training be as grueling as Major Ketkar says?" Lobo asked.

"You're in MOPs now, Lobo. I shouldn't have to answer that question."

CHAPTER 8

Glaser

The archives room on Makarhu was a dark, claustrophobic space filled with rows of blinking computer systems and humming servers. Lem was floating in the shadows back near a corner with his holopad plugged into one of the server inputs. A video of the attack on El Cavador played in the holospace above his pad. It showed a laser cutting through a pebble-killer on the hull of the free-miner ship. As Lem watched, the severed PK spun away and struck one of the free miners on spacewalk. Lem moved his hand through the holospace to stop the video, then he wiggled his fingers in the right sequence to rewind the video and play it again in slow motion. He couldn't be certain, but it looked like, as he had feared, he had killed the man.

The bump with El Cavador had been far more violent than Lem had anticipated. It was one thing to *talk* of lasers cutting through sensors and equipment. It was quite another thing to see it all unfold before your eyes as Lem had done—the entire attack had been recorded by several cameras and projected on the big holospace on the helm.

No, he mustn't use the word "attack." That sounded incriminating and prosecutable. "Attack" implied wrongdoing and sparked headlines on the nets like: LEM JUKES ATTACKS FAMILY OF FREE MINERS. Or: HEIR TO JUKE FORTUNE ATTACKS CHILDREN. No, "attack" was far too aggressive a word. It painted a completely inaccurate picture of events. It suggested malicious intent and automatically put people into false categories. Good versus evil. Black versus white. And in truth, there were no good guys and bad guys in this scenario. They were just two parties after the same asteroid, which, let the record show, didn't legally belong to anyone in the first place. Lem wasn't *taking* something from the free miners because it wasn't theirs to begin with. If they had possessed some deed perhaps or a bill of sale asserting them as the owners of said property, then yes, Lem would be in the wrong. But maneuvering someone away from an asteroid for which they had no right of ownership wasn't a crime at all.

Maneuvering. Yes, Lem liked that word much better.

The PK in the video spun away from the laser again and struck the man. Lem froze the video at the moment of impact. The man's neck was bent unnaturally to the side. Lem had never seen a broken neck before, but he was fairly certain that was what he was looking at.

"Mr. Jukes?"

Lem spun around, banging into two of the servers in the process. The archivist, a Belgian named Podolski, was floating at the end of the row of servers in his sleepsuit, looking at Lem with a confused expression. Lem felt panicked, though he worked hard to conceal it. The man should be sleeping. It was hours into sleep-shift.

"You startled me," said Lem, smiling and switching off his holopad.

The archivist stared, confused. A moment of silence passed.

"I hope I didn't wake you," said Lem. "I let myself in to review a few files."

"The system alerts me when anyone accesses the core files without my authorization code," Podolski said. "It's a security precaution."

"Ah," said Lem. He hadn't known that, or he would have figured out some way to circumvent the code. Lem chuckled. "How stupid of me. I'm so sorry. If I had known that, I would've come to you first during normal hours. I feel awful that I woke you."

"You do know, sir, that you can access any files we have here in the archives using your personal terminal in your room."

Of course Lem knew that. He wasn't an idiot. But he didn't want the ship to have a record of the files being transferred to his room—or to any other terminal on the ship for that matter. Nor did he want merely to look at the files; he wanted to erase the only copies in existence here on the main servers.

"I had some business to attend to in the mining bay," said Lem. "So I thought I'd slip in here and check a few things. I didn't know I'd make a stir."

It wasn't the best lie, but Lem had delivered it convincingly enough. And it could withstand scrutiny. The mining bay was close to the archive room, and in the days since the bump, the mining crew had been working long hours in the bay getting ready for the field test. It wasn't implausible to suggest that Lem had been there.

Podolski nodded. "Is there something I can help you find, sir?"

"Very kind, but no. Just finishing up here. Thank you."

Podolski nodded again, unsure what to do next. An awkward pause followed. "Well, if you need anything, sir, my quarters are right through that hatch over there."

Lem made a show of straining his neck and looking at the hatch even though he knew exactly where it was. "Thank you. If I need something, I'll let you know."

Podolski drifted away, an uncertain look on his face.

Lem waited for the hatch to close, then began erasing files quickly, not even bothering to review them first. Earlier, when Lem had decided to go through with this and erase any record of the bump, he had briefly considered giving the chore to Podolski, who was obviously more familiar with the servers and thus better qualified. But then Lem had realized how unsettled that would have left him: He would have always wondered if Podolski had made his own copy of the files in the hope of blackmailing Lem in the future. Some of Father's employees had tried such things over the years—their attempts had always ended in their own humiliation and never in Father's, but Father had found the experiences exhausting nonetheless. Plus, giving the order to Podolski would only raise the man's suspicions when most people on board, Podolski included, were still unaware of what had happened during the bump. No one but a few trusted senior officers knew of the incident with the free miner, and Lem thought it best to keep it that way.

When Lem finished erasing files, he checked and rechecked the servers and backups to make sure he hadn't missed anything. Then he ran a program that deleted any record of the erasing. The last step was patching up holes. There were now gaps in the video surveillance records, so Lem filled those in with random footage of space already on file. When he was done, every scrap of potentially incriminating evidence was gone.

Lem pocketed his holopad and made his way to the exit. He had hoped that by erasing the files he would also erase the sting of guilt that had been pecking at him ever since the bump, but as he left the archives room, he felt as anxious as he had before. He shouldn't have watched the video, he realized. If he hadn't watched the video he could have maintained the possibility in his mind that the man wasn't seriously injured. He could have led himself to believe that no lasting damage had been done. That wasn't an option now.

Why had the free miners been outside? It had been sleep-shift. You don't spacewalk during sleep-shift. That was reckless. In fact, now that Lem thought about it, if the free miner was in fact paralyzed or dead, the free miner deserved more of the blame than Lem did. Well, perhaps not *more* of the blame but certainly a good portion of it. Lem shouldn't carry *all* the blame.

Besides, it's not like Lem had hurt anyone intentionally. He hadn't even known the men were out there. The free miners had been working on the far side of El Cavador, obscured from Lem's view, when the attack—no, maneuver—began. And by the time the ship *did* detect them, the Makarhu was already moving and the laser-firing sequence was already initiated. Lem couldn't stop it. Not easily anyway. It was only dumb luck that the first target was the PK near where the three miners were standing.

And if you looked at the facts that way, if you chopped up the blame into portions, then part of the blame went to the free miner, part went to the computer, part went to dumb luck, and only a small part went to Lem. And even that portion shouldn't be entirely Lem's. It had been a group effort, after all. The crew was following Lem's orders, true, but they could have objected, they could have said no.

Someone had, Lem reminded himself. Benyawe. She had filed a formal objection. Had he erased that as well? He must have.

He left the archives room and made his way to the mining bay to give credence to the lie he had told. Lem didn't expect Podolski to investigate the matter—Podolski had no reason to disbelieve him. But what if Podolski mentioned in casual conversation to someone that Lem had been in the mining bay? No, it was best to play it safe.

The mining bay was a large garage where all the digging and mineral-extraction equipment was housed. Normally a ship this size would employ forty to fifty miners, with twenty to twenty-five WDs—or wearable dozers, the large exoskeleton diggers that most corporate miners wore for cleaning out mineshafts and pulling up lumps. Since this was a research vessel at the moment, the mining crew consisted of only ten men, whose only duties for the trip were to collect rock fragments from the field tests for analysis. The miners had intended to use the scoopers for this, which were long-armed diggers that could extend out from the ship and grab rocks in space. But since the engineers had only conducted a single field test and had not even bothered to collect the rock fragments from said test, the miners were insane with boredom. Lem had alleviated that a week ago when he had gone to them and told them of his intent to pull in as many minerals from the asteroid as the ship could hold. It would require modifications to the equipment, but the men were so hungry for an assignment that they had readily accepted the challenge. Lem could say his visit tonight was to check up on their progress.

To Lem's relief, five of the miners were working in the bay when he arrived, including their crew chief, who was anchored to one of the scoopers, welding on large metal plates.

"This is a surprise, Mr. Jukes," said the crew chief, lifting his welding visor and turning off his equipment. "Early for you, isn't it, sir?"

"Couldn't sleep. How goes the equipment for the mineral extraction?"

The crew chief smiled and gave the scooper an affectionate slap with his palm. "We're making good time. We've got two scoopers prepped. Two more will be ready by the time we fire the glaser."

Lem had decided to wait a full week after arriving at the asteroid to fire the glaser. He wanted to give El Cavador enough time to get far enough away that they wouldn't be able to see the field test take place. Lem could blow up a pebble and not arouse any curiosity, but if anyone saw him annihilate an asteroid this big, they'd know Juke had developed a revolutionary technology—a fact Father would rather keep secret.

"We've turned the scoopers into giant magnets, sir," explained the crew chief. "If what the engineers tell us is true, that glaser will blow the rock to dust. So to separate the detritus from the minerals, all we've got to do is wave a magnet through the dust cloud and let the magnet attract the metal fragments. Then we bring the scooper load into the smelter, switch off the magnets, dump the metal, then go back out and do it again. Pretty soon you'll have metal cylinders all stacked up neat as you please, sir."

"How long will it take to bring in the metal?"

The crew chief shrugged. "Depends on the size of the dust cloud and the amount of metal we find. Could be as quick as a week. Could be as long as eight. That's really your decision, sir, we'll keep making cylinders for as long as you want."

Lem thanked the man then went back to his room and zipped himself up in his hammock. He had two hours before sleep-shift ended, though he knew he wouldn't fall asleep; the image of the free miner's bent neck was too fresh in his mind. He might have erased the files and covered his tracks, but he couldn't erase the memory of it. Lem lay there in silence. He knew he was deluding himself to think that anyone else bore the responsibility of what had happened. It was his crime, his doing. And no sneaking around in the dark could ever delete that fact.

A week after the bump, Lem was up in the observation room with Ben-yawe and Dublin, ready to fire the glaser. Lem was looking out the window at the asteroid, now a considerable distance from the ship.

"You're sure we're far enough away?" asked Lem.

"No question, Mr. Jukes," said Dublin. "We've been working on the math all week. I went over it myself. The gravity field won't reach us this far out. We're already several kilometers farther out than we need to be. I've taken every precaution."

Lem nodded, though he couldn't help but feel a bit uneasy. When the glaser hit the asteroid, it would create a field of centrifugal gravity inside of which gravity would cease to hold mass together. And the larger the object hit, the larger the field of gravity.

"We can't be too far away in my opinion," said Lem. "Can we still hit the asteroid with accuracy if we back up, say, another five kilometers?"

"We should be able to," said Dublin. "But it's overkill."

"I would rather commit overkill than *be* killed," said Lem. He touched his holopad, and a holo of Chubs's head appeared. "Back us up five more kilometers, Chubs."

"Yes, sir."

"And give me the latest on our area scans. I want to be certain there aren't any ships close enough to see what we're about to do here."

"Rest easy, Lem," said Chubs. "We're all by our lonesome. El Cavador was closest, but they're long gone now. We're not even picking them up on our scans anymore."

"Good," said Lem. "Then let's get started. Send out the sensors."

"Sensors away," said Chubs.

Lem watched out the window as the sensors flew away from the ship in a burst of propulsion, heading toward the asteroid, a long anchor line unspooling behind each one. The sensors, once in position, would record every aspect of the explosion for later analysis.

"Sensors are in place," said Chubs.

"Fire the glaser," said Lem.

"Yes, sir."

Lem clicked off his holopad and waited in silence with Benyawe and Dublin. After a moment it began. The asteroid exploded outward into large chunks, which quickly exploded again into smaller chunks, racing outward in a growing sphere of destruction. The large fragments continued to burst again and again, getting smaller and smaller, the cloud getting thicker, wider, more massive, moving outward with incredible speed. Now four times bigger than the original size of the asteroid. Five times. Six.

"Hmm," said Dublin.

Eight times.

Benyawe looked confused. "I think perhaps it would be wise to . . ."

"Jettison the sensors!" Lem yelled into his headset. "Fire retros. Maximum power. Back us up now!"

The sensors were cut away. The ship backed up suddenly. Lem, Dublin, and Benyawe were thrown forward into the observation glass. The sphere kept growing. Lem pushed himself up from the glass and watched as the sphere engulfed the sensors he had jettisoned, which instantly exploded into smaller and smaller pieces. But the cloud didn't stop there. It grew more, now a massive ball of dust and particles and gravel. It reached the spot where the ship had been positioned, then grew farther still, expanding outward, the dust getting thinner now.

Then finally it stopped. The particles within the field were small enough and far apart enough that the gravity field was too weak to sustain itself and dissipated into nothing. All was quiet. Lem stared out the window, eyes wide, heart racing. Had he not given the order instantly, if he had waited for dithering Dublin to make a decision, the field would have reached the ship and they all would have been torn to pieces.

He whirled around to Dublin, furious. "I thought you said we were in the clear."

"I . . . I thought we were," said Dublin. "Several of us did the math."

"Well your math is kusi! You almost killed us all!"

"I know. I'm . . . I'm sorry. I'm not sure how we could've gotten that wrong."

"Benyawe told me we couldn't predict the gravity field," said Lem. "I see now I should have listened to her instead of you. You are excused, Dr. Dublin."

Dublin looked helpless, his face red with embarrassment. Lem watched the man leave then turned to Benyawe. "Is it over? Are we clear?"

She was tapping at her holopad. "It appears to be. Our sensors aren't as good as those we jettisoned, but it seems as if the field is gone. I'd want to do more analysis before giving a definitive answer, though." She looked at Lem, her voice shaky. "If you hadn't reacted so quickly—"

Lem spoke into his headset. "Stop the retros. Bring us to a full stop."

The ship slowed. Lem pushed himself away from the glass and looked out at the massive cloud of dust that was once an asteroid.

"You can't blame Dublin for this," said Benyawe. "Not completely."

"Oh?"

"If we had done more tests on pebbles as this mission was designed to do, Dublin would have had more data and been more accurate in his calculations."

"So this is my fault?"

"You went against his counsel and mine and tackled an asteroid a hundred times larger than we were prepared for. It strikes me as hypocritical to point the finger solely at him."

Lem smiled. "I see now why you've lasted so long with my father, Dr. Benyawe. You're not afraid to speak your mind. My father respects that."

"No, Lem. I have lasted so long with your father because I am always right."

Lem slept badly the next few days. In his dreams, the gravity field chewed up everything around him: the furniture, his terminal, his bed, his legs, the man with the broken neck; all of it exploding into rock fragments again and again until only dust remained. Lem took pills to help him sleep, but they couldn't keep him from dreaming. He had ordered the engineers to analyze the dust cloud to ensure that the gravity field had indeed dissipated—he didn't want to move into the cloud and begin collecting minerals until he was sure the field was gone and the area safe. On the morning of the fifth day, alone in his room, he got his answer.

"The field is gone," said Benyawe. Her head was floating in the holospace above Lem's terminal. "We built a sensor from old parts and sent it into the cloud. It didn't explode or experience any change in gravity whatsoever. We can begin collecting metal dust whenever you're ready."

"I want to see the data from the sensor," said Lem.

"I didn't know you could decipher this type of data."

"I can't. But seeing it will make me feel better."

Benyawe shrugged and disappeared. A moment later columns of data appeared on Lem's holodisplay. The numbers meant nothing to him, but he was pleased to see so many of them. Lots of data meant conclusive results. Lem relaxed a little, wiped the data away, and entered a command. The mining crew chief appeared in the holodisplay.

"Morning, Mr. Jukes."

"We've been given the all-clear," said Lem. "We'll be moving into the dust cloud within the hour."

"Excellent. The scoopers are ready. Once we bring in the dust, we'll start making the cylinders."

Lem ended the call and hovered there beside his terminal, at ease for the first time in weeks. He had taken a risk, yes, but now, finally, it was going to pay off. He put his hands behind his head and wondered what type of metal they would find. Iron? Cobalt? Curious, he returned to his terminal and pulled up the going rates for minerals. The prices were at least a month old, but barring some dramatic shift in the market, the rates should be fairly close to accurate. He was about to rotate one of the graphs and more closely study the data when the charts suddenly disappeared.

An old woman's head took their place in the holospace.

"Mr. Jukes," the woman said. "I am Concepción Querales, captain of El Cavador, which you attacked in an unprovoked assault."

Lem froze. Was this a joke? How was he getting an unprompted message to his personal terminal? Had El Cavador sent them a laserline? Who had authorized this?

"I have programmed this message to play for you long after we're gone," Concepción said. "I would have preferred to speak to you directly, but your irrational and barbaric behavior suggests that you are not a man with whom I can have any semblance of a normal conversation."

Lem tapped at his keyboard to make the message stop, but the terminal didn't respond.

"You cannot attack us now," said Concepción. "Nor can you track us. By now we are far beyond your reach. I have taken this risk and left you this message because I wanted you to know that you killed a man."

Lem stopped tapping at the keyboard and stared.

"I doubt you'll care," said Concepción. "I doubt you'll lose any sleep over this fact. But one of our best men, my nephew, is dead. He was a decent man with children and a loving wife. You, because of your arrogance and obvious disregard for human life, have taken all that away from him." Her voice was quavering, yet there was steel behind it. "I doubt you are a man of faith, Mr. Jukes. Or if you are, you must pray to gods so cruel of heart that I am glad I do not know them. In my faith, I am taught to forgive those who offend me seven times seventy. I fear that you have damned yourself and me as well, Mr. Jukes, because I don't see myself forgiving you in this life or the next."

The holo blinked out, and the mineral pricing charts returned. Lem tapped at his keyboard and saw that he had control again. His mind was racing. They had planted a file in the ship's system. They had penetrated their firewall and planted a file. How the hell had they done that?

He found his headset and called Podolski to his room immediately. The archivist arrived a few minutes later looking wary. Lem had put his greaves on and was pacing the room.

"They accessed us," Lem said. "El Cavador accessed our system. You want to tell me how that happened?"

Podolski looked confused. "Accessed us? I don't think so, sir."

"I just watched a holo on my display from the captain of their ship. Now, unless I am completely losing my mind, which I know I am not, they accessed our system."

"You say you watched a holo, sir?"

"Are you deaf? They planted a damn holo on my personal terminal. Now if this is someone's idea of a joke, I want to know who that someone is, and I want him jettisoned from this ship. You understand?"

Podolski seemed uneasy. "I assure you, Mr. Jukes. No one on this ship can access your personal terminal except for you and me, and I would never play a joke like that, sir."

Lem believed him. It wasn't a joke. It couldn't be a joke. Very few people even knew that someone had been injured in the bump.

"I thought our firewall was impenetrable," said Lem.

"It is, sir. Best design in the company. We're carrying proprietary tech on this vessel, sir. Every layer of security was employed. Nobody can get in here."

"Well they did. And I want to know how."

Podolski moved to Lem's holodisplay. "May I see this file, sir?"

"It played automatically. I don't know where it is."

Podolski tapped at Lem's display. Lem felt a momentary panic. He didn't want Podolski seeing the file. He didn't want anyone seeing the file. It was incriminating.

"I see where there was *something*," said Podolski, "but it had a track-backer program on it, which means it self-erased after playing."

"You see? They accessed our system."

Podolski squinted at the display and moved very quickly after that, windows opened and closed in quick succession. He entered passwords, accessed screens and icons that Lem had never seen before. He scrolled through long lists of what appeared to be random numbers and code. He worked for several minutes in silence, his eyes racing up and down through the holospace. Lem tried to keep up but couldn't.

Lem's first thought was for the gravity laser. Had the free miners seen it? Had they accessed its schematics? Were they after those files? If so, if they had seen them, if the secrecy of the glaser had been compromised, Lem would be ruined. His father and the Board would never forgive him. It would be devastating to the company. And what about the videos of the bump? The files he had erased. Had El Cavador seen those?

Podolski stopped typing suddenly and stared at the dozens of different windows and lines of code in the holospace. "Oh," he said.

"What?" said Lem. "What does 'oh' mean? What are you oh-ing about?"

"The system does a backup every forty-five minutes, sir. It's procedural. But it looks as if the system did an unscheduled backup recently."

"What does that mean? 'An unscheduled backup.' What are you saying?"

"I can't be certain, sir," said Podolski, turning to Lem, "but I think it means some of our files were copied to a foreign target."

"Foreign target? What? Like a snifferstick? When? When did this happen exactly?"

Podolski tapped the keys again to find the answer. "Exactly twenty-three minutes after we bumped El Cavador, sir."

CHAPTER 9

Scout

One week after the corporate attack, Victor was in the engine room making needed repairs to the generator when Father came for him. "How close are you to getting this thing back online?" Father asked.

"A day," said Victor. "Maybe less. Mono's in the workshop now fixing the last of the circuits. I'm putting in some new rotors. Barring another breakdown, we should be good to go. Why? What's wrong?"

"You better come with me."

Father didn't even wait for Victor to follow. He simply turned and left the engine room. Victor, sensing Father's urgency, quickly put his tools aside and caught up with him in the corridor. They both were wearing greaves, and they moved down the corridor in long, leaping strides.

"Have we detected the Italians?" Victor guessed. "Is that what this is about?"

The ship was speeding toward the Italians' position—or rather, what everyone hoped would be the Italians' position. With communication still down, El Cavador couldn't send a message ahead to confirm that the Italians were still at the location. There was a good chance they'd get there and find nothing but empty space.

"No idea," said Father. "But I don't think it's good. Concepción called a few minutes ago to ask if the PKs were ready."

"Why should that alarm you?" asked Victor. "We've got two working PKs out of six. That's hardly an adequate collision-avoidance system. Maybe we've got a debris field ahead. Maybe Concepción wants to be certain we don't hit anything."

"Maybe," said Father. "But I don't think so. It was the way she asked. She sounded concerned. Afraid even."

Afraid? Concepción? Victor couldn't imagine it. "Of what? Another corporate? The starship?"

"I don't think it's the starship. Toron and Edimar said it was several weeks away at the earliest, and more likely several months away. This is something else."

After the corporate attack, Victor and Father had divided up the repairs. Victor and Mono were to focus exclusively on the generator, while Father would put all of his efforts into repairing the sensors the corporates had cut away from the ship. The miners had successfully plucked a few of the sensors from space, but many of the most critical instruments, including the laserline transmitter, had never been found.

Father didn't even knock before entering Concepción's office. Inside, Concepción and Toron were gathered around Concepción's desk, studying a mapped quadrant of space floating above the desk in the holospace.

Concepción only barely looked up when they entered. "Close the door," she said.

Father did so. Victor glanced at Toron, but the man's face was unreadable.

"There are ships at the Italians' position," said Concepción. "We're close enough now for the Eye to detect them. It's not the cleanest data, and without communication we can't confirm their identity, but what data we do have suggests that they are in fact the Italians."

"That's good news," said Father. "We desperately need help with repairs."

"And a new laserline transmitter," said Victor.

"Even if the Italians don't have a spare transmitter," said Concepción, "we can use theirs to send as many laserlines as we need to, I'm sure. But that is not why I called you in here. Edimar and Toron have made another sighting."

"A second starship?" Victor asked.

"We don't know what it is," said Toron. "But I don't think it's a starship." He maneuvered his stylus in the holospace. A dot appeared in the top corner. "This is the starship, or what we're all assuming is a starship."

He moved his stylus, and a second dot appeared at the opposite end of the holospace. "This is the Italians." Toron made another hand gesture, and a third dot appeared between the first two dots, though relatively close to the Italians. "And this thing is a giant question mark. It's something, but we don't know what. We know it's small, at most the size of El Cavador, but probably smaller. Which is why we didn't see it before now."

"You think it's related to the starship?" Victor asked.

"Maybe," said Toron. "Edimar is more certain than I am, but we've been following its trajectory for a few hours, and it looks as if it came from the direction of the starship."

"That could be a coincidence," said Father. "It could be a family or clan ship coming in from way out whose angle of approach makes it seem as if they're coming from the starship. Look at the distance between the two anomalies. That's a lot of space. Connecting the two is kind of a leap, don't you think?"

"That was my reaction," said Concepción. "But Toron made me think otherwise."

"It's way too fast to be human," said Toron. "We've picked it up at a few spots now. It's moving at fifty times our top speeds, easy."

Victor was surprised. There were plenty of ships much faster than El Cavador. But fifty times faster? Unheard of.

"Could it be a comet?" Father asked. "Or some other natural object?"

Toron shook his head. "It's no comet. The Eye recognizes comets easily. This is something else. It's tech. It has a heat signature."

"A scout ship," said Victor. "From the starship. Has to be. Whoever they are, they've sent out a scout to scan the area. This is new territory for them, and they're playing it safe. They're getting the landscape."

"That's a possibility," said Toron. "But if it's true, that puts us in a very precarious situation. Let's assume for a moment that this is in fact a scout ship. If so, why is it heading straight for the Italians?"

"Maybe it can detect life-forms," said Victor.

"At that range?" said Father. "I doubt it. It's possible, I suppose. If it can travel at near-lightspeed, who's to say what it can do? But it's more likely that it can detect movement in much the same way the Eye does."

"The Italians aren't moving," said Victor. "They're stationary; have been for at least ten days now. If the scout were attracted to movement, it would come to us instead of them. We're the ones who are moving. Maybe it picked up the Italians' radio frequency. Radio is tech. Radio implies intelligent life. If I picked up radio waves in another solar system, I would definitely want to check them out. And the Italians use radio all the time. They have four ships. That's how they communicate with each other."

"And our radio is down," said Father. "Which would explain why it didn't come to us."

"How soon could you have our radio up?" asked Concepción.

"Within the next day or two," said Father. "I'm working on it now. But again, that's for blanket transmissions. Not focused ones. We need a laser-line for that."

"Finish the repair," said Concepción, "but don't transmit anything. Not even to test it. We're silent right now, and we'll stay silent until we know what we're dealing with." She turned to Toron. "How far away are we from the Italians?"

"Three days," said Toron.

"And when will this scout ship reach them?" asked Concepción.

"It's already decelerating," said Toron. "Best guess: a day and a half, if not sooner. It'll arrive long before we do."

Victor suddenly felt sick. A ship, likely an alien ship, was moving toward the Italians. Toward Alejandra.

For the past week, Victor had been trying to ignore the fact that El Cavador was heading toward Janda's position—she was a closed part of his life now; he had no business thinking of her. Yet, somehow, often without him noticing it happening, his mind kept circling back to her. He would wonder, for example, which Italian ship El Cavador would dock with when they arrived. Would it be Vesuvio, Janda's ship? That seemed probable; Vesuvio was the largest ship and, therefore, the most likely to store the spare parts El Cavador needed. And, if the two ships did dock, would Janda board El Cavador to see her family? And if so, would she see Victor as well?

Then Victor would realize he was having such thoughts and he'd throw himself even more into the repairs, frustrated with himself for letting his mind wander.

Now here Toron was telling them that Janda might be in danger.

"Given the uncertainty of this situation," said Toron, "we have to consider the worst-case scenario. This could be an attack on the Italians. We have no evidence to suggest that, but we would be foolish not to consider it. And if that's the case, what do we do?"

"We get to the Italians as fast as we can is what we do," said Victor.

"And do what?" asked Toron.

"Help. Fight back. Whatever it takes."

"With two PKs?" said Toron scornfully. "That's hardly enough for collision avoidance. We couldn't possibly defend ourselves."

"We don't know that," said Victor. "We have no idea what that ship's defenses are. Two PKs might be more than enough to take it down."

"And they might not," said Toron. "They might just aggravate it. You want to take that gamble?"

"Absolutely."

Toron threw his hands up, then turned to Concepción. "We are in no position to jump into a fight, if it comes to that. Look at us. We don't even have our main generator up. Everything's running on the backups, which barely put out enough juice for life support. We've got half our lights off to ration power, so we're all bumbling around in semidarkness. The temperature on board has dropped twenty degrees because the heaters aren't getting the power they need. We have no communication. We're one step above a crippled ship. We can't even help ourselves. And we're considering fighting? The corporates just wasted us. Did we not learn anything from that experience?"

"That was different," said Victor. "They took us by surprise."

Toron scoffed. "Oh, well, I'll make sure the aliens play by all the rules of chivalrous warfare and treat us 'fairly' when they attack." He turned back to Concepción. "We can't defend ourselves, much less anyone else. It might be more sensible to come to a full stop now and read the data that comes off the Eye. Let's wait and see what happens when this ship reaches the Italians."

"Do nothing?" said Victor. He couldn't believe what he was hearing. "Sit here and watch the scout ship attack them?"

"We don't know if it's a scout ship," said Toron. "Nor do we know if it intends to attack. And stopping here is not inaction. It's intelligence gathering. It's getting the information we need to choose the safest course of action."

Victor pointed at the dot in the holospace. "Your daughter is on one of those ships."

"And my wife and other daughter are on this one," said Toron. "Do you think I don't know Alejandra is there? Do you think I've forgotten that fact? I'm quite capable of keeping track of my daughter's whereabouts, thank you."

"Let's calm down," said Concepción. "These walls aren't soundproof. We're all adults here."

"He isn't," said Toron, gesturing to Victor.

Concepción ignored him. "Toron is proposing a legitimate concern, Victor. There are a lot of unanswered questions here. We have a responsibility to protect our people."

"Maybe so," said Father. "But I agree with Vico. We can't sit back and wait to see what happens. If it were us out there, and the Italians out here, we'd want them with us, supporting us. I say we push on. The Italians might need us in a critical moment."

"Each of the Italians' ships is faster and better equipped than ours," said Toron. "And there are four of them. If we made any contribution to a fight it would be minimal and a day and a half late. Do we really want to risk losing everything for that?"

"We're better defended than they are," said Victor. "That accounts for something. Their ships are fast, yes, but we have better armor. That might prove critical."

"Again," said Toron, "you're basing these assumptions on human technology. Who's to say this scout ship, or whatever it is, doesn't have a weapon that can't penetrate any armor."

"Where was this violent imagination of yours when I wanted to warn everyone?" said Victor. "You were perfectly content to deflect any suggestion that this thing was dangerous before. Now you seemed convinced it's programmed to kill."

"I am urging caution," said Toron, "just as I did before. And I don't need to explain myself to you."

"That's enough," said Concepción. "We get nowhere by arguing. The fact is, if this thing can move at fifty times our speed, we're already in the fight, if there is one. The ship could easily overtake us if it wanted to, even if we turned now and ran. Yes, it's possible that it doesn't know we're here, but I find that unlikely. We'd be wise to assume that it can do anything we can and more." She turned to Father. "Segundo, you said that some of the PKs are ready to be installed."

"We've fixed three of the four," said Father. "The last one needs parts we don't have and can't jury-rig. We intended to reinstall the three as soon as we reached the Italians. We obviously can't do a spacewalk now at our current speed."

Concepción looked at Victor. "And the generator?"

"I need a day at the most," said Victor.

Concepción nodded. "What we do about this scout ship is a decision for the Council. I will call a meeting immediately. Segundo, you are excused to conduct whatever repairs you need to. I will see to it that your views are expressed to the Council. Toron will present what he's found, and I will make my recommendation, which is that we decelerate and install the repaired PKs now. Then we punch it and get to the Italians as quickly as possible. We are wise to be cautious, but I suggest we prepare for the worst and hope for the best."

Toron didn't argue; Father nodded in agreement; and Concepción excused them all. Victor and Father made their way down the corridor, heading back to their respective repairs. "Toron isn't your enemy, Vico," said Father. "I know he can seem callous, but he really does love Alejandra. He would do anything for her or this family. But if he has to choose between the two, he will always choose the family, which is the right choice."

"Then why did you agree with me back there?"

"Because if it were you with the Italians, I wouldn't hesitate to go get you. I'd go in with no PKs and no generator if I had to, even if that meant endangering everyone aboard. That's not rational. It's reckless and irresponsible. But that's what I would do."

"Then I'm glad *you're* my father and not Toron."

"Toron isn't a coward, Vico. His suggestion to stop here and wait may seem like cowardice, but it isn't. I've known Toron a long time. He isn't motivated by self-preservation. He cares about Edimar and Lola, his wife, and Concepción and your mother and me and everyone aboard. Even you."

"I think he'd rather see me tossed from the ship."

"My point is, he loves Alejandra as much as I love you, son. If Toron could change places with her, he would do so in an instant. His willingness to hand her over to fate to protect the rest of us shows, to me at least, a greater courage than I possess. It's the smarter choice. The Italians aren't defenseless. They can hold their own. Keeping our distance and being safe is the rational thing to do. It's because of people like Toron that this family is still alive, Vico. Were I running things, we all would have died a long time ago." He smiled and put a hand on Victor's shoulder. "I fear I've made you too much like me, rash and bullheaded. Never for your own sake, but for those you love. That's a good trait to have. But one day you may run this family, Vico, and if that happens, you'll need to have some of Toron in you, too."

Victor wanted to tell him then. All he had to do was open his mouth and say, "I'm leaving Father. I don't know how. I don't know when. But I will never lead this family because I can't stay. I can't take a wife here. I can't raise children here. Not when everything I see around me reminds me of Janda."

But Victor said nothing. How could he? The family needed Victor now more than ever? How could he even think of leaving? It was selfish. It was abandonment. Yet what could he do? Try as he might to seal off that part of his brain where memories of Janda were stored, he couldn't. She was forever tied to this ship, and no event, not the starship, not the corporate attack, nothing could ever change that. Father left before Victor found the courage to say anything, and Victor removed his greaves and flew back to the engine room. He found Mono there, replacing a few of the burned-out circuits. "We've got a day to get this thing online, Mono."

"Good luck," said Mono. "It's a piece of junk. It should have seen a scrapyard four hundred years ago."

"They didn't have space flight four hundred years ago. Besides, we don't have a choice."

He told Mono about the scout ship. He knew he probably shouldn't, but the Council would find out soon enough, and then everyone on the ship would know. At first, Victor was worried that the news would frighten Mono. But to his surprise it had the opposite effect, with Mono all the more determined to get the generator up and running.

They worked long into sleep-shift. When they finished, nearly twelve hours later, they were both exhausted and filthy. "Flip the switch, Mono."

Victor got the fire extinguisher ready, just in case, while Mono went over to the switch box and turned on the power. They had tried to reboot the generator several times over the past few days, but every attempt had failed: knocking sounds, burning components, an array of sparks. On several occasions they had cut the power as quickly as they had turned it on. Now, however, the generator slowly came to life. The readout screen flickered on. The motor whirred and grew stronger. The turbines spun and gained speed. No knocking. No sparks. No screeching of metal.

Ten seconds passed. Then fifteen. The roar of the turbines grew louder. Victor watched the numbers on the readout screen, his heart racing. The turbines were at 60 percent. Then 70. Then 85. The turbines were screaming now, the sound rattling the entire engine room. Then 95 percent. Victor looked at Mono and saw that the boy was laughing. Victor couldn't hear the laughter over the roar of the generator, but the sight of it—along with the sudden release of all of Victor's pent-up anxiety—set Victor to laughing, too. Laughs so big and long that tears came out of his eyes.

Victor stood in the airlock in his pressure suit, waiting for the ship to stop. Father was beside him, along with ten miners, all of them facing the massive bay doors. The three repaired PKs floated among them, with the miners holding them in place with bracing cables. Victor could hear the retros firing outside, slowing the ship. After a moment, the rockets stopped, and then Concepción's voice sounded in Victor's helmet. "Full stop, gentlemen. Let's make this repair quick, if we can."

The Council had agreed to Concepción's recommendation: El Cavador would come to a complete stop, Victor and Father would install the repaired PKs, and the ship would accelerate to the Italians, still a day away. It hadn't been an easy decision. Mother had told Victor after the fact that quite a heated discussion had preceded the vote, with many people siding with Toron and urging extreme caution, preferring to stop immediately and observe the scout ship among the Italians from a safe distance. The final vote to continue on as soon as repairs were made had passed by the slimmest of majorities.

Victor punched a command into the keypad on the airlock wall. There was a brief warning siren followed by a computer voice telling them the wide cargo doors were about to open. The computer voice counted down from ten, then the doors unlocked and slid away. All of the air inside the airlock was sucked out into space, and the star-filled blackness of the Kuiper Belt stretched out before them.

Victor's HUD in his helmet immediately got to work. The temperature outside was negative three hundred and seventy degrees Fahrenheit, prompting the heating mechanism on his suit to compensate. Other windows of data told him oxygen levels, heart rate, suit humidity, and the vitals of everyone else in the group. A note from Mother also popped up: CHILI WAITING WHEN YOU GET BACK. BE SAFE. KEEP AN EYE ON YOUR FATHER. LOVE, PATITA.

Father led the group outside, moving slowly in their boot magnets as they stepped beyond the airlock and out onto the hull. The miners pulled the weightless PKs along like floats at a parade. Once everyone was outside and clear, Father led them to a spot where one of the PKs had been sliced away. Victor had made new network and power sockets to replace those that had been cut, and he spliced in the new socket while the miners applied the new mounting plates. Victor then drilled in new holes for the bolts and stepped clear. Father and the miners moved the PK into position, and Victor bolted it in and plugged in the new socket. When done, Victor blinked out the necessary commands to reboot the laser and restore it to the collision-avoidance system.

Two hours later, after they had finished installing the last of the three lasers without any problems, Father asked them all to gather in a circle. Victor had known this moment was coming, but he hadn't been looking forward to it. Gabi, Marco's wife, had asked Father to release Marco's ashes, as was the custom, and Father had agreed.

Victor and the ten miners silently formed a circle around Father, their boot magnets clinging to the hull, their hands folded reverently in front of them. Father pulled a canister from his hip pouch and spoke into his helmet comm. "We're ready," he said.

There was a moment's pause, then Concepción's voice answered on the line, "We're here, Segundo. Gabi and Lizbét and the girls and I. We're all here on the line."

Victor pictured Marco's family gathered around one of the terminals at the helm. The crew would be giving the family space, standing off to the side, silent, with heads bowed.

Father crossed himself, placed a hand on the canister lid, and said, "Vaya a Dios, nuestro hermano, y al cielo más allá de este." Go to God, our brother, and to the heaven beyond this one. Father unscrewed the cap and gently shook the canister upward. The ashes left the canister in a clouded clump and moved away from the ship without dispersing. The men in the circle slowly dropped to one knee, crossed themselves, and repeated the words. "Vaya a Dios, nuestro hermano, y al cielo más allá de este." The men then held their position in silence while the family on the bridge bid their farewells.

"Vaya a Dios, Papito," said eleven-year-old Daniella.

"Vaya a Dios, Papá," said sixteen-year-old Chencha.

Their voices cracked and trembled with emotion, and Victor couldn't bear it. He blinked out a command and muted the audio in his helmet. He didn't want to hear Gabi say good-bye to her husband, or hear four-year-old Alexándria bid farewell to a father she would not likely remember a year from now. Marco deserved to raise his daughters. And Gabi, widowed and broken, deserved to grow old with such a man. Now, however, none of that would happen. Thanks to Lem Jukes all of it was lost.

Victor watched the ashes drift away, surprised that so great a man could be diminished to so little.

Victor and Father fixed the radio that evening in the workshop, though they had to dismantle a few holodisplays to get the parts they needed. When they were certain it was fixed, they took it directly to Concepción's quarters, which she shared with three other widows on the ship. Concepción had insisted that they wake her the moment it was ready, and the three of them took the radio into one of the more spacious storage rooms and sealed the hatch.

"Have you checked all the frequencies?" asked Concepción.

"Only two," said Father. "Just enough to know it's working."

Concepción took her handheld and called Selmo to the room. When he arrived, still drowsy from sleep, he began working with the radio. The four of them sat in silence while Selmo checked every frequency, searching for chatter. Once, they caught a few faint clicks and snippets of speech, but it was so fragmented and the moments of sound so brief and so sparse that they couldn't make out anything.

"The Italians?" asked Concepción.

"Maybe," said Selmo. "Hard to say. I thought we'd get a better transmission as close as we are. If I had to guess, I'd say this was probably just rubbish from somewhere far away."

"So the Italians are silent?" asked Concepción.

"Seems odd that we wouldn't hear something," said Victor. "They have four transmitters. They should be talking to each other. We're still a distance away, but not too far that we shouldn't pick up something." He turned to Concepción. "How long ago did the scout ship arrive at their position?"

"Eighteen hours ago," she said.

"And no one has left their position since?" asked Father.

"Not according to the Eye," said Concepción.

"Maybe this scout ship is causing interference," said Victor.

"Maybe," said Concepción.

"Or maybe they're not transmitting because they can't transmit," said Selmo.

They were all silent a moment. Victor had been thinking the same thing. They all had. Either something had happened to all four of the Italians' transmitters or something had happened to the Italians.

"How long until we reach their position?" Concepción asked.

"Twelve hours," said Selmo.

Concepción considered this.

"There's still time to turn and run," said Father. "I'm not advocating it.

I'm just saying that if we start decelerating now, we could stop and change course if you wanted to."

"We're not stopping," said Concepción. "We're all going to bed and getting some sleep. Especially you and Victor. You haven't slept in two days. Selmo, get whoever is working the helm tonight on this radio, checking frequencies. They are not to transmit, only listen. Wake me if anything changes."

Alejandra was floating in the corridor in a white gown. The material was thin but not so thin that Victor could see through it. Her hair was down, floating out beside her in zero gravity. He thought it odd to see her dressed this way. Janda didn't own any gowns—certainly not ones so white and pristine and that fit her so well, as if made only for her. The Janda he knew wore jumpsuits and sweaters, all frayed and worn, having been handed down by other girls before her. Never something so new or unblemished or womanly.

Nor did she ever have her hair down, not out in the corridor at least, not where everyone could see it. Once, Victor had seen it down when he had gone to her family's quarters and found the door ajar. Janda's mother was inside the room braiding Janda's hair. It had surprised Victor to see how long and full it was. He had left immediately before anyone had noticed him, feeling awkward, as if he had witnessed something no boy should ever see.

Yet now, seeing her here, he had no such feelings. This was how her hair and dress should be, how he was meant to see her.

Janda smiled to him, and Victor felt such instant relief. He had worried that the scout ship had done something to her, harmed her somehow, yet here she was. He had so many questions. What was the scout ship? Had she made any friends among the Italians? Had she spotted any potential suitors whom she might one day consider taking as a husband? It lifted his heart to consider that last question without feeling a pang of guilt or loss. It meant he was moving on, that Janda was still the friend he had always taken her to be and not someone he had fallen in love with. It meant they could see one another and not be clouded with awkwardness and shame.

She beckoned him to follow her, then turned her body and pushed off with her bare feet. They moved through the ship. The halls were empty. Neither of them spoke. They didn't need to. Not yet. They were with each other, and for now that was enough. She looked back and smiled often, seeing him there behind her, still following her.

The airlock was open. The bay doors were open. They went through both of them. There were stars everywhere, silent and small. They faced one another. A star behind Janda moved, sliding across the sky to her, as if attracted to her, as if it were hers and she were calling it home. It reached her and disappeared, winking out. Then other stars came, slowly at first and then all at once, sweeping to her. Janda seemed not to notice. Her eyes were on Victor, her smile still strong.

His hands were in her hair. Her hand was around his waist, drawing him. Her lips were warm.

A hand shook Victor awake. He was in his hammock. Father looked down at him. "The scout ship has gone."

Victor was out of his hammock instantly. He and Father went directly to the helm. Toron was moving his stylus through the holospace above the table, drawing a line across the system chart. "It left ten hours ago," Toron was saying. "We didn't know it because the Eye is only giving us muddy data now."

"Why?" asked Concepción.

Toron shrugged. "We may be hitting some dust. I don't know. It's not clean data around the site, that's all we know. As for the pod, it's now heading in this direction, away from us, which is good."

"Pod?" Victor asked.

"That's what Edimar and I are calling the scout ship now," said Toron. "It's not shaped like anything we've seen before. It's very smooth, very aerodynamic."

"Any word from the Italians?" asked Father.

"Still nothing," said Selmo. "Radio is silent."

There were a lot of reasons why the data from the Eye might be "muddy" or unclear—any obstruction in space, however small, could throw off the data. But all of the reasons that Victor could think of, all of the reasons that Toron no doubt had already considered, seemed unlikely save one. There wasn't dust between El Cavador and the Italians' position. There was dust *at* the Italians' position. Where there had been four solid ships, there was now something else, something harder for the Eye to interpret. Smaller, more random pieces that didn't coincide with any ship design within the Eye's database. Moving dust, spinning scraps, unrecognizable clumps of steel. Victor refused to believe it. It was too dark a possibility. The Italians were fine. Janda was fine. El Cavador was a piece of junk. Why should they put any faith in the Eye? It was just another part on a ship of broken parts and barely-held-together machines. Muddy data meant nothing.

They flew for eight more hours, but by the time they reached the site Victor knew what they would find. The wreckage from the four ships was a scattered trail of scorched debris at least five kilometers wide.

CHAPTER 10

Wreckage

Victor flew down to the lockers in the cargo bay, moving fast. He landed, threw open his locker, grabbed his pressure suit, and quickly began putting it on. There were miners all around him doing the same, stepping into suits, grabbing rescue equipment: winch hooks, coiled cable, medical pouches, hydraulic spreaders, and shears. Victor's mind was racing. The Italians were dead. The pod had attacked, and the Italians were dead. Janda. No, he wouldn't think it. He wouldn't even consider the idea. She wasn't dead. They were putting together a search party. They would look for survivors. There were big pieces of wreckage out there. Some would have people inside them. Janda would be one of them. Shaken perhaps, frightened even, an emotional wreck, but alive.

How long ago had the pod left? Eighteen hours? That was too long to go without fresh oxygen. If there were survivors, they would have to have masks, with plenty of spare canisters of oxygen. Most canisters held up to forty-five minutes of air, but maybe the Italians had canisters that held more. It was possible. Plus there would be air in whatever room the survivors had sealed themselves up in. And that's what survivors would do. They'd seal themselves off in a room somewhere that hadn't been breached and wait for rescue. The Italians were smart. Surely they had rehearsed for emergencies like this. Surely they had emergency gear throughout the ship. They would be prepared. They would have a stockpile of canisters and masks. Both for adults and for children.

But air wasn't the only problem, Victor told himself. They would need heat as well. Without battery heaters or warmer blocks or some other emergency heat source to keep out the cold, survivors would freeze to death. It wouldn't take long. The cold this far out was relentless. It made Victor nervous. That was too many variables. If the survivors had sealed themselves off, and *if* there were no breaches, and *if* they had masks and canisters to spare, and *if* they had a heat source, then maybe they had a shot.

The locker beside Victor opened abruptly, startling him. It was Father, who grabbed his own pressure suit and hurriedly climbed into it.

"What are someone's chances after eighteen hours?" asked Victor. "Seriously."

"This could have happened more than eighteen hours ago," said Father. "The pod was here for twelve hours. It might have attacked when it got here instead of immediately before it left. In which case we're thirty hours in, not eighteen."

Victor had considered this, but he said nothing. Thirty hours was too long. That drastically reduced the likelihood of them finding anyone alive, and he wasn't going to accept that as a possibility. Besides, it didn't seem likely anyway. Why would the pod stay after it attacked? To scan for life? To make certain the job was done? No, it seemed more plausible that it had tried to communicate or observe or scan. And when those efforts had ended or failed, it had attacked and run.

Father closed his locker and faced Victor. "You sure you're up for this, Vico?"

Victor understood what he was asking. There would be bodies. Death. Women. Children. It would be awful.

"You've never seen something like this," said Father. "And I would rather you never did. It's worse than you can imagine."

"I can help you, Father. In ways none of these miners can."

Father hesitated then nodded. "If you change your mind, if you need to come back, no one will think less of you."

"When I come back inside, Father, it will be with you and with survivors."

Father nodded again.

Bahzím, who had replaced Marco as chief miner, was calmly shouting orders from the airlock entrance. "Have two people check your suit and lifeline inside the airlock. Two. Head to toe. Every seam. Do not rush inspections. The debris outside will be jagged and sharp and will puncture your suit or your line. Keep your line slack to a minimum. Stay with your partner. Segundo, I want you and Vico on saws."

Father nodded.

Victor went to the equipment cage and took down the rotary saws. They were dangerous tools outside since they could so easily slice suits and lines, but the blades had good guards and Victor and Father had experience using them. Victor carried them to the airlock.

Toron entered from the corridor, flew down to the airlock, and faced Bahzím. "I'm coming with you."

"This is for experienced walkers only, Toron. I'm sorry."

"I know how to spacewalk, Bahzím."

"You don't have enough hours, Toron. If the sky was clear, I wouldn't have any issue, but there's a lot of debris out there. Anything could happen."

"My daughter is out there."

Bahzím hesitated.

"There's one lifeline left," said Toron. "I just counted. You have room for one more person."

"He can come with me and Vico," said Father. "We'll need someone to hold our lines clear while we work the saws."

Bahzím looked unsure. "You don't have a suit, Toron."

"He can wear Marco's," Victor said. "They're about the same height."

Bahzím considered this then sighed. "Hurry. I'm closing this hatch in two minutes."

Toron nodded his thanks to Father and Victor then quickly changed into Marco's suit.

They hurried into the airlock, and Bahzím sealed the hatch behind them. Everyone unspooled a lifeline from the racks along the wall and attached it to the back of his partner's suit. Then came the helmets. Bahzím typed in the all-clear, and fresh air and heat filled Victor's suit. Everyone took a moment to inspect the suits and lifelines of those around them. When all was clear, Bahzím punched in another command, and Victor's HUD blinked on. Live video of the wreckage outside appeared on Victor's display, taken from the ship's cameras. El Cavador's spotlights cut through the darkness, lighting momentarily on a piece of wreckage, as if considering it, judging by its size and shape if it were a likely candidate for survivors. Apparently it wasn't. The lights moved on. Victor's heart sank. There was so much debris. So much destruction. How could he possibly find Janda in all this?

The first bodies appeared shortly thereafter. Two of them. Men. Stiff with death. The spotlights rested on them, but the men were thankfully at such a distance that Victor couldn't make out their faces. The lights moved on.

A few minutes later the ship came upon a large piece of wreckage. El Cavador's retrorockets fired, and the ship slowed and then stopped alongside the wreckage.

"Listen up," said Bahzím. "We're opening the doors. First ones out are Chepe and Pitoso. They'll do a quick scan while the rest of us hang tight. If they detect something, the rest of us go in."

The wide bay doors opened, and what had been video became a reality. The wreckage in front of them was a mangled heap of destruction: bent girders, severed conduit, twisted pipes, torn foam insulation, crunched deck and hull plates. It looked as if it had been ripped from the ship instead of cleanly cut away by a laser. Victor searched for markings on the hull that might identify it as Vesuvio, Janda's ship, but there were none. Bahzím gave the order, and Chepe and Pitoso were out in an instant, flying down to the wreck and moving fast.

They flew to the hull side of the wreck where the surface was smooth and there were fewer protrusions that might snag or cut their suits. There were several windows, and Chepe went to those first, shining his helmet lights inside. The first few windows were quick looks, but at the fourth window they stopped. "There are people inside," said Chepe.

Victor's heart leaped.

"But they're not moving," said Chepe. "I don't think they're alive. Some are wearing masks, but it looks like they died from anoxia. They must have survived the attack, though. I see emergency heaters set up in the room. We just didn't get here in time."

"Is Alejandra with them?" asked Toron. "Do you see Alejandra?"

"It's hard to see faces through the masks," said Chepe. "And many of them are turned away from me. Plus the window's small. I can't see the whole room, especially around the corners."

"Maybe they're not dead," said Toron. "They could be unconscious. Maybe we could revive them."

Isabella's voice came on the line. "Chepe, it's Isabella. I'm at the helm. Can you send your helmet vid feed over the line?"

The video from Chepe's helmet appeared on Victor's HUD. Now everyone saw what Chepe saw. There were bodies drifting in a dark space. The room—what Victor could see of it—looked like barracks, with hammocks and storage compartments for clothes and personal items. Glow rods in the room offered some light, but they had dimmed to almost nothing. Chepe's helmet lights illuminated a few faces, and Victor saw at once that there was no reviving these people. Some had eyes open, staring into nothing, the look of death forever frozen on their faces. Men. Women. A young child. Victor recognized a few of them from the week the Italians had spent with them. That woman there had been holding an infant back on El Cavador during one of the feasts—Victor distinctly remembered—but she held no infant now. And that man, he had sung with a few other men during that same feast, a song that had left them all laughing.

"Bang on the hatch," said Isabella. "See if anyone responds. Watch for movement."

Chepe took a tool from his pouch and banged it hard against the hatch. Victor watched. Chepe's lights swept the room through the glass, pausing at each person. He banged again. A third time. A fourth. No one moved.

Janda wasn't among them. Victor was sure of it. Even those who were turned away, whose faces he could not see, he knew the size and shape of her body enough to know she wasn't here.

"We could put a bubble over the hatch and send in Chepe to run vitals on those people," said Isabella. "But that's going to take time, and right now every second counts."

A bubble was a small inflatable dome that could be hermetically sealed over an external hatch. If Chepe was inside the bubble when it inflated and sealed over the hatch, then he could open the hatch and go inside without exposing the room beyond to the vacuum of space. Bubbles could be dangerous, though, as they required you to momentarily detach your lifeline to climb inside. The lifeline was attached to a valve on the bubble's exterior. This fed to an extendable lifeline inside the bubble, which restored

air and power to the suit wearer. But detaching your lifeline, even momentarily was a risk.

"I'd say it's highly unlikely we'll find anyone alive in there," said Isabella. "I suggest we press on and look for signs of life."

"Agreed," said Concepción. "Return to the ship. Let's keep moving."

"We're just leaving them there?" said Toron.

"There's nothing we can do for them, Toron," said Concepción. "But
there may be others we can reach in time."

Victor felt hopeless then. These people had survived the attack. All the
factors that Victor had considered critical for survival had been met.
And yet all of them were gone. He pictured them alive, huddled around a
heater, clinging to each other, speaking words of comfort. How long had
they lasted? Twelve hours? Fifteen? Had they known El Cavador was
coming? Had they believed rescue was imminent? Or did they think themselves all alone, waiting out the inevitable?

Victor looked at Toron beside him and saw that Father had a hand on
Toron's shoulder, comforting him. Toron looked pale, even in the low light
of the cargo bay.

"They had masks and heaters," said Father. "That's a good sign, Toron.
It means there's equipment out there."

"Little good it did them," said Toron.

Chepe and Pitoso landed back in the airlock, and the ship moved on.
The bay doors remained open as they continued to patrol through the destruction. Twice more they stopped, and twice more Chepe and Pitoso flew
out to investigate. One of the wrecks was empty. The other had a massive
hole in the back that hadn't been visible until Chepe and Pitoso went in for
a closer look. There were no signs of survivors.

The ship moved on. As they continued patrolling they passed more
bodies. Most were men. But there were women, too. And children. One
burned terribly. Victor turned away.

Once, a corpse floated uncomfortably close to the open airlock, right
there in front of them. It was a man. A boy, really. No more than twenty.
He could have been a suitor for Janda if he wasn't married already. His
eyes were—thankfully—closed. The miners nearest the edge could have
reached out and touched him, and for a horrific moment Victor thought

the body might float inside. But the ship moved on, and the body slipped past.

No one spoke. Several of the miners glanced back at Toron to see how he was taking it, the compassion evident on their faces. Toron never said a word, and as the minutes stretched into an hour, Victor's hope began to dissolve. There was too much wreckage. They had come too late. Nineteen hours was far too long. Perhaps if they hadn't stopped to install the pebble-killers or scatter Marco's ashes, if they had accelerated then instead of *de*celerating, maybe they could have saved someone; maybe they could have stopped this whole thing from happening.

No, they couldn't have arrived before the attack. Even if they had pushed themselves and never slowed. And what good would it have done if they *had* been here? They'd be just as dead as everyone else.

A large piece of wreckage came along the ship. The biggest piece yet. El Cavador's retros fired, and the ship slowed. Victor couldn't imagine how anyone could be alive inside. The whole structure was twisted, not just the ends. And none of the sides were smooth with hull plating, suggesting that it had come from somewhere deep inside a ship.

Approaching it would be difficult. Sharp twisted beams and other jagged structural pieces protruded from all sides in a random fashion, like a crushed metal can wrapped in iron thorns. Chepe and Pitoso flew down cautiously, circling the wreckage from a distance. "I see a hatch," said Chepe. "It's solid. No windows."

"Can you get close enough to bang on it?" asked Bahzím.

Victor watched Chepe's approach via the man's vid feed. Chepe drifted to the hatch slowly, steering clear of the jagged girders and beams.

"Watch his line, Pitoso," said Bahzím.

Chepe settled on the hull beside the hatch. "The space around the hatch looks smooth," he said. "We could get a bubble around it if we needed." He banged on the hatch, then pressed his hand against the metal. He wouldn't hear a knock response from anyone inside, but he would feel the vibration of it. Chepe waited a full minute and knocked again. After a pause, "I don't feel anything."

The wreckage was drifting and rotating. One of the jagged beams was coming close to Chepe's lifeline. "Back off," said Bahzím. "She's spinning."

Chepe and Pitoso pushed off from the wreckage and floated a short distance away as the wreckage slowly spun in front of them. The far side of it, which hadn't been visible before, turned into view of the cargo bay. It was a mess of twisted channel beams and girder framework, bent and mangled together, worse even than the other sides. But through that, beyond the web of distorted metal, was a corridor, maybe ten meters deep, like a shallow cave, with the entrance to it pinched half closed. Victor zoomed in with his visor and strained to see through all the obstructions, trying to see down into the corridor.

Then he saw it.

A flicker of light. A movement. There was a hatch at the end of the corridor with a small circular window in the center. And in that window there was a light. A glow rod. Wiggling in someone's hand. "There's somebody inside!" Victor shouted, and before he knew what he was doing, he had pushed his way to the end of the airlock and jumped out into space.

"Vico, wait," said Bahzím.

But Victor wasn't waiting. He had seen someone. Alive. "There's someone down there." He hit the trigger on his thumb, and the propulsion pushed him toward the corridor entrance. He jinked left, avoiding a protruding beam, then jinked right avoiding another.

"Slow down," said Father.

Victor rotated his body, got his feet under him, and slowed. He landed expertly atop the bars and metal that bent across and blocked the corridor. He stepped to the side, squatted down, and looked through a hole in the web of metal down into the corridor, as if peering down a well. He could see him clearly now. A man. The circle in the hatch was smaller than the man's face, but he was clearly alive and looked desperate. He wasn't wearing a mask, either, meaning he had none, or the canisters had run out. Victor zoomed in, switched on his helmet vid, and blinked out the command to send the feed to everyone else.

The reaction was immediate. Bahzím started giving commands. "All right. Listen up. I want cables on this wreckage. Moor it to us. Lock it down. I don't want it spinning. Segundo, I want you and Vico cutting away that debris at that entrance. I want the other shears at the hatch Chepe found. We might be able to reach survivors through there. Chepe and Pitoso, circle the wreckage another time and look for another way inside. Nando, I want you with a board and marker down there with Segundo and Vico communicating with whoever's inside. I want to know how many are alive and what their status is."

Father and Toron gingerly landed beside Victor, carrying the saws and hydraulic shears.

"He must have heard Chepe knocking," said Victor. "There might be other people in there."

"And we're going to get them out," said Father, handing a saw to Victor. "Try the saw first. If it gives you problems, go with the shears. Let's cut these channel beams away first." He indicated the ones Victor had avoided. "We need a clear path in and out of here."

Victor wanted to say something to the man at the hatch. "We're here. We're going to get you out. You're going to live." But no one could reach the hatch yet with all the obstructions in the way, and Victor had no means of communicating with the man anyway. Father took the beam on the left, Victor the one on the right. Victor fired up his saw. The blade spun.

"Clean cuts," said Father, "as close to the bottom as you can. Don't rush."

Victor's blade cut into the metal. He couldn't hear it, but the saw vibrated in his hands as it ate through the beam. Nineteen hours. Someone had gone nineteen hours. It looked like a big space. There had to be more people inside. Maybe it was their version of the fuge, the designated place for an emergency. Maybe lots of people had gone there. The saw felt slow in his hands. He pulled the blade free and killed the power. "Toron, give me the shears."

Toron passed them, and Victor wiggled the pincers into place and started the hydraulics. The shears went much faster, cut-crunching their way through the beam, opening and closing like a ravenous animal, making easy work of the metal.

Bahzím was giving more orders, sending two more miners down with hydraulic spreaders.

The shears bit through the last few inches, and the beam snapped free.

"Easy," said Father. "Push it away slowly, not by a jagged edge."

Their gloves had an outer layer of leatherlike material and were built to withstand heavy use and scrapes, but Victor was overly cautious anyway.

The beam drifted away. Nando was down near the web of metal covering the corridor entrance, writing on the small light board with a stylus. He wrote, "How many people?" and turned the board around for the man. The man in the hatch placed nine fingers against the glass.

"Nine people," said Nando.

"Vico," said Father. "Don't take your eyes off what you're doing. Pay attention."

Victor turned away from the hatch. Father was right. He couldn't cut and watch Nando or the man at the hatch. He focused on the girder beam he was cutting and guided the shears through the metal. Nine people. So few. The Italians had close to three hundred people.

"He's writing on the glass with his finger," said Nando. "One letter at a time. He's moving slowly. He seems half out of it. Air. He's saying they need air."

"I don't see any other entrance besides the hatch we knocked on," said Chepe. "We've been around the whole thing."

"Ask him if Alejandra is in there," said Toron.

"Ask him first if he can reach the outer hatch," said Bahzím. "We might be able to get a docking tube sealed over it. Then they could open the hatch and fly right up to us."

Victor continued to cut metal while Nando wrote. Shards of twisted bulkheads and deck plating fell away as Victor's shears chewed through them.

"He's shaking his head no," said Nando. "They can't reach the hatch."

"Why not?" asked Bahzím. "Because they sealed off that room or because it's not accessible from where he's at?"

"I can't fit all that on the board," said Nando.

"Just figure out a way to ask him," said Bahzím.

Nando wrote. Victor allowed himself a glance down the corridor. The man in the window looked half asleep. His eyes kept drooping. "He's passing out," said Victor.

"Keep cutting, Vico," said Father. "Stay focused."

Victor returned to his work, cutting furiously, pushing pieces away, trying to clear a path.

"He's writing again on the glass," said Nando. "H . . . U . . . R . . ."

"Hurt?" suggested Bahzím.

"Hurry," said Chepe. "He's saying hurry. They're out of air. Now he's drifting away. We're losing him."

"We've got to get air in there now!" said Toron.

"Chepe," said Bahzím. "You and Pitoso get a bubble over that hatch you found. Get nine masks and canisters. I want you to find another way to reach these people and get them air as fast as possible."

Victor guided the shears through a particularly thick girder. There was still so much to cut away, still so much work to do. We're not going to make it, he realized. We have nine people just a few feet away, and we're not going to reach them in time.

Chepe shot upward from the wreckage, twisting in such a way that his lifeline easily avoided the sharp protuberances. Protecting your line was the most critical part of flying, but it was also the first thing most novice flyers forgot. Everyone was always in such a rush to shoot forward that they never took the time to look back. Which was a mistake. If you wanted to avoid snags, kinks, knots, and cuts, you had to "keep your mind on your line," as the saying went, and Chepe always did.

The hatch he and Pitoso had found was on the opposite side of the wreckage, so Chepe flew straight up to a distance that he figured was at least twice the distance to the hatch and begin his descent, moving, as always, in an arc. Most young flyers assumed that the best route between two points was a straight line, but Chepe knew different. Tall arcs worked best. You avoided the obstructions that could snag your line, and wherever you were going, you always arrived with plenty of slack.

Pitoso appeared beside him, keeping pace, moving in a parallel arc, with their lines trailing behind like a parabolic tail. They both slowed at the same instant as they approached the jagged debris around the hatch. As soon as they landed, Pitoso pulled the deflated bubble from his bag and unfolded it. Chepe then helped him spread it over the hatch. Bulo, another miner, arrived carrying a bag of masks and canisters, and Chepe took them and slid them under the bubble canopy. Then he reached back and detached his own lifeline. His suit powered off. His comm went silent. His

HUD disappeared. He climbed under the canopy, found the ripcord and pulled it. The bubble inflated into a clear dome that sealed itself to the hull with Chepe and the masks inside. Pitoso plugged Chepe's detached lifeline into the external valve on the bubble while Chepe took the internal line and plugged it into his back. Power returned to his suit, and with it, fresh air and heat.

"I'm set," said Chepe.

"Go," said Bahzím.

Chepe removed the emergency lid from the center of the hatch to access the manual wheel lock. Then he gripped the wheel and turned. At first he strained, but the wheel suddenly loosened, and it spun quickly thereafter. Finally he felt the lock snap free, then slowly lifted the hatch. He felt no rush of air as the vacuum of the bubble was filled from air inside. He checked his sensors on his wrist and confirmed what he already suspected. "There's no air beyond the hatch. There must be a leak inside."

"Then we don't need the bubble," said Bahzím. "Take it off so you have more mobility to look around."

Chepe found the release valve on the bubble and pulled it. The bubble deflated, and Chepe returned his normal lifeline to his back. The room beyond was dark and cluttered with floating debris. Chepe floated through the entrance, intensified his helmet lights, and saw—

A dead man's face just inches from his own. Chepe recoiled. The face was gaunt and white in the bright lights, eyes closed, mouth slack, a man in his fifties, an apron around his waist. No mask.

"Push him to the side," said Pitoso, coming in through the hatch. "There's bound to be more like him."

Chepe set his feet against the wall and reluctantly reached out and pushed the man in the chest, sending him back into the darkness to the right.

Pitoso came forward, pushing other debris away. "Looks like a kitchen," he said.

Chepe took in their new surroundings. The room had once been a large kitchen, maybe twenty meters square. But now it barely resembled one. The walls were all slightly bent, twisted to one side in the attack, creating awkward angles and shadows, with the floor sloping up slightly in one place and dipping down in another. Debris was everywhere. Pots, food, appliances, all scattered throughout as if everything had broken free and banged around in the explosion. Structural material stuck out from the walls: conduit, pipes, support beams. They would need to tread carefully in here.

"Come on," said Pitoso. "Let's find another way to the survivors."

They advanced slowly, lightly tapping their propulsion triggers to push themselves forward, brushing aside debris as they went: cutlery, tubs of dry goods, boxes. Another body floated to their right. A woman, wearing an apron.

"I see a hatch," said Pitoso.

Chepe looked where Pitoso was pointing, and his heart sank. A hatch was indeed ahead, but there was no way of reaching it. Not easily anyway. The whole floor had broken upward right at the hatch, as if pulled apart, bending deck plating and support beams up and onto the bottom half of the hatch. The hatch itself looked undamaged, but getting to it and clearing a path wide enough to open it would take hours at least, even a day maybe. The bigger problem, though, was the wall around the hatch. It was bent and pinched in places.

"We can't get to those people this way," said Chepe. "There's no way we'll get a bubble seal over that hatch, even if we cut all this debris away. Look at the wall."

Pitoso shined his light around the edges of the hatch. "Then we need to find another way."

But there wasn't one. They circled the entire room. They found storage rooms and another hatch, but this led to a corridor where the walls pinched completely closed, and beyond it was space anyway.

"We got nothing," said Chepe. "The only way to reach the survivors is through the blocked corridor where Vico and Segundo are cutting."

"Then we're in trouble," said Pitoso. "Because even if they get air in there, there's no way to get those people out."

"Back up," said Victor. "We're cutting the last pieces free."

Nando and Toron backed away from the opening, while Victor and Father cut the last of the girder framework away, clearing the entrance of debris. Their work wasn't done, however. The entrance was still too narrow for anyone to pass through and reach the hatch; the walls had been pinched close together when it tore away from the ship.

"Get those spreaders in there," said Bahzím. "Make that entrance as wide as possible."

Victor and Father stepped aside for those with the hydraulic spreaders. The men placed the two ends of the spreader on opposite walls of the entrance and then started the hydraulics. The spreader bars expanded, pushing the walls father apart, making an opening. Finally, after several minutes that felt like an eternity, the walls were wide again. Victor didn't even wait for the miners to remove the spreaders. He ducked under the machine and flew down to the hatch.

Through the window he could see people inside. Those that were moving looked on the verge of falling asleep.

"Do you see other people?" asked Father, coming up behind Victor.

"Do you see Alejandra?" asked Toron.

"No," said Victor. "But I can't see everyone. Some of them are alive. Barely." He turned to Father. "We need to get air in there immediately."

"How?"

Behind Father, running parallel along the corridor wall, were a series of pipes. Victor moved to them, identifying them by their shape and type. Fresh water. Sewer water. Electrical. Air. The air pipe disappeared through the wall near the hatch. Victor knew there would be a valve on the wall on the other side. As soon as the corridor decompressed, the emergency system would have sealed the valve automatically so that no air from the room escaped through the severed pipe in the corridor.

"If we can get someone inside to open the air valve," said Victor, "we can attach one of our lifelines to the pipe and feed them fresh air."

"Disconnect someone's line?" said Father.

"Either that or they die," said Victor. "I've been watching Chepe's vid as we were cutting. There's no reaching them any other way."

"He's right," said Bahzím. "If you don't get air to them here, they die. I'm not too keen on cutting someone's line, though."

"If you got a better idea, let's hear it," said Victor.

"I don't," said Bahzím.

Victor looked at Father. "Decision time."

Father hesitated. "All right. But we use my line."

Toron was at the hatch window, looking through.

"Move over, Toron," Victor pushed him aside and looked through the window. "There. Across the room. On the right side. There's another valve. That means there's another air pipe over there. We need to flood this room. Two lines pumping in a hundred times what the lines are feeding us now. Take Nando and see if you can find the pipe that feeds to that valve. Leave the light board. Toron and I will do this pipe."

Father looked through the window of the hatch, spotting the valve, judging where the corresponding pipe would be on the other side of the wreckage. He turned back to Victor. "I don't like this."

"Me neither. But we don't have time to discuss it, do we?"

Father sighed. "Be careful."

Father went. Nando followed. Victor looked at Toron and handed him a wrench from his tool belt. "Bang on the hatch. Get someone's attention. They need to open that valve."

Toron began banging on the hatch. Victor took the saw, fired it up, and cut easily through the pipe. Then he killed the saw, set it aside, and used another tool to pry the pipe that led to the room away from the wall.

"He's coming back," said Toron. "The guy from before. He's back. But he looks half asleep."

"Anoxia. Lack of oxygen. Mental confusion. Impaired thinking. Write on the board. Tell him he needs to open the valve. Keep knocking so he stays with us."

"I can't knock and write at the same time."

Victor took the wrench and banged. Toron wrote then held up the sign. "Open the valve," Toron said.

The man inside read the sign and furrowed his brow.

"He doesn't understand," said Toron.

"Point to it," said Victor. "Show him where the valve is."

"I can't see it," said Toron.

"It's probably to the right of the door. Our right. His left. Flush against the wall."

"There," said Toron, pointing. "Look there. That valve, can you see it?"

The man's eyes followed Toron's finger, but then he blinked and wavered, confused, as if the last string of understanding had been cut. He tried to look but his eyes wouldn't focus. He was drifting, seemingly unaware of his surroundings.

Toron banged on the hatch with his fist. "Open the damn valve!"

The man shook his head, getting his bearings, and blinked again. Then he came to himself, as if a switch had flicked on in his mind, and he saw the valve. Comprehension registered on his face. He reached for something out of sight. "He's going for it," said Toron.

"Put your hand over the end of this pipe," said Victor. "So that none of their air escapes if he opens the valve before we're ready."

Toron pressed his hand against the pipe's end.

"Bahzím," said Victor. "As soon as Toron tells you to, increase my lifeline air supply to maximum, as much oxygen as you can pump in."

"We're ready," said Bahzím. "But you realize you're cutting off your own air."

Victor grabbed the saw and fired up the blade. "I'll be fine. I've done this before." Which was only partially true. He had lost power to his line when the corporates attacked, but he had never lost his line entirely. No one had. No one that lived to tell about it later, anyway.

"Here. Use my line instead," said Toron. He reached back to detach it, but Victor was faster; his hand was already on the release latch of his own suit. Victor squeezed the mechanism, and the line came free. The power in Victor's suit went off. His HUD winked out. The chatter of communication went silent. Now all he heard was the sound of his own breathing. The safety valve on the back of his suit had sealed the hole where the lifeline connected, preventing Victor's suit from deflating like a balloon. He brought the detached line forward and pressed it down over the saw blade, slicing through it easily. He tossed the severed head of the line aside, then got a firm grasp with both hands on the longer portion of the line that extended back to the ship. There were several hoses and wires inside the lifeline, held together by the protective outer tubing. Victor took out his knife and cut down the side of the lifeline, slicing through the outer tubing but being careful not to cut the air hose inside. Then he pulled the outer tubing down, freeing the air hose from the other hoses that supplied heat and electricity and communication. He took two wire clamps from his pouch that were wider than the air hose and slid them onto it. Then he nodded to Toron to remove his hand and Victor shoved the air hose onto the pipe. The air hose was bigger, but not by much. Victor quickly tightened the wire clamps, so the air hose clung tightly to the pipe and wouldn't shoot off when more air came through. Then he gave Toron a thumbs-up and watched as Toron relayed the order.

The air hose stiffened as oxygen surged into the pipe. The question was: Was the air getting through or was it blocked by the valve? Had the man opened it, and if so, had he opened it all the way? Victor looked inside the hatch window but couldn't see the man. Several people inside were stirring, as if hearing the rush of air.

"I think it's working," said Victor. But of course no one heard him.

He noticed then that his fingers and feet were cold. His visor was fogging up. The air in his suit was stale. He felt pressure applied to his back, and his suit came to life. Air poured in. Heat. His HUD flickered on. Only it wasn't *his* HUD. All the data boxes were positioned in all the wrong places. He turned. Toron was behind him; he had given Victor his lifeline. Bahzím's voice said, "The air's going through, Victor. He opened the valve. Good work."

"Victor, your father has the other pipe ready," said Nando. "Send someone over here to open this valve."

Victor turned back to the window. Several people had mustered the strength to gather at the hatch, breathing the fresh air. Victor grabbed the board and wrote, then banged on the hatch. A young but haggard woman came to the window, read Victor's note, and nodded, comprehending. She looked to where Victor was pointing, saw the valve on the far wall, and nodded again. She seemed weak, drained of life, but somehow she pushed off the floor and drifted over to the valve. She put her hand on it then turned. At first Victor didn't think she had the strength to turn it, but she persisted, and the valve opened wide. Air rushed through the valve, blowing the woman's hair to the side. She inhaled deep, eyes closed a moment, then burst into sobs, burying her face in her hands—whether from relief at having survived or from grief for those who hadn't, Victor could only guess.

"Toron will share his line with you until you're both back on the ship," said Bahzím. "I want you back in the airlock. No one outside without a lifeline."

"How are we getting these people out?" Victor asked.

"We've been discussing that. The docking tube is too wide to get down that corridor and seal around the hatch. Do you think we could get a bubble over that hatch? Maybe we could fill a bubble with suits. Then they open the hatch, suit up, and quickly fly up to us."

Victor inspected the wall around the hatch. "It's too narrow in here. And even if we get the spreaders down in here, the wall is too damaged to hold a seal. What if we pull the wreckage into the airlock? Then we fill the space with air and they open the hatch and walk out."

"The wreck's way too big," said Bahzím.

"Then we cut it down with one of the PKs, slice away all the rooms that are compromised and keep only the room with survivors. If we shave enough away, it might be small enough to squeeze inside."

"Laser cutting around these people?" said Concepción. "That's extremely dangerous."

"Bulo's a good cutter," said Victor. "He could sign his name on a pebble if he wanted to."

"I could do it," said Bulo, who was listening on the line. "If the ship is holding steady, if we anchor the wreckage so it doesn't move. I can slice off the deadweight easy."

Concepción asked, "Segundo, what do you think?"

"I don't know of a better option," said Father. "The downside is time. Anchoring and cutting and moving them inside. That all will take a lot of time. I'm guessing five or six hours at the least. And there might be more survivors out there who need immediate help. We'd be essentially ending the search."

Victor was watching Toron, who was at the hatch window with a light board. He wrote something that Victor couldn't see and showed it to the man on the other side of the glass. The man read the board then shook his head. Toron released the board and turned away from the hatch. The board drifted away and Victor saw the single-word question written there: "Alejandra?"

CHAPTER 11

Quickship

Victor plugged the lifeline back into Toron before the two of them left the wreckage. Toron didn't object or play hero. He understood that if they were both going to arrive safely back at the airlock, they needed to share the line. Toron nodded his thanks to Victor, but Victor could tell Toron's mind was elsewhere. All hope of finding Janda alive here had shattered, and Toron's face showed only despair.

It almost relieved Victor that he and Toron couldn't communicate since they were sharing a line. What would Victor say? It's my fault that Janda's here? It's my fault she may be dead? It wouldn't be untrue. If not for Victor, the Council would never have sent Janda away. She'd be on El Cavador. Safe and alive.

He flew up out of the corridor of the wreckage, leading the way, with Toron behind him. Since Victor couldn't call for help if he needed it, it made sense for him to be up front where Toron could see him. Most of the jagged protrusions around the entrance to the corridor had been cut away, but it surprised Victor to see that many still remained. It had been dangerous and reckless of him to fly down here as quickly as he had. But he had been thinking of Janda then. He had been clinging to the hope that she was here, inside, alive, ready for rescue. Now he knew she wasn't.

A hand grabbed Victor's shoulder. It was Toron, already plugging the lifeline into Victor's back. Toron seemed agitated. He flew forward in a rush toward the ship, and Victor followed. The chatter in Victor's helmet continued.

"We don't have a choice, Toron," said Bahzím.

"It's not Toron anymore," said Victor. "It's Victor. He just gave me the line. What's going on?"

"He objects to suspending the search for more survivors to rescue the people trapped inside," said Father. "He says there might be a hundred people out there who need rescuing."

"He's right," said Victor. "There might be."

"Unlikely," said Bahzím.

"But possible," said Father.

Toron landed back in the airlock. Victor was right behind him. Father and Nando were coming in as well, the two of them sharing a lifeline also. The airlock was busy with activity. A team of miners was working the big winches, pulling in the mooring cables they had already anchored to the wreckage. The intent was to bring the wreck close to a PK to be extremely precise with the cuts.

There was a limited supply of the longer lifelines, but there were several short lines for working here in the airlock. Toron grabbed one from the wall, plugged it into his back, and approached Bahzím.

"I want to go back out there," he said. "I'm not staying here while we cut these people free. I want to keep looking. Even if I go alone."

"You can't, Toron," said Bahzím. "You can't leave the ship without a lifeline."

"I can plug the emergency regulator into my lifeline jack and connect air canisters. It's been done before. That will give me all the air I need."

"And what about heat? You'll freeze to death."

"I'll carry one of the battery packs. That'll give me enough heat and power for a few hours, at least."

Bahzím shook his head. "I can't let you do that, Toron."

"My daughter is out there, Bahzím. Dead probably, but maybe alive. And as long as there is a chance of me finding her alive, as long as that is the slimmest of possibilities, I will not sit here and do nothing. If you want to stay and help these people, fine. That's your choice. If it were up to me, we'd cut them loose now and look for Alejandra."

"You don't mean that."

"The hell I don't. And if it were your daughter you'd do the same."

Father stepped over. "Think, Toron. Everyone here loves Alejandra. All of us want to keep looking, but we need to go about it safely. If you rush out there, there's a good chance you'll die. Too much can go wrong, and you know it. Think about Lola. She can't lose a daughter and a husband."

"Don't talk like Alejandra is already dead," said Toron. "We don't know that."

"All right," said Father. "Let's put family aside and think about this practically. You can't carry that much equipment. You'd need a dozen canisters of air at least. Plus spare propulsion tanks. Plus the battery pack for power and heat. Plus rescue gear. Spreaders, shears, saws, the bubble. Are you going to carry all that?"

"If I have to."

"You can't," said Father. "It's too much for one person. It's too much for *five* people to carry. But even if it weren't, what would you do if you found someone? You can't get them back to the ship."

"I could keep them alive until you came for us."

Bahzím sighed. "None of us wants to delay the search, Toron. But we can't desert these people here. As soon as we cut away the other wreckage and get them inside, we can push on."

"That will take five to six hours at least," said Toron. "These people were minutes away from death. We barely reached them in time. If there are more out there, they won't last five hours."

Bahzím and Father exchanged glances. There was no arguing that the prospect of finding more survivors grew thinner by the minute.

Father sighed. "It wouldn't work, Toron. Look at the debris out there. It extends for kilometers in every direction. You can't cover that much ground in a propulsion pack."

"He could take one of the quickships," said Victor.

Everyone turned to Victor, who was standing off to the side, listening to the whole exchange.

"Quickships are cargo carriers, Vico," said Bahzím. "They're not made for carrying people."

"Doesn't mean a person can't climb inside," said Victor. "And there would be plenty of room for rescue gear and air canisters and batteries."

Bahzím shook his head. "Wouldn't work. Quickships are programmed to go directly to Luna."

"Every quickship has two programs," said Victor. "We only use the one that sends the ship to Luna, the one that operates the rockets, the one for long-range flight. The other one is the LUG program, the one Lunar Guidance uses when the quickship arrives at Luna. It overrides the first program and gently flies the quickship into port using the battery and a light propulsion rig. It doesn't run on the rockets. We've never used it before because we've never had any need for it."

"We've never used it," said Bahzím, "because we can't access it."

"I can," said Victor. "I've made repairs to quickships before. I've noodled around with the system. I know how to get to it and how to initiate it. We can fly it manually."

Bahzím shook his head again. "Those batteries don't carry a lot of juice, Vico. They're made to fly the ship a short distance into port, not patrol for kilometers on end through a debris cloud. If the battery runs out while you're cruising along, you won't be able to fire the retros. You'll sail on forever into oblivion. Besides, Toron has no idea how to fly one of these things."

"He doesn't have to fly it," said Victor. "I will."

They all stared at him.

"It wouldn't be that difficult," said Victor. "Simple, really. You know I could do it, Father. You've seen me tinker with the program. I wouldn't even have to leave the ship. Toron could wear a cable harness anchored to the ship when he leaves to check out a wreck. That way, he's not out there floating in nothing. He's anchored to someone who could fly him back to El Cavador if something goes wrong. And the battery isn't a problem either. I know how to monitor the power supply to ensure that we don't use up all the power without leaving us enough juice to stop and return to the ship. I can do this."

The men looked at one another.

Finally Father said, "I can't let you go out there, Vico. It's too dangerous. If anyone is flying that ship it's me."

"I know the system better than you do, Father. That's no fault of yours. You had no reason to study what we don't use. I did study it. It's much safer if I fly it."

"I'm sorry," said Bahzím. "It's not that I doubt your abilities, Vico. But we've never practiced this. And right now my job is to protect this family."

"Alejandra *is* family," said Victor. "And so is Faron. They may have left with the Italians, but they are still part of us."

That gave Bahzím pause. He looked at Father, who still seemed unsure.

"At least let him try," said Toron. "Let him show you he can fly it. Or let Segundo try. There's nothing more the three of us can do for the survivors we've found. It's in the miners' hands now. If Victor can prove it's possible and safe, you can't deny me the chance to save my daughter."

"Have you been listening to this, Concepción?" Bahzím asked.

"Every word," said Concepción, who was still at the helm with the flight crew. "I can't overrule Segundo's decision," she said. "Whether he allows Victor to go is his choice. But if there's a way to find more survivors we should try it."

There was a long pause as Father considered. "Two conditions," he said. "Show me you can fly this thing. And I'm coming with you."

The quickships were docked in a holding bay at the rear of the ship. Victor and Toron brought one outside, and Victor climbed into the space that would serve as a cockpit. He wired his handheld into the ship's computer and located the Lunar Guidance program. Since the quickship was automated, there were no flight controls for Victor to steer with. Instead, he devised a way to enter flight commands directly into the program by typing them into his handheld. It would be a slow and precarious way to maneuver the ship since only one command could be entered at a time and it didn't allow for quick reactions—he wouldn't be able to jink or dive or spin like he did when flying with a propulsion pack. It would be more like flying a freighter: slow to turn and decelerate.

Even still, Victor was fairly confident he could fly it with at least enough accuracy to reach the larger pieces of wreckage. With more time, he would have installed shields against solar radiation as well as seats with safety harnesses. But there was no time, and as soon as he had strapped himself to the structure, he detached his lifeline and replaced it with an air regulator and oxygen canister. Getting power to his suit was trickier. Victor taped one of the smaller batteries to his belt and hardwired the power inputs directly into the suit. The lights on his HUD were noticeably dimmer, but he had enough heat to get by with, and the radio worked. When Toron saw that Victor was set, he flew back to the airlock with Victor's detached lifeline and watched with the others.

It was then that Victor realized how alone he was. He was completely untethered from El Cavador. It was only moments ago that he had severed his own lifeline to rescue the survivors, but that hadn't been a risk really. Toron had been right there beside him—a link and anchor to El Cavador had been only an arm's length away. Now, for the first time in his life, El Cavador was beyond his immediate reach.

He began typing in the command to fly forward when it occurred to him that the LUG program was based on the quickship having a full load of mined metal, meaning a lot more mass. Victor stopped himself. Had he entered the command, he realized, he might had rocketed himself into oblivion. Brilliant, Victor. He shook his head, annoyed with himself for being so careless, then adjusted the program and typed in the first command. The propulsion pushed him forward gently, much to his relief. He flew away from the ship and did a wide loop that brought him eventually back to the airlock in what he hoped was a display of some piloting proficiency.

Father, Bahzím, and Toron flew out to the quickship, carrying larger batteries and rescue equipment. It meant they had agreed to try it. Father plugged an audio cable from his helmet to Victor's, while Bahzím anchored the equipment in the cargo hold. Victor then hardwired portable power supplies into Father's and Toron's suits, and soon everyone was settled.

"That wasn't the best flying I've seen, Vico," said Bahzím, "but it should be good enough for our purposes." He put a hand on the spare air canisters. "You've got about eight hours of air, but I want you back here in three. The less time you spend out there the better. The wreckage is unstable and drifting. This ship is small. It can't withstand a collision. Give yourself a wide berth wherever you go. As for communication, Concepción still has us on radio silence in case the pod can detect radio. Use the helmet-to-helmet audio cables to speak to each other, but keep your radios on just in case. Above all, be safe. Don't take risks. If all of you don't agree that something is safe, don't do it. Even to save another survivor. Your first priority is your own safety. Get back here alive."

Bahzím did a quick final inspection of all cables, canisters, and equipment, then he wished them well and flew back to the airlock.

Toron looked at Victor and Father. "Thank you," he said. "For doing this, for coming with me."

"We may not find anyone," said Father.

"We will have tried," said Toron. "I couldn't live with myself if I didn't at least do that."

"Take us out, Vico," said Father. "Nice and slow."

Victor entered the command, and the ship pulled away, heading in the direction El Cavador was pointed. After patrolling for a while, Toron spotted a large piece of wreckage a few kilometers below and ahead of them. Victor saw it and entered what he hoped would be the right commands to maneuver the quickship alongside the wreckage. He had to judge the distance and angle of approach by sight alone, however, and his first attempt was way off, far beyond the reach of their safety cables. He apologized, circled wide, and tried a second approach. This time he fired retros too late and overshot.

"I thought you said you could fly this," said Toron.

"He's doing the best he can," said Father. "No one's done this before."

Victor entered another series of commands and this time judged it right, coming alongside the wreck within ten meters of an accessible hatch.

"Toron and I will check it out," Father said to Victor. "You stay put and watch for collisions. Don't let anything hit the quickship, or we're all in trouble." Father detached the audio cable that connected him to Victor then flew down to the wreck, carrying a load of gear. Toron followed, and once they landed, they spread the bubble over the hatch, detached their safety cables, climbed under the bubble with the gear, then pulled the ripcord. The bubble inflated and sealed, and the hatch opened easily. Father and Toron then flew inside and disappeared from view.

Five minutes passed. Then ten. At fifteen minutes, Victor began to worry. At twenty-five, he was near panicked. Something had gone wrong. They shouldn't be taking this long.

Victor considered calling Father on the radio, even though he'd be disobeying orders and possibly putting the family at risk, but then he thought better of it. Father had asked him to wait, and so he would. Wait and pray.

Edimar was in the crow's nest on El Cavador, trying not to burst into tears. The data streaming through her display goggles from the Eye was so constant and in such volume that Edimar was beyond overwhelmed. Column after column of nonstop digits, all demanding to be analyzed immediately and marked EXTREMELY URGENT.

The problem was the debris. There were thousands of pieces of wreckage all around the ship, and since all of them were drifting through space and relatively close, the Eye had mistakenly labeled each piece of debris, however small, as a possible collision threat. And once an object was so tagged, the Eye's programming insisted that the Eye track its movements. This meant the Eye was now tracking thousands of objects at once and sending all of that data in a deluge of information directly to Edimar's goggles.

It was too much. And worse still, it was inaccurate. Of the thousands of objects the Eye currently considered a threat, only a handful were truly dangerous. It meant the real threats, the objects that Edimar *should* be tracking, were being lost in a sea of unnecessary alerts.

She blinked open a line to Concepción at the bridge. "I can't do it," said Edimar. "I need help."

"What's wrong?" said Concepción.

"It's too much. I can't process all the data the Eye is sending me. You've got to get my father back up here. I can't chew through the information as fast as he can. I'm too slow."

"You're father left on a quickship to look for more survivors," said Concepción.

"Quickship? I didn't think we could fly those."

"Apparently Victor can. Tell me what you need."

"Four clones of my father." She explained as quickly as she could how the Eye was giving her too much information and leaving her blind to immediate threats.

"I'm sending Dreo your way," said Concepción. "He might be able to tweak the Eye's programming. Rena and Mono will come as well and help however you need them. In the meantime, I'll put spotters at every window to look out for drifting debris. Don't worry. We'll figure this out."

"Thank you," said Edimar, and ended the call.

She felt so relieved that she could no longer hold back the tears. She removed her goggles, covered her face with her hands, and sobbed. Some of her tears were for the Eye and all the stupid pent-up frustration it had caused, but most of them were for Alejandra. Her sister. Jandita. Her best friend. The only person with whom she had ever been able to talk to about Father's temper or wearing a bra or what it would be like to get zogged one day, things she could never bring herself to discuss with Mother. And now Alejandra was out there. Gone perhaps. And Edimar would never speak with her again.

There was a noise in the tube that led to the crow's nest, and Edimar quickly composed herself, wiping at her eyes and taking deep calming breaths.

Three people floated into the room, and the sight of them further put Edimar at ease.

"Give me a pair of goggles," said Dreo. "I want to see the code on this thing."

Edimar handed him a pair. "It's tagging every piece of debris as a collision threat. I need to create perimeters that will isolate only those objects that are indeed too close. But I don't know how to do that."

Dreo had the goggles on. "All you need to do is write in a simple script. Toron didn't teach you how to do that?"

"I'm sure he knows how, but he doesn't want me tinkering with the programming."

"Then he shouldn't be leaving you alone," said Dreo. "It's irresponsible and puts all of us in danger. How old are you anyway?"

Rena put an arm around Edimar's shoulders. "Yes, yes, Dreo. Why don't you worry about the Eye and let Mono and I tend to Edimar."

"Don't give her all of that chili," said Dreo.

Rena was holding a container with a hot pad.

"I could use some of that, too, you know," said Dreo. "We haven't eaten on the helm in hours."

"Fix this Eye, Dreo, without further harping on Toron or Edimar," said Rena, "and I will make you your very own pot."

That put a smile of Dreo's face. "I'll be silent as space."

Rena took Edimar's hand, and they flew over to the other side of the room with Mono.

"Did my Father really leave on a quickship with Vico?" asked Edimar.

"Yes," said Rena. "And with my husband. They're looking for more survivors."

Edimar bowed her head. "They won't find any. It's been too long."

"We don't know that," said Rena. "We didn't expect to find anyone when we got here, and so far we've found nine."

"Believe me," said Mono. "If anyone can find more people, it's Vico. He might even find Alejandra."

Rena tensed slightly at this and glanced awkwardly at Edimar. "We certainly hope so, Mono," said Rena. "We're all praying for that very thing."

Edimar wanted to feel bolstered by the boy's innocent optimism, but she knew it was hopeless. And she could see that Rena thought so, too, only pretending to be optimistic for Edimar's sake. "Here," said Rena, handing Edimar the container of chili. "This is probably cool enough to eat. You must be famished." She popped off the lid on the straw and the aroma of beans and meat and cilantro wafted up to Edimar, who suddenly realized how hungry she was.

"Thank you," said Edimar.

"I can smell that, too, you know?" said Dreo. "You're making it difficult to concentrate over here."

Edimar sucked up a mouthful. It was warm and spicy and exactly what she needed. She wanted to cry again. Rena seemed so much like Alejandra in that moment. Edimar knew it was silly to even think it—Rena was old enough to be Jandita's mother—but the way she had pulled Edimar aside and showed her kindness was exactly what Alejandra would have done.

"What kind of parameters should I set up in the program?" Dreo asked.

"I wish Father were here," said Edimar. "He would know better than me."

"Well, he isn't," said Dreo. "You have to decide."

Edimar thought for a moment. "Cancel out all the debris that's beyond two hundred meters of our position yet within ten kilometers. That should cancel out most of the objects the Eye is tracking but pose no real threat to us. The one exception should be the quickship. We should continue to track that."

"I don't know which of these objects is the quickship," said Dreo. "I can't isolate that."

Edimar put on her goggles and found the quickship easily. "That one," said Edimar, moving the icon for the object into Dreo's monitor field.

"All right," said Dreo. "The quickship is still on the watch list. What else?"

"Now we're primarily looking at debris within two hundred meters of us," said Edimar. "Plus whatever we can see beyond the debris cloud."

"That's still over eight hundred objects," said Dreo.

"Most of the objects are merely drifting, though," said Edimar, "so we really don't have to worry about the small ones. They won't damage the ship. It's the big ones we have to track. Cancel out all debris that's less than two meters in length. That should remove all small debris and bodies from the watch list." She remembered that Mono was listening and removed her goggles enough to glance at him.

"I know what a dead body is," said Mono. "You don't have to talk different just because I'm here."

"Takes you down to fifty-three objects," said Dreo. "Much less than you started with."

"Can you put the objects in order of priority based on their distance from the ship?" asked Edimar.

"Done," said Dreo.

Edimar adjusted her goggles and smiled at the list. This was certainly more manageable. This she could handle, even without Father's help. She started at the top and scanned down to the bottom. The last object on the list instantly wiped the smile from her face. It was only a few thousand kilometers out and moving in their direction at incredible speed.

"What is it?" asked Rena. "What's wrong?"

"It's the pod," said Edimar. "It's coming back."

CHAPTER 12

Tech

Captain Wit O'Toole moved through the forest under the cover of night. His footfalls were soft and silent. His P87 assault rifle was at his shoulder. His body was slightly crouched, keeping a low center of gravity. His helmet had no visor or eye slits but covered his face completely with blast-resistant metal. His body armor was lightweight and camouflaged for darkness. Beside him, six MOPs in identical gear, carrying identical weapons, kept pace with him as he advanced up the slope of the Parvati Valley in northern India, weaving through the pine and fir trees as quiet as the wind.

Inside Wit's helmet, his HUD projected a 180-degree view of the terrain in front of him, as bright as if it were day, allowing him to see every detail of the forest. The computer helped further by flagging any obstacles in his path. A root, a low branch, a patch of uneven ground.

A female computer voice said, "One hundred meters to target."

"Full stop," said Wit.

The six MOPs stopped their advance and moved into a tight circle, dropping to one knee with their backs to one another, rifles up, covering their position from every approach. It was a simple tactical move, but it was done swiftly and silently, without hesitation or missteps, as fluid as a practiced dance.

"We're a hundred meters from the target," said Wit. "Now what?"

"Threat assessment," said Bogdanovich.

"How?" asked Wit.

"Satellite feed," said Lobo, "I'll patch us in."

A window popped up on Wit's HUD showing an overhead view of their position taken from a satellite. Wit blinked out a command, and the satellite image shifted, scrolling upward over the treetops in the direction the team was headed. The tree line ended, and a wide meadow came into view. A concrete two-story building, with an almost bunkerlike appearance, stood in the center of the meadow. The Indian military had built it here for military exercises like this one. Several armed guards patrolled the perimeter.

"What a lovely mountain resort," said Pinetop.

"The brochure said five stars," said Lobo.

Tonight's mission was a rescue operation. Calinga was acting the part of a foreign diplomat being held hostage by Islamist extremists. The extremists were actually fellow MOPs and Indian PCs eager to play the bad guys for once.

It was the tenth field exercise in as many days, and Wit had no intention of letting up.

He had devised all kinds of different scenarios: rescue operations, refugee protection, urban warfare, demolition, counterinsurgency measures—each with its own different cultural consideration, terrain, and enemies. One day he'd tell them they were being dropped into a dry mountain valley in Tadzhikistan. The next day they were being dropped at a beach in New Guinea with nothing but jungle as far as the eye could see. The idea was to train for every contingency and enemy.

"I count five guards around the perimeter," said Chi-won. "But there are probably others we can't see with the satellite. I say we go thermal from here on in."

He meant switching their helmet cams to detect heat signatures. "Agreed," said Wit. "What else?"

"There are more of the enemy inside," said Pinetop. "We need a floor plan."

"Coming up," said Lobo.

A three-dimensional schematic of the structure appeared on Wit's display. "If you were holding hostages, where would you keep them?" Wit asked.

"Away from windows," said Chi-won. "Terrorists prefer to keep hostages close, and they're terrified of snipers. A centralized room is best, probably on the second floor since there's no basement or attic. And the stairwell can easily be defended. If they were going to hide a hostage, I'd say they'd do it here."

A blinking dot appeared on a room on Wit's floor plan.

"Other ideas?" asked Wit.

The men briefly discussed other possibilities but everyone agreed that Chi-won's assessment was probably accurate.

"Now what?" asked Wit.

"We could send in a peeker and scope out the interior," said Pinetop.

Peekers were small, near-silent hover drones that carried a through-wall radar. Land one on a roof or a wall, and its signal processing could detect any movement on the other side.

Wit voiced no objection. Pinetop took a peeker from his backpack and flew it upward through the trees using his HUD. They all watched the vid coming from the peeker as it flew high over the meadow and settled on the building's roof. Three minutes later, they had confirmed Chi-won's assumption: The hostage was indeed being held on the second floor in the centrally located room.

"Pinetop, you take point," said Wit. "From here on in, I'm a grunt. You're in charge."

Pinetop responded without hesitation, giving out orders to everyone. His instructions were clear, thorough, and intelligent, as if he had been planning his strategy for months.

They advanced up the slope quickly, fanning out, rifles at the ready, approaching the meadow from multiple angles. Thermal imaging revealed three enemy guards hiding in the forest, but the MOPs took these out easily. Their P87 rifles fired almost silently, and the three enemy guards dropped, their dampening suits stiff.

The MOPs crouched at the tree line in the shadows. The guards in the meadow hadn't noticed the takedown and continued to patrol the perimeter without any sign of alarm. One of the guards walked within a few feet of their position, and Chi-won leaped out of the underbrush and hit the man with a spider pad. The man's suit stiffened, and Chi-won dragged him back into the darkness.

Four down.

"There's too much open ground between us and the building," said Pine-top. "We'll sniper the rest."

They extended the barrels of their rifles and made adjustments to the weapons for longer-range fire. Wit put his rifle to his shoulder and blinked a command in his HUD that caused the arms, shoulders, and upper back of his body armor to stiffen. This minimized the slight movements in his hands and made his upper body as steady as a tripod, greatly enhancing the accuracy of his shots. The computer then highlighted each of the targets on Wit's display. Seven guards total, one for each of them.

Wit watched his display as, one by one, the targets were marked with the name of the MOP who had selected it for takedown. Wit chose the last unselected target.

Pinetop gave the order. The MOPs all fired, and the seven guards went down.

After that it was a matter of following Pinetop's instructions. They rushed forward and stormed the building. The enemy combatants were exactly where the computer told them they would be. The peeker, which was still attached to the side of the house, warned them whenever new threats charged toward them from elsewhere in the house, giving Wit and his team plenty of time to seek cover or move into a position to neutralize the enemy.

Wit made every shot count, getting up the stairs just behind the others, stepping over the enemy that had already fallen. Calinga was waiting for them in the room. The last enemy guard, who was taking his role as a terrorist rather seriously, attempted to use Calinga as a human shield. But the advancing MOPs fired in unison, and five spider rounds hit the terrorist's helmet in nearly the same spot. The man's suit went stiff, and he released Calinga. He didn't even bother dropping to the floor as was the rule of the game. It was all over at that point.

"About time you got here," said Calinga. "It's no fun being the hostage. I don't get a weapon, and they wouldn't even give me something to read."

When they got outside, Wit ended the exercise. He blinked the command to unfreeze everyone's suits and had them all gather in the meadow for a debriefing, both MOPs and terrorists alike. The men sat in a wide circle all around him under the moonlight.

"What did we learn?" Wit asked.

"That Calinga makes a terrible hostage," said Deen, who had played a terrorist. "He wouldn't stop whining. We almost shot him to shut him up."

The men laughed.

"I almost shot myself," said Calinga. "Boring as hell, this crew."

The men laughed again.

"Here's what I learned," said Wit. "Seven MOPs prevailed against twenty-four equally trained commandos. Why? Because we're better soldiers? Because we're smarter? Faster? No. We won for two reasons: One, you bad guys were sloppy. You weren't taking proper cover. We picked you off way too easily."

"We were giving you the real thing," said Deen. "Terrorists are always sloppy."

"Don't give me the real thing," said Wit. "Give me you, one of the finest trained, most intelligent soldiers I know. Be merciless. I don't want realism. I want worse than realism. I want a hundred times more difficult than realism. Do everything in your power to annihilate us. That way, when the bullets are real, when our lives are on the line, we will do our duty with exactness. We will never lose. I should have seen nothing when we approached this compound. You should have been completely invisible to me and the satellite. You should have killed us before we left the trees. Why didn't you?"

"You were with the new guys," said Deen. "We thought we'd make it a little easier for them."

"Do you think they need any hand-holding?" asked Wit. "Do you think that just because they're new to this unit that they're not good enough or experienced enough to take you at your best? If so, you're in for the surprise of your life tomorrow when we do this again. From here on out, we pull no punches. If you lose, it's because you screwed up and were bested and not because you *let* someone win."

"I was actually trying," said one of the guards. "Chi-won jumped out of the bushes so fast, I nearly pissed myself."

The men laughed.

"Good," said Wit. "I'm glad you only *nearly* pissed yourself. Had you actually done so your suit might have short-circuited and given you quite the shock."

"Smoked sausage," said Deen, to another round of laughter.

"From here on out," said Wit, "you act as if your life is on the line. No more going easy. No more pretending that the enemy is inferior or less intelligent than you. Which brings me to the second reason why you failed. We MOPs had better tech. The enemy had older rifles, no computer assistance, no satellites, no peekers, no thermal vision. This was a tech war, and we won because of our equipment. Pinetop, if I had stripped you of all of your gear, could you have taken the hostage?"

"I don't think so, sir."

"Why not?"

"I'd be unarmed."

"So you're only an effective soldier if I arm you? You're only good if I give you better equipment?"

Pinetop hesitated. "No, sir. It's just more difficult. If I had been unarmed, I would have taken down one of the guards and confiscated his weapon. Then I could have picked off the others."

"And what if you didn't know how to operate the enemy's weapon?" said Wit. "What if it was tech you had never seen before?"

"Then I'd be in a pickle, sir."

"So you would have given up?"

"No, sir. I would just have a harder time of it. I'd need to devise ways to beat my enemy using what little resources were at my disposal."

"Such as?"

"The forest could supply me with spears, for example."

Deen laughed. "Spears? Against twenty-four armed men holding a defensive position?"

"Does that seem unlikely to you, Deen?" asked Wit.

Deen saw that no one else was laughing. "Forgive me, sir, but that sounds a touch impossible, doesn't it?"

Wit stared at him for ten long seconds. "Are you a MOP, Deen?"

"Yes, sir. To the core, sir. Absolutely."

"Then I expect you to take down twenty-four armed men, using only a spear. I expect you to take down a thousand men with a toothpick. We are not soldiers until we know how to go stark naked against a fully armed enemy and kill him."

Deen nodded, humbled. "Yes, sir."

Wit turned to the others. "We have become too reliant on our tech. Who's to say we will always have the technological advantage? What if there were an enemy with capabilities and weapons far beyond our own? Do we give up?" He waited for a response. "I said, do we give up?"

The men shouted in unison, "No, sir!"

"This is an inevitability, gentlemen. Sooner or later we will face a threat whose tech surpasses our own. Or we will face an enemy who figures out how to completely neutralize our tech. Weapons, communication, GPS, drones, rifles, explosives, everything. Let's figure out how to fight them no matter *what* they do and no matter *how* hard it is." He paused, coming to a decision. "From here on out, we will also train for missions without tech. Zero. Then we'll train for missions without gunpowder. Then we'll train for missions in which the enemy can always see us. Whatever the situation is, we will always be at the severe disadvantage. It's time we reminded ourselves what makes us PCs and MOPs. It is not the chips inside our rifles. It is the gray matter between our ears. The enemy may outgun us, but they will never outthink us." He turned to the six MOPs with whom he had taken the compound. "Gentlemen, leave your rifles and tech here. Carry only a pouch of spider pads. These will serve as your spears. Wear only your dampening suits. No helmets. Head into the hills, no farther than three miles. In two hours, twenty-four soldiers equipped with all the tech we possess will come hunt you down and kill you unless you kill them first."

The six MOPs stood and began removing their gear.

"And Deen," said Wit, turning to the man. "I'd like you to go with them. You may doubt your own abilities, but I don't. I will be coming for you personally. Take me down before I find you."

Deen stood and smiled, pleased for the chance to redeem himself. "Thank you, sir."

The MOPs ran away from the group at a sprint into the forest. Deen ran after them, hopping over the underbrush at the tree line and disappearing under the cover of trees.

CHAPTER 13

Files

Lem looked through the mining reports in the cargo bay and tried his best to appear pleased. The crew chief was beside him, smiling, waiting for Lem's praise. By the look of the reports, the man deserved plenty of praise indeed. The numbers were impressive. The scoopers were bringing in so much metal from the dust cloud that the men couldn't smelt it into cylinders fast enough. Iron-nickel, cobalt, magnesium, all the big-money metals. Thousands of tons of it already. It was more than Lem could have hoped for. Yet Lem's mind was so plagued at the moment by El Cavador and the files that they had stolen from the ship's computers that he couldn't even enjoy the good news.

"Hard to believe, isn't it?" said the crew chief. "I've been in this business for twenty years, Mr. Jukes, and I've never seen anything like this. This is the fastest I've ever brought in ferros."

Ferros, or ferromagnetic metals, the most valuable of minerals extracted from asteroids.

"The scoopers are working well, I take it?" said Lem.

"It's like trolling for fish, Mr. Jukes. We stick out the magnetized scoopers, move the ship back and forth through the dust cloud, and when we bring the scoopers back in, they're teeming with ferro particles. My whole career has been digging and scraping and blasting away at rock to get metal up out of a mine, but this glaser turns that whole model on its head. Now we blast the rock to dust, wave some magnets in the cloud, and the minerals come to us." He laughed and shook his head. "Damndest thing I ever saw."

"Yes, yes. This is all very impressive."

"We picked the right asteroid for it, too," said the crew chief. "It's no wonder those free miners were camped here. This rock was the mother lode. All kinds of high-value metals, and plenty of them to go around. Most miners see a rock this good once every few years or so. I got to hand it to you, Mr. Jukes, you picked one helluva rock to blow up."

Lem was only half listening. "Yes, wonderful. Well, keep up the good work. Is there anything you need?"

"More people," said the crew chief. "This is a research vessel, so we're shorthanded. Our boys smelting the dust and making the cylinders are already working two shifts."

"How many do you need?"

"Another ten would work wonders."

"I'll have Chubs send some people down."

"Thank you, Mr. Jukes." He pulled off his hat and scratched at his head, looking hesitant. "Now, you're sure you don't want us to load up a few quickships? We'll get a much bigger haul if we send some of these cylinders straight on to Luna."

"No," said Lem. "I don't want to send anything back ahead of us. Once we load the cargo bays, we'll pull out."

The crew chief shrugged. "Seems a shame to leave the cloud when there's so much metal here for the taking. We only have four cargo bays on the ship, and we'll fill those easy. That's quite a big load, to be sure. But using quickships, we could double that. That's a lot of money we're letting slip through our fingers."

"I appreciate your dedication to the company bottom line," said Lem. "In any other circumstances, I'd agree with you. But I don't want my father or the Board to know we have a full load. I'd like it to be a surprise when we arrive."

The crew chief winked. "Smart thinking, Mr. Jukes. Those suits will be surprised all right. They'll probably give us all a hearty bonus when this is all over."

Lem knew the man was fishing, and he obliged. "If they don't give us a bonus, I'll give you one myself. You've done exceptionally well."

The man beamed. "Thank you, Mr. Jukes."

The man looked like he was going to speak further, but Lem didn't give him the chance. He turned and flew away, heading back to the push tube. The Board would be surprised all right. And when Lem told them that their files had been compromised and that the schematics for the glaser were likely in the hands of free miners, or that the same free miners likely had incriminating video of a Juke vessel *killing* someone, video that would almost assuredly result in a public-relations nightmare of a lawsuit, they'd be much more than surprised.

Lem could see the Board of Directors now. Fine mission, Lem. Well done. Too bad you killed a man and lost us billions of credits in R&D and the very future of this company. Too bad you made a jackass of yourself. Other than that little snafu we'd say the mission was a smashing success. We were warming up this seat here at the board table for you, but you see, we have a strict policy against idiots. We'll have to give it to this spineless Ivy League bastard instead. So sorry. I'm sure you understand.

Lem climbed into the tube and spoke the order for the helm, shooting away.

These people have stained me, he told himself. These damn free miners have stained me. Thank you, Concepción Querales. Thank you for taking the last two years of my life and flushing them down the crapper. No, not just the last two years, but my *whole* life, everything I've worked for. This will cancel out all of my previous achievements. My reputation will be ruined. And not only that—now that he thought about it—but his fortune as well. The company wouldn't just sue him, they'd take him for every-thing he was worth, which was no small sum. They'd tag the whole ordeal as gross negligence and roast him alive. And Father wouldn't do anything to stop it. He'd turn a blind eye. He'd chalk it up as another of Lem's "life lessons." You got yourself into this mess, Lem. You can get yourself out.

No, he was going to correct this. The Board would never know. By the time they reached Luna, all would be resolved. The free miners might be beyond their reach at the moment, but he was certain there was a solution, even if he had no idea at the moment what it might be.

He reached the helm and pulled Chubs aside into one the conference rooms. Chubs floated near the entrance, but Lem felt like walking. He turned on his greaves and vambraces and paced back and forth in front of the window, beyond which was the murky dust cloud and the dotted black of space.

"We have a situation," said Lem. "One that I would prefer to keep very quiet."

"All right," said Chubs.

"When we bumped the free miners, there were three men on the hull. One of them was struck with one of the sensors we cut away."

"I remember," said Chubs. "It looked ugly."

"Yes, well, ugly is putting it mildly. The man is dead. We killed him." Lem put a little emphasis on the word "we," hoping to spread the blame around.

Chubs furrowed his brow. "How can you possibly know that?"

Lem told him about the message from Concepción.

Chubs whistled. "Podolski know about this?"

"I called him to my room, and he checked the system. You ready for the fun part? They downloaded us. Not only did they hack us and leave us a lovely little message, but they also took our files. Everything."

Chubs swore under his breath. "Are we sure about this? Podolski confirmed?"

"They used a snifferstick. They poked their little noses in here without us knowing it and they copied us clean. Podolski showed me on the records. They duped us."

Chubs swore again. "Not good, Lem."

"No, not good. Schematics of the glaser. All of our research. The engineers' journals. And my favorite part: all the video of the bump."

Chubs stopped rubbing his eyes and looked up at Lem.

"Yes," said Lem. "They have video of us killing one of their crew. Do you know what the press would do with that? What the courts would do with that?"

"It was an accident," said Chubs. "We weren't aiming for the guy. We didn't even know he was out there."

"Prosecutors won't care," said Lem. "Besides, it doesn't look that way in the video. I reviewed it myself. In slow motion. It looks like we were gunning for him. They'll call it incontestable. And when they do, corporate will cut us off at the knees. They'll sue us as well. If we don't do something about this, you and me and everyone on this ship is malja. Toast. Game over."

"They stole from us," said Chubs. "That has to account for something. They stole corporate secrets."

"That will win us no sympathy. You think people will shed tears for the largest, wealthiest corporation in the world? Oh boo-hoo. Poor Juke Limited. Those fat, greedy corporate executives will only get a hundred billion credits on their yearly bonus this year instead of a hundred and twenty. What a shame. No. No one will care. The media would have a field day with this. The poor and middle class will dance in the streets. They eat this stuff up. They can't be happy until everyone else is brought down to their level."

"We can fix this," said Chubs.

"How? We can't track them. I already asked the navigator. They're long gone. We could go looking for them, but there's no guarantee we'd find them. We probably wouldn't."

"We don't have to find them," said Chubs. "We just have to know where they're going and be there first, waiting for them when they arrive."

"We don't know where they're going," said Lem. "I told you. They didn't exactly leave a forwarding address."

"But we do know where they'll go eventually," said Chubs. "Weigh Station Four is the only outpost this far out. All the families and clans go there for supplies. El Cavador headed out into the Deep, so they obviously don't yet know what's in our files. As soon as they figure out what they have, they'll rush to Weigh Station Four and try to sell the schematics on the black market. That's the only place even remotely close to here where they can do that."

"They could head back into the inner system," said Lem. "Maybe they won't go to Weigh Station Four. Maybe they'll think they'll get a better price closer to home."

Chubs shook his head. "Not families. You have to know how these people think. They don't take risks like that. Most of them came out to the Deep to get away from trouble. When they try to sell, they'll use a reliable source, someone they trust, someone they use often. That's more important to them than getting a better price. They wouldn't fly down to Mars or the Asteroid Belt. A, it's too far, and B, they'd want to stay as far away from corporates as possible. They took something of ours, and they know we'll want it back. Believe me, they'll play it safe. Weigh Station Four is where they'll go."

"Fine. But how will we recover the data?"

"The same way they took it from us. We'll hack their ship and steal it back. And maybe erase their servers in the process, just to be certain."

"They could have moved the data onto a mobile device, a portable drive or something."

Chubs shook his head. "Families use handhelds. Old models. If they want to port the information, they'd use those. But the handhelds are rooted to the ship's main servers. When we wipe the servers, we wipe the handhelds, too."

"It's not flawless," said Lem. "They still could have the data stored somewhere else."

"Maybe," said Chubs, "but I doubt it. We'll never be one hundred percent sure. Hitting their servers is as close as we can get."

Lem considered this a moment then realized a snag. "It won't work," he said. "If we go to Weigh Station Four, they'll see us. They'll see the ship. It's not a very big outpost. They'll know we're waiting for them. They'll turn tail and run."

"They won't see us," said Chubs, "because our ship won't be there. By the time El Cavador arrives, we'll be heading back to Luna."

"Then how will we wipe their system?"

"We'll leave Podolski. He's the only one of us that can do this anyway. We drop him off at Weigh Station Four and have him stay there until El Cavador shows up, which, after all, could take months. We can't hang around that long without arousing a lot of suspicion anyway. But Podolski and a few security guys can blend in. We'll even dress them up as free miners so they don't draw attention to themselves. El Cavador arrives. Podolski swipes them. Then he and the security team hop on the next freighter to Luna. Simple."

"Podolski will never go for this," said Lem. "We're essentially banishing him to a dump outpost. He'd make a stink about this with corporate."

"No. He won't," said Chubs. "All we have to do is convince him that this whole thing is completely and utterly his fault. He's not doing us a favor. We're doing *him* a favor."

They brought Podolski into the conference room and had him stand at the end of the holotable. Lem put on a grave, disappointed face while Chubs stood over in the corner, arms folded across his chest, scowling, playing bad cop. The idea was to unsettle Podolski immediately, and Lem could see by the man's expression that it was working.

"I've just informed Chubs here of our dilemma," said Lem. "I've tried to keep this quiet for as long as I can for your sake, Podolski, but I can't put it off forever. We need to address this issue."

Podolski shifted his feet, uncomfortable. "Issue, sir?"

"Don't act like you don't know what we're talking about," said Chubs. "El Cavador swiped our files on *your* watch. This was supposed to be the tightest firewall in the solar system, and a bunch of ignorant gravel suckers waltzed in here and cleaned us out. You screwed us, Podolski, and I'll be damned if I take any heat for your mistake."

Lem thought Chubs was laying it on rather thick, pointing and nearly shouting and even turning red with anger, which Lem found particularly impressive—a man who could do that on command belonged on the stage. But it seemed to be working. Podolski recoiled a step and held up his hands, palms out, in a gesture of surrender.

"Wait. Hold on a minute. You can't peg this thing on me."

"We can't?" said Chubs. "Then who's responsible? The cooks? Janitorial? Or maybe you think Mr. Jukes here is to blame. Is that what you're saying?"

"No, no, of course not," said Podolski.

"The firewall is your territory," said Chubs. "That's what this company pays you for. It's your job to keep this ship as tight as a drum. Perhaps you've forgotten what we're carrying on this vessel. Maybe it simply slipped your mind that the schematics and notes and research for the gravity laser, the most expensive prototype of any tech this company has ever developed, I might add, is on our servers. Did you forget that, Podolski?"

"No, sir."

"You didn't?" said Chubs, feigning surprise. "Well, that's astonishing. That boggles my mind. Because I can't fathom why anyone would allow a group of uneducated free miners to steal that information from us, knowing how valuable it is."

"I don't know how it happened," said Podolski. "Nobody's cracked us before. We're impenetrable."

"You see?" said Chubs, turning to Lem. "Listen to him. 'We're impenetrable.' He's not even admitting it happened. He's in denial. He's not going to do anything about it. We have to go to your father, Lem. Ukko needs to hear about this personally. The Board as well. Podolski isn't going to fix it."

Lem moved to Chubs and began speaking in hushed tones, though just loud enough for Podolski to hear. "We can't go to my father," said Lem. "He has zero tolerance for mistakes like this. Especially when there's this much money and company resources invested. He'd string Podolski up. He would ruin him. Maybe even sue him. Podolski can't afford that."

"We don't have a choice," said Chubs.

"Wait," said Podolski. "I'm not the only one who wrote the security measures, you know. I helped, yeah, but there are over two hundred coders on Luna working on this stuff. I can't be the fall guy here. This wasn't my fault."

Chubs looked at him with contempt. "Yes, Podolski, we'll tell that to Ukko Jukes. We'll explain to him that the man at the controls can't be blamed. He's innocent. Did he even notice the attack take place? No, he had to wait for someone to point it out to him. Did he do anything afterward to rectify the situation? No, he twiddled his thumbs. I'm sure Mr. Ukko Jukes will be pacified by that argument and absolve you of any and all blame."

Podolski considered this. "All right. There's no need to go to Ukko. I can fix this. Honest. Please. Give me a chance on this."

"What could you do?" asked Lem.

"Get me close to El Cavador and I'll hack them back. It would be easy. Free-miner security is a joke. I could get in and wipe their system without them even knowing I was there."

Lem visibly relaxed, smiling, and turned to Chubs. "There. Satisfied? I told you Podolski would own up. Problem solved."

"It's not that easy," said Chubs, shaking his head. "We don't know where El Cavador is. We can't track them."

Lem frowned, all hope vanishing. "Right. That is a problem, yes." He sighed. "Then there's nothing to be done."

Podolski seemed desperate. "Maybe we could ask around, hit up some of the other clans or families for information. Someone has to know where they are."

Chubs looked painfully amused. "You think free miners are going to offer up any intel to corporates? They hate us. They'd never sell out one of their own. And whom would we ask anyway? There's no one close."

Lem brightened, as if the idea had just struck him. "Weigh Station Four. El Cavador will need supplies. We'll go there and wait them out."

"They'd see the ship," said Chubs. "They wouldn't stop. It wouldn't work."

"Drop me off," said Podolski. "Let me stay there, while you go off a ways. I'll clean their system, they leave, I call you back, you pick me up."

Chubs shook his head. "Ships like theirs have incredible sky scanners. They'd see us from way out. The only way that would work is if El Cavador believed we were heading back to Luna."

Podolski paused, staring down at the holotable, his face taut with tension. Finally he looked up. "Then that's what we do. You drop me off at Weigh Station Four with some gear and money. Then you head back to Luna. I wait them out, clean their system, then buy passage back on a freighter."

Lem and Chubs looked at one another.

"You know," said Chubs, "that just might work."

CHAPTER 14

Pod

Concepción stood at the holotable at the helm, watching one of the PKs cut through the wreckage of the Italian ship. The miners outside were sending her live video to the holospace in front of her. Everyone who worked at the helm was gathered around Concepción, their faces taut with worry. For her part, Concepción did her best to appear poised and in command, though inside she felt tense and helpless. Whittling down the wreckage with a laser was taking an incredible risk. If the wreckage were to shift or rotate unexpectedly while they were cutting, even only slightly, the laser might cut into the room where the survivors were waiting, breaching the airtight walls and killing everyone inside within moments.

Concepción shuddered at the thought. It would be a cruel death, made all the more horrible because the people trapped inside now believed they were being rescued. *Right as we fill their hearts with hope, we screw up and give them a death more terrible and traumatic than what they would have suffered had we never come along.*

But no, the wreckage wouldn't shift, she told herself. The miners were taking every precaution. They had set up mooring cables and two long pylons that extended from El Cavador out to the wreckage, holding the wreckage in place and preventing it from drifting into the ship. It was a precarious procedure, yes, but they were doing everything they could to protect those inside.

The laser finished a cut, and the severed section of wreckage broke free and drifted away. There was an audible sigh of relief from the crew, and a few of them even applauded and embraced one another. Concepción remained still and unresponsive. The job was nowhere close to being finished, and she had learned through sad experience never to celebrate prematurely. They were not out of danger yet. Whatever had done this to the Italians was still out there.

The laser beam stopped cutting. The miners turned on the winches and pulled on the mooring cables, rotating the wreckage into a different position in preparation for a second cut. Since the wreckage was unstable and had lifelines attached and people inside, the miners didn't rush the process. They rotated the wreckage slowly, being careful not to jerk any of the lines. It made Concepción realize how tedious and lengthy a process this would be: cutting and rotating and cutting and rotating until they had whittled down the structure small enough to fit inside the airlock.

It relieved her to know that Victor and Segundo and Toron were out there somewhere continuing the search. The work with the laser drill hadn't put a full stop on the rescue efforts.

Of course, sending the three out in the quickship didn't exactly put her mind at ease either. Under any other circumstances she wouldn't have taken such a risk, especially with the only two mechanics in the crew. If something happened to both of them, who would keep the ship operational? Not Mono. He was too young, too inexperienced. He had barely had enough time to learn the fundamentals, if that. I should have considered that before blessing the mission, she thought. That had been careless. But what could she have done? Only Victor could fly the quickship, and Segundo wouldn't have let him go without accompanying him.

The laser started cutting again.

Concepción watched a moment, then her handheld vibrated. She put it to her ear and answered it.

Edimar's voice was rushed and panicked. "It's coming back," she said. "The pod. It's already close and moving fast. We have about twenty-eight minutes before it reaches the debris cloud."

Concepción leaped forward to the holotable and swiped her hand through the holospace. The video feeds disappeared. "Show me," she said.

The people around her recoiled, sensing her alarm. "What is it?" asked Selmo.

A system chart with dots of light appeared in the holospace. One light was marked EL CAVADOR. Other smaller dots of light immediately around the ship represented debris. Concepción ignored those and focused instead on a distant dot of light off to the side, alone out in space. As she watched, a computer-rendered line representing the ship's trajectory extended from the dot across the holospace and landed directly on El Cavador.

The crew stared. They all knew what it meant.

"How much time do we have?" asked Selmo.

"Less than twenty-eight minutes," said Concepción.

"Everyone to stations," said Selmo. "Move!"

Selmo stayed by her side while the crew hurried to their workstations. Dreo entered from the corridor and flew to the holotable, coming in from the crow's nest. Concepción spoke into the handheld. "Watch the pod's progress, Edimar. If it changes speed or its trajectory notify me immediately." She ended the call and turned to Dreo and Selmo. "What are our options?" she asked.

"Hard to say," said Selmo. "We don't know what we're up against. We know next to nothing about this pod."

"We know it destroyed the Italians," said Dreo, "one of the best defended clans in the Belt. We know it's lethal. We know the Italians' death wasn't an accident. The pod destroyed four ships, not just one. You can't chalk that up as a mistake. It wiped them out. This was an intentional kill."

"Agreed," said Selmo. "But we don't know if it considers us a threat as well."

"It's heading straight for us," said Dreo. "It's not coming here to play a hand of cards. It likely thinks we're part of the Italians. And for whatever reason it considered the Italians a threat. We don't know why, but it's probably safe to assume that the Italians didn't provoke it. That would be foolish. The Italians wouldn't endanger themselves. They'd play it cautiously. Which would suggest that this thing killed them indiscriminately. But in my mind that isn't even the question we need to answer. The 'why' is irrelevant right now. We need to know the 'how.' How did it wipe them out? What are its weapons capabilities? Can it attack from long range? Are we already within its reach? Consider the debris. The pieces of wreckage aren't clean cut. The edges aren't straight. This doesn't look like laser work. It looks like explosions, like something ripped the ships apart. How did it do that? And more importantly how do we defend against it?"

"Maybe we can't," said Selmo. "Unless the pod attacked and destroyed the Italians incredibly fast, the Italians would have fired back. They would have given the pod everything they had. Yet their weapons, which are much stronger than ours, apparently had little to no effect on this thing. What makes us think we can take it down when the Italians couldn't?"

"Then what do you suggest?" asked Dreo. "We can't run. The pod's too fast. It would catch us easily. Plus running only makes it harder to defend ourselves or to hit it with the lasers."

"If the pod thinks we're with the Italians," said Selmo, "if we're an enemy by association, then perhaps we should move out of the debris cloud. If we distance ourselves from this place, the pod might disassociate us from the Italians and leave us alone."

"If we move out of the cloud, we'll be exposed," said Concepción. "The debris is the best defense we have right now. It provides some cover and it likely throws off the pod's sensors."

"If it even has sensors," said Dreo.

"Point taken," said Concepción. "We need information about this pod, and the only people who can provide it are the survivors inside the wreckage." She punched a command into her handheld and called Bahzím, who was supervising the effort outside. When he answered, she told him the situation and asked if there was any way to speak with the survivors.

"The only way to communicate with them is by light board," said Bahzím. "We write, and they give simple responses, nodding their head or writing words on the glass of the hatch one letter at a time."

"We don't have time for that," said Dreo. "Look, these survivors are hindering our maneuverability. We won't be able to move around the debris field quickly if we're moored to a massive hunk of wreckage. They're an albatross. I hate to be the one to say this, but we need to consider cutting them loose."

"Absolutely not," said Concepción.

"We could come back and get them when it's over," said Dreo.

"They can't survive without us," said Selmo. "We're supplying them with oxygen."

"Think," said Dreo. "These are nine total strangers. Are we willing to handicap ourselves and risk everything for people we don't know?"

"They're not strangers," said Concepción. "The moment we started helping them they became a part of this crew. End of discussion. Selmo, have the miners remove the pylons and pull the wreckage in close with the mooring cables. That will give us more mobility. Dreo, contact the quickship. Get Victor and Segundo and Toron back here immediately."

Dreo hesitated, as if he would argue further, then went to his workstation.

Concepción turned to Selmo. "We need a better defensive position. I want us behind a large chunk of debris if there is one. Then put our best men on our five pebble-killers."

"That may not be enough," said Selmo.

"It's going to have to be," said Concepción.

Victor floated in the quickship, watching the large, twisted piece of wreckage beside him. An hour had passed since Father and Toron had gone inside through the hatch, and Victor was on the verge of flying to the wreck to investigate. Just as he began unspooling cable to produce a makeshift safety line, a voice crackled over the radio.

"Quickship, this is El Cavador. If you can hear us, respond. Repeat. Victor, Toron, Segundo, if you can hear us, respond."

Victor dropped the cable. El Cavador was using radio, which meant one of two things. Either the ship had determined that radio wasn't what had attracted the pod, or the pod was no longer a threat. A different voice sounded in Victor's helmet. "El Cavador, this is Segundo, we copy. Over."

Victor relaxed. It was Father. He didn't sound injured.

"Toron here as well," said Toron.

Victor swallowed, composing himself. "And Victor. I'm here, too. Over."

"Get back to the ship immediately," said Dreo. "The pod's coming back."

Victor's relief at hearing Father's voice was gone in an instant. They weren't prepared for the pod; they had five pebble-killers. The Italians had been armed with as many as twenty-five, and the pod had wasted them. Father began asking questions, and Dreo shared what he knew.

"We can't come back immediately," said Father. "Toron and I are still inside one of the wrecks. We're moving back to the quickship now, but it will be ten minutes before we reach it. We won't get back to you in time. Don't wait for us. If you need to run or move elsewhere, do it now. We'll catch up to you later if we can."

"Concepción won't like that," said Dreo.

"She doesn't have much choice," said Father.

El Cavador clicked off. Victor hit his talkback: If the ship had abandoned radio silence, there was no need for him to adhere to it now. "Father, what happened?"

Father sounded solemn. "We found Faron shortly after we came inside. He was dead. There were a lot of people in this one, Vico. None of them made it. We had to cut through some heavy debris in one of the corridors to reach the rear of the wreck. We knew it would take a while, but we went for it anyway. It didn't pay off."

Victor said nothing. Faron. Dead. Here inside this wreck. That meant this was Vesuvio, Janda's ship; it meant that if they were going to find Janda, it would likely be here. Faron would have stayed close to her; he would have protected her. Yet Father and Toron hadn't found her; Father would have said so if they had.

They weren't going to find her, Victor realized. Ever. It had been an unlikely possibility from the beginning, but Victor had still clung to hope. Now that lingering chance was gone. Alejandra was dead. Nine survivors was more of a miracle than they could have hoped for.

Father and Toron emerged from the hatch. They deflated the bubble and flew back up to the quickship. Toron looked vacant as he climbed back into the cockpit. Victor watched him, seeing that Toron had reached the same conclusion he had: Janda was gone.

Concepción's voice came over the radio. "We've moved to a more defensive position, but don't come to us if you have enough air. The pod is nearly here, and you may be safer where you are. We've managed to get a communication line to the survivors, and we've learned more about what we're up against. The survivors believe the pod is drawn to heat. It stopped at their position and sat there for hours doing nothing. The Italians tried communicating with it, but the pod was nonresponsive. Then, without provocation, it flew to the rear of one of their ships, clung to it with grappling arms, and began probing the ship's engines with long, thin drills, like needles almost. The drills went in like a 'knife through hot butter,' they said, hardly any resistance at all. The pod was systematic about it, as if looking for something. The first ship blew up before anyone knew what was happening. At first the Italians thought the pod had planted an explosive, but it appears the probing of the engines is what caused the detonation. That's why the debris looks ripped apart. It blew up from within. As for the pod, it sustained no visible damage. Not even the needle drills. The other ships fired their lasers, but the pod moved quickly to the engines of the second ship and repeated the process. The pod took several direct hits, but again, no damage. Either it's shielded or its hull is impermeable to lasers. It might not attack us, but if it does, we'll destroy it. Bahzím has a team of miners already outside with penetrating tools. If it lands on our engines, we'll rip it to shreds."

"Did it have any other weapons?" asked Father.

"None that the Italians could detect. Just the probing needle drills. It's also much smaller than we thought. Maybe a quarter the size of El Cavador. The Italians believe it's designed for atmospheric entry and exit, though probably not in really strong gravity, by the looks of its engines and design. It could land on and leave from, say, Earth, but it might have trouble with Jupiter. That's conjecture, though, and not necessarily helpful."

"Anything is helpful," said Father. He quickly gave her his own report and informed her that they had found Faron's body but no survivors.

"I'm sorry to hear it," said Concepción. "Once we destroy the pod and make needed repairs, if any, we'll resume the search. In the meantime, hold your position. If you don't hear from us afterward, come to us. We may not be able to contact you, and we'll likely need you for repairs." She paused a moment, then added, "Qué Dios les proteja." May God protect you.

"Y ustedes también," said Father. And you as well.

The radio went silent, and no one spoke for a moment.

"She doesn't think they'll survive an attack, does she?" Victor asked.

"I don't think so, no," said Father. "And she has every reason to believe so. The Italians tried to stop it and couldn't. It got all four of their ships, and they all were desperately fighting to the end."

"El Cavador doesn't have a chance," said Toron. "This thing took laser fire. Direct hits. We can't let it reach the ship."

"What do you suggest?" asked Father.

"Bahzím has a team outside with penetrating tools. We have the same tools here. Spreaders, shears, cold sprayers. We're closer to the pod than they are. It will be coming from this direction. When it passes, we get behind it and attack it from the rear. We'll have to come in slightly from the side to avoid its thrusters, but we hit its hull, climb out, anchor ourselves to whatever we can, and destroy anything that moves with the tools. Maybe we can disable these grappling arms or needle drills. If we cripple it enough, it can't inflict any damage."

"It's going to be moving," said Father. "If we're off on our approach, even slightly, we'll miss it." He turned to Victor. "You only just learned to fly this thing, Vico. Can you do this? Can we hit it?"

Victor blinked. They were going to attack the pod. Alone. With rescue gear. "I'd need to make some adjustments to the program to give us more propulsion; we can't match it with our current speed. We'll need to be much faster. But even then, I won't have a guidance system. It will be like shooting a bow, with us as the arrow. If I track it right, and judge our speed right, it might work. But it will largely be guesswork. The challenge will be securing ourselves to the hull once we reach it. How do we anchor? We'll need to cling to the hull long enough to get out of the ship with tools."

"Leave that to me," said Father. "You worry about getting us into a position to attack." He clicked on the radio. "El Cavador, this is Segundo. Give me the exact location, trajectory, and speed of the pod based on our current position."

"What are you planning?" asked Concepción.

"A bit of sabotage," said Father. "We might be able to do some damage before it reaches you. And don't argue with us. You know it makes tactical sense, and we're doing it whether you approve or not. We'll simply have a better chance of success if you help."

After a pause, Concepción answered, "Selmo will give you the coordinates. Be careful, Segundo. I need my two best mechanics and my sky scanner alive."

"You need everyone on board El Cavador alive," said Father.

Selmo gave them the coordinates. The numbers meant little to Victor. But for Toron, a sky scanner, the coordinates were a second language he spoke fluently. Even without instruments, using only the placement of stars around them, Toron knew precisely where the pod would be coming from. He gave directions to Victor, who turned the quickship around and flew them through the debris, weaving this way and that until Toron felt certain about their position. Victor fired the retros and settled in a patch of shadow behind a large piece of debris.

"He'll be coming right through here," said Toron, making a sweeping gesture with his arm, showing them the expected trajectory.

Victor rotated the quickship so it was pointed in the direction to intercept the pod once it passed. Toron gazed outward with his visor zoomed to maximum, searching the sky for the pod, waiting. Father worked furiously behind Victor, making hooks for the cables. Using the shears, he snipped bars from the quickship's walls and bent them with another hydraulic tool, jury-rigging a hook.

A few minutes later Toron saw it.

"There," he said, pointing.

Victor strained his eyes and zoomed in with his visor. At first he saw nothing. There was wreckage clouding his view, and the sunlight through the debris was dim and heavily dappled with long shadows that kept most of their surroundings in near darkness.

Then he saw it. Or at least a glimpse of it, there in the distance, behind a scattering of debris, moving toward them.

Then the debris thinned, and the whole pod came into view. Victor's heart sank. It was a ship, yes, but with its grappling hooks and needle drills already extended, it looked more like a smooth-shelled insect. It wasn't human. Whatever was inside it piloting it couldn't be human. It wasn't shaped for humans. It seemed too narrow in the body. And what was that on the nose of the ship? A drive? For the first time in Victor's memory, he was mechanically stumped. Typically he could look at other ships and know just by the shape of them and the placement of their sensors and engines how the ship flew and operated. Even ships he had not read about and whose designs were completely foreign to him, even those Victor could understand if he looked at them long enough.

Except this one. This was like nothing he had ever seen before. Had it not been flying through space in front of him, if he had seen only an image of it on the nets, he wouldn't have believed it was a ship at all. He wouldn't have believed it even existed.

El Cavador can't stop it, Victor realized. Concepción isn't prepared for this. Nothing is prepared for this.

"What the devil is that?" said Toron.

"It doesn't matter," said Father. "We don't have to understand it. We just have to stop it. Check your safety harnesses. Make sure your cables are secure. If you're not tethered and you slip, you're gone. The ship will be moving. Use your hand and boot magnets. Strap a second pair of magnets to your knees. Stay as flat as you can. Crawl, don't walk. Toron, once we land, bring out the tools. We'll target the needle drills and grappling arms first." Father reached up and turned on his helmet cam. He was going to record everything. "You can do this, Vico," he said. "Wait for the pod to pass. Then pull up alongside it and land on its surface."

Yes, thought Victor. Land on its surface. How simple. Just plop a quickship—which was never intended to be piloted, never intended to hold people at all, and operated with rudimentary flight controls—onto a moving alien target. Easy.

Victor watched the pod approach. It decelerated as it sunk into the debris cloud, yet it still moved faster than Victor thought safe for a debris field. It must be incredibly nimble, he thought. It must be able to shift direction quickly. And just as he considered this, it happened. The pod jinked and spun to avoid a chunk of debris and then returned to its previous trajectory with inhuman agility. Again, like a flying insect, zipping to the side and back with ease. How was he supposed to land on something that could change direction that fast?

Ten seconds passed. The pod drew closer, getting larger. For a harrowing moment, Victor thought it was coming directly for them, that it had seen them moving through the debris and decided to attack them instead.

But no, now it slowly began to veer to the side. They were beside its trajectory, not on it.

Finally it passed by, not a hundred meters from their position, slick and smooth and moving fast.

Victor slid his finger down the screen of his handheld, and the quickship shot forward. Earlier he had devised a dial to increase the propulsion by simply sliding his finger across the screen, but as soon as the ship took off, he knew that he had misjudged it: They were accelerating too quickly. He had intended to start slow and then rush at the end, but it was too late for that now. He would have to rely on retros to slow them down in the final moments just before impact.

The quickship raced forward, not aiming at the pod, but at a point in space ahead of it, where Victor hoped the two ships would meet. He had to hit it right, he knew. If he came late, they might fly up into the pod's rear thrusters, burning themselves up in whatever heat or radiation was emitted there. Too early and they'd put themselves directly in the pod's path, only to be crushed by the subsequent collision. It was the middle of the pod or nothing. And not at too sharp an angle either or they'd only bounce off or, worse, collide with such force that they'd kill themselves instantly.

Victor kept his eyes focused on the point of interception. The pod was to his right, slightly ahead of them. They were too fast, he realized. He was going to overshoot.

"We're coming in hot," he said. "Hold on to something."

He fired up the retros to a quarter power. The straps across his chest tightened as he felt his body pressed forward in sudden deceleration. Then just when he thought he had slowed them enough, he released the retros, hit the propulsion, and they shot forward again. Victor waited one more moment then killed the propulsion. Now they were in a fast dead drift, closing in on the ship.

Three more seconds. Then two. One.

The impact was hard, and Victor's body jerked against the straps. He hit the propulsion again to keep them from bouncing off, but he could already feel the ship deflecting away. He saw Father's body fly by, and for an instant Victor thought Father had been thrown from the ship. But no, Father had launched forward, using the speed and force of the impact to get clear of the quickship, and hurled himself onto the pod. Two cables uncoiled behind him, and Father raised the hook in his hand. He hit the surface of the pod and snapped the hook around the base of one of the long grappling arms. His body flipped around, still full of momentum; and it would have flown off into space if not for the cable attached to his safety harness, which snapped taut and whipped him back to the surface of the pod.

The cable attached to the hook snapped taut next, and the quickship swung back to the pod like a pendulum, slamming hard against the side of the pod. For a moment, Victor felt dazed and disoriented, then he tore at his restraints, pulling himself free, crawling out. He set his boot magnets to the hull and was relieved to feel them attracted to the metal. Toron was right behind him, magnet pads in his hands, crawling out onto the pod with two hydraulic shears strapped across his back.

Victor grabbed the heat extractor, and crawled forward. Toron was right beside him. Debris whipped by overhead. They reached Father. Toron handed Father one of the shears, and Father immediately went to work, firing up the hydraulics. They had aimed for the drills, but Father was attached to a grappling arm, and he set the shears to work there first. The teeth bit at the metal but they didn't sink in. He tried again, setting the teeth at a different angle, but again to no effect.

"I can't bite through," said Father. "The metal's impermeable."

"What do we do?" said Toron.

"Vico, get the heat extractor here at the base of this grappling arm," said Father. "We'll suck the heat off of it. Freezing it will make it brittle."

Victor moved quickly, attaching the claw of the heat extractor around the narrow grappling arm. Then he watched the meter as the heat of the arm quickly dropped.

After ten seconds, Father said, "Good enough. Take it off."

Victor snapped the claw free, and pulled the extractor away. Father was instantly at the frozen spot with the shears again. This time the shears bit through, but instead of tearing, the metal cracked, splintered, and then shattered. The entire grappling arm snapped free and hovered there in space a moment before Father pushed it away from the ship.

One arm down. Three to go. Plus the drills.

"That one next," said Father, indicating the grappling arm two meters to their right. Victor began crawling for it, following Father, sliding his knee magnets across the smooth surface, keeping himself low and his grip on the pod secure. A flicker of movement in his peripheral vision stopped him. He turned toward the nose of the pod and saw a hatch open. A figure emerged wearing a pressure suit and helmet. It wasn't human. It was three-quarters the size of a human, with a double set of arms and a pair of legs. All six appendages stuck to the surface as the creature shuffle-crawled forward with incredible speed, racing toward them, an air hose trailing behind it.

Victor couldn't move. His whole body was rigid with fear.

The thing paused, lifted its head, and regarded them. Victor saw its face then. It wasn't an insect exactly—there was skin and fur and musculature. But it *was* antlike. Large black eyes. Small mouth, with pincers and protuberances like teeth. Two superciliary antennae that bent downward across its face.

"Son hormigas," said Toron. They're ants.

The creature moved its head, eyeing their equipment. Then, seeing that Victor had the largest piece, the heat extractor, and perhaps the most threatening, the hormiga shot forward toward Victor with its first set of arms raised.

Victor cried out. And just before the arms seized him, the blunt end of a pair of shears struck the hormiga on the side of the head, knocking it away. It was Toron. "Help your father! I'll hold it back."

The creature slid away and then tumbled off the ship, spinning into space. Its air hose snapped taut and held firm, however, and as soon as the hormiga got its bearings, it shimmied up the hose like it was climbing a pole and was back on the surface of the pod. Toron hurried to the hose and severed it with a quick snip of the shears. Air poured from the hose, and the creature lunged at Toron, pinning him to the surface.

Victor moved to intercede, but Father was quicker, crawling past him and lunging at the creature. "Get the extractor on that grappling arm," Father yelled. "Now!"

Victor moved for the arm and snapped the claw around the base of it.

He cranked the setting up to maximum and pulled out as much heat as he could. He looked back to Father and Toron and saw that the creature was gone, knocked off the ship by one of them. Toron was on his back, his knee magnets turned around to the back of his legs, holding his lower body against the hull. Father was kneeling over him, clinging to the stomach of Toron's suit.

"Victor. Help me," said Father.

Victor hurried over and saw at once that Toron was badly wounded. The front of Toron's suit over his abdomen was ripped and bloody. Father was trying desperately to hold the punctured suit closed. Toron was coughing up blood into his helmet, and his eyes weren't focused.

"What do I do?" said Victor.

"We need to seal the suit," said Father. "Hurry."

Victor tore at his hip pouch for the tape.

Every suit had a fail-safe system inside it in case of a puncture: Straps would tighten and rings of airtight foam would inflate inside the suit to seal off the punctured area and prevent an oxygen leak. Without these emergency sealants, you'd quickly lose all air pressure and die in fifteen to thirty seconds. The problem was, the seals were never perfect. Air always seeped out, sometimes quickly, sometimes slowly, but air always found a way. If anything, the sealants were designed to give you a few extra minutes at most to get back inside the ship before you asphyxiated or your body fluids began to boil. Tape could help seal the puncture if the hole was small enough, but it wasn't the golden solution, especially on a puncture as big as Toron's.

Victor found the tape and hit the mechanism on the side to eject a foot-long strip of adhesive.

"Put it here," said Father, "where my fingers are. Hurry."

The suit was red and wet, and the tape wasn't sticking because of the fluid.

"We have to stop the bleeding first," said Victor. "We have to put pressure on the wound."

"He's losing air," said Father.

"He'll bleed to death if we seal the suit," said Victor.

A hand grabbed Victor's arm. It was Toron, looking up at him. "You find my daughter. You keep looking. You make sure I don't die in vain."

"You're not going to die. We're going to get you back," said Victor, though he knew it wasn't true.

Toron tried to smile. "Don't think so."

"Put your hand on the wound and hold it there," Father said to Victor. "I'll try to seal your hand inside the suit."

Toron turned his head to Father. "Always trying to fix things, eh, cousin? This one's even beyond you." He coughed again, and winced, then gasped from the pain of it. Father held his hand. The pain passed, and when Toron spoke again his voice was strained and weak. "Save the ship. Save Lola and Edimar. Promise me that."

"I promise," said Father.

"I was hard on Edimar. I was a bad father."

"Stop talking," said Father gently.

Toron winced again.

Father handed Victor the shears. "Cut the grappling arm."

Victor hesitated. He didn't want to leave Toron.

"Do it now, Vico," said Father.

Victor moved, crawling across the surface. He pulled the claw of the heat extractor away. The metal was cracked and brittle. Victor turned on the shears, and the second grappling arm snapped away.

"Don't stop," said Father. "Take out one of the needle drills next. No matter what happens, keep going. Break off as much as you can."

A second figure emerged from the hatch. Father had the other pair of shears in his hand. He rushed the creature, staying low, jabbing the shears forward. Victor reached the drill. It was narrower than the arm. He snapped the claw around it and waited for the heat extractor to do its work, sucking the heat away. Victor glanced to the side and saw Father fighting the creature. Father kept lunging with the shears, but the creature was easily swatting the attacks aside. If Victor didn't help, the creature would soon get the upper hand.

Victor glanced back at the extractor. It was done. Victor quickly removed the claw and snipped with the shears. The drill snapped free, and Victor pushed it away before glancing again at Father. The creature was off the ship, dangling in space at the end of its hose, not moving, its body mangled from the shears. Father crawled forward and snipped the hose, severing the creature from the ship.

"Are you hurt?" asked Victor.

Father sounded winded. "No. Keep going."

Victor went to the next drill. Froze it. Snipped it. Pushed it away.

They were approaching El Cavador. Victor could see it far ahead in the distance. Father was at the hatch, looking inside. It was a small hole, too narrow for his shoulders. "There's another one inside," he said.

Father reached in with the shears. There was a struggle. Father's arms jerked right and left. The creature had incredible strength, and for a moment Victor feared that the magnets anchoring Father to the surface of the ship would break their hold and Father would be slung out into space.

But the magnets held, and Father continued to lunged downward, fierce and fast.

Finally the struggling stopped. Father exhaled, coughed, and sounded exhausted. "It's dead," he said. He shined a light down into the hole. "I think this is the cockpit. I don't see any other way to get into this room except through this hatch. No doors. No access points. I think these three were the entire crew."

Victor crawled toward him. "We have to stop it if we can. Do you see any controls?"

"I see a lot of levers and dials. And a few screens, but they only display images. There's no data. No writing, no symbols, no instructions, nothing that suggests measurement or coordinates or directions. No language marks or symbols. Nothing. I wouldn't know how to stop it."

Victor reached him and looked inside. The creature was snipped in half, floating in the air, limp and oozing liquid. Victor averted his eyes, suddenly hit with a wave of nausea. He shined his light toward the flight console instead, which was a ring around the front window, filled with dozens of levers and switches.

"We need to widen this hole," said Victor. "I'll freeze it with the heat extractor. You cut behind me as I move around the circle." He reached down and pinched the inner ring of the hatch with the claw of the heat extractor then slowly slid the claw along the inner ring. Father followed behind with the shears, cutting and cracking the metal away. They worked quickly, and when they were done, the hole was more than wide enough for the both of them to float inside. Victor pushed the creature aside with the claw of the heat extractor and flew down to the console. The levers varied in size and shape, but there was nothing to indicate their purpose. No markings, words, numbers, nothing. Some of the levers would no doubt be for the drill and grappling arm while others must be for the engines. But which ones? Victor looked around him, searching for clues. The room was large and filled with equipment. There were long tubes of smoky gases and odd-looking plants. The screens showed images of the Milky Way, the solar system, and a slightly blurry image of a planet.

"That's Earth," said Father.

Victor thought so, too. "Yet there's no data," said Victor. "No labeling, no markings of any kind. Just images. Are you recording all this?"

Father scanned the room. "Trying to."

Victor focused his attention back on the console, searching for any symbols or markings that might suggest the purpose of any of the levers. It was useless, he realized. There was nothing to guide him.

"Trouble," said Father, pointing.

Victor followed Father's finger and looked out the window. The pod was heading toward a large piece of wreckage a kilometer or two ahead.

"We don't know how to stop it," said Father. "We need to bail."

"Give me a second," said Victor, reaching for one of the levers. He pulled back, and one of the grappling arms extended out in front of them.

"We don't have time, Vico."

"We need to save this ship, Father. There might be information here."

The debris was approaching. The ship would collide in moments. Victor studied the levers. There were three other levers like the one he had tried. Those would all be grappling arms; not what he wanted.

"We need to go now," said Father.

Victor tried another lever, and the ship accelerated slightly.

"Whoa," said Father.

Victor pulled back in the other direction, and the ship slowed. But not enough.

"Pull it back more," said Father.

"That's as far as it goes."

They were nearly on top of the debris. It was at least four times the size of the pod, with twisted beams and mangled steel protruding from every direction, all coming clearly into view fast. Father grabbed Victor's hand. "Move. Now!"

Victor launched up through the hole and crawled out onto the hull. Father came up behind him. The shadow of the debris covered the pod. They were seconds from impact.

"We need to jump," Father said. "Take off your line."

Victor fumbled with the D-ring on his safety harness. His fingers slipped. He couldn't get it lose.

Snip. The shears in Father's hands cut the line. "Go!"

They launched upward. Victor looked back. The pod crashed into the debris below them. Beams from the debris pierced the cockpit window. Glass shattered and twinkled away into space. The quickship flew forward, spinning awkwardly, still tethered to the pod, and careened into the debris, bending, bouncing off, wrecked. Dust and tiny debris scattered in every direction, clouding the collision.

"El Cavador. El Cavador," Father was saying. "Do you read? Over."

The wreckage was getting smaller below them. They were still flying upward with the force and speed of their launch. They weren't tethered to anything. They had nothing in hand to stop themselves. Father was off to Victor's right, with the distance growing between them by the second. They had launched at slightly different angles, and now they were drifting farther apart. Unless El Cavador retrieved them immediately, they would fly in these directions at these speeds forever.

"El Cavador," Father said again. "Can you read?"

There was a crackle over the line, then Concepción's voice said, "Segundo. We see you. We're coming for you now."

Victor looked back and saw El Cavador emerge from behind a section of debris.

"Get Vico first," said Father.

"We're getting you both," said Concepción.

Victor turned his head back to Father, who was a great distance away now, getting smaller by the moment.

"Toron didn't make it," said Father.

"We know," said Concepción.

The ship moved closer, pulling up beside him. A miner with a lifeline leaped out from the ship and wrapped his arms around Victor's chest, stopping Victor's flight. It was Bahzím.

"Got you, Vico."

Victor clung to him as Bahzím thumbed his propulsion pack and turned them both back toward El Cavador. Down the side of the ship, a distance away, another of the miners was grabbing Father as well. Victor watched until he was certain Father was secured, then he turned his head and looked back at the wreckage now far below, where Toron was lost among the dust and debris.

CHAPTER 15

Warnings

Victor gathered with the Council in the fuge two days later after a search for more survivors proved unsuccessful. He had hoped to accompany the search party to look for Janda, but Concepción had asked him and Father to comb through the wreckage for salvageable parts instead. It was a long shot, but if Victor and Father could find enough parts to build a laserline transmitter, they could restore the ship's long-range communication. Father had said that finding what they needed would be like finding needles in a haystack that had been ripped to shreds and strewn across a county mile, but he agreed to look nonetheless. When he and Victor came up empty-handed, Concepción convened the Council meeting.

The nine Italian survivors who had been trapped in the wreckage were in attendance. They stood huddled together off to one side, the horror of their ordeal still evident on their faces. None of them had been terribly injured in the pod attack, but they looked like broken people nonetheless. Weeks ago, when the Italians had docked with El Cavador, the Italians had been full of song and laughter and life. Now they were like ghosts of the people they had been, silent and solemn and heavy of heart. For the past two days they had patiently awaited the return of the search party, desperate for news of lost loved ones. But both days had ended in disappointment, and now whatever hope they clung to had to be paper thin.

"I'm ending the search for survivors," said Concepción.

Jeppe, an elderly Italian who had become a spokesman for the survivors, objected. "There have to be places we haven't searched," he said.

"There aren't," said Concepción. "As painful as I know this must be, we all must accept facts and move forward."

"What about the bodies?" asked Jeppe. "We can't leave them out there."

"We can and we will," said Concepción. "The recovery effort could take weeks to conduct safely, and we've stayed here too long already. Under other circumstances I would agree, but these are not normal circumstances. We need to move now. I remind you that there are three members of my own family among the dead who have not been recovered. All of us are making sacrifices."

She meant Toron, Faron, and Janda. The miners never found Janda's body in their searches, and now that the search was over, no one ever would. Victor felt a pang of guilt as he pictured Toron in his mind, dying there on the pod, pleading for Victor to find his daughter.

Concepción continued. "Our primary mission now is to warn Earth and Luna and everyone in the Belts that this near-lightspeed ship is coming. The pod is incontrovertible evidence that the ship is alien and that the species flying it has malicious intent. If we had a laserline transmitter, we could send a warning immediately, but at the moment, we have no reliable long-range communication. The radio is working, but without a laserline, I doubt we'll send a message at this distance with any accuracy. I suggest we set a course for Weigh Station Four and try to hail them as we approach. We can then use their laserline transmitter to send a warning from there."

"Agreed," said Dreo. "But sending the warning via laserline isn't a sure thing. We can't count on our message getting through. We're still a long way from Earth. Any message we send in that direction will have to pass through several hands and relay stations along the way before it reaches Earth. If the message isn't passed on, if it stops somewhere along the chain, it dies there. It happens all the time. You know how these relay stations work. Corporates and paying accounts get top priority. Those are relayed first. The computers do that automatically. We're free miners, the dregs of space, ignorant roughnecks. The station attendants would push our messages aside only to be sent out when the server space becomes available."

"We'll mark the message as an emergency," said Concepción. "We'll tag it as high priority."

"Of course," said Dreo. "But that's overused. Some clans mark all of

their messages as emergencies in hopes of getting top placement and being quickly sent through. Believe me, when I worked for corporates, I had
to deal with these relay stations all the time. Seventy to eighty percent of
the laserlines they get every day are marked as emergencies even though
most of them aren't. 'Emergency' means nothing."

"But we have an overwhelming amount of evidence," said Father. "The
helmet-cam footage shows that the pod had images of Earth. The Eye has
given us mountains of data to suggest the ship is moving in that direction.
We have eyewitness accounts of the pod attacking without provocation. We
even have footage of the hormigas themselves. No one can refute this."

"Yes," said Dreo, "but no one will know any of that until they *open*
the message. Which these relay stations won't do. And even in the remote
chance that someone *does* open the message, they might dismiss what little evidence they look at as either a hoax or simply a mistake of our equipment. And if they think that, they'll do more than not pass it on, they'll
delete it."

"You make it sound hopeless," said Mother.

"I'm being realistic," said Dreo. "I'm telling you how the system works."

"We'll get other clans and families involved," said Father. "We'll tell
them where to look in deep space, something we should have done a long
time ago. We'll turn everyone's attention out here to the alien ship. Whoever has a sky scanner as good as our Eye would detect the ship and send
a warning message to Earth. Maybe if we build a swell of warnings, if we
make enough noise, something will get through."

"Maybe," said Dreo. "Probably. But how much time do we have here
before it reaches the Kuiper Belt? Six months? A year?"

"I've asked Edimar to give us a status," said Concepción. "She'll up-
date us on the ship's trajectory and position. Edimar?"

The crowd parted, and Edimar stepped forward. It was the first time
Victor had seen her since Toron's death. She looked exhausted and small.
Victor's heart went out to her. She had lost her father and sister in a few
short weeks. And now, with Toron gone, she had the overwhelming responsibility of being the family's only sky scanner. Her face was expressionless, and Victor knew that Edimar was doing what she always did:
burying her pain, holding everything in, closing everyone else out.

"As has been mentioned," she said, "we now know with some degree of certainty that the ship is on a trajectory with Earth. It could change its speed at any moment, but based on its current rate of deceleration, it will arrive at Earth in little over a year."

There was a murmur of concern among the Council.

"As for when it will reach the Kuiper Belt," said Edimar, "we obviously have much less time. I've run through the data over and over again now and it looks as if the ship will be relatively close to us in less than four months."

Everyone started talking at once, alarmed. It was loud and chaotic and Concepción called for order. "Please. Quiet. Let Edimar finish."

The talking subsided.

"We can't even reach Weigh Station Four in that time," said someone in the back.

"You're probably right," said Edimar. "I've done the math. The starship will likely pass by Weigh Station Four before we get there."

"Pass by?" said Dreo. "You mean the two will be close?"

"They won't collide," said Edimar. "There's little chance of that. Weigh Station Four will be a hundred thousand kilometers away from the ship's trajectory. That should be a safe distance."

"In relative space terms, that's not all that far," said Mother. "That's only a quarter of the distance from the Earth to the Moon. That's too close for comfort. We have to move now. Immediately. We need to warn the weigh station as soon as possible."

"We need to be clear about our warning, though," said Dreo. "We know plenty about the pod, but less about the ship. Such as its size. Do we even know how big it is?"

"Not precisely," said Edimar. "It's heading toward us, so we don't know its length. We can only detect the front of it. But even that is big. At least a kilometer across."

This time the reaction in the room was a stunned silence.

Victor thought Edimar had misspoken. A kilometer? And that was the ship's *width,* not its length. That couldn't be right. What could possibly be that big?

"Any of you are welcome to check my calculations," said Edimar. "I hope you can prove me wrong. But you won't. I didn't believe it myself until I rechecked it the fifth time. This ship is big."

And filled with creatures like those that killed Janda and Toron and the Italians, thought Victor. How many could fit in a ship that size? Thousands? Tens of thousands? And what about pods and other weaponized ships? How many pods could squeeze into a ship a kilometer across?

Sending a laserline wasn't enough, he realized. Dreo was right. A warning might get through, but not as quickly as it needed to, if at all. Any number of things could go wrong, and then Earth would be caught off guard. We need a contingency plan, he told himself. We need a way to get the evidence to Earth and in the right hands as soon as possible. No delays, no middleman holding up or deleting the warning. We need a person on Earth presenting the evidence to people that matter, decision makers, political leaders, government agencies. That was the only way it was going to get noticed.

It all became clear to him then. He understood in that moment what he needed to do.

"A quickship," said Victor.

Everyone turned to him.

"We need to send a quickship to Luna. The laserline is one approach we should pursue, but it shouldn't be the only one. If Dreo is right, there's too much of a chance the message won't get through. We can't risk that. There's too much at stake. We have to have a second means of warning Earth."

"What are you suggesting?" asked Concepción. "That we put all of the evidence on a data cube and send the cube on a quickship to Luna?"

"If we just put a data cube on the ship, it probably wouldn't get noticed," said Victor. "All of the quickships go directly to the mineral docks. They don't pass through human hands. And even if someone did notice the cube, we can't be certain that person would recognize its significance and put it in the right hands. What I'm suggesting is that we send the data cube with an escort. Someone rides in the quickship to Luna with all the evidence and then gets passage to Earth to deliver that evidence to the people who need to see it."

There was a pause as everyone stared at him.

"You can't be serious," said Selmo.

"Victor," said Concepción. "Flying a quickship around on a rescue mission with docking propulsion is one thing. Riding in one to Luna is another matter entirely. The quickship isn't designed to accommodate a passenger."

"I can fix that," said Victor. "I can build a seat and cover the cockpit with shields to block out cosmic rays and solar radiation. I can make it safe. The cargo hold is more than big enough for batteries and one of the large air tanks. And the suits are already designed for food intake and waste removal. It's just a matter of stockpiling the needed supplies."

"That trip takes six months," said Selmo. "You're proposing that someone ride in a quickship for six months?"

"A full cargo of mineral cylinders takes six months," said Victor. "A quickship with only a passenger and gear will take longer. You wouldn't want to accelerate and decelerate as quickly with a human inside. Too much G-force. Seven months or so is probably more accurate."

"You want to strap someone between two deep-space rockets and fire him like a bullet to Luna?" said Selmo. "That's insane. Who would be crazy enough to do such a thing?"

"I would," said Victor.

The room was silent. They looked at him. No one moved. To Victor's surprise, Mother didn't seem alarmed. Her face, instead of shock or disagreement, displayed a pained acceptance, as if she had been expecting this moment, as if she had known all along that Victor would propose such a thing, even though the whole idea had only just occurred to him. He had said nothing to her about his need to leave, about how his love for Janda had made it impossible for him to stay here. But from the look on her face, Mother somehow already knew.

He would apologize to her later in private for his suggesting to leave without first consulting with her and Father. But he knew, even as he considered this, that if he *had* conceived the idea beforehand, he wouldn't have mentioned it to them first. Not because he didn't respect them or because he thought they might object, but because it would mean admitting to their faces that he was leaving them, which he knew would break their hearts.

But wasn't it crueler to do it here, in front of everyone, where Mother and Father couldn't contest the matter as they would in private? No. Because here they could set emotion aside. Here, in the presence of everyone, it was easier to think of the greater need.

"I know it's dangerous," said Victor. "I know it sounds next to impossible. But if it *can* be done, aren't we morally obligated to do it? We can't rely on a single method of warning, particularly one as uncertain as an Earth-bound laserline. We need a backup. There are all kinds of considerations, I know. I wouldn't have greaves or a fuge or simulated gravity. So muscle atrophy is a concern, as is bone density, and blood volume. But if anyone is going to attempt a trip like that and put that much strain on a body it should be me. I'm young. I'm healthy. I'm at my prime. Plus I was born in space. I have an advantage over those of you who are older and were born on Earth and whose bodies have had to adjust. More importantly, I can make repairs. If anything happens to the rockets or the shields, I can fix them. No one knows quickships better than me."

"We can't afford to let Vico go," said Dreo. "He's too valuable a mechanic."

"We can't afford *not* to let me go," said Victor. "Everything we know so far about this alien ship suggests that it's a threat, maybe to the entire human race. This is bigger than El Cavador, bigger than all of us. Father knows more about this ship than I do. If something breaks, he can fix it. You have Mono, too. He's small, but he's incredibly capable. We can't think about what's best for us anymore. This is about Earth now, about home."

He had never called Earth home before, not out loud anyway. No one did, even those who had been born there. El Cavador was their home. The Kuiper Belt was home. But no one argued the point. They all agreed that their deeper allegiance lay with Earth.

"He's right," said Concepción. "If Victor can prove that a quickship flight is possible, for the sake of Earth, we should do it. I suggest we set out for Weigh Station Four immediately while Victor prepares one of the quickships. Once it's ready, we'll decelerate enough to drop him off and continue on to Weigh Station Four. If there are objections or better ideas, let's hear them now."

The crew was silent. Mother remained still, watching Concepción. Father put a hand on Victor's shoulder.

"Then let's move," said Concepción.

Victor worked for two weeks on the quickship in the cargo bay. Building the shields was the hardest part. Since he wouldn't be attempting any atmospheric entry, he could make the shields as heavy as they needed to be, which was good. He worried about cosmic rays penetrating the shields and interacting with the metal to form radioactive neutrons, so the thicker the better. He didn't stop there, however. He also installed water tanks all along the cockpit's interior to create another layer of protection. Then he packed radiation detection equipment and additional shield plates and tools in case he needed to make adjustments en route.

Mono helped of course, doing simple welding and cutting jobs, all while trying to convince Victor that he, Mono, should be allowed to come along. "What if you get hurt?" Mono asked one morning. "What if something happens to your suit? You might need someone to help you."

"I can't think of anyone I'd rather have at my side, Mono," said Victor. "But you can't come. It's too dangerous."

"Why is it too dangerous for me but not too dangerous for you?"

"It *is* dangerous for me. But I'm bigger. My body can take more of the abuse."

"I'm tough," said Mono, offended. "I can take abuse."

"It has nothing to do with toughness," said Victor. "It's more about body size and structure. You can't help how small you are. You're only nine. And believe me, it's not the kind of trip you'd want to go on anyway. It will be extremely boring. You know how it feels to be grounded to your room for a day?"

"It's cruel and unusual punishment."

"Right. Try doing that for two hundred and twenty days or so. No birthday parties. No Christmas. No playing with friends. No time with your parents. No fun repairs on the ship. No exploring. No desserts or cookies or fun treats. I won't even get to chew my food. I'll have to suck up vitamin mush through a straw in my helmet."

Mono made a face. "Gross. I hate that stuff."

"You and me both," said Victor. "And I'll be eating it every day for seven months. With no seasoning, no spreading it on bread to make it tolerable, no mixing it with sugary oatmeal, just straight, bland mush. Plus I have to wear a catheter and another device that's so disgusting that I'm not even going to explain what it is or how it works. Suffice it to say, it won't be comfortable. Then there's the abuse. My bones will thin and become susceptible to fracture. My muscles will weaken. My vertebrae will spread apart. My discs will swell with fluid, giving me backaches. I'll likely have decreased blood volume; maybe calcium deposits as my bones weaken, which will likely gather in my kidneys and result in stones; fatigue; not to mention possible impotency from radiation exposure."

"What's impotency?"

"Means I wouldn't be able to have children. But I'm hoping that's not the case. That's why we've got the shields and water tanks. My point is, it's not a party."

"But you'd be with me," said Mono. "That would be fun at least."

Victor smiled. "Trust me, Mono. You'd get sick of me. I'm pretty certain that *I'll* get sick of me."

Mono hung his head and began to cry. "I don't want you to go, Vico. I don't want you to get sick."

Victor set down his tools and floated over to Mono. "Hey, monkey brains. I'm going to be fine. I'm exaggerating everything. Isabella has all kinds of pills for me to take throughout the trip that will counter a lot of the discomfort. I'm not going to get sick. I may need some gym time once I arrive to get the muscles back up, but I'll be fine."

"But what if the hormigas get you?"

"The hormigas aren't going to get me, Mono. They're not going to get any of us. That's why we're hurrying to warn everyone, so that no one else gets hurt."

Victor wanted to tell Mono that he would return soon and that the two of them would be a team again when this was all over. Mono could continue as his apprentice. They'd learn the rest of the ship together. They'd invent things, build things, repair things.

But Victor said none of that because he knew it wasn't true. He wouldn't be coming back. Probably ever.

"El Cavador needs you here, Mono. My father needs you. When I'm gone you'll have to do more repairs around here. He'll be counting on you for all the small-hand work. He can't do it all himself. Listen to him. He's the best mechanic in the Belt. He'll teach you far more about this ship than I can."

"I don't want anyone else teaching me about the ship. I want to be *your* apprentice." Mono threw his arms around Victor's neck and cried into his shoulder.

Over the next few days Father ignored his work elsewhere on the ship and spent his time in the cargo bay helping Victor and Mono make final preparations for the ship. Mother found excuses to be there as well, doing small jobs to the quickship to make it as comfortable as possible. Father inspected Victor's work and kindly pointed out a few flaws. The two of them then selected the appropriate tools and addressed the issues together. It reminded Victor of all the years he had spent as Father's apprentice, following Father around the ship and handing him tools whenever Father needed them. Father had been indestructible then, as far as Victor was concerned. There was no machine in the universe Father couldn't repair. And even now, with Victor older and all of Father's weaknesses glaringly obvious, Victor still regarded Father with that same sense of awe—though now Victor's respect wasn't born from Father's capacity to fix things; it came from Father's capacity to love, his willingness to make any sacrifice for Victor and Mother and the family. Victor could see that now. Father and Mother were making the biggest sacrifice of their lives here. As painful as it was for them to see Victor go, somehow they knew that it would be more painful for him if he stayed.

Victor left the following morning. Nearly the whole family came to see him off. The quickship was ready in the airlock, having passed Father's meticulous inspection. All the supplies were boarded and secured. Victor's modified suit, which several of the women had prepared under Isabella's and Concepción's instructions, fit him better than he could have hoped. He noticed the catheter and the other uncomfortable devices he had to wear, but he found them more manageable than he had expected.

Isabella embraced him and made him promise he'd take his pills and follow the diet plan she had outlined. Victor carried his helmet under his arm, and Bahzím and the other miners knocked on it for good luck.

Edimar hugged him. "Get to Earth safe, Vico. When humans kill all the hormigas, I want to know it was you who told them to."

Next came Concepción. "The data cube is in the ship," she said. "Don't let anyone ignore you because you're young. Even though you have overwhelming evidence, it's going to be tough to find anyone to listen to you. You're a free miner. You're space born. That's two strikes against you on Luna. Don't give up. Find someone you can trust and follow your instincts."

"I'll do my best," Victor said.

Mother embraced him and gave him a small data card for his handheld. "This is from your father and me. Don't watch it until you're a month out."

Victor didn't question her. "I promise."

"I love you, Vico. If you weren't as smart and resourceful as you are I'd be scared to death. But if anyone can do this, you can."

"I love you, too, Mother."

Father wrapped him in his long, thick arms. "I'm proud of you. Don't take risks. Your goal is to get to Earth alive. Be smart. Whenever you have to make a decision ask yourself what your mother would do and then do that. She hasn't made a mistake yet that I know of."

Mother smiled.

Small arms wrapped around Victor's waist, and Mono looked up at him. "I'll be waiting for you, Vico. When you get back, I'll know this ship better than you do."

Victor smiled and tousled Mono's hair. "I don't doubt it, monkey brains."

He didn't linger after that. He moved into the airlock and climbed into the cockpit. Two miners in suits removed the anchor harnesses, opened the airlock, and pushed him outside.

All was silent. Before strapping himself in, Victor allowed himself one last look back at El Cavador. The airlock was already closed. As he watched, the ship began its slow acceleration toward Weigh Station Four.

He was alone. He looked at the data card Mother had given him and slid it into the slot on the side of his handheld. The icon appeared on the screen, but he didn't click it. He checked and rechecked his hoses and attachments. He did a sweep with the Geiger counter and found no signs of radiation, though he didn't expect to, not this early in the trip. He put the gear away and buckled in. The gel cushioning of the seat was thick and malleable. Once the rockets engaged, he would be pressed against it like a fist into bread dough. He clicked through his handheld and found the launch program to Luna. He had watched the miners initiate the program countless times before as they sent cylinders on to Luna. The rockets would accelerate quickly, far faster than a human could withstand. Victor had already researched human tolerance levels and altered the program to decrease the acceleration and lessen the Gs. But as his finger hovered over the launch button, he wondered if he had pulled back the rockets enough. He needed to get up to speed as quickly as he could, but he needed to be careful, too. He hadn't trained for this. His body wasn't ready. He pulled back the acceleration setting a little more, just to be sure, then pressed the button.

The program initiated. The rockets flared. The ship moved forward, slowly at first. Then the rockets went hot, and the quickship took off. Victor felt himself pushed back into the seat and knew immediately that he had misjudged. He should have pulled back farther. His face felt slack. His body felt heavy. He reached out for the handheld but his hand wouldn't obey him. His vision began to tunnel. His windpipe felt constricted. He was going to die. Two minutes into his journey and he was going to die. He thought of Janda and wondered if he would see her after this life. Mother believed such things, but Victor wasn't so sure. He hoped it was true, of course. He wanted nothing more than to see Janda again. Only, not now. Not yet.

His mind went blank.

Then all went black.

He woke sometime later, his body weightless. The ship was moving at an incredible speed, but it was no longer accelerating. No more Gs; this was a cruising speed. Victor shook his head and blinked his eyes, feeling foolish for his mistake. This didn't bode well for a successful trip. I nearly kill myself right from the start. Brilliant.

He blinked his eyes again. They no longer felt like they were boring into the back of his skull. His throat felt open and free. His whole body felt numb, as if all of his muscles were asleep from lack of circulation, which they probably were. His head pounded from a migraine. He felt nauseated and disoriented.

I need a fail-safe, he realized. If I have to decelerate and accelerate, I can't risk passing out and losing control again. He thought of the biometric sensors all over his body monitoring his vitals and wondered why he had never thought to connect them to the ship's operations. That had been a foolish oversight. He quickly whipped up a simple program on his handheld that would tell the ship to decelerate if his heart rate or blood pressure dropped below certain levels. He next devised a program to ask him questions periodically, to identify a number perhaps or to retype a word. If he couldn't, if he had lost his mental faculties for whatever reason, the ship would decelerate until he came to himself.

But what if I don't come to myself? he thought. What if I'm dead? If I die then the ship will decelerate and stay out here and never reach Luna. That wouldn't do. It would be better if he reached Luna as a corpse with the data cube than never reach Luna at all. He altered the program so that if his heart monitor flatlined for at least twenty-four hours, the rockets would accelerate to maximum and get his corpse and, more importantly, the data cube to Luna as quickly as possible.

Over the next few weeks, he occasionally accelerated and decelerated simply to train his body to withstand the forces, increasing the speed of acceleration and deceleration a little more each time. He blacked out often, but the ship responded well and decelerated whenever it happened, allowing him to come to himself quickly. Eventually he could stay conscious for two hours of fast acceleration. Then three hours. Then four.

In other areas, he wasn't doing as well. Eating had become a chore. Victor had assumed that he would eventually come to accept the vitamin mush over time, that eating it would become tolerable simply out of habit. But it didn't. If anything, the mush became more unappetizing with every meal, and he had to force himself to eat it while suppressing his gag reflex.

One of Father's ideas turned out to be a lifesaver. He had suggested that Victor bring along a hatch bubble to inflate periodically on a flat surface inside the quickship. With Victor inside and with the bubble filled with air, Victor could get out of his suit briefly and clean the suit tubes and brush his teeth and sponge his skin and do everything else he needed to keep himself sanitary.

The biggest challenge of the trip, even more taxing than the physical stress or the food or the cramped confines of the ship, was the sheer boredom of it all. He had assumed that loading his handheld with books and recordings and games and puzzles would be enough to stimulate his mind for seven months, but here he was wrong as well. His eyes strained from looking at the screen after a few days, and soon even listening became tedious. As he approached the month mark, his mind continually returned to the message Mother had left him. He considered opening it early—what difference would it make, after all?—but he always decided against it. He had made a promise.

He was so eager for something different, so desperate for a break in the monotony, that he found it hard to sleep the night before the message was to be opened. Eventually he slipped into slumber, and when he awoke, he clicked on the icon. Father had installed a holopad attachment to his handheld, and Mother's head appeared in the holospace. He lifted it and turned it toward him so that it was as if she were looking directly at him. Even before she spoke, Victor felt more alone and more isolated than he had ever felt in his life. He had six months more to go and already he hated this existence.

"You're a month out, Vico," Mother said. "And by now you're probably ready for this trip to be over. Hang in there, Viquito. Whenever you feel lonely watch this message. Know that your father and I are thinking about you and praying for your safe arrival. We're proud of you, and we know you'll be fine."

Mother paused to gather herself. Her voice had begun to break. She swallowed and sounded like herself again.

"But that's not why we've made this message. You're my son, Vico. My only child, the light of my life, so know that what I am about to say I say because I love you and want the best for you. Don't come back. Don't return to El Cavador. Under your seat, you'll find a disc with access codes to an account your father and I have set up for you. It's not much, but it's all we have. Concepción has donated all her savings as well. Use that money to enroll in a university on Earth after you give warning. Your mind is too valuable to waste in the Belt, Vico. You can do great things, but not here, not with us." Mother was crying now. "I'll always love you. Make us proud."

The message ended. Mother disappeared. They were releasing him. They were giving him a way to move on. He had wondered what he would do and where he would go after he had given the warning, and now he had his answer. The feeling of loneliness left him. He felt renewed, determined. He could endure six more months. For Mother and Father and Earth, he could endure it.

CHAPTER 16

Weigh Station Four

Lem was on the helm at the window when Weigh Station Four finally came into view. At first it was just a distant dot in space, indistinguishable from the countless stars behind it. But the navigator assured Lem that it was in fact the outpost, and Lem made the announcement to the crew. They answered him with whistles and applause, and a few of the crewmen nearest him gave him a congratulatory slap on the back, as if Lem had built the thing himself.

Lem didn't mind all the positive attention. He had told the crew months ago that they would be stopping here for supplies and a bit of shore leave before pushing on to Luna, and ever since then the crew had treated him warmly, smiling when they saw him, nodding as he passed. Suddenly he wasn't the boss's son. He was one of them.

Granted, supplies and shore leave weren't Lem's true motivation for the visit, and he felt a slight stab of guilt at all the celebration. The real reason for coming was to drop off Podolski so he could wipe El Cavador's computers. But since everyone did in fact deserve a little break, no harm no foul.

"Chubs, turn our scopes on Weigh Station Four and bring it up here in the holospace," said Lem. "I want to see what amenities await us."

In the Asteroid Belt, weigh stations were enormous enterprises, with all manner of entertainment for miners desperate to escape the monotony of their ships. Casinos, restaurants, movie houses. One near Jupiter even had a small sports arena for zero-G wrestling matches and other theatrics. So when the image of Weigh Station Four appeared large in the holospace for everyone on the helm to see, Lem knew at once that it was nothing like what everyone was hoping for.

The applause died. The whistling ceased. Everyone stared.

Weigh Station Four was a cluster of old mining vessels and sections of retired space stations connected haphazardly together through a series of tubes and tunnels to form a single massive structure. It had no symmetry, no design, no central space dock. Retired ships had been added to it over the years in a seemingly random fashion, connected to the structure wherever there had been room. It was like someone had rolled up a space junkyard into a sad little ball and decorated it with a few neon lights. It wasn't a weigh station; it was a dump.

Lem could see disappointment on everyone's faces.

"Well," said Lem, clapping his hands once. "I'm not sure which is uglier, a free-miner weigh station or free-miner women."

It wasn't particularly funny, but Lem had hoped to elicit at least a polite chuckle. Instead he got silence and blank stares.

Time to change the mood.

"The good news," said Lem, smiling and trying to stay chipper, "is that your stay at this delightful oasis of the Kuiper Belt is my treat. Drinks and food and entertainment are on me. Consider it an early bonus courtesy of Juke Limited."

As he expected, this news prompted another round of applause and whistles. Lem smiled. He had been planning to spring this surprise on the crew regardless of the station's condition, and now he was particularly relieved that he had thought of it beforehand. He would sell a load of cylinders to pay for the expense, but again Podolski was the real motivation here. Lem needed cash to fund Podolski's stay on the station and subsequent flight home, and he didn't want to use any corporate account for the expenses. Giving everyone a bonus was an expensive, albeit effective, cover for getting Podolski cash.

Lem ordered the crew to dock the ship near the depository, a massive warehouselike structure nearly as large as the station itself. Here free miners who didn't use quickships dumped and sold raw minerals or cylinders to the station at below-market value. The weigh station then sent it all to Luna in quickships for a profit. Most established families and clans had their own quickship system and used the weigh station only as a source of supplies. But the newcomers and start-ups without the full array of equipment still sold their mining hauls here.

Lem and Chubs left the airlock of the ship and stepped out into the docking tunnel. The drop master was waiting for them. He was a dirty little man in a jumpsuit and a mismatched pair of greaves on his shins who carried a holopad that looked like he had beaten it against the floor a few times. The air was warm and thick with the scent of rock dust, machine oil, and human sweat.

"Name's Staggar," the man said. "I'm the drop master here. You boys are Jukies, eh? Don't see too much of your type around here. Most corporates stick to the A Belt."

"We're testing the waters, so to speak," said Lem. "There are a lot of rocks out here."

Staggar laughed—a cackle that showed a train wreck of teeth. "Snowballs are more like it. If you can get through the frozen water and ammonia, you might find something. Otherwise, this is no-man's-land."

"You're out here," said Lem. "Business must be going well for you."

"Business doesn't do well for anybody out here, mister. This place used to be booming, long time ago maybe, but a lot of the clans have left. We scrape by like anybody else."

"Where do the clans go?" asked Lem. "I thought this was a free miner's paradise."

Staggar laughed. "Hardly. Most of the clans scurry back to the inner system, to the A Belt. They can't take all this space or the cold. I take it this is your first time out in the Deep."

"It's not deep space," said Lem. "It's only the Kuiper Belt."

Staggar scoffed. "Only the Kuiper Belt? You make it sound like a vacation spot. Got a summer home out here, do you, Jukie?" He laughed again.

"We'd like to sell some cylinders," said Lem. "For cash. Whom would we speak with about that?"

"You'd speak to me," said Staggar. "But I should warn you, you won't get the same prices here that you'll get elsewhere. We have to adjust to reflect the greater distance we find ourselves at. This is the outer edge. I'm sure you understand."

I understand that you're a crook, Lem thought. But aloud he said, "We're prepared to negotiate."

"I'm not promising we're buying, though," said Staggar. "Depends on what you're selling. We get a lot of folks trying to pass off gangue. So if that's what you're intending, don't waste my time. We don't want any worthless crap. We may look dumb to hoity-toities like yourself, but dumb we ain't, and you'll be wise to remember that fact."

"You strike me as a shrewd businessman," said Lem. "I wouldn't dream of conning you. I think you'll find our cylinders of high quality."

Lem nodded to Chubs, who had been holding a sample cylinder all this time. Chubs gently floated the cylinder in the air toward Staggar, and the man easily caught it. Staggar limped over to a scanner on the wall— apparently his mismatched greaves had a different polarity and affected his gait—and he slid the cylinder into the designated slot. In a moment the reading came back. Staggar tried to appear unimpressed.

"Your scanner doesn't lie," said Lem. "That's some of the purest iron-nickel I'll bet you've seen in a while."

Staggar shrugged. "It's decent. Nothing special, really."

"So are you interested or not?" asked Lem.

Staggar removed the cylinder from the scanner and turned to them, smiling. "Depends. You see, I got this little tickle in my brain that I can't seem to scratch. Why would a bunch of Jukies want to sell cylinders here? You boys have your own depository down near Jupiter."

"Jupiter's a long way off," said Lem, "and I'm eager to give my crew a break. All the cash you give us will likely go back into the economy of your weigh station here. So the way I see it, this is a win-win situation for you."

Staggar studied their faces, his smile broadening. "Well, aren't you the generous captain." He turned the cylinder on its side and began expertly spinning it in the air in front of him on the tip of his finger. "You're doing this out of the kindness of your heart, is that it? Giving the boys and girls on board once last hurrah before setting out for home?"

Lem didn't like where this was heading. "In so many words, yes."

Staggar laughed. "I told you I wasn't dumb, Mr. Hoity-Toit, and I meant it. A, a corporate never says what he means, and B, corporates never do squat for their crews unless there's something in it for them."

"You think I have some devious motivation," said Lem, acting amused. "Did it not occur to you that perhaps I want a break as well?"

Staggar shook his head. "No, it seems to me you boys want this one off the books, am I right? Don't want old Ukko Jukes to know you're skimming a little off the top for yourselves. Under-the-table mining, eh? Then you can scoot on home and tell your corporate stuffies that you didn't quite mine as much as you hoped. And everything you sell here, as far as they're concerned, never existed, while you drop a load of cash into your private bank accounts." He laughed. "I wasn't born on an asteroid, boys. I know a pocket scheme when I see one."

"Is this how you always do business?" Lem asked. "By insulting your customers first?"

"We ain't doing business until we understand one another," said Staggar. "You corporates must have iron balls to show yourself around here. This ain't the headquarters of the corporate fan club, if you catch my meaning. Lot of people here won't be particularly happy to see you."

"We didn't come to make friends," said Lem. "We came to sell a few cylinders and have a decent time. I doubt your merchants will mind us giving them our money."

"My money, you mean," said Staggar.

"How much per cylinder?" asked Lem.

"Can't answer that until you have an account," said Staggar. He began typing on his holopad. "Whose name should I put this in?"

Lem and Chubs exchanged glances.

"We'd rather avoid any record," said Lem.

"I'm sure you would," said Staggar, "but I can't buy without adding it to the inventory. You boys can skimp off your boss, but I can't skimp off mine. You get an account or no sale."

"Put in my name," said Chubs. "Chubs Zimmons."

Staggar looked at Lem. "Not your name, mister? Fancy clothes like that and from the way you were talking, I figured you for the captain."

"My name," said Chubs.

The drop master shrugged. "Suit yourself." He typed some more. With his eyes still down he asked, "Out of curiosity, where did you boys find this iron-nickel?"

"We'd rather not say," said Lem. "Trade secrets. I'm sure you understand."

Staggar smiled. "I figured as much. How much of this do you want to sell?"

"Depends on the price," said Lem.

"I'll pay you by the tonnage," said Staggar, "not by the cylinder."

"What price?" said Chubs.

Staggar told them.

Chubs was furious. "That's outrageous. It's worth twenty times that amount."

Staggar shrugged. "Take it or leave it."

Chubs turned to Lem. "He's trying to rob us."

"That's the cash price," said Staggar. "If you want to trade in food or fuel, I might be able to go a little higher."

"A little higher?" said Chubs, angry. "You're crazy if you think we'll accept that."

"You came to me," said Staggar. "I'm telling you my price. You don't like it, go elsewhere."

"He's right," said Lem. "We should have gone to Jupiter. Come on, Chubs. We're wasting this man's time." Lem turned and moved back toward the ship.

Chubs squinted down at Staggar. "Yes, you seem to have so much business here, why not let a big shipment like ours slip away? It's not like you need the money." He looked Staggar up and down, showing his disgust at Staggar's appearance, then turned away and followed Lem back to the ship.

Lem had his hand on the airlock when Staggar shouted at them.

"Wait. I have another price in case you boys got all stubborn and annoying, which you have."

"And what price is that?" said Lem.

Staggar told them.

"Double that amount and you've got a deal," said Lem.

"Double!" said Staggar.

"You'll still make a fortune," said Lem. "Which, if my calculations are correct, is more than the alternative. Zero."

Staggar glowered. "You corporates are all the same. Cocky thugs, the whole lot of you."

"From one thug to another, I'll take that as a compliment," said Lem.

Lem had his senior officers dole out the cash to the crew. It was less than Lem had hoped to give them but more than enough for a two-day break. Because of the low price he had received for the cylinders, he had been forced to sell more than he had intended, but he didn't worry. He still had more than enough to make an impression with the Board.

The inside of the weigh station was more attractive than the exterior, though not by much. Wherever Lem and Chubs went, merchants clamored for their attention, selling all variety of mining tools and worthless trinkets. It surprised Lem to see how many people lived here: several hundred if he had to guess, including children, mothers with infants, even a few dogs, which Lem found especially amusing since these had learned to jump from wall to wall in zero gravity. Lem soaked it all in, feeling at home for the first time in a while. He didn't belong in space. He belonged in a city, where the energy was palpable and the sights and sounds and smells were always changing.

They found a woman in the marketplace selling men's work clothes, and Lem bought nearly everything she had. Podolski and the two security guards might be on the weigh station for a while, and Lem thought it would be better for them to blend in and dress like free miners. He didn't know if the clothes would fit perfectly, but since no one at the weigh station had any concern for fashion and all the clothes were baggy anyway, Lem didn't think it mattered.

He paid the woman a large tip to deliver the clothes to the ship, and when the woman, who had a young boy with her, saw the sum of money in her hand, she was so overwhelmed with gratitude that she teared up and kissed Lem's hand. Lem could see that she was poor and that the child was hungry, so he gave her another large bill before sending her on her way.

"You getting soft on me?" asked Chubs.

"It looked like she had sewn the clothes herself," said Lem, shrugging. "Work like that should be paid well."

Chubs smiled as if he knew better.

They found a shoemaker next. Lem guessed at Podolski's and the security guard's boot sizes and then argued with the man about the prices. When they left, after the purchases were made, Chubs laughed. "I think you were trying to overcompensate for being nice to that woman," he said. "You took that shoemaker for a ride."

"He was trying to cheat us," said Lem.

"We could probably go back and find that woman," said Chubs, teasing. "Your father would be thrilled for you to come home with a bride."

Lem laughed. "Yes, my father would love a peasant free miner as a daughter-in-law. Especially one with a child. Father would be tickled pink."

They entered the food court area, where a dozen aromas assaulted them at once: pastries, pastas, breads, stews, even a few cooked meats, though these were exorbitantly expensive. They ran into Benyawe, and the three of them took a standing countertop at a Thai restaurant. It wasn't big enough in Lem's opinion to call itself a restaurant—there was only room for six people at the most—but Lem preferred the privacy.

Late in the meal Chubs raised his bottle. "To our captain, Mr. Lem Jukes, who salvaged our mission and turned a profit in the process."

Benyawe raised her bottle and joined the toast, but she didn't seem particularly agreeable to it.

"You shouldn't toast me," said Lem. "Our real thanks goes to the lovely Dr. Benyawe here, who tirelessly prepped the laser and conducted our field tests with aplomb. Without her brilliance, perseverance, and patience with her hot-tempered captain, we'd still be shooting pebbles out of the sky."

"To Dr. Benyawe," said Chubs.

Benyawe smiled at Lem. "Toasting me doesn't make you any more tolerable," she said.

"Of course not," said Lem. "I barely tolerate myself."

"And we would be wise to remember that our mission isn't over until we return to Luna," said Benyawe. "We're months behind schedule, and there are many on the board who no doubt have written this mission off as a cataclysmic failure."

Chub's smile faded.

"I'm not trying to spoil our evening," said Benyawe. "I'm merely reminding us all that we're still a long way from home."

"She's right," said Lem. "Perhaps we're a little premature in our celebrations." He raised his glass again. "Still, I'll toast Benyawe again for being such a wise counselor and an expert party pooper."

"Hear, hear," said Chubs, raising his bottle.

Benyawe raised her own bottle and smiled.

"Lem Jukes." The words came from the doorway.

Lem and the others turned to the entrance and saw a mountain of a man standing at the threshold. He was flanked by three other men, all rugged and dirty and not the least bit friendly looking.

"So you *are* Lem Jukes," said the big man. "Mr. Lem Jukes himself. Son of the great Ukko Jukes, the richest man in the solar system. We're practically in the presence of royalty."

His three friends smiled.

"Can I do something for you, friend?" said Lem.

The man stepped into the room, ducking his head through the door frame as he entered. "I am Verbatov, Mr. Jukes. And we are not friends. Far from it."

"What grievance do you have with me, Mr. Verbatov?"

"My friends and I were part of a Bulgarian clan working the Asteroid Belt four years back. Nine families in all. A Juke vessel took our claim and crippled our ship. Our family had no choice but to break up. Each of us went our separate ways, working what ships would take us on. The way I see it, Juke Limited owes us for damages. The value of our ship and all the hell we've been through since."

A silence followed. Lem glanced at Chubs and chose his words carefully. "You were done an injustice, sir. And for that I am sorry. But your fight isn't with me. We aren't the people who took your claim or damaged your ship."

"Doesn't matter," said Verbatov. "You're Juke Limited. The son of the president. You represent the company."

"Our lawyers represent the company," said Lem. "I'm about as far down the chain of command as you can get. If you have issue with how you've been treated, I suggest you take it to the courts."

Verbatov laughed. "The courts near Mars or Luna, you mean? Billions of klicks from here? No. I'll take an out-of-court settlement, thank you. And don't bother telling me you don't have the cash. I have it on good authority that you just came into a bit of money and have a sizable load on your ship."

"Staggar is a friend of yours, I take it," said Lem.

Verbatov smiled.

"What's the agreement you two have?" asked Lem. "You get back his money for him, and he gives you a cut? I find that surprising, Mr. Verbatov. You don't seem like the type of person who gives back much of anything."

Verbatov chuckled. "Am I that transparent, Mr. Jukes?"

"You are indeed," said Lem.

"Pay us what we rightly deserve," said the man.

"The money isn't mine to give," said Lem. "It belongs to Juke Limited."

"Which owes us," said the man.

"Write a complaint," said Chubs. "We'll see that it gets to the right people."

Verbatov's smile faded. He motioned to one of his men behind him. "You'll pay us what is rightfully ours, Mr. Jukes, or we'll be forced to have more conversations with your crew."

One of Verbatov's men entered, pulling a weightless body behind him. It was Dr. Dublin. His face was bloody and swollen, but he was alive.

"Richard!" said Dr. Benyawe, starting to move to him.

Chubs grabbed Benyawe's arm, stopping her.

Dr. Dublin looked dazed, unaware of his surroundings.

"Dr. Dublin has been quite the chatterbox," said Verbatov. "He told us all about this gravity laser you have on your ship. Turns rock into powder, he says. Very fascinating. Sounds like an entirely new way to mine rock. My brothers and I would appreciate a gift like that. That ought to cover our damages if Dr. Dublin was telling the truth, which I suspect he was, considering he broke a few of his fingers in the process."

Lem said nothing.

Verbatov looked down at Dublin and patted the man's head, gently pushing Dublin's floating body down toward the floor. "Unless you and I reach an agreement, Mr. Jukes, Dr. Dublin may accidentally break his legs as well."

The dart struck Verbatov in the throat, and for a moment Lem didn't know what was happening. There was a series of pops, and the men with Verbatov each slightly recoiled as darts buried into their chests, faces, or throats. Lem was confused until Chubs launched from the table toward the door, the weapon in his hand. Chubs pushed past Verbatov and moved outside, sweeping his aim to the right and left, looking for stragglers. Verbatov's eyes flickered and then closed. His shoulders slumped, but he stayed upright in zero gravity, his feet still held to the floor by his greaves. Chubs went back to him and put three more darts into his neck at point-blank range.

"What are you doing?" said Lem.

"My job," said Chubs. He grabbed Dr. Dublin and pulled his body toward the exit. When he reached Verbatov, Chubs pushed the man's upper body aside. Verbatov's feet, like the trunk of a tree, didn't move, but his torso bent to the side enough for Chubs to pull Dublin through the door and out into the hall. Lem and Benyawe followed.

Verbatov's men stood motionless like their leader, shoulders sagged, eyes closed. Chubs checked the men's necks for a pulse, clearly hoping not to find one.

"You killed them," said Benyawe.

"You can thank me later," said Chubs, pecking away at his handheld. "And I just sent an emergency command to every member of the crew on the station to get their butts back to the ship now."

Lem's own handheld at his hip vibrated as the message was received.

Chubs quickly pulled all the darts out of the men and deposited them into a small container.

"You killed them," Benyawe repeated.

The owner of the Thai restaurant approached, shocked. Chubs instinctively raised his dart gun. Benyawe stepped between him and the restaurant owner. "Enough. We're not killing innocent people."

Chubs shrugged then turned to Lem. "We need to move. I'll lead. You and Benyawe pull Dublin. Upright if you can. Not too fast. We don't want to draw attention."

Chubs put his hands in his coat pockets, concealing his weapon, and began walking quickly through the tunnels. They passed small pubs, kiosks, shops, and vendors. Everywhere they went they got looks from people—Dublin's bloody face was hard to miss—and people stepped out of their way, giving them plenty of room. The closer they got to the ship, the more crewmen they encountered. Several joined them as they went, took one look at Dr. Dublin, and quickened their step.

They didn't meet any resistance until they reached the docking tunnel. Staggar was blocking the way with four men. He carried a dart rifle draped across one arm. He saw the approaching crowd of Juke crewmen and smiled. "What's the hurry, Mr. Jukes? Leaving so—"

A dart buried in Staggar's chest, and an instant later his eyes closed. The rifle slipped from his grip and hovered in space in front of him.

The men with Staggar reached under their coats, but before they could extract anything, a cluster of darts embedded into their chests, necks, and faces. In seconds they were all silent and still.

Lem couldn't believe what he was seeing. All around him seven or eight crewmen had their weapons out, having just fired. Lem hadn't even known they had weapons.

"Are you out of your mind?" Benyawe shouted at Chubs.

Chubs turned to one of the crewmen, ignoring Benyawe. "I want every dart accounted for. No traces."

"Yes, sir."

The man and the other crewmen began removing the darts from the dead. Lem watched in amazement. No shock in their faces. No panic. Just quick unquestionable obedience. As if the crew had trained for moments such as these.

Benyawe stared at the standing corpses, then hurried to catch up to Chubs, who was moving for the ship. "You can't just shoot people like that and expect there to be no consequences," she said.

"The consequences of us staying here were far worse," said Chubs.

"They will come looking for us," said Benyawe.

Chubs stopped and faced her. "Who? The police? This is a weigh station, Doctor. We probably just did every store owner and trinket vendor the biggest service of their lives by killing off the thugs and criminals who have been pushing them around." He gestured to the dead. "These men are bad men. That simple enough for you? Probably murderers. Did you see the restaurant owner's face when Verbatov came in? The man was scared witless. There was a history there. By tomorrow, he and his store owner pals will be building a statue of us in our honor. Now, if you'd like to stay here and wait for the station security guard so you can apologize all formal like, be my guest. But this ship is leaving in six minutes or less, and I suggest you get on it."

Chubs went to the scanner Staggar had used earlier and called into his handheld. "Podolski, get out here."

In moments Podolski came out of the ship wearing the free-miner clothing Lem had purchased for him.

"Erase our existence," said Chubs, motioning to the scanner. "Every trace of this ship and our visit to this place is to be deleted. You understand?"

Podolski looked uneasy. He noticed the dead men at the end of the docking tunnel. "What's going on? What happened to those people?"

"It's nothing you need to concern yourself with," said Chubs. "Just do your job."

Podolski nodded.

"Now," said Chubs.

Podolski hopped to it, tapping at keys on the scanner.

Chubs turned to Lem. "You'll excuse me if I'm overstepping my authority here, Lem. It should be you giving these orders, not me."

Lem looked at Chubs, as if seeing him for the first time. "You're more than a ship's crewman for my father, aren't you?"

Chubs grinned. "You could say that."

"My father sent you on this mission to protect me. To keep me from getting myself killed."

"Basically," said Chubs.

Lem nodded. "Good. Keep it up." Lem turned to the gathered crew and spoke loud enough for all to hear. "My apologies, everyone. Our stay here is cut short. But frankly, if your day on this dump was half as unpleasant as mine was, getting back on this ship probably feels like a good idea."

Lem opened the airlock. Two of the crew went in first, carefully escorting Dr. Dublin inside. The other crew followed.

Podolski took another moment at the terminal then turned to Chubs. "Scanner's clean. We were never here."

Two crewmen came out of the ship wearing free-miner clothing.

"I took the liberty of choosing two of our best men," said Chubs.

"Good," said Lem.

Podolski looked frightened. "I've been thinking about this agreement we made," he said. "And I don't think it's a good idea anymore. This place isn't safe."

Chubs slapped him on the arm good-naturedly. "You'll be fine. Mangler and Wain here will provide all the security you need."

Lem regarded the two men. They stood there expressionless, like two cold soldiers. No, not *like* soldiers; they *were* soldiers. Father had loaded this ship with security personnel and Lem hadn't even known it.

"You can't leave me here," said Podolski. "What if these people think I'm responsible? What if they know I'm a corporate?"

Chubs and Lem joined Benyawe in the airlock.

"You'll be fine," said Chubs. "Think of this as a vacation."

Podolski opened his mouth and shouted a response, but the airlock door was already closed. Lem watched the man through the small window. Podolski looked panicked and furious. The two security personnel stood behind, not moving. Farther down the tunnel, Staggar and the other corpses stood with their boot magnets stuck to the floor and their arms out loose beside them.

"I don't suppose you're going to tell me why we're abandoning three of our crew," said Benyawe.

"Couldn't you tell?" said Chubs. "They wanted to stay."

Edimar flew down the corridor on El Cavador without looking at anyone. There were people all around her, going about their business, brushing past her, hurrying along their way, but Edimar pretended not to notice them. She couldn't bear to see their faces. Among them would be one or two people who still looked at her as if she were a fragile child. It had been months since Father's and Alejandra's deaths, yet there were still some in the family who always gave her that pitying look that said, "You poor thing. Your father and sister dead. You poor, poor child."

I am *not* a child, Edimar wanted to scream at them. I do not need your pity. I do not want your sympathy. Stop professing that you "know" what I'm going through or that you "know" what it feels like it or that you "know" how hard this must be for me. You don't know anything. Was it *your* father who was ripped open by an hormiga and left to bleed to death? Was it *your* sister who had likely been blown to bits or had the air sucked from her lungs? No, it wasn't. So stop pretending that you're some fountain of emotional wisdom who understands everyone's grief and pain. Because you don't. You don't know a thing about me. And you can jump in a black hole, for all I care.

She didn't mean it. Not that last part anyway. But she did hate the sympathetic looks and the mournful sighs they gave on her behalf, as if all life was hopeless now, as if nothing mattered in the world and she was resigned to spend the rest of her life wallowing in misery.

The single most infuriating moment had been when her aunt Henrika had told her, "It's all right, Edimar. You can cry." As if Edimar needed permission from this woman. As if Edimar had been damming back all of her emotion and was just waiting for some grown-up to cue her to open the floodgates. Oh thank you, Aunt. Thank you. How kind of you to grant me the right to cry in front of you and humiliate myself just so I can prove to you and your snotty, gossiping sisters that I am in fact sad. Happy, Auntie? Look, here's a tear, dropped from my very own eye. Take note. Spread the word. Edimar is *sad*.

It was so hurtful and demeaning and presumptive when her aunt had said it that Edimar almost *had* cried, right then and there in front of everyone in what would have been a burst of immediate tears. She had come so close. She could feel herself there at the precipice, so close to sobbing that the tiniest change in her breathing or the slightest tightening of her throat would have pushed her over the edge into uncontrollable sobs.

Yet fortunately, in some miraculous display of willpower, Edimar had kept her face a mask and not betrayed the horror and shock and pain she felt at Aunt Henrika's words. How could people, in an effort to be helpful, be so clueless of heart, so thoughtless and cruel?

It was especially infuriating because Edimar *did* cry. Every day. Sometimes for an hour at a time. Always alone in the darkness of the crow's nest where no one could see or hear her tears.

Yet apparently for the likes of Aunt Henrika, unless you're crying in front of everyone, unless you wore your grief on your sleeve and paraded your tears for all the world to see, you had no tears to shed.

Edimar turned a corner and pushed off a wall, shooting up the corridor. She knew she shouldn't be so petulant. No one was feigning sympathy. They all had her best interests in mind. Even Aunt Henrika, in her sad, condescending way. The problem was, the people who should shut up were the ones talking the most. It made Edimar grateful for people like Segundo and Rena and Concepción, people who didn't baby her or even broach the subject of Father's and Alejandra's deaths but who simply asked her about her work and told her about theirs. That's all Edimar wanted: to be treated like a person who could handle her situation instead of being expected to act like a sad, blubbery sack.

Dreo was waiting for her outside the dining hall. They had agreed to meet here before going on to Concepción's office to give their report. After Father's death, Concepción had asked Dreo to assist Edimar with the Eye whenever she needed it, and Dreo, like the eager commander he was, had relished this new authority. Edimar didn't need his help and certainly didn't want it, but Dreo still found opportunities to insert himself into her work. For propriety's sake, Dreo wasn't to visit Edimar in the crow's nest without another adult with him, and fortunately this had mostly kept Dreo away. Which was best. He knew next to nothing about how the Eye worked or how to interpret its data. He understood the operating system and nothing more. But just because you know how an oven works doesn't mean you can bake a soufflé.

"Did you bring your holopad?" Dreo asked.

So he was going to treat her like a child again. She kept her face expressionless and held up the holopad for him to see.

"Good. Is the presentation on it?"

Did he really think her an idiot? Or was Dreo this patronizing with everyone? Aloud she said, "You're welcome to look at it if you want."

He waved the idea away. "If there are flaws, I'll talk through them. Let's go." He turned and moved for the helm, expecting her to follow.

How kind of you, thought Edimar. You'll talk through my "flaws." What a team player you are, Dreo. Good thing we have your great intellect to rescue us from my flawed presentation.

Edimar sighed. She was being bratty again. So what if Dreo is a pain. So what if he takes all the credit. The world could be coming to an end. There are more important matters than me getting my feelings stung.

They reached Concepción's office and were invited inside. Concepción wasn't alone. Segundo, Bahzím, and Selmo were also present as well.

"I've asked a few of the Council to join us," said Concepción. "I want their input on this. I hope you don't mind."

"Not at all," said Dreo. "We prefer it."

It annoyed Edimar that Dreo would presume to speak for her. He was right of course; she did prefer more input. But Edimar hadn't expressed that to him, and she didn't like him making assumptions about her.

"We now know what the hormiga ship looks like," said Dreo. "It's close enough and moving slow enough for the Eye to create an accurate rendering. I'll let Edimar give the presentation, and I'll clarify points where necessary."

Oh, he'll "let" me give the presentation, thought Edimar. How kind. As if Dreo could give the presentation himself but was merely humoring a child, as if he knew the material better than she did, when in fact it was Edimar who had done ninety-five percent of the work. And he would clarify points? What points exactly? What did he know about the ship that she didn't?

She didn't look at him, worried that she might let her annoyance show. Instead she busied herself with the holopad, anchoring it to Concepción's desk and raising the various antennae. When it was ready, she turned on the holo. A computer-rendered image of the hormiga ship appeared in front of them.

The room went quiet. As Edimar had expected, everyone had the same slightly baffled expression. The ship was unlike anything humans had ever conceived. It was a large, bulgy teardrop shape, seemingly smooth as glass, with its pointy end facing in the direction it was traveling. Near the front was a wide-mouthed opening that faced forward and completely encircled the tip.

"To give you a sense of scale," said Edimar, "here's what El Cavador would look like beside it." A rendering of El Cavador appeared next to the hormiga ship. It was like holding a grape next to a cantaloupe.

"How can a ship that big move that fast?" said Bahzím.

"It doesn't even look like a ship at all," said Selmo. "It's circular. There's no up or down. It looks more like a satellite."

"It's too big to be a satellite," said Segundo. "Besides, we know the pod came from inside the ship. How it left the ship at such a high speed is anyone's guess, but it must have. What stumps me is that I can't see any obvious entrances or exit points."

"What about this wide opening here at the front?" said Bahzím, pointing.

Segundo shook his head. "If I had to guess, I'd say that was a ram drive. Victor suspected the pod was powered by one, and this looks like a similar design. The ship scoops up hydrogen atoms, which at near-lightspeed would be gamma radiation, then the rockets shoot this gamma plasma out the back for thrust. It would be a brilliant propulsive system because you'd have an infinite amount of fuel, and the faster you move, the more hydrogen you'd pick up and therefore the more acceleration and thrust you'd generate."

"Scoop-field propulsion," said Concepción.

"Is that even possible?" asked Bahzím.

"Theoretically," said Segundo. "It would only work on a ship built in space and intended for interstellar travel, though. You couldn't use a propulsion system like that to exit a planet or atmosphere. Too much G-force. You'd die instantly. But in a vacuum, you could accelerate quickly, safely. I wouldn't exactly call it a clean form of propulsion, though. It would be putting out massive amounts of radiation. You wouldn't want to fly behind it. Even at a great distance. If it's powered by gamma plasma, the plasma would likely interfere with electronics and sensors as far back as, say, a million kilometers or so. Stay in its propulsion wake too long, and it would cause tearing on the surface of the ship. And at closer distances, you'd probably get a lethal dose of radiation. Be right behind it, and you'd be disintegrated instantly."

"Lovely," said Selmo.

"What I don't understand," said Bahzím, "is how they can even see where they're going. I don't see any windows or visible sensors. The surface is completely smooth."

"It looks smooth, but it isn't," said Edimar. "At close inspection you can detect seams, indentations, and ridges. Like these circles." She typed a command, and four massive circles appeared on the ship, side by side, around the bulbous end of the teardrop. "We don't know what these are," she said. "Doors maybe. Or perhaps smaller ships that detach from the main ship. Whatever they are, they're massive."

"The whole thing is massive," said Bahzím. "Which makes me wonder about defense. How does it protect itself against collision threats? It would get pulverized by asteroids without a good PK system. But look at it. No pebble-killers. No guns. No weapons whatsoever."

"I couldn't discern any weapons either," said Edimar. "But it *does* have a PK system. I've seen it. Any object on a collision course is completely obliterated. Asteroids, pebbles, comets. All vaporized by lasers from the surface of the ship."

"The surface?" said Bahzím. "Where?"

"That's just it," said Edimar. "From *any*where on the surface. It can fire from any spot on the ship. It's like the entire ship is a weapon."

"How is that possible?" said Bahzím. "Lasers have to come from something."

Edimar shrugged. "Maybe there's some system below the surface that unleashes them. Maybe it has thousands of pores all over its hull that open and release the lasers. However it works, it's more powerful than anything humans have because it can fire as many of these as it wants at once. So instead of firing a single beam from two cannons like we do to hit a collision threat, the hormigas can fire a whole wall of laser fire."

The room was silent a moment.

"That's not exactly comforting," said Concepción.

"Nothing about this is comforting," said Selmo.

"Do we know what the lasers are composed of?" asked Segundo.

"No," said Edimar. "But I don't think it's photons. Their beams can be up to a meter thick and they act differently than our lasers. If you're right about the ram drive, if they're using gamma plasma as propulsion, it's not far-fetched to suggest that they use coherent gamma rays as their weapons, too. I mean, why not? If they can harness gamma plasma for propulsion, why not harness it and laserize it as a means of defense?"

"Weapons and fuel from the same substance," said Concepción. "That's certainly economical."

"Laserized gamma plasma?" said Selmo "That makes our PKs sound like a joke."

"They are a joke," said Bahzím.

"The composition of the lasers is all speculation," said Dreo. "What we *do* know is that their lasers only target collision threats. The hormigas aren't blasting everything in sight. They're conservative with their fire. They follow the same protocol of any other ship in that regard. Unless the object is set to collide with them, they ignore it."

"That's good news for us," said Edimar. "We're moving in the same direction as it is alongside the starship's trajectory. We're not on a collision course. When it passes us, it should ignore us."

"Unless it's blasting every ship in sight," said Bahzím. "Just because it didn't blow up a bunch of rocks out there, doesn't mean it won't gun us. What do we know? Maybe its mission is to destroy every human ship it sees. It didn't exactly leave the Italians alone, and they weren't a collision threat, either."

"We won't be close to it when it passes," said Dreo. "We're moving parallel to its trajectory but at a great distance. It's never fired on anything remotely close to this range."

"So it will pass us before we reach Weigh Station Four?" asked Concepción.

"Yes," said Edimar. "Which obviously means it will pass the weigh station before *we* reach the station, though not by much."

Concepción turned to Segundo. "Any luck with the radio?"

They had been trying for weeks to contact the weigh station, but without any success.

"Radio's only working for short distances," said Segundo. "We've been sending out messages to the station, but all we hear back is static. There's a lot of interference."

"Maybe the hormigas are scrambling radio," said Bahzím.

Segundo shrugged. "Who's to say they even know what radio is? They may have another communication system entirely. Or the problem might be the radiation their ship is emitting. Maybe that's disrupting transmissions somehow. Even at this distance. I don't know."

"So the station still doesn't know the ship is coming?" asked Bahzím.

"Not unless they've detected it themselves," said Segundo. "Which is possible, but I doubt it. It's not heading directly for them—it will miss them by a hundred thousand kilometers—so their computers probably won't alert them. And you know the guys they have manning the control room. They're overworked dockworkers, picking up overtime. They're not experts like Toron or Edimar. If it's not a collision threat, what do they care? If I had to guess, I'd say the station is completely unaware."

"The upside," said Dreo, "is that based on the hormiga ship's prior behavior, it will probably leave the weigh station alone and move right on by. We'll get there a day later, and we can use their laserline then."

Concepción leaned forward, staring down at the starship in the holospace. "For the sake of everyone on board that station, I pray to God you're right."

Podolski was hiding in a small rented room adjacent to a noodle shop on Weigh Station Four when the authorities found him. They kicked in the door after Podolski didn't answer it, and he cowered to the back corner of the room. He could tell at once that they weren't real police officials. They were rough men, dressed like the men Chubs and the ship's crew had killed at the docking tunnel before rocketing away and leaving Podolski here, stranded.

"Hello there," said the big man in the front. He had a European accent Podolski couldn't place. "You're a tough bird to find, friend. I had to ask three different people before we tracked you down." He laughed. "That was a joke, friend. Come on now. No need for tears. We just want to ask you a few questions."

Podolski wiped at his eyes. Was he crying? He hadn't noticed. He wondered where Mangler and Wain were. They were supposed to be protecting him. They were supposed to be right outside.

"Who are you?" said Podolski.

"You might say we're the keepers of the peace around here," the man said. "And seeing as how there's been a disruption in the peace recently, our first question is: Who are the new people on the station? Maybe they have some information on this. You follow me? Logical detective work."

"I don't know anything," said Podolski.

The man smiled. "Now, now, friend. Don't cut yourself so short. You know lots of things I'm sure. Like your name for instance. You know that much, don't you?"

"Gunther Podolski."

"Podolski," repeated the man, smiling. "You see? You do have information. Now, what ship did you come in on?"

"Where are my friends?" asked Podolski, finding his courage now. "The ones who were outside."

The big man tried to hide his annoyance. "Your friends are being cooperative, Podolski. We're asking them questions, and they're happy to answer them. You should answer them, too. It'll make it easier for everyone."

Podolski said nothing.

The big man eyed Podolski's bag anchored to the table and opened it. Inside were various holopads and equipment for accessing and wiping El Cavador. The big man whistled. "You're not packing light, are you Mr. Podolski? These are some fancy machines, all so shiny and new. If I didn't know any better I'd say this was corporate gear."

Podolski said nothing.

"I won't lie to you, Mr. Podolski, this is bad news for you." He held up the bag. "This is incriminating evidence. One of the honorable entrepreneurs of this weigh station was robbed and murdered two days ago along with several of his employees, and this bag makes you a prime suspect. Personally, I didn't much care for the man, but he was one of our citizens, and more importantly, he owed me a good deal of money. Then suddenly I find you, Mr. Podolski, a stranger with all this equipment for robbing people."

"That's not what it's for," said Podolski.

The man raised an eyebrow. "Oh? Got other plans, do you? Enlighten me."

Podolski said nothing.

The big man sighed. "You're not being cooperative, Mr. Podolski. I'm no lawyer, but that makes you look guilty." He took a step closer. "Now if you have Mr. Staggar's money, this could all be resolved rather easily."

"I don't have his money," said Podolski. "I don't know who you're talking about."

The man smiled. "You may not know his name, but you know the man. I'll refresh your memory. Dead guy. Docking tunnel. Ugly as a rock, probably from getting hit in the face over the years for being obstinate just like you."

The man's hand was suddenly around Podolski's neck, squeezing. Podolski gagged. His windpipe felt crushed. The man's fingernails dug into Podolski's skin.

"These aren't difficult questions, Mr. Podolski. I'm trying to be reasonable, and you're not meeting me halfway. So I'll be clearer for your sake. You give me whatever cash you took from Mr. Staggar, and I'll do a poor job with the paperwork and forget you and I shared words. That strikes me as a reasonable proposition. What do you say?"

Podolski saw spots. His lungs screamed for air. He wanted to assure the man that he didn't have what he was looking for. He tried to say, "I can't give you what I don't have." But all that came out in a wheezy desperate whisper was, "I can't."

The man took it as defiance.

Podolski was flying. The man had thrown him, and Podolski was weightless. Podolski went through the doorway and out into the marketplace, his arm striking the door frame as he passed. He heard something snap. His body spun. People screamed and dodged. He hit something else midflight—he didn't know what—then struck the shielded glass wall opposite and bounced away. The big man caught him in the air and slammed him back face-first against the glass. Podolski's arm was broken. He could feel it bent awkwardly behind him. The man was at his ear, saying something, but Podolski couldn't make it out. Everything sounded muffled and distant.

Beyond the glass was space, black and silent and sprinkled with stars. Podolski wanted to tell the man that he had money for passage to Luna. The man could have that. Podolski didn't care. But the words wouldn't form in his mouth. They were buzzing around inside him, but he couldn't grasp them and get them out.

He is going to kill me, thought Podolski. I am going to die here, alone, eight billion klicks from home.

There was a distant flash of light in space.

Then the sky was no longer black. It was a wall of green, flameless fire rushing forward. And in the microsecond before it consumed everything and burned up the world, Podolski realized that death was coming after all, though not in any way he had expected. Nor was he—it turned out—going to die alone. Wasn't life full of surprises?

CHAPTER 17

Allies

Concepción called the Council to the helm even though it was the middle of sleep-shift. The adults quickly gathered, groggy and unkempt and alarmed. "Weigh Station Four has been destroyed," Concepción said. "We just received the data from the Eye a few moments ago."

Their faces showed shock, horror, confusion. Those who had been half asleep were now wide awake.

"The hormiga ship unleashed a massive burst of its weapon as it was passing the station," said Concepción. "The station subsequently went dark. No light. No power. The main structure is mostly intact, but several pieces have broken off. We don't have any contact with the station, so we have no way to determine if there are any survivors. We've been trying to reach them for some time now, but without success. Segundo believes the weapon could be laserized gamma plasma. If that's accurate, then it's likely the station received a fatal dose of radiation."

"How many people?" asked Rena.

"We don't know," said Concepción. "Several hundred at least."

One of the Italian survivors began to cry, a woman, Mariana, who had lost her husband and four children. Rena put an arm around her, comforting her. The news was reopening a still-healing wound.

"I thought the hormiga ship was a distance from the station," said Segundo.

"It was," said Concepción. "Which is one of the reasons why we suspect this may not have been a tactical strike."

"Not a strike?" said Bahzím. "What could it have been? An accident?"

"Edimar will explain," said Concepción.

Edimar stepped forward, and a rendering of the hormiga ship appeared behind her in the holospace above the table. "It wasn't an accident," she said. "The hormigas deliberately fired their weapon. But based on what we've learned from the Eye, it's not clear if the hormigas were targeting the station."

"What else could they have been targeting?" said Rena. "If they hit it with a focused burst, it's too much of a coincidence to suggest they weren't aiming for it."

"That's just it," said Edimar. "The ship didn't fire a focused burst. It fired in every direction at once."

She hit a command on the holotable, and a simulation began. Gamma plasma ejected from all sides of the hormiga ship at once, growing outward, getting larger, until the ship stopped emitting the plasma, and the fast-growing wall of destruction became a giant ring with the hole in the center, continually getting larger as it stretched out in every direction.

"The hormiga ship didn't fire *at* the weigh station," said Edimar. "It fired at everything."

The simulation was on a loop and began again from the beginning.

"If it fired in all directions at once," said Rena, "and has a long range, why didn't we get hit?"

"Because we're much farther away," said Concepción. "Well behind the ship. Over two million kilometers. We're probably getting some radiation, but it has greatly dissipated by the time it reaches us. Not enough to damage us. Not a lethal dose. We were lucky."

"Don't know if I'd call this lucky," said Rena. "This means the ship's weapons are far more powerful than we thought."

"What if they *aren't* weapons?" said Segundo. "Or at least, maybe the ship wasn't using the radiation at that moment *as* a weapon."

"What do you mean?" asked Concepción.

"If it's sucking up hydrogen atoms at near-lightspeed and taking in all this radiation, it has to expulse it somehow," said Segundo, "especially when it's trying to slow down. It doesn't want to shoot it out the back like it normally does. That would only give it massive thrust. And it doesn't want to accelerate. It wants to *de*celerate. So it must be getting rid of the buildup some other way."

"And if its weapons and fuel are the same substance like we suspect . . . ," said Concepción.

"Then its weapons are the means of releasing all that buildup," finished Segundo. "Notice how the weapons fired in all directions at once at the same amount. That's logical, because if it released the plasma on just one side or if it released more plasma on one side than on the other, the plasma would generate enough thrust on that side to change the ship's course, which the ship doesn't want to do. Its course is set."

"So Weigh Station Four was destroyed by the ship's exhaust?" asked Selmo.

"If you want to call it that," said Segundo. "It's the one drawback of their weapon. The ship never stops collecting hydrogen. And when they're decelerating, that's a problem because they have no other way besides their weapons to dump all the excess. So they blast it out in every direction, and whatever happens to be right outside, tough luck."

"That's irresponsible," said Bahzím. "If you have a system like that, you have to make sure nothing is in the way."

"Apparently the hormigas don't care what gets destroyed," said Segundo.

"So the weigh station was at the wrong place at the wrong time?" said Rena.

"No," said Concepción. "The weigh station was destroyed by a careless species with no regard for human life."

There was a silence among them.

"What are we going to do?" asked Segundo.

"I've made a decision," said Concepción. "Only because one had to be made immediately. If you think I'm wrong, it's not too late to change that decision. But I don't think I'm wrong. I told Selmo not to decelerate. Rather than move for Weigh Station Four, we're moving to intercept the ship and attack it."

The reaction was fierce and loud as everyone began speaking and shouting at once. Concepción raised her arms to quiet them, but the tumult continued.

Segundo's voice thundered over everyone else's. "Quiet!"

The voices died.

"Let's hear her out," said Segundo.

"Thank you," said Concepción. "I know what I'm suggesting is extremely dangerous, but consider our situation. As far as we know, no one else is aware that this ship is headed to Earth. No one else knows it's killed hundreds of people, or that it has a weapon powerful enough to annihilate anything within a hundred thousand kilometers of it or more; or that its creatures care nothing for human life and will attack without provocation. We're the only people who know that. And right now we don't have any means of issuing a warning. Weigh Station Four is gone. We can hope that Victor will reach Luna and warn Earth, but he's still several months away. The hormigas will cover a lot of space in that time. And if we let them, if we do nothing, more people will die."

"How can we possibly stop it?" said Dreo. "We can't compete with its tech and weapons. A whole fleet of warships couldn't stop it. You thought going up against the pod was impossible? This would be a thousand times worse."

"We don't have to destroy it," said Concepción. "It might be enough to cripple it. That would give Earth more time to build a defense, or it would give military ships enough time to come and destroy it."

"And how would we cripple it?" asked Dreo. "We have five PKs. Five. Have we forgotten how big this thing is? We're a fraction of its size. Five PKs might not inflict any damage."

"I don't know how we'd do it," said Concepción. "That will require thought. But doing nothing isn't an option. If we let it go, families will die. Whole clans maybe."

"No offense," said Dreo, "but that's not our problem. We did our part. We destroyed the pod. We saved nine people. We sent Victor to Luna. We lost Toron and Alejandra and Faron. We've made our sacrifices. We've done our duty. What you're suggesting will get us all killed. This is out of our hands now. It's too big for us to solve."

"I agree with Concepción," said Edimar. "If we can make an attempt to stop it, we should."

"Of course *you* agree," said Dreo. "You lost half your family. You're angry. I, for one, would like to live. Besides, did we not just establish that they have a weapon that can destroy *everything* around it? How could we even get close enough to attack it?"

"Don't think of it as a weapon," said Segundo. "Think of it as exhaust."

"What difference does it make?" said Dreo. "If it fires it, we're just as dead."

"It does make a difference," said Segundo. "Because if it just unleashed a massive amount of exhaust, then it stands to reason that it won't release *more* exhaust for some time. If we're going to strike it, now is the time."

"You can't be serious," said Dreo. He looked at those around him. "Am I the only one who thinks this is insane? What about our children? Are we willing to risk them, too?"

"We don't have to do this alone," said Concepción. "There are other ships ahead of us. If we can contact them, we can enlist help. Maybe we could load the children onto another ship and keep that ship out of the fray."

"We're not a warship," said Dreo. "This isn't our fight."

"It *is* our fight," said Concepción. "It is most definitely our fight. That ship is a threat to every human alive. Now, if all of you tell me I'm wrong, if all of you disagree, then I'll stop the ship. Otherwise, we're attacking that ship."

"How can we enlist help with all this interference?" asked Rena.

"The radio will work for up to a few hundred kilometers," said Segundo. "It's the long-distance messages that can't get through. If we get close enough to another ship, we can get a high-bandwidth message through. Holo to holo."

"Who would help us?" said Bahzím.

"We'd have to be selective," said Concepción. "The only mining ships that could likely intercept the hormigas are ones that are already moving in this direction at a high velocity. There isn't time for other ships to change their course and accelerate up to our speed. Selmo, what ships ahead of us qualify?"

Selmo wiped his hand through the holospace and busied himself with the data from the Eye. "I've got ten ships in front of us, but only two of them are matching our speed and moving in our direction."

"Two ships?" said Bahzím. "That's not much of an assault, especially if one of them is going to take the women and children."

"What are the two ships?" asked Concepción.

"One's a WU-HU ship," said Selmo. "D-class. A drill digger. About half the size of us. Not much of a fighter, really."

WU-HU was a Chinese mining corporation, a direct competitor of Juke Limited, though they were small potatoes in comparison. Concepción liked WU-HU. They stayed to themselves and didn't resort to claim jumps or clan bullying. If anything, they respected free miners. Whoever the captain was, Concepción was almost certain he or she would help.

"What about the other ship?" asked Concepción.

Selmo looked at the data and frowned. "It's certainly a fighter. Well defended. Plenty of guns. Strong hull. But I'll be damned if we want *his* help."

Concepción knew at once whose ship it must be.

"It's Lem Jukes," said Selmo.

Lem grabbed a meal box and found Benyawe already eating at one of the dining counters. "I have an idea that I'd like you to pursue, Dr. Benyawe. Something to keep you busy on the flight home."

"We're not exactly twiddling our thumbs in the lab, Lem. We do work."

Lem smiled. "Naturally this would be in addition to your current duties with the glaser."

"And if I refuse? Will you abandon me at the next stop like you did Podolski?"

"Podolski had a special assignment and will be well taken care of," said Lem. "He has passage to Luna. We didn't abandon him. The whole thing was his idea."

"He must've forgotten that when we left him behind. He didn't seem too eager to stay."

"Going to the weigh station was a mistake," said Lem. "I take full responsibility. I had no idea it was crawling with criminals. We took decisive action, and I don't think anyone can begrudge us for self-defense. How's Dr. Dublin?"

"Recuperating. The doctors reset the finger breaks. He's in a cast and taking meds."

"Good." Lem pulled the tab on his meal box, allowing the food to float to the top of the container where he could suck it up with the straw.

She studied him a moment. "Did we kill those men because they knew about the glaser?"

Lem sighed. "*We* didn't kill anyone, Doctor. Chubs and his security team, working under my father's instructions, saved our lives. And no, they didn't kill them to protect corporate secrets. We were threatened. You were there. Now, put it out of your mind. I need that brain of yours focused on other matters."

"Your idea."

"I agree that gravity focusing is the future of the company, but not in its present state, not as a glaser. It's too unstable. The subsequent gravity field is too unpredictable."

"We've been working sixteen-hour days for almost two years, nearly getting ourselves killed to demonstrate this glaser for you, Lem, and suddenly you're not interested?"

"On the contrary. I'm very interested. But I think you'll agree our current model needs some work. I'm merely making a suggestion on how to improve it. If it's a terrible idea, you'll tell me. You're the engineer, not me."

"What's the idea?"

"Two glaserlike devices connected to each other like a bola that can be placed on opposite sides of an asteroid. Like earmuffs. They operate under the same principle, but their gravity fields counter each other, so the asteroid is still ripped to shreds by tidal forces, but the gravity field doesn't grow to unstable levels. It's far more contained. The rock is still ground to powder, but nobody dies."

"I'll put a team on it," said Benyawe. "I'll oversee it personally. It's a good idea. It's worth exploring."

Lem was surprised. He had expected a polite, yet slightly condescending lecture on how the idea was appreciated but far too impractical, a verbal pat on the head that essentially said, "Why don't you leave the thinking to the grown-ups?" After all, how could he presume to think of something they hadn't? They were the most brilliant minds in their fields. He wasn't a scientist; he didn't know physics, not to their level anyway. Yet Benyawe was going with the idea. Or was she merely placating him? No. It *was* a good idea. It *did* have promise. And isn't this what entrepreneurs do? They have ideas, and they call on people who can make them happen. Isn't that what Father had done?

Lem left the dining hall with a spring in his step, which was easy in zero gravity. Everything was finally working out. It was all coming together. He had four cargo bays nearly full of cylinders as a gift for the Board. He had successful tests with the glaser. Podolski was handling the snafu with El Cavador, so that would go away. And now, if Benyawe and her team pulled through, he might return to Luna with plans for the next generation glaser, an idea for which he could largely take credit.

Lem smiled.

He had gone through a rocky patch, yes, but the old Lem Jukes was back. He stopped and checked his reflection in one of the shiny metallic columns positioned throughout the ship. He hadn't shaved in two days, but he liked the stubbly facial hair. It was that rugged, devil-may-care look that women he had known seemed to swoon over. He put his shoulders back and checked his profile. It was the look of a leader, a face that demanded to be followed. He had Father to thank for that.

He straightened his jacket, checked his other profile, and continued on. He hadn't gone far when he passed a female crewmember—someone who worked in the kitchen by the looks of her. He gave her his best smile, and the woman nodded and blushed, continuing on her way. So he still had it. After almost two years out of the game, he hadn't lost his appeal.

He took the tube to his quarters and wondered whom he should call on when he returned to Earth. It probably wasn't too early to think about that. If he achieved a more prominent place in the company as he expected, it would pay to have a woman at his side. Not necessarily a wife, per se. But someone who could accompany him to corporate engagements and charm members of the Board.

Lem put on some music, took off his greaves and vambraces, and floated over to his computer terminal. There was no shortage of beautiful women in his contact list: women of enterprise, medicine, science, entertainment, even a Danish countess, though Lem had found her rather self-absorbed eventually. He clicked through their photos and smiled at the memories. Many had progressed to a third or fourth date, but rarely had they gone any further. Lem traveled too extensively and worked too heavily.

The most recent entry was over two years old, he noticed, but that was to be expected: Lem had been in space. Other entries were as old as seven or eight years, which surprised him. Had it been that long? Worse still, he hadn't maintained contact with any of them, even though he had promised to stay in touch with them all. He suddenly realized how foolish he would sound trying to contact them when he returned. Hey, remember me? We had dinner seven years ago and I was completely charming and then never called. Shall I pick you up at eight?

How classy. Lem allowed his eyes to readjust until he saw his own reflection on the terminal screen. He was kidding himself, and he knew it. He pushed off the desk, found his razor, and shaved. Stubbly hair indeed.

He was towel-drying his face when an alert popped up in the holospace above his desk. Lem waved his hand through it, authorizing the message. Chubs's head appeared in the holospace. "We're getting a high-bandwidth radio message over an emergency frequency, Lem. And you won't believe who it is."

"Someone we know?"

"El Cavador," said Chubs.

Lem froze. El Cavador? How was that possible? "I thought the radio was down. I thought we had interference." They hadn't received any messages for days now.

"The interference mostly affects long-range transmissions," said Chubs. "If a transmission is close enough and strong enough, it gets through apparently."

"How close is El Cavador?"

"A day behind us. Matching our speed."

Lem swore under his breath. A single day. They were practically on top of them. Well that was just perfect.

"It's worse than you think," said Chubs. "They're asking for you personally."

Lem closed his eyes. Everything was coming apart again. Podolski couldn't have wiped El Cavador already. It was too soon. The free miners had been tracking him. They must have read Lem's files and now they're coming to name their price for the files' safe return.

"What do I tell them?" asked Chubs.

For a moment, Lem considered not taking the transmission. If he ignored them, maybe they'd go away. But no, if extortion was their agenda, they'd only go somewhere else and sell the data, which would be worse. "Put it through," said Lem. "But I want you watching and recording this holo, Chubs. You alone."

"Understood."

Chubs winked out, and the woman's head appeared in the holospace. She looked exactly as she had months ago: old and commanding and made of steel.

Lem checked his collar then leaned his face into the holospace so that she could see him as well. There would be a time delay in their conversation, and the length of the delay would depend entirely on how close the two ships were.

The old woman spoke first. "Mr. Jukes, I had hoped that our paths would never cross again, but circumstances demand it. I am Concepción Querales, captain of El Cavador. We are contacting you because we require your assistance. Weigh Station Four has been destroyed. I am sending you all the files I have to prove this fact to you and your crew."

Lem said nothing. If files were coming, he knew Chubs would immediately start combing through them. But Weigh Station Four destroyed? Impossible. Lem had left there, what, less than a week ago? This was a trick. They were plotting something.

As if Concepción could read his mind, she said, "Everything I am about to tell you will sound ludicrous to you, and you will no doubt think this some ploy on our part to seek revenge for your attack on our ship. I assure you this is not the case. I am contacting you, Mr. Jukes, because we are desperate for your assistance. An alien ship has entered our solar system. Among the data I have sent you are its trajectory and coordinates. You can look for yourself and see that it's there. This ship is already responsible for the deaths of an estimated six hundred people, including everyone aboard Weigh Station Four and three members of my own crew. Among the data I've sent you is a video of the alien species. This is not a joke, Mr. Jukes, and I would not be contacting you unless we were in dire need. I am sending you rendezvous coordinates. A WU-HU vessel in the area has agreed to join us in an attack on the ship six days from now. Our hope is that you will add your ship's strength to ours. The alien ship continues to decelerate, and if we all accelerate and change our course slightly, we can intercept it and save countless lives, perhaps Earth itself. I will give you and your crew three hours to review our data and respond. Please acknowledge message received and intention to respond."

Lem didn't move, trying to keep his face free of any surprise. "Message received. We will respond. Makarhu out."

He pulled his face out of the holospace. Chubs's head appeared almost instantly in front of him. "We got their files. I thought it might be loaded with a virus, but it's clean. The navigator ran the coordinates she gave us for the ship."

"And?"

Chubs shook his head. "You better get up here, Lem. There's something out there. Something like I've never seen."

Lem and Chubs spent two hours going over all of the data from El Cavador. When they finished, they immediately went looking for Benyawe. They found her down in the engineering room with six other engineers, drawing rudimentary designs on the wall of Lem's new idea for the glaser.

Benyawe smiled when Lem entered. "Mr. Jukes, we were just discussing this bola-shaped design of yours. Perhaps you could explain to the engineers what you explained earlier to me?"

"Some other time," said Lem. He touched a button, made the drawings disappear, and turned to the gathered engineers. "If you'll excuse us, we need a moment with Dr. Benyawe in private on an urgent matter." He gestured to the door. The engineers exchanged glances, startled, then quickly gathered their things and left. Chubs locked the hatch behind them.

"You've got my attention," said Benyawe, with a look of concern.

Lem first played the holo message from Concepción. Then he played the vids from El Cavador on the wall. Benyawe watched everything in silence, showing little reaction, like a calculating scientific observer. She didn't even jump as Lem had when the hormiga showed itself on the surface of the pod. When the vids were over, she asked specific questions, and Chubs answered by putting the rest of the data from El Cavador up on the wall. Benyawe was silent as she read through it, clicking through the various windows, checking the math, rechecking the coordinates.

When she finished, she turned and faced Lem. "We can't call them hormigas. That's Spanish for 'ant.' The scientific community would never approve of a living language classification. It needs to be the Latin. Formic. At least that's my professional recommendation."

Lem blinked. "Who the hell cares what we call them? I've just showed you a damn alien species, Benyawe. What difference does their name make?"

"All the difference in the world," said Benyawe. "This is the greatest scientific discovery in our history, Lem. This changes everything. This answers the most fundamental scientific question out there. Are we alone in the universe? The answer, obviously, is no, we are not. And further, we're not the most technologically advanced species, either, which will sting every human's pride, I suspect."

"I am not interested in science, Doctor," said Lem. "Your scientific mind might be tickled pink at this discovery, but my mind, my logical, practical, reasoning mind, is peeing in his mind pants. There is an alien ship out there rocketing toward Earth with unimaginable firepower and likely malicious intent. Now, if there is any chance whatsoever that this is a hoax and Chubs and I are gullible idiots, tell me now."

"No," said Benyawe. "This is legitimate. The evidence is incontrovertible."

"No doubt in your mind?" asked Chubs.

"None. We need to relay this information to Earth immediately."

"We can't," said Chubs. "Long-range comm is currently shot because of the interference."

"Even the laserline?" asked Benyawe.

"The transmitter's out," said Chubs. "El Cavador believes the venting of the alien ship may have damaged external sensors as far away as a million kilometers. We hadn't tried sending a laserline in a while or we would have noticed the problem sooner."

"Now you know what we know," said Lem. "How do we respond to El Cavador? I've already gotten Chubs's opinion. Now I want yours."

Benyawe looked surprised by the question. "We tell them we'll fight, of course. We tell them we'll be at their side, giving them everything we've got. We have to stop that ship, Lem. Destroy it if we can, though I suspect their captain is correct. Crippling it is the best we can hope for. But as for our answer, it must be a resounding and absolute yes. The Makarhu will join the fight."

Lem nodded gravely. "That's what I thought you would say."

"You disagree?" asked Benyawe. "It's my vote against both of yours?"

"No," said Lem. "The decision's unanimous. We attack these bastards."

CHAPTER 18

Formics

Two heads floated in the holospace in front of Concepción: Lem Jukes and Captain Doashang of the WU-HU Corporation. Their ships were still several days away from intercepting the Formic ship, but they were now close enough to each other that a three-way conference was possible without much interference. Concepción, despite feeling exhausted and suffering through a flare-up of arthritis in more places than she cared to count, put her best face forward in the holospace. Let them see my eyes and know that we as a family will not fail them.

There were introductions. Doashang seemed a most capable captain. Lem Jukes had an air of his father about him, which was to say confident in a way that was both alluring and off-putting at the same time. He was in his mid-thirties if Concepción had to guess. A child, really. Less than half her age. Goodness she was old. She had still been on Earth when she was that age, working in her father's bodega in Barinitas, Venezuela, convinced that she would be stuck there in the heat and dust for the rest of her life, selling cold bottles of malta to the banana farmers as they came down from the fields.

How wrong she had been.

After the introductions, Lem wasted no time getting into tactics. He had surprised Concepción by accepting the call to help so readily, and Concepción had assumed that it was Lem's conquering spirit—his need to subdue and bully—that had motivated him. But now, as he offered up ideas and showed concern for the safety of the other ships as well as his own, it occurred to Concepción that perhaps Lem's compulsion to help might be driven by a genuine desire to protect Earth. That put Concepción's mind at ease. Selfish motivations led to abandonment and betrayal in a fight, and if any of them hoped to survive, they would have to trust each other implicitly.

"If the pod took direct hits from the Italians and suffered no visible damage," Lem said, "we can only assume that the main ship has the same shielding."

"We won't win this with lasers," said Concepción. "The moment we open fire, the Formics will know we're there. The instant they're aware of us, we're in trouble. They could vent their weapons like they did near Weigh Station Four, and we wouldn't know what hit us."

"Then how will we attack them?" asked Doashang.

"The Italians couldn't damage the pod with laser fire," said Concepción, "but a few of my men were able to land on the pod and cripple its sensors and equipment with tools."

"There are no sensors or equipment on the surface of the Formic ship," said Lem. "It's smooth. There's nothing to attack. Besides, it's moving at a hundred and ten thousand kilometers per hour. Are you suggesting we put men on the surface of that ship at that speed?"

"That's exactly what I'm suggesting," said Concepción. "The only way we know of to penetrate their shielding is to be on the surface, right there on the hull. We know the surface of the pod was magnetic, so there is a high probability that the surface of the main ship will be as well. If our men are equipped with magnets, they could crawl on the surface of the ship and plant explosives. We could set these on a timer with enough of a delay to get our men back to our ships and to move the ships a safe distance away. If we're lucky, we can get in and out without the Formics even knowing we were there."

"That avoids a firefight," said Doashang. "I like that aspect."

"What if the hull is so strong that explosives don't damage it?" asked Lem. "We don't know what material the ship is made of. It could be impervious to attack. It could be ten meters thick."

"If that's the case, then nothing we do can stop them," said Concepción. "But we won't know that until we at least try. And if the hull is impenetrable, then we've learned something valuable. That's intelligence that will help whoever fights them next."

"I'm assuming you have explosives," said Lem.

"I'm assuming all of us have explosives," said Concepción. "Don't you occasionally use explosives to break up surface rock or open up a shaft?"

"I'll have to check with our quartermaster," said Lem.

"Aren't you outfitted?" asked Concepción. "You very forcefully took our dig site. I assumed you wanted it for mining purposes. What were you going to do with it if not extract minerals?"

There was an awkward silence. Doashang looked back and forth between them.

"I'll check with our quartermaster," Lem repeated.

"You do that," said Concepción. "Because the more explosives we plant, the more damage we'll obviously inflict."

"How would this work?" asked Doashang. "How do we safely get men onto the surface of the ship after we match its speed?"

"We make ziplines using mooring cables," said Concepción. "Then we fire cables with magnetic anchors down to its surface. When the cables are secure, our miners clip onto the line and fly down to the surface with their propulsion packs. They can't be wearing lifelines because we can't fly that close to the Formic ship. But they could wear portable oxygen and batteries. They plant the explosives, crawl back to the mooring cable, then they either fly back up or we pull them up with the winch."

"That's a lot of moving parts," said Doashang. "A thousand things could go wrong. What if the magnetic anchor hitting the ship alerts them? Or what if the surface of the ship can detect movement?"

"Possibilities," said Concepción. "But unlikely. When we attacked the pod, the Formics only surfaced after we had damaged their equipment. We literally crashed into the side of them and spent several minutes on their hull before they responded."

She was silent then, letting them mull it over.

Finally Doashang said, "I don't have a better idea. And I agree that stealth is best. We don't have a winch on our ship, though. So we'd be no help with the cables."

"Actually I was going to suggest that your ship stay out of the fight entirely," said Concepción.

"Why?" asked Lem.

"One of us needs to stay behind," said Concepción. "The intelligence we have is too important to die with us. We sent one of our crewmen to Luna with much of this intel, but we have no way of knowing if he'll arrive alive or if anyone will take him seriously. If this attack fails, someone needs to communicate everything we know with Earth. I suggest that be your ship, Captain Doashang. You can record everything from a distance. We can load all of the women and children from our ship onto yours prior to the attack in the event that something happens to us."

"I agree," said Lem. "Your ship is the smallest and least armored, Captain Doashang. If anyone stays back it should be you."

Doashang sighed. "I don't like being an observer. But I agree that everything we know must be relayed to Earth. If I'm to take on your noncombatants and children, we'll have to dock our ships in flight at high speed, which is dangerous. We can't decelerate to dock or we'll never catch the Formic ship."

"We'll have to trust our computers and pilots," said Concepción. "I'll have our crew make preparations immediately."

Rena went to the docking hatch at the designated time, carrying a small bag with a single change of clothes. Segundo stood beside her, an arm around her shoulders. There was commotion all around them: infants crying, mothers shushing them, small children flying about despite their parents' stern commands to be quiet and still. A few of the women were crying too, particularly the younger mothers and brides, clinging to their husbands who were staying behind. Rena refused to cry. To cry was to acknowledge that something terrible might happen, that this parting between her and Segundo could be their last, and she refused to believe it.

The proximity alarm went off, startling her. It meant the WU-HU ship was close now, preparing to dock. Frightened children flew into their parents' arms, and everyone watched the docking hatch at the end of the corridor. The hatch was solid steel without windows, but Rena stared at it as if she could see the approaching ship on the other side.

Segundo's hand went to his handheld and turned off the alarm. Silence retuned to the corridor, then Segundo's voice was loud. "There may be a jolt when they dock. Everyone get close to a wall and hold on to something."

Parents immediately pulled their children in close and floated to one of the walls, clinging to a pipe or a handhold. Segundo and Rena moved to a corner and anchored themselves.

"Docking the ships like this is ridiculously dangerous," said Rena quietly, and not for the first time.

"It's necessary," said Segundo.

"It is *not* necessary. We should be staying on the ship. Or at least I should. There's no reason for me to go. I don't have small children. Our only son isn't even on the ship anymore. I should be staying with you. I'm useless on that ship."

"You're not useless," said Segundo. "You have a talent for comforting others. These women need you, Rena, now more than ever. You can be a strength to them."

"I can just as easily be a strength to you."

He smiled. "And you always will be. But you can't be by my side through this. I won't be on the ship."

She turned her head away from him. She didn't want him speaking about the attack. She knew the particulars; he had told her the plan and the risks he would be taking, but she didn't want to think about it. To think about it was to imagine every possible thing that could go wrong.

He put his arm around her waist again. She turned back to him and saw that he was smiling at her gently. It was the smile he always gave her when he realized it was pointless to argue with her and he was conceding defeat. Only this time he couldn't concede. She couldn't stay. It would cause a panic. Other women would then insist on it, and those with children who wanted to be near their husbands would then be torn. Leaving would suddenly look like abandonment and not a command they were forced to obey.

Rena felt safe right then. Despite the docking, despite the hormigas or Formics or whatever they were called now, she felt safe with his arm around her. She had wanted to argue with him and to object again to the whole stupid affair, but his smile had burned away the fight in her.

There was a violent jolt as the WU-HU ship touched down, and several people screamed. The lights flickered. Rena put a hand to her mouth, stifling her own cry. Then it was over. The ship steadied, and for a moment all was quiet. Muffled noises then sounded on the other side of the docking hatch as someone secured a seal and pressurized the airlock.

The light above the hatch turned from red to green, and two sharp knocks clanged on the hatch. Bahzím opened the hatch, and an Asian man floated through. His uniform suggested that he was the captain, and Concepción approached him and greeted him. Words were exchanged, though Rena couldn't hear. Concepción then turned to everyone in the corridor and said, "Captain Doashang here has taken a great risk to dock with us, and we appreciate his kindness in taking you onto his ship until this matter is over. Please show him the same courtesy you have always shown me. Now let's do this quickly. Single file, keep the line moving."

The people closest to the hatch began to gather their things and move.

Rena suddenly felt panicked. It was happening. They were moving already. She hadn't said good-bye. This was too quick. She turned to Segundo. He was looking down at her. He put his hands on her arms and smiled in that disarming way again, the way that blocked out everything and everyone around her, that look of his that could silence all the world for her.

People around them were moving into position, getting into line.

Rena ignored them. There were a million things she wanted to say to him—nothing that hadn't been said already every day of their married lives, nothing that he didn't already know. But still she wanted to say them. Yet "love" suddenly felt like such a small word. It wasn't love that she felt for him. It was something much greater, something that she didn't have a word for.

He slid something into her hand. She looked down. It was two letters sealed in envelopes. Her name was written on one. The other was for Victor. Her tears came instantly. No, she was not taking letters. A letter is what husbands write to their wives when they don't think they're coming back. And he was coming back. This wasn't good-bye. She wouldn't even entertain the thought. She shook her head, pushed the letters back into his hand, and closed his fingers around them.

"You can read me that when this is over," she said. "And you can give that letter to our son someday."

He smiled but seemed a little hurt.

"I'll make you dinner," she said, wiping at her eyes. "Then we'll squeeze into a hammock, and you can read me every word. Nothing would make me happier."

"Aren't you curious to know what it says now?"

She put a hand on his cheek. "I already know what it says, mi cielo. And I feel the same way."

He nodded. His true smile returned. He put the letters back in his jacket. "I get to pick the hammock," he said. "A very small hammock. It may be crowded. You'll have to float very close."

She embraced him, holding him tight, wetting his shirt with her tears.

The line was moving. Half of the people were already gone.

"You better go," he told her.

She cleared her throat and composed herself. What was she doing crying like this? She took a deep breath and wiped at her eyes. This was absurd. She was overreacting. Everything was going to be fine. He took her bag and offered her his arm.

"I can carry my own bag, silly," she said. "It's weightless."

"Never deny a man his chivalry," said Segundo.

She shrugged, relenting, then linked her arm in his and let him escort her to the hatch.

When they reached the hatch, he gave her back her bag. The line never stopped moving. Their arms parted. She was going through; there was no time to stop. She looked back and saw him once before she was forced to turn a corner. A hand took hers and gently pulled her into the WU-HU ship. It was a female member of the crew, young and Chinese and beautiful. "Huānyíng," the woman said. And then in English, "Welcome."

"Thank you," said Rena.

The lights on the WU-HU ship were brighter than she was accustomed to. She squinted, letting her eyes adjust. The ship was sleek and modern, with tech everywhere, nothing like El Cavador. She moved to where the other mothers and children were gathered, giving words of comfort and embraces where she knew they were needed.

The hatch closed. The two ships separated. The crew moved Rena and the others to their quarters. The rooms were small, but everyone would have a hammock at least, and besides, it was only for a few days. Rena moved to place her bag in the designated compartment and saw that the bag was open. Odd. She was sure she had closed it. She looked inside and found items she hadn't packed. Two sealed envelopes. One addressed to her, the other addressed to Victor.

Mono wasn't getting on the WU-HU ship. Of that he was certain. He had come to the docking hatch with Mother and all of the other women and children, but just because he was nine and small and technically a child didn't mean he couldn't help on El Cavador. Hadn't Victor told him that he would have to step up and help Segundo more? Wasn't that his job? Who would do the small-hand work for Segundo if the ship needed repairs? No, he was staying. He had a duty. Except for one problem. Mother. She was holding his hand like a vice. For this to work, Mono was going to have to lie. And he hated lying, especially to Mother.

He watched as the docking hatch opened, and the WU-HU captain floated into El Cavador. The man spoke briefly with Concepción, and then Concepción made an announcement. Show the captain respect. Be good. Blah blah blah. The same instruction every adult always gave. Of course everyone would be good. We'll be staying on someone else's ship. Guest rules. Everybody knows that.

Except Mono *wouldn't* be staying there. He'd be staying right here. He turned to Mother and saw that she was crying. Not openly, not big tears like girls his age would shed just so an adult would come running, but real tears, quiet tears, the ones Mother never wanted Mono to see.

He squeezed her hand and spoke gently. "It's going to be all right, Mother."

She wiped her face, smiled, and lowered herself so they were eye to eye. "Of course it will, Monito. Mother is being a blubbery boo." It was a word she used whenever he caught her crying this way, and he smiled. He knew he was probably too old for such childish words, but they always helped Mother stop crying when she said them, and so Mono didn't mind.

He noticed then how the other women were clinging to their husbands and saying their good-byes. Mother had no one. Father had gotten sick when Mono was too young to remember, and the medicine Father had needed hadn't been on board.

Mono watched as Mother gathered their things and moved into the line, still wiping at her eyes. How could he leave her now? She would be terrified to discover him not on the ship. It would break her heart. She would be furious.

But hadn't she told him that he was the man of the house? Hadn't she called him her little protector? Always in a way that was cute, yes, always in a way that suggested she really didn't mean it. But wasn't it true? He *was* the man of the house. He *was* her protector. And if he could prove that to her, if he could make it real for her, maybe she wouldn't cry so much. Maybe all the sadness she felt for Father would go away.

"I want to go to the front of the line with Zapa," said Mono. Zapatón, or Big Shoes, was a boy Mono's age—probably his best friend if you didn't count Victor or Mother or Segundo.

"Stay with me, Monito."

"Please. I want to see inside the ship."

"We'll be in the ship in a moment."

"But Zapa's father gave him a handheld that has a Chinese translator on it so we could greet the crew in Chinese."

It was a lie. And it was the lowest of lies to use on Mother. He knew that if he inserted another child's father into the story, if he made it seem like he was missing out on some privilege or opportunity because he had no father to give him such things, Mother would relent.

She sighed, annoyed. "Stay where I can see you."

Mono didn't wait for her to change her mind. He launched upward, grabbed a handhold, turned his body, launched again, and landed beside Zapa, who was sniffling and wiping at his eyes.

"What are you crying for?" asked Mono.

"My papito. He's staying behind." Zapa had six bothers and sisters, all of whom were ahead of him in line, as was his mother.

"I need you to pretend that I came with you on the ship," said Mono.

Zapa wiped his nose across his sleeve. "What?"

"I'm not getting on the WU-HU ship, but I need you to make it look like I did."

"You're not getting on the ship?"

"Listen. When you get inside, my mother is going to come looking for me. Tell her I'm in the bathroom."

"Which bathroom?"

"The bathroom on the WU-HU ship."

"But you said you weren't getting on the WU-HU ship."

"I *won't* be in the bathroom, meathead. I'll be here, hiding on El Cavador."

Zapa's eyes widened. "Are you stupid? You're going to get me in trouble."

"I need to stay and help. Just tell my mother I took the handheld with the translator into the bathroom to study Chinese."

Zapa made a face. "You're talking loco, Mono. Está tostao."

"Just tell her."

They reached the hatch. Mono looked back. Mother was talking to someone else, not paying attention. Mono stepped away from the line and hid behind some crates as Zapa and his family went through the hatch. Mono stayed there, not moving until long after the hatch closed and the WU-HU ship flew away.

Lem brought up the rendering of the Formic ship and enlarged it as much as he could in the holospace over his desk in his room. Benyawe and Chubs floated nearby, watching him. "Why not simply shoot the thing with the glaser?" asked Lem. "Why not blast the Formics to smithereens and be done with it? None of this flying down to the surface and planting explosives. We fire the glaser and turn the ship to dust."

"It wouldn't work," said Benyawe. "The Formic ship is too big and too dense. The glaser wasn't designed for that type of mass. It was designed for rocks."

"Asteroids are filled with dense metals," said Lem. "Compositionally they're essentially the same thing."

"Let's not forget what happened that last time we fired the glaser," said Benyawe. "It's too unstable. We have no idea what type of gravity field would result, if any at all. Nor can we assume that the same metals we find in asteroids are the ones used to construct this ship. The Formics may use alloys unlike any we've ever seen. All we know is that the surface of that ship is designed to resist collisions and high radiation at near-lightspeed, which means they're incredibly strong. Far stronger than any asteroid."

"If that's the case, then what good will explosives do?" asked Chubs.

"How the ship responds to the explosives will tell us a great deal about the hull's strength," said Benyawe. "But that's not the only reason why I question the glaser. Consider our speed. We're traveling at a hundred and ten thousand kilometers per hour. The glaser wasn't built for that. If we extended it out of the ship to fire, it would likely be struck by something and ripped to shreds. Even tiny space particles would render it useless. It was designed to fire from a stationary position. Our spacesuits have heavy shielding. The glaser doesn't."

"Then we build some shielding for it," said Lem. "You're engineers. You figure it out."

"Easier said than done," said Benyawe. "This would require time we don't have and resources we may not have."

"We've got four cargo bays full of metal cylinders," said Lem. "You have all the metal you need."

"Yes, which would require smelting and reshaping and building," said Benyawe. "We're engineers, Lem. We're not manufacturers. We draw up plans. Someone else makes them."

"Free miners can build engines with space junk and bonding glue," said Lem. "Surely we can build a shield for the glaser."

"I am not a free miner," said Benyawe. "I wish I had the capabilities you'd like me to have, but I don't. We can poll the crew and perhaps find people with all the skills required, but again, the glaser is not the answer, even with shielding. In all likelihood, all the glaser would do is alert the Formics of our presence and seal our own doom. We'd accomplish nothing, and they would blow us to dust before we knew what hit us."

"Well then," said Lem. "That's a pessimistic position if ever I heard one."

"You asked for my scientific opinion," said Benyawe, "and as an engineer on the very weapon you want to use, I'm giving it to you. You're the captain, Lem. You're the one who will decide, not me. I'm merely giving you considerations so that you can make an informed decision."

Lem sighed. "I know. I'm being a snot. It's good counsel. I'll relay to El Cavador that we have explosives." He excused them then, put his face in the holospace, and called El Cavador. After a short delay, Concepción's head appeared.

"We can contribute twenty-five men," said Lem. "We're not operating on a full crew, so I'm putting in all the men I can afford. And we have explosives."

Concepción showed no emotion. "Thank you."

He waited for her to say more, but she didn't. "Now to another matter, Captain," he said. "When we last met, you downloaded files from my ship."

"When we last met, you killed one of my crew, crippled my ship, and risked the lives of everyone in my family, including women and children."

He had to be careful how he responded. She was probably recording this transmission, and he couldn't make any statement that could be used against him in court. An apology would be an admission of guilt, as would telling her that he hadn't intended to hurt anyone. But it was best to avoid such statements anyway. Unless he broke down and sobbed like a penitent churchgoer, she'd probably think him insincere. Better to ignore the issue entirely.

"Downloading our files constitutes theft," he said.

"Killing my nephew constitutes murder."

Lem resisted the urge to sigh. "Come now, Captain," he wanted to say. "Must we play this tit for tat game of who is guiltier of the greater crime? Besides, it would be involuntary manslaughter, not murder, and probably a much lesser charge if Juke lawyers jumped into the fray." But aloud he said, "What are your intentions with this data?"

If she was going to blackmail him, he wanted to be done with it. If she intended to sell it to a competitor, maybe he could convince her otherwise. He was more than willing to dip into his personal fortune to make this go away.

"Our intentions were to find out who the captain of your ship was," said Concepción. "We wanted to know who would be cruel enough to do such a thing."

"Yes, but what are your intentions now?"

She seemed confused. "What do you expect our intentions to be? That we will use your corporate secrets against you, sell them on the black market perhaps, contact one of your competitors?"

"Yes, actually."

She laughed. "We're not like you, Lem. As difficult as it might be for you to believe, there are decent people in the universe who don't scheme or push aside others for profit. I haven't given your files any consideration since we took them. We've been occupied with trying to stay alive. If you would like me to erase them from our system, I will gladly do so. They are of no use to me."

"Right now?" Lem couldn't believe what he was hearing. "You'll erase them immediately."

"I'll give the order, the moment we terminate this call."

"How do I know you're not lying? How do I know you won't keep them or sell them?"

She shook her head, pitying him. "You won't know, Lem. You'll have to take my word for it." She moved as if to end the call, then turned back. "Incidentally, we sent you a laserline before you attacked us, warning you about the Formic ship. But since you had left your position to conduct your unprovoked strike against us, you didn't receive that message. Which is too bad. If you *had* received it maybe you wouldn't have killed my nephew and destroyed our laserline transmitter. Which means we could have warned Weigh Station Four and everyone else a long time ago. If you have an ounce of soul, Lem, I suspect that knowing that—knowing the ramifications of your decision, knowing how damaging your selfishness really is—will keep you up at night far longer than losing your precious corporate files."

Her face disappeared, ending the transmission.

How dare she, thought Lem. How dare she blame him for the destruction of Weigh Station Four. He pushed away from the desk. Free miners. Dirty little scavengers. He shouldn't have mentioned the files. Now she'll suspect they have great value. She's probably contacting the WU-HU ship to try and sell them right now.

No. He knew that wasn't true. She was erasing them. She hadn't been lying.

But had she really sent him a laserline warning him of the Formics? Or was that some ploy to make him feel guilty? What had Father said? "Guilt is the greatest weapon because its cuts rarely heal and it aims for the heart."

No, Concepción Querales was nothing like Father. Father might try to burden Lem with guilt for some personal gain, but something told Lem that Concepción didn't play that game. Deceit and dominion and the twisted manipulation of human emotion weren't the old lady's style.

Mono stood in the cargo bay, twisting his pinkie finger and wishing he were a million klicks away.

"What were you thinking?" said Concepción. "You disobeyed direct orders and you terrified your mother."

Mono felt himself shrink a little. All of the men who had stayed behind, along with Concepción, stood nearby, looking down on him, furious. Even Segundo, who never got angry, now looked as if he was ready to give Mono the spanking of his life. Mono cursed himself. He should have thought his plan through a little better. Of course Mother would eventually figure out that he wasn't on the WU-HU ship. She would realize Zapa was lying sooner or later. He couldn't pretend Mono was in the bathroom forever. But Mono hadn't thought that far ahead. He hadn't considered what would happen next. Mother had gone to the WU-HU captain in tears, according to Concepción, and the captain had radioed immediately to El Cavador. After that it was just a matter of Concepción getting on the ship's loudspeaker and telling Mono, wherever he was on the ship, to get his butt to the cargo bay immediately.

"What do you have to say for yourself?" asked Concepción.

"I wanted to help," said Mono. "I'm good with the small-hand work. Vico said so. You might need that."

Concepción rubbed her eyes.

Segundo turned to Concepción. "What are we going to do? I wouldn't recommend we dock again. The WU-HU ship hit us hard. We took a little structural damage, nothing to be concerned about, but enough to weaken the area around the docking hatch. I wouldn't risk another high-speed dock if we don't have to."

"You've put us in a very difficult position, Mono," said Concepción. "I thought Vico had trained you better."

That did it. He could bear the angry looks of two dozen men; he could tolerate a good tongue-lashing; but to think that this would disappoint Vico, to think that Vico would disapprove, that was too much for Mono to bear. He covered his eyes and began to cry. "Don't tell Vico. Please. Don't tell Vico."

To Mono's surprise, they responded with silence. No one lashed out. No one told him he couldn't be an apprentice anymore. They just stood there and watched him cry. Finally Concepción spoke again, and this time her voice was calm. "From now on Mono, when I give you an order or when your mother gives you an order, you will obey it. Do I make myself clear?"

He nodded.

"I want to hear your answer," said Concepción.

"Yes, ma'am."

"I appreciate your willingness to help, Mono, but lying to your mother and getting others to lie for you is not how we operate. We are family."

He wanted to tell her that it was *for* the family that he had stayed and *for* the family that he had lied, but he didn't think that would help his situation.

She made him stand off to the side while the men checked their equipment. Helmets, suits, propulsion packs, magnets, helmet radios. Mono watched them work, feeling foolish and angry with himself. He had frightened Mother when all he ultimately wanted to do was drive her fear away.

Segundo set up a workbench to assemble the timers and magnet discs to the explosives. The explosives weren't live. That required a blasting disc, which the men would insert into the mechanism when they set the charges on the Formic ship, so there was no chance of them detonating prematurely. Segundo enlisted four men to help him assemble the timers, but it quickly became clear that the men were out of their element; they could set explosives, but they didn't know wiring and chip work. Finally, after forty-five minutes, Segundo excused the men and called Mono over.

"Don't think this means you're not in trouble," said Segundo.

Mono kept his face a blank and didn't say a word. He worried that he might say the wrong thing or smile at the wrong time and anger Segundo and spoil his chance to help.

The timers were a cinch to assemble. He and Vico had done similar work on other things dozens of times. It was just a matter of cutting and rewiring and making a few taps with the soldering gun. The magnet discs were a little trickier, and Mono ended up changing the design Segundo had started. Instead of having the magnets *underneath* the explosive, which would dampen the explosive's damaging effect to the hull, Mono used smaller magnets around the rim of the device and increased their attraction with a second battery. It was nothing innovative, really. Mono was merely copying something Victor had done when they had repaired one of the water pumps. But Segundo, who had been watching him silently work, picked up the piece when Mono was finished and nodded. "This is the kind of thing Vico would do."

It was more praise than Mono could have hoped for, and even though he thought it might get him in trouble, he couldn't help but smile.

Segundo secured his helmet and stepped into the airlock. They were minutes away from reaching the Formic ship, and a quiet intensity had settled among the men. They had drilled their maneuvers so many times over the past few days—using a wall in the cargo bay as the hull of the Formic ship and setting down dummy explosives over and over again until it was second nature—that Segundo didn't feel nearly as much anxiety as he thought he would. They could do this.

Once everyone was in the airlock and the door secured, Bahzím had them check and recheck each other's equipment. Segundo was especially thorough with those around him and found nothing out of order. Concepción then gathered them in a circle for prayer, asking for protection and mercy and that a heavenly hand watch over the women and children. At the "Amen," Segundo crossed himself and offered his own silent prayer for Rena and Victor.

Everything moved quickly after that. Bahzím ordered them to clip the D-rings of their safety harnesses onto the mooring cable that would be shot down to the surface of the ship. Segundo positioned himself at the front of the line so that he would be the first one on the Formic ship. He knew that many of the younger men were watching him closely, and he suspected it would put them at ease to see him leading out. Concepción strapped herself into the seat on the winch. She would pull everyone in once the charges were set. Segundo couldn't remember the last time he had seen her in a suit and helmet.

"Remember," Concepción said. "Your suits weren't designed for spacewalks at this speed. They'll protect you from collisions with space dust, but anything bigger will rip through you like shrapnel. So the less time you spend outside the better. Bottom line, move fast. Set the explosives, click back on the cable, and I'll reel you back in. Nothing to it."

Right, thought Segundo. Nothing to it. Just perform a spacewalk at an insane speed, cling to magnets for dear life, and take down an alien ship fifty times our size. Easy.

He turned on his HUD, and windows of data popped up on his visor. He blinked through a few file folders until he found the family photo he was looking for. A candid shot of him, Rena, and Vico at some family gathering a few years ago. He smiled to see how small Vico was then, still a boy. He had grown to his man height so quickly. Segundo's smile faded. He wondered where Victor was at the moment, rocketing toward Luna all these months, his health slowly deteriorating.

Video taken from inside Lem Jukes's helmet popped up on Segundo's HUD. "We're in position," said Lem. "Give the word."

The Makarhu was approaching the Formic ship on the opposite side, and Lem, like Concepción, was manning the winch on his ship. The plan was for Lem to fire his cable onto the hull at the same instant El Cavador fired hers. Then both ships would send out their men.

"We're opening our doors," said Concepción.

The large airlock doors opened wide, and Segundo stared in wonder and horror at the size of the ship before them. El Cavador was over a hundred meters from the ship, yet the view of the ship filled the entire airlock doorway. Segundo had seen renderings and models of the ship, but until now he hadn't grasped the sheer immensity of it. It was larger than any structure he had ever seen, and yet it was so smooth and uniform and singular in its design that it didn't seem like a structure at all. It didn't seem like something *made*. It seemed like a giant drop of red paint falling from heaven to Earth. The color surprised Segundo, though he wasn't sure why. What had he expected? A menacing black?

These are not ignorant monsters, he realized. They are every child's worst nightmare. The monster that thinks. The monster that can build and move fast and defy every defense. I've been in denial, he realized. He had seen the pod, he had seen their tech, but the obstinate, dominant-species part of his brain had refused to believe that a face so horrific and antlike could be more innovative or intelligent than human beings. Yet here was the proof. Here was a whole kilometer of proof.

"Are you sure you want to go through with this?" asked Lem. "Are you seeing what we're seeing?"

"We see it," said Concepción. "And I'm more convinced than ever. We cannot let this reach Earth."

"You're right," said Lem. "But I don't like it."

Segundo agreed. He wasn't convinced that they'd be the ones to stop it, but it had to stop.

"Makarhu, are you ready to fire your cable?" asked Concepción.

"Makarhu ready," said a man's voice.

"On my mark," said Concepción. "Four. Three. Two. One. Cable away."

The mooring cable shot forward with a large round magnet at its end. Segundo watched the cable uncoil as it flew toward the ship. It seemed to go forever, and then it struck the surface, holding firm. Concepción gunned the winch, and pulled in the slack. The cable was taut. Bahzím was shouting, "Go, go, go!"

Segundo launched himself out and thumbed the trigger on his propulsion pack. He shot forward toward the ship, keenly aware that he was also moving in the direction of the ship at one hundred and ten thousand kilometers per hour. The smallest rock chunk would kill him, and the thought prompted him to press the thumb trigger harder. The Formic ship was coming up fast. A beeping message in Segundo's HUD warned him of an impending collision and urged him to reduce his speed. Segundo ignored it. He needed to get down fast or he'd slow down the line. Thirty meters. Twenty. He hit the second thumb trigger, and retro boosters on his thighs and chest quickly slowed his descent. Two seconds later he was bringing his feet up in front of him.

Touchdown. His boot magnets—thankfully—held to the surface. A disc magnet with a handgrip was already in his left hand. He reached down to the surface and anchored his upper body with the magnet while his right hand released the D-ring from the cable, all in one fluid movement as they had rehearsed.

He scooted to his right, getting clear of the cable, making room. The others arrived behind him. Chepe, Pitoso, Bulo, Nando, and the rest, with Bahzím picking up the rear. Segundo looked ahead of them. Lem Jukes's crew was coming down a cable from the Juke ship maybe three hundred meters away. Even at a distance Segundo could see that the Juke suits and gear were far superior than anything El Cavador men had.

"Spread out," said Bahzím. "Be back on the line in twelve minutes."

Segundo was on his hands and knees, crawling forward, keeping his body low, getting as far away from everyone else as he could. The idea was to disperse and set the explosives far apart to create a wide circle of damage. Segundo's knee and hand magnets held him securely to the hull, but they were cumbersome and difficult to move. He had to pull hard on each leg to momentarily break the attraction and lift the magnet enough to move it forward. It was agonizing and far more difficult than their re-hearsals. After twenty meters, his thighs were burning, and his breathing was heavy.

He could see now that the surface of the ship wasn't as smooth as it had appeared at a distance. There were thousands of closed apertures in rows running the length of the ship, like planted fields of crop. Each aperture was as big around as Segundo's helmet, and he knew that if any of them opened it would be to unleash their weapon. He tried not putting any weight on the apertures for fear that the magnet might trigger something and open them. It was like crawling across a minefield.

Finally he stopped and looked around him. The men from both ships were spread all over the surface. Some were laying explosives; others were still crawling forward; several explosives were already set, each with a small blinking green light, indicating the explosive was live. Segundo removed his first explosive from his pouch and set it gently on the surface. He inserted the blasting disc into the slot then set the timer to detonate three hours from now.

They had agreed to radio silence during this phase of the operation so that they could all concentrate on setting the charges without interruptions. But suddenly everyone was yelling. Segundo lifted his head and saw that one of the explosives had gone off prematurely, ripping through the hull and throwing up debris. The voices in his helmet were fast and frantic.

"What happened?"

"Pitoso's dead!"

"It blew up right under him!"

"What do we do?"

"Get back to the cable. Set your explosives and get back to the line. Move!"

Segundo's explosive was blinking green, set. He left it and turned toward the mooring cable at least thirty meters away, a good five-minute crawl. They weren't going to make it, he realized. Even if they got back to the line and up to the ship, they couldn't fly El Cavador away fast enough. The whole operation relied on them getting in and out and then a safe distance away without being detected, before the Formics could respond. That wasn't going to happen now. The Formics knew they were here.

Segundo crawled faster, not bothering to avoid the apertures this time. His thighs burned. His arms ached. Sweat ran down his forehead and into his eyes. The blast site was in front of him, between him and the cable—he would have to go around it. As he drew closer, up the curvature of the ship, the hole from the explosion came into view. It was a meter wide and stretched between two rows of apertures. Segundo looked down inside but saw nothing but darkness and shadows.

"Let's go," Bahzím was shouting. "Move!"

Segundo pulled out his last two explosives, set them on the ship's surface beside one another, and quickly slid in the discs. Before setting the timers, he glanced up. Two men had made it to the line. Segundo couldn't see who they were. He watched as they clipped their D-rings onto the line and launched upward, soaring away from the ship toward El Cavador.

Segundo returned his attention back to the explosives and began setting the timers. A moment later Chepe was shouting over the radio. "There's movement here. Something's coming up out of the hole."

Segundo looked up. Chepe had come to the edge of the hole but was now retreating back from it as shapes emerged from the darkness. Two Formics in spacesuits, carrying equipment, crawled out onto the surface quick and insectlike with the patter of many legs. Two more followed them. Then three after that. A few of the Formics carried thick plates. Others had oddly shaped tools and machines.

They're a repair crew, Segundo realized. They think something struck their ship and they've come out to fix it. They had no idea we were here.

The Formics stood still and kept their distance, regarding the men on the ship in a rather unemotional, calculating way, as if they were more intrigued by the humans' presence than threatened. Then one of the Formics looked directly at Segundo, and the demeanor of all of them changed in an instant. In unison, they all turned their heads toward Segundo, and their flat, yet frightening expressions became even darker and more menacing. It was as if they recognized Segundo.

Two of the Formics released their tools and charged him. Segundo couldn't retreat. There was nowhere to go. He gripped his hand magnets tightly, pulled his knees up away from the surface, twisted his body, and kicked out with his legs as hard as he could when the first Formic lunged. The creature wasn't expecting it, and Segundo felt his boots break bone as they drove into the Formic's chest. Its mouth opened in agony, and its hold on the ship broke. It flew off the ship in the direction it had been kicked.

"Help him!" someone was yelling.

The second Formic lunged. Segundo didn't have time to get his feet back under him. A kick struck him in the abdomen, then another. Pain shot through him. The Formics were small, but they had the strength of something three times their size. He swung out with the hand magnet, connecting with the Formic's helmet. The creature retreated a few steps, spread its lower legs apart in a fighting stance, and opened its mouth, bearing its mucus-laced maw and teeth. Segundo could almost hear it hissing.

Behind him he could see other men engaged with Formics. Two men flew away from the ship, Formics clinging to them. Lost. Segundo heard their screams but could do nothing to help them.

The Formic lunged again, but now Segundo was ready. He swept with his legs, surprising the Formic and causing it to stumble. Then he swung out with his hand magnet, connecting again and cracking the Formic's helmet. The Formic panicked, scrambling for purchase, and Segundo seized the moment to rotate his legs and lock them around the Formic's waist. The Formic kicked out, but its body was turned the wrong way. Segundo came down with the hand magnet again and again, striking the helmet visor with all of his strength. The Formic thrashed and bucked, but then the visor shattered under repeated blows. Segundo kicked the creature away from him, and the Formic flew upward, flailing its arms and legs. Its air hose stretched out until it snapped taut, but the creature continued to thrash about.

Segundo rotated, getting his legs back under him, and made for the cable. All over the surface of the ship, men were fighting off Formic attacks and hurrying to their respective cables. Two Juke men fell away from the ship. Then another. Then someone from El Cavador—Segundo couldn't see whom.

A Formic to his left was bent over one of the explosives, poking at it quizzically. The explosive detonated, vaporizing the creature and tearing another hole in the hull, momentarily blinding Segundo with the blast.

Instantly the Formics changed their tactics, abandoning those they were fighting and hurrying to the explosives nearest them, pulling the explosives away and throwing them out to space.

"They're peeling off the charges," said Bahzím.

A Formic near Segundo was trying to pry one of his explosives free. Segundo hurried toward him, but the Formic was faster, throwing the explosive clear of the ship. Segundo didn't stop. He swung with the hand magnet and connected with the creature. The Formic took the blow, but then, instead of fighting back, it reached for and pulled on Segundo's magnets, desperately trying to break Segundo's hold on the ship.

More hands were suddenly grabbing Segundo, pulling at him, punching him, yanking on the magnets that held him to the surface. Three Formics, then four, all of them swarming all around him. These new ones weren't wearing suits, he realized. They wore shoes on their feet that gripped to the hull and small, tightly sealed masks over their insect mouths, but otherwise they were unprotected, as if they hadn't taken the time to suit up before rushing outside.

They attacked Segundo with an unrelenting ferocity, pulling at his hand magnets, pulling at his knees. He kicked and shook and fought, but it was no use. One hand magnet came loose. Then the other one. Then the last knee magnet was disconnected, and Segundo was suddenly floating just above the surface of the ship. The Formics attacking him didn't let go to save themselves, but instead continued clinging to him, poking, stabbing, striking out. One of the creatures anchored to the surface pushed Segundo away, and that was all it took. He drifted away from the ship, swinging, punching, furiously trying to break the hold the Formics had on him.

Pain exploded in his leg. He looked down. One of the Formics without a helmet had pulled away its own mask and bit through Segundo's suit and into the meat of his calf. Foam inside the suit inflated around the puncture, sealing off the leak, but Segundo barely felt it over the hot, stabbing agony of the bite. He screamed, half in pain, half in fury, but if anyone could hear him, they didn't respond.

Lem clung to the side of the cargo bay and watched in horror as his men on the surface of the Formic ship scrambled for the cable. Chubs was beside him at the winch, waiting for the order to pull up the line. Lem zoomed in with his visor. Formics without spacesuits were pouring out of the breached holes and rushing to the men. When they reached someone, they pulled the man's magnets free and tumbled with him out into space.

"They're not even bothering with suits," said Lem. "They're killing themselves to peel us off the ship. They're dying and they don't even care."

Lem shifted his view to the base of the cable and watched as one of the Juke men clipped his harness onto the line. Just as the man was about to launch away from the ship toward Lem and the safety of the cargo bay, two Formics seized him from behind by the waist and wrestled him down. The man twisted and struggled and fought, but the Formics showed incredible strength and seemed unfazed by the man's attacks.

Lem extended a hand. "Chubs, give me your gun."

"You can't hit anything at this range."

"Give me your gun."

Chubs handed it over. It was a small and seemingly insignificant weapon, with its short barrel and tiny dart cartridges. Lem handled it carefully, having seen how lethal it could be back at Weigh Station Four. Tightening his grip around the gun, Lem widened his stance with his boot magnets and extended his arm, aiming at the two Formics struggling with the man at the end of the cable. The fight was fast and violent, however, and Lem quickly saw how dangerous it would be to fire into the melee. Even at close range he wasn't certain he could hit the Formics and not the man. Lem cursed under his breath and shifted his aim to one of the two holes where Formics continued to emerge in a steady stream. It stunned him to see so many of the creatures rush out into the vacuum of space with a feeble mask as protection—or in the case of a few, with no protection at all. It was suicide. Nothing could survive for more than—how long?— twenty seconds? Maybe not even that long. Didn't they know they were killing themselves? And if so, what kind of leader demanded and received that degree of loyalty?

Lem squeezed the trigger. A dart discharged. It flew toward the hole but then disappeared from view at a distance when it became too small to track. Lem lowered the gun. Chubs was right; it was pointless.

He returned his attention back to the base of the cable. The two Formics were gone, and the man who had clipped onto the cable looked dead. His body hung limp by the harness, floating in space, bent in an awkward position.

Two more Juke men reached the line. One of them unsnapped the dead man and pushed his corpse away, sending it out into space. As they attached their harnesses onto the line, two more crewmen arrived and buckled on as well. Rather than moving orderly up the cable, the men momentarily fought for position, struggling to be the first up the line. Their infighting would be their undoing, Lem realized, as he spotted three Formics racing toward them and moving fast.

"Pull up the line," said Lem. Saving four men was better than saving none at all.

Chubs turned off the magnet anchor and switched on the winch. The cable began to move away from the Formic ship, but not before three Formics grabbed at the men's feet and climbed upward. Now there were seven bodies at the end of the line, all of them lashing out, fighting, kicking, and spinning.

The winch continued to reel in the cable, moving faster now. One of the Formics scrambled past the twisting mass of bodies and was now climbing up the cable directly toward Lem.

Lem fired the gun, but he must have missed as the Formic kept coming, unharmed and unhindered.

"I'm cutting the cable," said Chubs.

"No," Lem shouted. "We have men on that line."

The Formic was moving faster now, scurrying up the cable, eyes locked with Lem's. Forty meters away. Then thirty.

"It'll get on the ship," Chubs said.

"Pull in the line," Lem said. "That is an order."

Lem could see the Formic's mouth now, clenched tight to keep it alive in the vacuum as long as possible. Fall off, Lem thought. Come on. Open your mouth and die.

He fired another dart, and this time the creature was close enough that Lem saw the dart miss. The men on the line were still fighting off the other two Formics, screaming and begging for Lem to pull the line in faster.

The climbing Formic had almost reached Lem. Ten meters. Five.

The cable snapped free from the winch, severed by Chubs, and the cargo bay door swished closed. Lem watched through the glass in the bay door as the Formic's momentum carried him to the ship. The creature bounced against the closed door and ricocheted away, its hands scratching at the ship for a moment, struggling to find purchase. The men on the cable cried out, begging not to be left behind. Chubs hit the command on his wrist pad to sever the men from the radio frequency.

Lem grabbed him by the front of the suit and slammed him back against the wall. "I gave you an order!"

"And your father gave me another order. Protect you at all costs. His word trumps yours."

Chubs opened a frequency to the helm. "Get us as far away from the Formic ship as possible. Now!"

"We can't leave El Cavador," said Lem.

"If the Formics are willing to send out men without air, they'll be willing to roast them with lasers if it means taking us down."

Lem's expression was hard. "You killed our own men."

"I saved your life, Lem. That's two you owe me."

Mono floated at the crow's nest window, his face pressed against the glass, his lip trembling. From here he could see everything: men peeling away from the Formic ship; Formics pulling off the explosives; a swarm of Formics coming out of the holes to fight, kick, bite, and attack. They were worse than any monster Mono had imagined, made all the more horrible by the sounds coming from the radio frequency, which Mono had opened on Edimar's terminal. Frantic shouts. Men screaming. The sounds of a struggle. Concepción telling everyone to hurry back to the cable. Mono wanted to go to the radio and turn it off, but he was too afraid to move.

He shouldn't have left Mother. That had been a stupid mistake. This was grown-up business. He shouldn't be here. He had helped, yes, and played an important part, but right now he didn't care. He would go back and *not* play an important part if it meant he could be on the WU-HU ship with Mother.

Why had he lied to her? He loved Mother, and now his last act to her would be a lie. And yes, it would be his last act. He was going to die. He knew that. He had heard everything the men had said over the past few days, even when they thought they were talking quietly enough for him not to hear. If the Formics discovered them, they had no chance.

I'm sorry, Mother.

He felt doubly ashamed because he knew Vico wouldn't be afraid. Vico wouldn't flinch at this. He would be down there with the others, fighting. And yet, even the mere thought of Vico gave Mono a touch of courage. He launched across the room to the radio and clicked it off. The room went silent. Mono took a deep breath. He could feel it calm him, so he took another one, a deep calming breath like Mother had taught him to take whenever he had cried so much that his breathing became rapid. "Easy now," Mother would say, gently taking him into her arms. "You're going to make yourself sick, Monito. Deep breaths." And then she would brush her fingers through his hair and hum into his ear until he got himself under control again.

It worked now, here in the crow's nest. Mono's lips stopped trembling, and his muscles relaxed. Outside the struggle continued, but inside, here in the crow's nest, Mono felt almost at ease.

A door opened on the side of the Formic ship, and a large mechanism extended. Mono couldn't begin to guess what it was for or how it operated. Vico would probably know. Vico could look at anything and know exactly how to fix it or what it was good for.

The mechanism rotated and pointed its many shafts at El Cavador. There was a flash of light, and then a wall of hot glowing globules of radiant plasma shot forth from the shafts, rocketing toward Mono like ten thousand balls of light.

Segundo tumbled through space, struggling desperately, fighting off the last two Formics clinging to his body. One of them crawled onto his back, opened its maw, and reared back its head, ready to bite and tear and puncture his suit. Segundo thumbed the propulsion trigger and hit the Formic with a blast of compressed air, startling it and knocking it away.

The last Formic was kicking at him, swatting, biting. Segundo spun it around, grabbed it below the jaw, and twisted its head until he heard things break inside. The Formic thrashed and kicked and then went still. Segundo released it and hit his thumb trigger, shooting away from it. His breathing was labored. He had little air. He was bleeding. There were holes in his suit. Several alarms were going off on his HUD. One showed a silhouette of his suit dotted with flashing lights, indicating where there was a rip or tear. The worst was on his leg where the Formic had bitten through. The emergency system had cinched his leg's strap tight, sealing off the escape of air in the tear, but it wouldn't hold for long. He fumbled for the emergency tape in his pouch. He pulled a strip free and placed it across a hissing puncture on his arm. He tapped the tape mechanism to release another strip. Then another. His gloved fingers were big and cumbersome and kept sticking to the corners of the tape strips before he could apply them. Twice he had to throw bent, twisted strips to the side, which was maddening since he knew he would need every strip. He covered as many holes as he could, but then the tape ran out. There were still a few torn seams, nothing big, tiny holes, but his HUD continued to sound its alarm.

Segundo blinked a command to shut off the alarm. The computer asked if he was sure since life-threatening damage to his suit was still unrepaired. He blinked the affirmative, and the alarm went silent.

His oxygen tank was nearly empty. He was desperate for air. He had a spare tank in his pouch with fifteen more minutes of oxygen, but he knew it probably wouldn't last him five. He ditched the spent tank and screwed in the spare. Cool oxygen came into his helmet. He'd enjoy it while it lasted.

He turned back toward the direction of the ships and saw nothing but empty space. He knew he was still moving incredibly fast in that direction, but he would never see the ships again. The WU-HU ship would have passed him a long time ago, trailing behind the Formic ship, recording everything. They wouldn't see him. He was a speck in a sea of black.

Rena.

She was safe at least. She would take this hard, but she was with others. They would comfort each other, strengthen each other. They would survive. He wanted her to know that she was the last thing on his mind, and that he hadn't died in agony. Well, not total agony; the wound in his leg had settled to a burning numbness. Some of the others had suffered much worse. He focused on the spot in space where he assumed the WU-HU ship would be and told his HUD to give the remaining power to the radio transmitter to boost the signal.

"Rena. I don't know if you'll receive this, but my suit is punctured and leaking air. Even if the WU-HU ship decelerated now and you knew exactly where I was, you'd still never reach me in time. So don't stop. Keep going. I don't know if El Cavador got out, but I don't think so. Tell Abbi that Mono was sorry for lying to her. Tell her he loves her. Tell her we couldn't have done this without him. It's the truth.

"The women will be looking for a leader, Rena, someone to help them navigate all this. Don't be modest. We both know they'd appreciate you guiding them. Work with the captain. He strikes me as a good man. Don't rush to Earth. I don't know what will come of this, but I'd prefer you stay away from it and survive. Do that for me, mi amor. I'm sorry we won't share a hammock when you read my letter, but know that I mean every word. Te amo, Rena. Para siempre jamás, te amo."

The air in his helmet was getting thin, and he didn't want her hearing him gasping for breath. He shut off the transmitter. He turned off his HUD. All was silent except for the weak rasp of the regulator, pumping in the last of the air. Segundo let his body go loose. He was cold and tired, but he ignored the cold. Around him stars shone. Some bright, some dim, the most constant things in life. Segundo smiled up at them, happy at least to be dying among friends.

CHAPTER 19

Interference

Rena listened to the transmission on the helm of the WU-HU ship. Static crackled throughout much of the message, and for several seconds Segundo's words were lost entirely. Rena got the gist of it, though. She knew Segundo well enough to fill in the blanks.

Captain Doashang apologized that they didn't get the complete transmission, explaining that the alien emissions interfered with the signal quality. He assured Rena, however, that the ship had decelerated as quickly as it could upon receiving the transmission, but that, sadly, they were unable to locate Segundo or any of the other men. "Thank you for trying," said Rena. "I appreciate you being considerate enough to play the transmission for me. It means more than you know."

"We took the liberty of making you a copy," said Doashang, offering her a small memory disc. "We thought you would want it for your personal records."

It was that act of kindness that pushed her over the edge. She broke down briefly and cried silent tears, covering her face with her hands. A female member of the crew consoled her with a gentle arm around her shoulders, and it was that touch that steeled Rena again. She stood erect and wiped at her eyes. "Forgive me," she said to the captain.

"There is nothing to forgive, Mrs. Delgado. You have my most sincere condolences. I will provide grief counselors from my crew for you and those from your ship."

"That is very kind. Thank you."

"I have prepared a few statements for your people to explain the events of the battle. I think it necessary to give the families an account of the bravery demonstrated by their husbands and fathers."

Doashang had politely asked the women and children to stay in their rooms for the duration of the attack so that he and his crew could perform their duties without interruption. Rena, pulled from her room moments ago, was the only person from El Cavador who knew it had been destroyed.

"Everyone is eager to hear news," said Rena. "Thank you."

Captain Doashang looked at her with compassion. "I want to be as sensitive as I can with the families, Mrs. Delgado. Now that I've met you and heard your husband's transmission, I wonder if the report of the battle would be better delivered by you."

"Me?"

"I will accompany you, if you agree. But you know these families best, and I wonder if such news is better delivered by a friend instead of a stranger."

It took Rena a moment to find her voice. "With all due respect, Captain, I don't know if I'm in the right emotional state to do that."

He nodded, blushing. "Of course. It was inconsiderate of me to ask, particularly in your own time of grief. Forgive me."

But before Rena excused herself, she reconsidered. If she could choose someone to tell her such devastating news, she would want it to be someone she loved, a friend, a fellow sufferer even, someone who could take her in her arms and weep with her.

"On second thought, Captain, I think you may be right. I will meet with the families individually. But first, I must hear the full account myself."

He showed her everything. She watched the vids and listened to the transmissions. She seethed when Lem Jukes's ship pulled away and fled. Her heart broke when El Cavador disintegrated before her eyes. Her home, the only world she knew, was gone.

Why hadn't Concepción come with her? Rena had insisted that she join them on the WU-HU ship, arguing that by Concepción's own orders, all women and children were to leave El Cavador. But Concepción had laughed this off. "Old, stubborn women are the exception," she had said.

Now she was gone. They were all gone. Bahzím, Chepe, Pitoso, Mono:

cousins, brothers, nephews, uncles. Half of everyone she knew and loved in the world. As well as the man she loved more than them all.

The vids ended. She knew everything she needed to know. Her back was straight. Her eyes were dry. "Come, Captain. You and I have work to do."

Captain Doashang stayed at Rena's side as she met with every woman from El Cavador. Doashang promised each of them protection and safe passage to the Asteroid Belt. The ship would have to ration its food supply—corporate hadn't planned for this many passengers—but neither Doashang nor his crew would get an ounce more food than anyone else. The children would not go hungry. The women wept in sorrow and gratitude, and one even kissed his hand as she cried.

In the corridor afterward, he faced Rena. "My senior officers and I will vacate our quarters for those families who do not yet have a room."

"That's not necessary, Captain."

"I have children of my own, Mrs. Delgado. We have quite a trip to the Asteroid Belt ahead of us. The more comfortable the children are, the more pleasant the flight will be for all of us."

She nodded. "True. I'll see to it. Thank you. Also, with your permission, I would like to organize a work detail. Those of us from El Cavador don't want to be a burden. We would appreciate being allowed to help maintain the ship however we can."

"Permission granted. Work out the particulars with one of my officers." His wrist pad vibrated. "Now if you'll excuse me."

Doashang hurried to the helm. His first officer, Wenchin, was waiting for him at the monitors. "We found a Formic drifting in space," said Wenchin. "It's dead. Or at least we think so. It wasn't wearing a suit. It must have fallen from the ship. I have a team outside checking it now."

On the monitors, five spacewalkers in WU-HU suits surrounded the Formic. They had attached various instruments to its body, but the men were keeping their distance.

"It couldn't have survived in a vacuum this long," said Doashang. "Restrain its limbs and bag it. Use every precaution. Treat it as if it were the most lethal of biohazards. Have the men outside decontaminate their suits. Then get the Formic to Dr. Ji to examine. The more information we can send to Earth about these creatures the better."

"Yes, sir."

Captain Doashang moved to the communications officer. "Any luck contacting Lem Jukes?"

"No, sir. The Formic ship is putting off all kinds of interference. It's causing a perturbation that randomizes the digital information. I'm getting transmissions, but at a much slower rate. A bit per second instead of a trillion bits per second. Which means what I am getting is basically nothing. It's not enough information to decipher anything. We can't send or receive long-range messages at all. Not as focused laserlines or as blanket spreads."

"That's unacceptable. I need to send a warning to the Asteroid Belt."

"I don't know what to tell you, sir. The only radio communication that works is short-range. And we've deviated from the main thoroughfare to follow the Formic ship, so no other ship is going to come even remotely close to this position. We could accelerate back to the major flight paths and wait until a ship comes close enough to hear our transmission. But that could be a long wait, sir. And there's no way to determine if the interference is still affecting that quadrant. If it is, whomever we contact won't be able to send long transmissions either. The most reliable way to get word to the Belt, sir, may be to go there ourselves."

"That's several months away."

The officer looked helpless. "It's not ideal, sir. But we're short on options."

"Is the Formic ship sending radio? How are *their* messages getting through?"

"Near as we can tell, the Formics are silent, sir. Even when we were close, I didn't pick up so much as a squawk."

Captain Doashang turned to Wenchin. "Set a course to the nearest station in the Asteroid Belt, moving as fast as our fuel supply will allow."

"What about Lem Jukes?" asked Wenchin.

"He's out of range, and I doubt he cares what happened to us anyway.

He abandoned his own men. He won't concern himself with us. He's probably heading for the Belt as well."

Wenchin relayed the order, and the ship quickly accelerated.

Doashang stayed on the helm until Dr. Ji called him to the medical offices several hours later. Ji appeared pale and shaken when Doashang arrived.

"Not the most pleasant postmortem examination you've performed, I'm guessing," said Doashang.

"That's putting it lightly," said Ji.

The two stood at a large window outside a room where a team of technicians was examining and videoing the dissected Formic.

"What are they?" asked Doashang.

"They're semivertebrate," said Ji, "in that they have a single neural column, but clearly they evolved from exoskeletal hexiforms."

"What does that mean?"

"They evolved from creatures very much like ants, but they left anthood far behind."

"So they're not insects?"

"*Descended* from insectlike creatures. Certain evolutionary changes have occurred. They're warm blooded, for instance. They insulate and perspire to regulate body temperature in much the same way we do. They have an endoskeleton covered with muscles and skin and fur. Most of their organs are a mystery to me, although we've documented everything. They have six legs obviously. The middle pair has musculature that suggests they can bear weight, though perhaps not as much as hips or thighs. The joint socket is extraordinarily flexible, even more so than human shoulders. Plus they have highly developed back muscles, which suggests they have enormous strength."

"We've already seen evidence of that. What I want to know is how do we kill them."

"They're not indestructible. They're tough and resilient, but they can be broken. What frightens me more than their physicality, though, is what we saw them do on the vids. They were immediately willing to give their lives to thwart any attack. No hesitation. No attempt to protect themselves. Just unbridled animal ferocity and completely unyielding devotion. These aren't just technologically superior creatures, Captain. This is a species that will never, ever give up until every last one of them is destroyed."

"On that point, Doctor, we will gladly oblige them."

Lem stood in the engineering room, which had been converted into a war room of sorts, and looked at all of the notes on the wall-screens around him. There were anatomical diagrams of a Formic; sketches of the Formic ship with various engineering theories on how the ship operated; photos and analysis of the weapon that had destroyed El Cavador; a systems chart showing the Formic ship's trajectory; as well as numerous other scribbles, lists, ideas, and theories. "We have all this intel," said Lem. "All this critical information that Earth desperately needs, and we can't do a damn thing with any of it." He turned and faced Chubs, Benyawe, and Dr. Dublin, whose hands were still in casts. "Unless we relay this to Earth, it's worthless," said Lem.

"We're at the mercy of our radio," said Chubs. "Until we get through the interference there's not much we can do."

In the weeks since the attack, the interference from the Formic ship had rendered long-range communication impossible. Lem had ordered the radio officers to continually broadcast a looped transmission about the Formics—detailing the ship's coordinates, flight path, dimensions, and speed—but as far as the radio officers could tell, nothing was getting through. Every day hundreds of the transmissions went out and zero transmissions came in. The Makarhu was screaming a warning, but nobody could hear a word.

"Then how do we get around the interference?" asked Lem.

"We don't know the limits of it," said Chubs. "Right now we're four million kilometers away from the Formic ship's trajectory. We could go farther out, but there's no telling how far we would need to go. Ten million? Twenty? A hundred? Also, if we distance ourselves any more from the ship, we won't be able to track it. It's so far ahead of us already that it disappears from our scanners for days at a time. We're out of range of its weapons, which is good, but if we deviate any more from our current course or speed, we'll get so far behind the ship that we'll lose it completely. We could do that, but it's a risk. We may not reach the end of the interference before the ship reaches Earth."

"I don't want to lose sight of the ship," said Lem. "But unless we do something to counter this interference, Earth isn't going to get much of a warning, if any at all. They'll be completely unprepared for an attack."

"We don't actually know if the Formics intend to attack," said Dublin. "We strongly suspect that, but we can't be definitive about what they'll do once they reach Earth."

"They're not coming to borrow a cup of sugar," said Chubs. "You saw what they did to El Cavador."

Lem cringed inside. El Cavador. He knew it wasn't his fault that they had been destroyed—they should have gotten out when he did. Still, he couldn't shake the nagging idea that he should have done more. What, he didn't know; there was nothing else he could have done, really. There was no saving the men stuck on the Formic ship; they were beyond rescue. El Cavador should have seen that. But no, Concepción had adhered to some foolish, self-destructive notion of "never leave a man behind," which was stupid. Lem was all for saving people, sure. But once it was clear that further rescue was impossible, what good was it to hang around? In the heat of the moment he had chided Chubs for ordering the ship to leave, but now he saw the wisdom of it. All El Cavador had accomplished by staying behind to rescue its men was its own sad demise.

But that was free miners. He respected their courage. But to ignore self-preservation for the sake of family didn't feel noble. It felt irresponsible.

There was one more thing, too. One he tried not to think about, since it made him feel shallow and callous. But there was no denying it either: The destruction of El Cavador meant the destruction of their copy of his files. Concepción had said she would erase them, but now he knew without a doubt that it had happened. There was the slim possibility that one of the women had carried a copy onto the WU-HU ship, but that was unlikely. They were worried about protecting their children and surviving. Burning Lem Jukes at the legal stake hadn't been on their minds. He was in the clear. The files were gone.

"My point is," Dublin was saying, "we don't yet know why they're headed to Earth. What do they want? Our resources? To make contact? To study us?"

"They didn't come to make contact," said Lem. "Their pod destroyed the Italian free miners."

"Yes," said Dublin, "but only after it had been among them for twelve hours. Maybe it was trying to contact them in all that time."

Lem shook his head. "Concepción told us everything. The Italians didn't pick up anything that resembled communication from the pod."

"Maybe they have a way of communicating that we don't know about," said Dublin. "Maybe they were trying to communicate, but humans don't have the tech to receive their transmissions."

"They *killed* the Italians," said Chubs. "If someone doesn't answer your hello, you don't waste them."

"I'm trying to look at this scientifically," said Dublin.

"It doesn't matter if they tried to communicate or not," said Chubs. "They wanted to kill us. Did you watch the vids? Did you see the face of that Formic climbing up the mooring cable? It wasn't coming to introduce itself. It was coming to rip Lem's head off."

Dublin held up two hands in a gesture of surrender. "I'm not defending them. I'm reminding us that they come from a completely different social structure with completely different behaviors and values."

"There is one theory we haven't discussed," said Benyawe. She walked to the sketch of the Formic ship on the wall, studied it, then faced them. "What if it's a colony ship?"

"Colony?" said Chubs. "Can't be. The planet's taken. We own it. No vacancy."

"Maybe they don't care," said Benyawe. "Maybe they come from a civilization where aliens share planets."

"Or maybe they intend to take it for themselves," said Lem. He turned and studied the diagram of the Formic. "We've been assuming all this time that they consider us as equals. But what if they don't? What if they think of us in the same way we think of houseflies or rabbits? If you want to build a house on a lot and you find a family of rabbits living on the land, you don't think of the land as belonging to the rabbits and build elsewhere. You shoot the rabbits or you scare them off."

"There are twelve billion people on Earth," said Chubs. "With cities and industry and tech. That's more than a family of rabbits."

"Fine. Pick a different animal. Say, earthworms. How many worms are on the plot of land? Thousands? Tens of thousands? Or what about ants? A million? They have colonies and homes, but what do we care? We level the land and build anyway. My point is, maybe they don't consider the planet ours. We only happen to live there. Maybe they see it as theirs for the taking."

"There's a hole in that theory," said Dublin. "The interference. If the Formics didn't consider as us equals or at least near their place on the species hierarchy, why are they working so hard to cloak their approach with the interference? What they're doing to our radio suggests they fear us and have developed tactics to avoid our detection. It implies they consider us a threat."

"Only if the interference is deliberate," said Lem. "But what if it isn't? What if it's nothing more than a by-product of their propulsion system? What if they have no idea they're wrecking our radio? Yes, it's working to their advantage, but that doesn't mean they *meant* for it to happen."

"If that's true," said Benyawe, "then Earth is in more danger than we thought. If the Formics aren't doing anything deliberate to hide their approach, if they don't care if we notice them or not, then they don't consider us a threat at all. They're so confident they can destroy us that it doesn't matter if we know they're coming."

The more they talked, the less Lem liked what we he was hearing. "So what do we do?" he asked. "We can't communicate with anyone. We can't surpass the ship and get ahead of it—not at its current speed anyway. It's moving too fast. We can't even catch it if we wanted to."

"Which we most definitely *don't* want to do," said Chubs.

"I see two options," said Benyawe. "We can either deviate and take a gamble that there's a way out of this interference. Or we can continue to track the ship and gather intelligence and hope that it decelerates enough for us to zip past it and beat it to Earth."

"Also a gamble," said Lem.

"There's no easy answer," said Benyawe.

"Option B gets my vote," said Dublin. "That puts us closer to Earth. That's our destination."

"I agree," said Benyawe. "There might be something else we can learn about the Formics, a weakness perhaps. That would be more valuable to Earth than anything. If we lose sight of the ship, we lose that chance."

"The Formics are leaving a wake of destruction," said Chubs. "People may need help. I say we stay the course."

Benyawe said, "An odd philosophy for you, considering you've left quite a wake of destruction yourself."

"Always to protect us," said Chubs, annoyed.

A navigator from the helm appeared on the wall-screen. "Sir, sensors indicate that the Formic ship has vented again."

"Decelerate immediately," said Lem. "I don't want us flying into the gamma plasma. Bring us to a full stop if necessary." It was the second time the ship had vented since the battle with El Cavador.

The navigator made a series of hand movements offscreen, then returned. "Deceleration commenced, sir."

"Were there any ships near the Formics that may have been affected by the plasma?"

"Don't know, sir. The only reason we can detect the Formic ship at this distance is because of its size. Anything smaller doesn't show up on the sensors."

"Keep scanning. Let me know if we find anything that might have been hit by the plasma."

"Yes, sir."

The navigator disappeared. Benyawe walked to the systems chart that stretched across one wall. A line representing the Formics' trajectory cut across space. Benyawe touched various points on the line, leaving blinking red dots. "The first venting happened here, near Weigh Station Four. The next venting was here, roughly six au later. Now we have a third venting that's approximately six au after that."

"So they vent every six au," said Dublin.

"Which means we can approximate where it will likely vent again," said Benyawe. She tapped her finger down the line every six au and left more dots. As she reached the inner Belt, she placed a dot near an asteroid.

"What asteroid is that?" asked Lem.

Benyawe enlarged it until it filled the screen. Lem thought it looked like a dog bone: thin shaft in the middle, with two knobby lobes at either end. "It's called Kleopatra," said Benyawe. "M-class. Measures two hundred and seventeen kilometers across. She moved her fingers on the screen and rotated the asteroid until the opposite side came into view. There, on the surface of one of the lobes, was a small cluster of lights.

"What is that?" asked Lem. "Zoom in."

Benyawe moved her fingers and zoomed in on the lights, revealing a massive mining complex at least five kilometers across. Buildings, smelting plants, diggers, barracks. A mini industrial city.

"It's a Juke facility," said Benyawe.

"One of ours? How come I've never heard of it?" asked Lem.

"Your father has over a hundred of these facilities throughout the Belt," said Chubs. "By building a facility, we're basically claiming the entire rock. We're sticking a flag in the ground and telling competitors to back off. Which is smart. That much iron is worth a fortune."

"If the Formics vent near Kleopatra, even if the plasma hits the opposite side of the asteroid, those people don't stand a chance," said Dublin.

"How many people work there?" asked Lem.

Benyawe tapped the complex with her finger, opened a window of data, and began reading. After a moment, she turned to them, troubled.

"How many?" asked Lem.

"Over seven thousand," said Benyawe.

CHAPTER 20

Solitude

At first Victor thought little of the pain in his back. After five months of traveling in the quickship, unexplained aches and pains had become second nature. His muscles were atrophying, his bones were weakening; dull aches were to be expected. But then the backache worsened and became so excruciating at times that it felt like a knife stabbing and twisting inside him. It came in waves, and no matter how Victor positioned his body in the quickship, the pain continued. Then the pain spread to his side and groin. Then blood appeared in his urine, and he knew he was in trouble.

All symptoms pointed to kidney stones. His bones were becoming osteoporotic and the released calcium was coalescing in the kidneys. Sleep was difficult. He felt anxious and nauseated and worried about being sick in his helmet. He drank lots of water, but it didn't help. He had brought a few mild pain meds, but he had taken those months ago to get through a few days of migraines. Now he cursed himself. The migraines were a gentle kiss on the cheek compared to this.

After three days, he worried that the stone might be too big to pass, and he wondered what would happen if that were the case. Would he get an infection? Could it kill him? Would Earth never receive warning because of a stupid clump of crystallized calcium?

He passed it on the fourth day, and the pain was so unexpectedly searing and intense that for a moment he thought he *was* dying. When it was over, he fell instantly asleep, exhausted.

He continued to drink a lot of water over the next few weeks, but it didn't stop him from having stones. He passed four in all. None of them were as painful as the first, but they all left him anxious and restless. He was now keenly aware of the fact that his body was deteriorating, and he constantly worried about a dozen other ailments that might afflict him at any moment. His bone density was his primary concern. Would the weight of his own body break his legs when he stood on Luna? Gravity on Luna was only a fraction of what it was on Earth, but perhaps it would be enough to overstress his weakening bones. Then there was the issue of his appetite. It had greatly diminished recently. Was he malnourished? And what about his heart? It was weakening, too. Would it give out before he reached the Moon? And what about radiation? Was the shield holding? He needed to strengthen it, he realized. He needed to add another plate to the exterior. He was sure he'd get cancer if he didn't.

Victor entered the commands in his handheld to initiate deceleration. The ship had been moving at a constant, high velocity for months, and if he maintained that speed and went outside, the ship would appear to him as if it wasn't moving at all since he would be moving at the same velocity. But going outside at a high velocity was risky. He'd expose himself to gamma radiation and the threat of micrometeoroids. Getting hit by a tiny rock particle would likely be fatal. Victor couldn't take that risk. Not with so much at stake. It would be safer to decelerate and repair the shields at a full stop. He'd add a lot of time to his trip, yes, and he wouldn't reach Luna as quickly as he had hoped, but he felt the extra shielding and precautions were worth the delay.

It took the ship almost two full days to decelerate. Victor didn't want to rush the process and put any undue burden on his body, weak as it was, so he had slowed the ship gradually. When it had reached a full stop, he detached his air hose and screwed a canister of oxygen into the back of his suit. Next came his tool belt, which he fastened around his waist. Then he opened the hatch and crawled outside. Using the handholds recessed into the hull, Victor pulled himself toward the back of the ship to check how the rear plates were holding up. His hand slipped from one of the handholds, and Victor instinctively reached for the safety cable fastened to his chest harness to steady himself.

Only the safety cable wasn't there.

In his haste to come outside he had forgotten to anchor himself to the ship.

Victor clawed at the hull, trying to get purchase, desperate to stop himself, but his body was in motion now, moving toward the rear of the ship, and he had already passed the last handhold. His bulky gloves slipped along the metal surface, stopping on nothing. He was screaming now, his voice hoarse and cracked from lack of use. He was slipping down the side of the ship. There was nothing to grab. He was going to die.

Then he saw it ahead of him. A tube of some sort, a small metal pipe at the back corner of the ship. Beyond it was space. If he missed it, he was gone. He would drift until he ran out of air. He approached the pipe, and just before he reached it he knew he wouldn't be able to grab it. It was too far away, just beyond the reach of his fingers.

In a single swift movement, his hand whipped to his tool belt and came back with a long wrench that he reached out and hooked around the pipe at the last possible moment, stopping himself. His heart was pounding. His breathing was labored. The wrench's hold on the pipe was slight and precarious. It could easily slip off. He gently pulled and drew himself back to the ship.

The wrench slipped from the pipe, but he was moving in the right direction now. He slowly drifted toward the cockpit, climbed inside, and fastened the safety cable onto his harness. He cursed himself for being so stupid. He had come all this way, risked his life, with intelligence that the whole world needed to see, and he nearly ruined it all by failing to fasten a single metal ring to his harness. Brilliant, Victor. Real genius.

With the cable secured, he returned outside, checked the plates, found them in order, but then decided to install the spare plates anyway on top of the existing ones. Might as well. The spares weren't doing any good inside the ship. Besides, he needed the labor. He needed to occupy his mind with work for a little while. He had built and engineered every day of his life since becoming Father's apprentice, and the past five months had been nothing but mind-numbing idleness.

When he finished the installation, he resealed the seams twice to be sure they would hold. He knew he was stalling. The seals were fine. He simply didn't want to get back in the ship.

Eventually, he returned to the cockpit. His hand lingered on the hatch for a moment before he closed it, his eyes scanning the expanse of space above him. He was only a few months away from Luna. He could endure this a little longer. He sealed the hatch and began to accelerate. The computer reconfigured his flight path to account for the delay and revised the time of arrival, putting him at Luna three weeks later than originally expected. Victor felt like hitting something. Three weeks. That was much longer than he had anticipated. But it was too late now. What's done is done, he thought. Sighing, he sat motionless in the flight seat as the quickship picked up speed.

A month later a feeling of hopelessness overcame Victor. He felt certain he was off course. Or the computer had a glitch in it. Or he was running short of air. He kept catching himself staring at nothing. Food lost all appeal. His sense of taste was gone. Or maybe the proteins in the food had broken down so much from radiation that the food no longer had any taste to deliver. Either way, he had no appetite. He lost weight. His wrists and ankles felt thin and flimsy. He had brought rubber strips for resistance exercises, which he had been doing religiously every day since setting out. Now he ignored all exercise. Why bother? Little good it was doing. His bones were probably twigs at this point. He had struggled for months with insomnia. Now he seemed to sleep all the time. He hadn't touched his handheld in days. There were books he had started and hadn't finished, puzzles he had left unsolved. He didn't care.

A hand was gently shaking his shoulder, rousing him from sleep. Alejandra was beside him, wearing the pristine and pressed white gown. She smiled at him and folded her arms across her chest. "You're losing your mind, Vico. You're psychologically frito. You've been cooped up in this thing so long and your sleep is so unregulated that you're only sane when you're dreaming."

Victor's voice was dry and frail, and the sound of it surprised him. "Am I dreaming?" He looked around him. Everything seemed normal. The instruments. The equipment. The air tanks.

"You won't find any pink elephants, if that's what you're looking for," said Alejandra. "*I'm* here. That should be evidence enough for you." She sat down in front of him, with her legs bent demurely to the side. "You've stopped exercising and eating. Have you looked at yourself? You're wasting away to nothing."

"I don't have a mirror."

"Probably best. You'd break it. Also, you need a haircut."

"I'm going crazy, aren't I?"

She ticked off his problems on her fingers. "Severe anxiety. Depression. You're ignoring life-sustaining food and exercise. Your sleep patterns are completely out of whack. You can't think straight, and you're talking to a dead person."

"It's a very good choice of dead person. That should win me some points."

She rolled her eyes. "Isabella gave you pills to help regulate your sleep. Why did you stop taking them?"

"I don't like taking pills. I like being in control."

"You're *not* in control. That's the problem, Vico Loco. You're not yourself. If you're not careful they'll throw you in a padded room when you reach Luna. It won't take much to convince them. They'll already think you're crazy for flying from the Kuiper Belt in a quickship. As soon as you start yapping about aliens, their suspicions will be confirmed. You need to be a model of sanity, Vico. Looking like you do now isn't going to help."

"You, on the other hand, look quite the opposite. I never told you how beautiful you are. I never even thought to say it, but it's true."

"We're talking about you at the moment."

"I wish we wouldn't. You're much more interesting."

She smiled and said nothing.

"They sent you away because of me, Janda. If I had known that's what they would do, I would have changed things."

"How? By pretending not to be my friend? By avoiding me? By being formal around me and treating me like a mere acquaintance? That would have been worse."

"These aren't your thoughts," he told her. "They're mine, projected on to you. You're only saying what my mind is telling you to say."

"But you knew my thoughts, Vico. You always did. The only reason why you didn't know that I loved you was because I didn't know it myself. But I did."

"Don't use the past tense," he said. "That means it's over."

He awoke. Alone. Everything was where it always was. The instruments. The equipment. The air tanks. He forced himself to eat. He drank water and took vitamins. He did the resistance exercises and was shocked to learn how weak he was. He checked the instruments. He had seven weeks to get back to health. He drank more water and did another rep of leg exercises.

There was traffic all around Luna, but the LUG system in Victor's quickship took over the flight controls long before he reached the mass of ships. Freighters, courier ships, passenger vessels moving back and forth to Earth, newer corporate mining ships heading out toward the Asteroid Belt, many of which were emblazoned with the Juke Limited corporate logo.

The quickship had decelerated hours ago, and now that he was here and close, he found the LUG system's docking speed maddeningly slow. Soon other quickships were gathering around him, coming in from all quarters, all being lugged toward the same destination; where exactly, Victor had no idea.

He could see Earth but he was greatly disappointed since he had expected it to be much closer. It was night on the planet's surface, and there were millions of lights twinkling below the atmosphere. All of those people, he thought, and none of them know what's coming. Or maybe they did know. Maybe word had gotten through. Victor hoped that was true. That would mean his work was done.

The settlements and industries of Luna constituted the tiniest part of the moon's surface. Victor had seen pictures, but they had been taken from space, so he expected a small outpost. When the moon rotated as the quickships approached, and the city of Imbrium came into view, Victor gaped in wonder. Factories, smelting plants, huge industrial complexes with so many lights and pipes and buildings that they seemed to be their very own cities. Then Imbrium proper came into view to his right. Buildings and lights and glass-topped walkways. It was more human-built structure than he had ever seen.

He could feel his body getting heavier. Gravity was seizing him. The quickships around him organized themselves into a line, all of them loaded with huge cargos of cylinders. Victor's eyes followed the line in front of him, and he saw that the LUG system was taking the quickships to a massive complex beyond the city.

Then suddenly his quickship deviated from the others and changed course, flying down toward a hangar with a ceiling at least a hundred meters high. The quickship's engines died. It drifted into the hangar. There were damaged quickships everywhere in various stages of repair, but there were no workers that he could see. Robot arms extended and grabbed the quickship. His forward motion stopped, and Victor was thrown against his restraining harness. The pain took his breath away, and he was certain he had cracked a few ribs. He coughed, trying to get his wind back. The ship rotated ninety degrees, with the nose pointed upward. Victor was on his back. The robot arms lifted him quickly and hooked the ship onto a long rack of quickships hanging by their noses ten meters off the ground. The robot arms released him and went elsewhere.

All was quiet. The ship swung lightly on the rack, an odd sensation caused by gravity that Victor had never experienced. He waited, but no one came for him. He unharnessed himself, still wincing from the pain in his chest. His body felt heavy. He climbed out of the seat and looked out the window. He was too high off the ground. He didn't trust the strength of his legs in partial gravity with a drop like that. He scanned the warehouse floor, looking for people. There were none. Everything was automated. A quickship suddenly slid onto the rack in front of him, pushing him farther into the rack, partially blocking his view. The robot arms were packing him in here. He needed to get out.

He tried the hatch. He couldn't open it. The other quickship was packed in too tightly. He went to the radio and tried a frequency. "Hello? Can anyone hear me?"

Again, the sound of his own voice frightened him. It was hoarse and crackly and barely above a whisper. No one responded. He heard only static. He tried another frequency. Still nothing. Then he tried another and got chatter. Men talking, giving numbers and data; Victor didn't understand it. He interrupted them. "Hello? Can anyone hear me?"

The chatter stopped. There was a pause. "Who is this?"

"My name is Victor Delgado. I'm a free miner from the Kuiper Belt. I'm stuck in a warehouse of some kind."

"Get off this frequency."

"Please. I need help. I have information that needs to get to Earth."

"Sanjay, I got someone on the frequency who won't get off."

A different voice—deeper, commanding, with an accent Victor didn't recognize. "I don't know who you are, mate, but this is a restricted frequency. Now get the hell off before I have you tossed."

"Please. I need to speak to someone in charge. All of Earth is in danger." The words sounded trite, even to him.

"You're the one in danger, mate. Marcus, triangulate that signal and find this prankster. I want this ash trash off my frequency."

Victor stayed on the frequency, but didn't say more. Let them triangulate it. Let them find him.

An hour later a police rover arrived. A single police officer in a suit and helmet got out with a light and began scanning the interior of the warehouse with bored disinterest.

Victor banged on the side of the ship with a tool to get the man's attention, but the man couldn't hear him. Victor lowered himself to the back of the ship, which was now the bottom. He turned on his cutting tool and began slicing through the ship's wall, showering the inside of the ship with small burning metal embers. He pressed harder, being careful not to damage his suit. The cutter broke through. Hot embers rained down from the ship into the warehouse. The officer saw him.

It was another hour before someone who could operate the machinery arrived to lower the ship from the rack. When the men lifted him out of the quickship and set him on the ground, Victor's legs gave out completely. He buckled and crumpled to the ground. He tried pushing himself up with his arms but couldn't. He lay there not moving while the officer attached an audio cable to his suit.

"I need to see some identification," said the officer.

"I don't have any. I'm a free miner."

"Space born, eh? Let me guess, you don't have any docking authorization, either."

"I came here from the Kuiper Belt."

The officer looked amused. "On a quickship? Sure you did."

"You don't believe me? Check the flight computer."

The officer ignored this, typing notes onto his pad. "So no permits, no papers, no entry codes, nothing."

"I need to speak with someone in charge."

"You need to speak with a lawyer, space born."

They carried him out to the rover and lifted him into the cargo trunk. Victor felt completely helpless—and to think this was only one-sixth of Earth gravity.

The officer drove him to a medical facility, where nurses put him on a stretcher and gave him IV fluids and ten different vaccinations. When they finished, an officer in a different colored uniform entered and wire-strapped Victor's wrists to the stretcher. It wasn't until the man started reciting a litany of legal rights that Victor realized he had been arrested.

CHAPTER 21

Imala

Imala Bootstamp wasn't trying to get anyone fired at the Lunar Trade Department, but it sure felt good when she did. The culprit was one of the big uppity-ups, a senior auditor on the fifth floor who had been with the LTD for over thirty years. Imala, a mere junior assistant auditor with the agency, was so far down the totem pole that it took her a month to get anyone with authority to actually look at what she had found.

She had tried going to her immediate boss, a perverted idiot named Pendergrass, whose eyes dropped to her chest whenever she was forced to bring anything to his attention. Pendergrass had only told her, "Get off the warpath, Imala. Put down your little tomahawk and focus on your job. Stop following tracks you shouldn't be following."

Oh Pendergrass. You're so, so clever. How witty of you to make reference to my Apache heritage.

She had thought the world had outgrown racial insults—she certainly had never heard any growing up in Arizona. But then she had never known anyone like Pendergrass, either, who called her cubicle her "wigwam" and who would always make a circle with his mouth and tap it with his fingers whenever she passed him in the break room. She could have gone to HR and filed a complaint a long time ago, but the HR bimbo assigned to their floor was actually sleeping with Pendergrass—a fact Imala found both repulsive and sadly pathetic. Besides, Imala didn't want anyone fighting her battles for her. When she felt the need to "go on the warpath," she'd be swinging her own tomahawk, thank you very much.

She couldn't go to Pendergrass's boss either. He was a pushover yes-man whose head was so far up his boss's ass that he wore a kidney for a cap. All she'd get from him was a nice condescending lecture on the importance of following the chain of command. Then Kidney Cap would go to Pendergrass and give him an earful for not keeping his Apache on a short leash. And if that happened, Imala would have hell to pay with Pendergrass.

So she did the slightly unethical yet wholly necessary next best thing: She lied her way into the director's office.

"Do you have an appointment to see Director Gardona?" asked the secretary, not looking up from her terminal.

"Yes," said Imala. "Karen O'Hara, *Space Finance* magazine. Here for the feature interview."

Imala felt ridiculous with her hair in a bun and dressed in such a fashionable jacket and slacks—which she had rented for the occasion—but she knew she needed to look the part. She wasn't concerned about the secretary recognizing her. The agency employed hundreds of people, and all the grunts on the second floor where Imala worked never hobnobbed with anyone up here on the fifth. They didn't even use the same entrances. It was like two neighboring countries whose borders were never crossed.

Imala had tried a week ago to set an appointment with the director as herself, but as soon as the secretary had learned that she was a junior assistant auditor, the secretary referred her to her superiors and hung up on her. Nor could Imala get an e-mail or a call through. All of the director's messages were screened, and every attempt to contact him had been blocked. It was ridiculous. Who did the man think he was? This was the Lunar Trade Department, not the damn White House.

So here she was, doing the stupidest thing she had ever done in her life, all to get an audience with someone who might take her seriously.

"This way please," said the secretary, leading Imala through two doors that required holoprint authorization. The secretary waved her hand through the boxy holo by the door, and the locks clicked open.

All the security made Imala nervous, and she was beginning to wonder if this was a good idea. What if the director didn't think her information important enough to overlook her unorthodox way of getting his attention? Or what if she was wrong about the data? No, she was sure about that. The last door opened, and the secretary ushered her inside. Imala stepped through, and the secretary disappeared the way she had come.

Director Gardona was standing at his workstation moving his stylus through his holospace, zipping through documents so fast, Imala couldn't imagine how he could possibly be reading anything. She put him in his early sixties, white haired, fit, handsome. The suit he was wearing was probably worth more than three months of Imala's salary.

"Come in, Ms. Bootstamp," he said. "I'm most interested to meet you."

So he knew who she was. Imala wasn't yet sure if that was a good thing or a bad thing.

He pocketed his stylus and faced her, smiling. "But tell me first, is Karen O'Hara a real journalist for *Space Finance* or did you pull that name from a hat?"

"Real, sir. In case you checked her on the nets."

"As if I have time for such things," he waved her to a cocoon chair, which resembled an empty sphere with the front quarter sliced off. They were great for minimal gravity, and Imala climbed inside. Gardona took the chair opposite her.

"Why did you agree to meet me, sir, if you knew who I was?"

Gardona spread his hands in an innocent gesture. "Why wouldn't I want to meet any of my employees? And such a good one, too, I'm told."

He was either lying or there were people watching her she didn't know about. Pendergrass and Kidney Cap would rather yank out their fingernails than give her a positive review.

"I apologize for the silly deception, sir, but reaching you by traditional means wasn't working."

"I'm a busy man, Imala. My secretary protects my time."

So he knew *how* she had tried to reach him as well. Or maybe he was simply assuming she'd gone to the secretary.

He laughed. "Disguising yourself as a journalist. That's takes guts, Imala. Guts or stupidity, I'm not sure which."

"Perhaps a bit of both, sir."

"And under the guise of doing a feature interview, too." He shook a finger at her. "Appealing to my narcissism, I see."

"It seemed the most believable story, sir."

"Well I'm flattered you would think me important enough to warrant a feature interview in such a reputable magazine." He crossed his legs. "Well, you have my attention, Imala. I'm all ears."

She got right to it. "I have evidence, sir, that Gregory Seabright, one of our senior auditors, has been ignoring and in many cases concealing false financial records from Juke Limited for the better part of twelve years."

"I know Greg, Imala. I've known him since grad school. That's a very serious accusation."

"There's more, sir. I also have evidence of financial payments to Mr. Seabright from a small subsidiary of Juke Limited in excess of four million credits."

Gardona was silent a moment. He was still smiling, but there was no longer any life behind it. "If such an allegation were true, Imala, which I doubt, I can't imagine Greg would be dumb enough to keep such payments on file or make them easily detectable. He's one of our top auditors. He would cover his tracks."

"Oh, he covered his tracks, sir. He covered them with so many layers it's taken me two months to piece it together. I had to snoop and dig in places not normally accessible to me. It's a very lengthy thread that I had to follow to connect Mr. Seabright with the payments, but if prosecutors are patient enough, I can connect the dots for them."

"Prosecutors?"

"Obviously. Juke Limited ships have been exceeding weight limits for transshipments to Earth year after year without paying the required fees and fines. We're talking about hundreds of millions of credits here. Juke has been paying him off to turn a blind eye and foster illegal tax and tariff practices."

"And you can prove all this?"

She held up a data cube. "Over three thousands documents."

"I see. And when did you research and compile all this?"

"After hours. I only stumbled on it because I was studying old files, trying to familiarize myself with some of our larger accounts."

"This is troubling, Imala. Who else knows about this?"

"Just my immediate boss, Richard Pendergrass."

"I see. Well I will have to look into this immediately. If this proves true, it would be devastating to the reputation of this agency. I would ask that you keep this quiet until we can conduct an internal investigation."

He started to get up.

"One more thing, Mr. Gardona. Juke Limited is our largest account. To conceal something this big for this long is too much for one person. I can't prove it beyond the legal definition of doubt, but I have six other names on this cube whom I suspect are aware of and participating in this practice."

He took the cube. "I hope you're wrong, Imala. Thank you for bringing this to my attention."

She left his office, and by late afternoon of the following day word was spreading that Gregory Seabright had been terminated. Not suspended. Not given leave. Terminated.

Imala stood at her cubicle—which was smaller than most refrigerators and sometimes just as cold since it was directly below one of the AC vents—and felt better than she had in a long time. She had beaten the Man. She had taken on the giant and slung her rock and hit him dead center in the forehead. Gregory Seabright, dirty money-grubber, was down. And not just Seabright but Ukko Jukes as well, the wealthiest man in the solar system. Or, as Imala knew all too well, one of the most crooked men alive. Yes sir, not even old Ukko Jukes was safe from her justice.

She slapped her desk with the palm of her hand. Now this was auditing. If only her father could see her now. "Auditing?" he had said, when she had told him about her plans for grad school. "Auditing?" He said the word like it left a sour taste in his mouth. "That's worse than accounting, Imala. You're not even counting beans. You're checking to make sure someone else counted beans. That's the most pointless, fruitless, meaningless career anyone could possibly choose. You're smarter than that. You can do anything. Don't waste your life being a bean-counter checker."

But oh how wrong Father was. Auditing was what made everything work. Without auditing, we'd live in financial barbarism. Markets would collapse. Banks would break. The whole system would crash.

But you couldn't explain that to Father. He'd throw up his hands at talk like that. But taking a crook, putting a bad guy in prison, that Father could grasp, that was something he could wrap his head around.

Once she saved up enough to send a holo to Earth and once Lunar prosecutors got involved and the media caught wind, she could contact home and say, "See, Father? Your little girl taking on Ukko Jukes. That big enough for you?"

Pendergrass poked his head over the wall of the cubicle. "You heard about Seabright?"

"Yeah, I heard."

"You have anything to do with that?"

She shrugged.

"Come on, Imala. You told me he was duping. I didn't think it was possible. I thought you were witch-hunting. You know, fresh out of school and ready to take on the world. All that idealistic crap. We get people like that sometimes."

Imala said nothing.

"Guess I was wrong," said Pendergrass. "I should've listened to you. My mistake."

Imala raised an eyebrow. "Are you actually admitting you were wrong?"

"Hey, there's a first for everything."

He smiled, and for once he didn't look at her chest.

"As a peace offering," said Pendergrass, "I want to buy you lunch."

Ah, thought Imala. So that's where this was going.

He must have sensed what she was thinking. "It's not a date, Imala. Hanixa is meeting us at the restaurant. It would be the three of us."

Nothing could be less appetizing than to share a table with Pendergrass and his little HR hussy, but Imala wasn't about to reject an offered olive branch. That would only make things worse. So she grabbed her coat and followed him outside.

The black car waiting at the curb was the first red flag. Pendergrass opened the back passenger door, still as friendly as ever, and Imala was climbing inside even though warning bells were going off in her head.

When the car door closed without Pendergrass joining her, Imala realized what a mistake she had made. A man was sitting across from her, his face hidden in shadow. Imala didn't need to see his features to know who he was.

"Hello, Imala. My name is Ukko Jukes."

The car pulled away from the curb and onto the track. Wherever they were going, Ukko had already programmed the destination into the system. Imala considered trying for the door handle and taking her chances jumping from the car. But they accelerated suddenly, and she figured he would probably have the doors locked anyway.

"Are you going to kill me?" she asked.

He surprised her by laughing, a big belly laugh that filled the car. "You don't mince words, do you, Imala. Rest easy, my dear. I'm not the villain you think I am."

"Then who's the villain? Gregory Seabright?"

Ukko frowned. "Director Gardona contacted me this morning and informed me of the investigation. I was as disappointed and shocked as he was. Furious, really. If this proves true, it means there are people in my company who think they can steal from me."

Imala couldn't hide the sarcasm in her voice. "So you had no idea this was going on?"

He looked affronted. "Absolutely not. Do you think I would be stupid enough to skimp like that? I'm a businessman, Imala. Some would even say a very savvy businessman. Do you think I would skate around regulations and risk losing shipping licenses that generate billions in monthly revenue? I'm no fool, Imala. Even if I were the three-headed monster you take me for, I'm not moronic enough to risk having my company broken up and dragged through the mud by international prosecutors all for a few hundred million credits."

"You say that like it's not a lot of money."

"Do you know how much I am worth, Imala? Do you have any idea how much money my corporation has generated in the time you and I have been talking?"

"I bet you pick up a lot of women with that line."

He laughed again. "Believe me, Imala, whatever my people were hiding with Gregory Seabright was a drop in my bucket."

He was exaggerating. Imala had a pretty good idea what he was worth. She hadn't seen all the files at the agency, so she couldn't be completely certain. But she knew enough to suspect that the load Seabright had helped conceal was no chump change. Plus Seabright was only one person. Imala was near certain Jukes was filling pockets all throughout the agency. Seabright was simply the one careless enough to get caught.

"So you kidnapped me to convince me that you're innocent of any wrongdoing?" asked Imala.

"Kidnapped? Goodness, Imala. You do gravitate toward the dramatic, don't you? No, I shared this car with you on the way to your lunch appointment so that I may make you a proposition."

"If you're going to offer me hush money, don't bother."

He chuckled and shook his head. "Honestly. I don't think I've ever met someone who thinks so little of me. I should have you around more often, Imala, just to keep me humble."

She folded her arms and said nothing.

"I want to offer you a job, Imala. You're still young, and you lack experience, so it's not a senior position. But you obviously have a passion for the work and you're very good at what you do. You uncovered a mess at the LTD that no one else saw for years."

"The other auditors look at the totals. I look at *all* the numbers."

"Exactly. You look at all the numbers. That's what I need, Imala. Someone who looks where others don't. There are people in my company who have cheated me, and I want to know who they are. I don't know whom to trust. I need someone above reproach who will report directly to me."

"You don't need me," said Imala. "Most of the files I found implicate people on your staff. Anyone on the investigation can follow those threads and give you a list of names."

"Yes, but how big is this problem? Did you find every file? Did you uncover every concealment? I fear this may be bigger than we think. These people are auditors, Imala. They know how to make their crimes disappear. I want to know who they are." His face darkened, and she saw a glimpse of the man he was rumored to be. "No one steals from me, Imala. No one."

Did he honestly not know this was going on? Was he actually innocent? Imala couldn't deny that it was possible. The man had hundreds of thousands of employees. He couldn't know the actions of all of them. And none of the evidence she had found implicated Ukko in any way, not directly at least.

Ukko said, "You and I both know that no one in the private sector will even glance at your résumé until you've done five years at the LTD, Imala. I'm offering you an early out. I know the bureaucracy you're dealing with. I know you must hate it. And you've been there, what, six months?"

Seven months, thirteen days, thought Imala. Enough time to know she loved the work and hated the people. Aloud she said, "It didn't cross your mind that hiring me would be a conflict of interest considering the pending investigation? I can't possibly accept, Mr. Jukes."

"I haven't even told you the salary."

"It doesn't matter. It would taint the investigation. It would *look* like hush money."

He told her the salary.

It was a lot of money, though not *too* much that it looked like a bribe. It was probably comparable to what people with a few more years experience than her were making these days in the private sector. And hadn't she proved that she was just as capable as they were, if not more so? It was exactly the salary she knew she deserved. For a moment she hesitated. More income meant she could get out of that closet of an apartment she was staying in and start paying off her student loans. Maybe even send money home.

No. What was she thinking? He was buying her off. Just as he had bought off Seabright and Pendergrass. How could she forget Pendergrass? The snake had tossed her into the lion's den.

"Stop the car," she said.

"Am I to take this as a no to my offer?"

"You may take it as a hell no and you can shove it up that wrinkly white butt of yours. You're not buying me off."

His expression remained impassive. "You're making a mistake, Imala. I am offering you an opportunity here."

"You're removing me from the investigation," she said. "You're mopping up. Make me go away, and your stooges in the LTD make the whole investigation go away. Tell me if I'm getting warm here."

Ukko flicked his wrist, and the car pulled to the curb. Imala's door opened.

"Enjoy your lunch, Imala. I hope you'll show more respect the next time someone merely offers you what you deserve."

She started to get out.

"And one more thing," said Ukko. "A bit of unsolicited advice. Get to know people before you write them off as black-hearted scoundrels. You're a quick judge of character, Imala. And you're not always right."

She got out. The door closed. The car zipped back into traffic and disappeared.

She looked around her. She was in the French Quarter, an upscale part of town with quaint shops selling chocolates and perfumes and ridiculously priced clothing. Every street in the city was covered with shielded domes that protected against solar radiation and that kept in air and heat, but only in the French Quarter were the dome ceilings painted the light blue color of Earth sky with the occasional white of fluffy clouds. Imala hated it. It was like everyone she worked with at the LTD. Fake and phony.

Across the street was a restaurant. Pendergrass and his dimwit vixen were sitting at a table outside, eating pasta through semi-sealed containers. Imala must have been doing circles with Ukko if Pendergrass had beaten her here. He saw her, smiled, and waved at her to come join them. Imala turned on her heels and began walking back toward the office, ignoring him. If she crossed the street and approached Pendergrass she was fairly certain she'd grab his pasta and smear it in his face.

It took Imala well over an hour to get back to the LTD, and that was after removing her greaves and taking big moon leaps down the sidewalk in the lesser gravity. She got contemptuous looks from people since moonwalking was unfashionable in the French Quarter, but Imala didn't care. It's the Moon, people. Get over it.

A message was waiting in the holospace at her cubicle. It read, COME TO MY OFFICE. ROOM 414.

Imala checked the agency directory, worried that the room was assigned to one of the auditors she had fingered. She was relieved when she saw that it wasn't. A senior auditor named Fareed Bakárzai, whom Imala didn't know, occupied the space. She felt leery about being summoned to a stranger's office so soon after meeting with Gardona and Ukko Jukes. It couldn't be a coincidence.

She took the tube up to the fourth floor and knocked on the office door. "Come in."

Fareed Bakárzai's office was an organized disaster. There were stacks of discs, boxes, and files everywhere, all strapped to the floor with long bands. Rows of old tariff and tax-code books lined shelves, though they had to be years, if not decades, out of date. It was the most paper Imala had seen since coming to Luna.

Fareed flicked off his holospace and faced her. He was about the same age as Director Gardona, but the similarities stopped there. Fareed reminded Imala of a few professors from Arizona State: cardigan, beard, slightly unkempt appearance, the kind of person you'd find running an antique store filled mostly with junk.

"Ms. Bootstamp," he said, extending a hand. "I'm Fareed. Welcome. You probably don't know this, but I'm the man who brought you here. To Luna, I mean. I read your paper on iron trade discrepancies and found it naïve in places but mostly on the nose. Very keen observations for a grad student. I had HR do a little digging. When they saw that you had actually submitted an application, I had them pull it from the slush pile and told them to interview you."

Imala was momentarily speechless. She had no idea. "I don't know what to say. Thank you, sir."

He shook a finger. "Not 'sir.' Fareed." He gestured to the mess. "I'd offer you a place to sit down, but there isn't one and we're nearly weightless up here anyway."

She looked around and said nothing.

"You're wondering why I brought you here," he said. "And I'll be forthright with you. It's not good news." He took a moment and sighed. "Essentially you were terminated about half an hour ago."

"What!"

Fareed held a hand. "Now, before you get angry and say something you might regret, hear me out. You are *not* terminated. The executive team met, and I fought for you."

"Wait. I'm not fired?"

"You were. I talked them into keeping you on, though not with your old job. That was out of the question. You're getting a new assignment."

"Why was I terminated in the first place?" But as soon as she asked the question she knew the answer. Ukko. She had turned him down an hour ago, and Ukko had wasted no time getting a holo to whomever he owned in the agency.

"Does Ukko Jukes own Director Gardona?" asked Imala. "Is that what this is?"

"Careful what you say, Imala. These walls are thin. There were several legitimate reasons for your termination."

She folded her arms, furious. "Such as?"

"You pretended to be a journalist and lied to a fellow employee, violating the agency's code of ethics."

Imala threw a hand up. "I lied to a *secretary*. And I did it in the interest of the agency. Gardona wouldn't see me otherwise."

"You also snooped around agency files for which you had no authorization to access."

"I was conducting an investigation into illegal practices. I couldn't exactly go to Seabright and ask to see his files."

"There are channels to follow for this kind of thing, Imala. You skipped them all and played sheriff."

She couldn't believe this. Here she had done what no one else in the agency had the courage to do—and maybe even the brains to do—and they were vilifying her.

"Whom was I supposed to go to?" she asked. "Pendergrass? Because I *did* go to him. He blew me off."

Fareed seemed surprised. "When was this?"

"A month ago."

"Do you any have documentation of this? E-mails? Holos?"

She tried to remember. "No. I pulled him aside and showed him everything in person."

Fareed was disappointed. He shrugged. "He'd probably only say he thought you were being zealous and admit he made a mistake."

"That's exactly what he said. Right before he led me outside and put me in a car with Ukko Jukes."

Fareed was startled. "When?"

"An hour ago. That's where I was at lunch."

"I see." Fareed went back behind his desk, paced a moment, then turned to her. "I can't get you your old job back, Imala. Even knowing that you went to Pendergrass. The executive team was adamant."

"Of course they were. Ukko Jukes has them in his pocket. They're trying to shut me up and make the whole scandal with Seabright go away."

"It already is going away," said Fareed. "Jukes has agreed to pay all the back taxes and tariffs as well all fees and fines. Both the agency and Jukes will conduct separate internal investigations, and that will be the end of it."

"Tell me you're joking. We should be taking this to prosecutors."

Fareed shook his head. "Not going to happen, Imala. They're going to bury it."

"Then I'll go to the press. I'll tell whomever will listen."

"No one will listen, Imala. There are influences here much greater than you realize."

He was telling her that Ukko owned the media as well; that anything she did would be squashed by Jukes. Unbelievable. They were letting this man bully them. Even Fareed—who seemed like a decent enough guy and who probably didn't take a dime from Ukko—was stuck under Ukko's thumb simply because he was in a system Ukko controlled.

"I got you on at Customs," said Fareed. "It's not glamorous, but it's working with people, which you need."

"What is that supposed to mean?"

"You're a little rough around the edges, Imala. You haven't made any friends since you came here. You despise everyone. This could be good for you."

"I don't despise everyone."

"Name one person in your department with whom you have a friend-ship."

"They all kiss up to Pendergrass. They don't care about the work. They make constant mistakes."

"How would you know they make mistakes?"

"Because I've checked their work. It's sloppy."

"Yes, and I'm sure they greatly appreciate you, a junior assistant, comb-ing their work for mistakes."

"Pendergrass sure isn't going to do it."

Fareed sighed. "You're done, Imala. I stuck my neck out for you when the guys upstairs were ready to put you on a shuttle back to Earth. You can at least pretend to act grateful and take this job. Who knows? In a few years, I might be able to help you get on with a private firm."

Imala wasn't sure if she should punch the wall or cry. A few years? He *might* help her in few years? This was his gift to her? This was him pulling a favor? She wanted to tell him no. She wanted to shut him down the same way she had rejected Ukko. But what good would that do her? The moment your work permit was tagged as terminated, you were gone. If she walked out of here without a job, she'd be shipped to Earth no questions asked. And then what? Back to Arizona to face her father and tell him how right he had been? No, she couldn't do that.

"What would I be auditing at Customs?" she asked.

"You won't be auditing. You'd be a caseworker."

"A caseworker? I'm not trained for that."

"Show them how smart and nice you are, Imala, and I'm sure they'll give you more responsibility."

He handed her a data drive.

"What's this?" she asked.

"Your first case. A free miner who came in a week ago from the Kuiper Belt on a quickship. No identification. No docking authorizations. Deal with it."

"How? I don't know what to do with this."

"You know customs law, Imala. You know the regulations. The rest is paperwork. If you smile occasionally, you might actually be good at this."

She walked out of the office, holding the data drive. She stepped into the down tube and slowly descended, feeling numb. She had come to Luna because she believed she could do something important with her life, something meaningful. Now she was relegated to resolving petty customs violations. Pendergrass was right. She had gone on the warpath and picked a fight she had no chance of winning.

She didn't bother going to her desk. There was nothing there she needed.

She paused in the lobby and connected the data drive to her wrist pad. There was a single file. A thin dossier on Victor Delgado. It didn't tell her much, other than the fact that Delgado had been asking to speak with someone in authority since he had arrived. Imala found this amusing. Sorry, Victor. You're stuck with a blacklisted former junior assistant. I'm about as far from authority as you can get.

CHAPTER 22

MOPs

Wit O'Toole sat in the passenger seat of the Air Shark attack helicopter as it flew south from the village of Pakuli in Central Sulawesi, Indonesia. Below him, dense lowland tropical forests began to mix with shorter, montane trees as the chopper left the river valley and moved up into the foothills. Breaks in the trees revealed small, isolated family farms with simple wooden homes built amid fields of maize or coffee. As the chopper rose in elevation, terraced rice fields came into view, clinging to the slopes of the highlands like a staircase of green climbing up the landscape. If not for the burning villages and corpses rotting in the sun, Wit might think this a paradise.

Indonesia was having two civil wars at once. The government of Sulawesi was fighting an Islamist extremist group known as the Rémeseh here in the mountains, while the government of New Guinea was fighting native insurgents on that island. Civilians were stuck in the crosshairs, and the situation was getting bloody enough that the developed world was almost beginning to care. News of the burning church might be exactly the sort of human-interest story to make the media take notice. People's eyes glazed over headlines about mountain farmers murdered in Indonesia. But tell them that Islamist militants had locked a congregation of Christians in their small mountain chapel and burned the building to the ground with the people inside, and suddenly you've got news people care about.

Wit hoped that was true. The people of Indonesia needed help—more help than the MOPs could provide. And if the church incident would turn the world's eyes to the plight of Sulawesi then perhaps the people burned alive hadn't died in vain.

Wit turned to Calinga sitting in the pilot's seat. "Take vids of every-thing. But be discreet about it, don't let the people *see* that we're taking vids."

Calinga nodded. He understood.

The cameras on the helmets and suits were small enough and con-cealed enough that Wit wasn't too concerned about the villagers taking notice—most of them had probably never seen tech like that anyway. He was more concerned about him and Calinga getting the right kind of shots. The smoldering bodies. The blackened, charred remains of a child's toy or doll. The weeping women of the village mourning the loss of loved ones. The media was starving for that type of horror, and if Wit could give it to them, then he *might* be able to begin the sequence of events that *might* eventually result in aid for the people of Indonesia.

That effort would take months, though. The war on apathy moved much slower than real wars fought on the ground. Enough citizens and human rights groups would have to see the vids and get angry enough and com-plain to legislators enough that eventually someone with authority would actually take action. It wouldn't be easy. If the economy took another dive or if some politician or celebrity was caught in a sex scandal, the media would go back to ignoring Indonesia and no aid or protection would come.

Wit wasn't on a mission to turn public opinion, though. Getting the vids was a tertiary objective. His first order of business was to recover the body of one of his men who had died in the attack. Then he would deal with the Rémeseh who had burned the church, either taking them into custody—which was never ideal—or taking them down—which was never pretty.

Wit saw the pillars of smoke long before they reached the village of Toro. The chapel would be little more than a smoldering heap by now, but the terrorists had set other fires, and the wind had likely blown some of the flames into the grasslands.

Calinga set the helicopter down in the village a block south of where the church had burned. Hundreds of villagers were gathered, but they gave the helicopter a wide berth and turned their heads away from the wind of the rotor blades. Wit and Calinga climbed down in full combat gear, and Wit could see the villagers' faces change from fear to relief. They knew who MOPs were and the protection they provided. Some cheered. Some wept openly, clasping their hands in front of them. Others, especially children, crowded around Wit and Calinga, motioning them to follow them up to the chapel. Everyone was speaking Indonesian at once, and Wit could only pick up bits and pieces. They were telling him his man was dead.

They meant Bogdanovich, one of the MOPs from Wit's most recent round of recruits. Wit had sent the Russian to the village weeks ago with Averbach, a more senior MOP, to protect the village from strikes the Rémeseh were conducting all across the highlands. When a firefight to the south had broken out between the Rémeseh and a group of farmers, Wit had ordered Bogdanovich and Averbach to go and offer support.

Bogdanovich, however, had refused to leave the village, fearing the firefight was a distraction for a coordinated strike on the village. Averbach ended up going south alone. When he had returned, the chapel was burning, and Bogdanovich was dead in the street.

Wit arrived at the chapel and found Averbach carrying out bodies. Several of the corpses already lay in the street covered with sheets, and villagers were wailing and crying and raising their arms heavenward as they identified the dead.

There were other bodies, too. About ten men. All riddled with bullets or other wounds, lying in circles of their own blood. Several women and children were throwing rocks at these corpses, spitting and shouting curses and screaming through their tears. Bogdanovich hadn't gone down without a fight apparently.

An elderly woman was kneeling beside another body, this one wrapped in bloody sheets and sprinkled with flower petals. The villagers and children pointed at the body and told Wit what he already suspected. It was Bogdanovich.

Wit nodded and thanked them, then went directly to Averbach, whose face was covered in soot and sweat, and who had gone back into the chapel to retrieve more of the dead. Wit and Calinga pulled on their latex gloves and fell into step beside him. Without speaking they delicately helped Averbach lift another body from the ashes and onto a sheet, which they then used as a stretcher to carry the body out into the street. It was gruesome, horrific work. The air was thick with the scent of charred human remains, and the timbers and ashes continued to smolder, burning Wit's eyes with the smoke. It took a great deal of concentration for Wit to control his gag reflex and maintain a reverent composure.

When they finished, twenty-six charred bodies lay in a line, some of them burned beyond recognition. Many of them were children. A block away another fire was burning in the street. Some of the villagers had dragged the dead Rémeseh militants into a heap and set the bodies on fire. Bogdanovich remained untouched, and now more of the village's elderly women kneeled beside him, offering their respect and prayers.

Wit spoke in his broken Indonesian to one of the men, asking if anyone in the village had seen in which direction the surviving Rémeseh had fled. As he suspected, no shortage of people came forward. They all pointed to the south.

"I will leave one of my men here with you," Wit told them in Indonesian. "He will protect you. He is as good a soldier as Bogdanovich, if not better."

"No one is better," the crowd cried. "No one is braver. More would have died if not for him."

Wit got the stretcher down from the chopper, then he and Calinga delicately lifted Bogdanovich into a body bag. They kept him wrapped in the sheets, then loaded the body into the Air Shark. Calinga stayed behind. Wit took the pilot's seat, and Averbach sat shotgun.

When they were up in the air, Averbach said, "This is my fault. Bog had gone local. He had fallen in love with one of the women in the village. Nothing ever happened between them. They were never alone. But I noticed the furtive looks she gave him. And I noticed that *he* noticed and didn't seem to mind. He never said anything to me, but I should have told you. We should have pulled him out. It clouded his judgment."

"I figured as much," said Wit. "It wasn't like Bog to disobey an order."

"The villagers said Bog would have taken down all the Rémeseh if not for the chapel. The woman was inside. When the Rémeseh set it on fire and padlocked the door, Bog went for it. He tried to give himself enough cover to reach the door, but it was a trap. They had three snipers waiting. They burned the church, not to kill the people inside but to flush Bog out."

Averbach shook his head. "I should have been with him. I could have taken the snipers."

"I sent you south," said Wit. "You obeyed orders. That's what you should have done."

They flew south, but saw little through the jungle canopy. After an hour of searching they headed back to Pakuli and delivered Bogdanovich's body to the medical team who would prepare it for shipment back to Russia.

Another one lost, thought Wit. That was four in Indonesia. Four too many.

He had hoped that the Indians would join in the fight. He could use the PCs; they were excellent trackers. But the Indians were being skittish. The PCs were willing, but the powers that be didn't want to commit troops.

I need more men, thought Wit. I should have taken that Maori bastard, Mazer Rackham. I could use him about now.

He sent a squad up into the jungle south of Toro village, but he didn't expect them to find much. The Rémeseh were long gone by now—they had likely been long gone before Wit had even reached the village.

He returned to his tent and set up his terminal. Calinga had collected all the video he had taken at the village and sent it to Wit's inbox. Wit reviewed the footage along with his own and edited a three-minute piece that showed the horror and suffering in Toro. He didn't censor himself. He showed everything. The bodies. The mourning. The ashes. He added no music. He didn't need to sensationalize it. The raw video would speak for itself. He titled the file "Victims of the Rémeseh," then added the date and location. He then uploaded it to the nets and waited. The following morning several news organizations had picked up the video, though even these had buried it.

The story getting the most attention on the nets was an unexplained interference of space communications. Scientists on Earth and Luna said it was an increase in cosmic radiation, although no one could determine a source. In fact, the interference seemed to be coming from all directions at once, raising background noise to a shout and making it impossible to communicate in space. A reputable astronomer was doing the rounds on the talk-show circuit prattling on about unexplained gamma bursts, but he offered up no explanation. Many commercial and passenger flights to and from Luna were temporarily suspended, and representatives from the space-mining industry were making official statements to the press, assuring the families of corporate miners that the companies were doing all they could to ensure the safety of their employees and to determine the source of the problem.

Wit's first thought was terrorists. It was a brilliant way to cripple commerce and devastate the economy, particularly in those countries that had become so dependent on the space trade. But he eventually dismissed this idea. He couldn't imagine a terrorist group with enough scientific talent and resources to construct a device powerful enough to pull off this level of interference, to say nothing of getting the thing in space.

What's more, the inference was gradually getting louder: The background noise was increasing in volume, suggesting that the device in space was either increasing in power, or whatever was causing it was getting closer to Earth.

A news site had a related headline stating: NUTTY NETTERS PEG INTERFERENCE ON ALIENS.

Wit selected the link and read the article. The reporter was having a laugh at the hundred or so vids that had popped up on the nets recently, claiming that the interference was caused by aliens. Wit followed the links and watched a number of the vids. Many were talking heads: mostly conspiracy theorists rattling off quasi-science and making vague references to government cover-ups. (Nutty indeed.) Others were quite entertaining. They ranged from the ridiculous to the comical to the sadly pathetic. Poems, songs, even a puppet show, which Wit couldn't help but laugh at. Most of them had zero production value, but several had been made using every device of movie magic to create creatures and environments so lifelike and so believable that Wit had to watch them two or three times to find the imperfections that disproved their authenticity.

The comments for most of the vids were what he would expect. Hate, mockery, cruel personal attacks. But occasionally, particularly on those vids that had re-created aliens with striking realism, the comments were more congratulatory: Well done! Looked real. You almost had me. Peed my pants!

Wit knew the vids were fake. But he couldn't help but wonder: What if the radio interference *is* aliens? What if the conspiracy theorists were right? What if an alien army was approaching Earth at this very moment? It was a far-fetched idea, yes, but it *was* possible. And if it were true, his troops would be completely unprepared. He couldn't allow that. He had to train them for such a contingency. They would scoff, yes, laugh at him even, but he had his duty. And yet, how do you train soldiers for an enemy you don't understand? How do you prepare them for a completely unpredictable situation? Would the aliens be hostile? There was no way to tell for certain until it was too late. No, the only training I can give my men is to analyze before they act in a strange situation, and to presume hostile intent in all cases.

The following morning, Wit gathered all of the MOPs in Indonesia. Many were in the camp in Sulawesi and joined him in the mess hall. The others stationed in nearby villages or in New Guinea joined him via holo.

Wit stood in the holospace facing them. "I have some vids I want you to see," he said. He played them a few of the alien vids from the nets. Their reaction was not unlike the comments online. They laughed. They scoffed. They mocked. They applauded and whistled at the realistic endeavors.

"Hey Deen, is that your girlfriend?" someone shouted when a particularly nasty alien roared on-screen.

"Couldn't be Deen's girl," someone else shouted, "she's much uglier."

More laughter.

"I'm surrounded by comic geniuses," Deen deadpanned.

When the vids finished, Wit stepped back into the holospace.

"What gives, Captain?" Lobo asked. "We gearing up for some aliens?"

"Maybe," said Wit.

The room laughed, but when Wit's expression stayed flat, the laughter quickly died and a confused awkwardness took its place.

"You can't be serious, Cap," said Deen. "I've seen a hundred of those vids. They're all bogus."

"Is that what you do with your free time, Deen?" said Chi-won.

"Hey, what is this? Pick on Deen Day?" said Deen.

"Seriously, Captain," said Mabuzza. "Haven't we been seeing alien invasions since, like, the nineteen hundreds?"

"But that doesn't mean it won't happen," said Wit, "and that it won't be terrible when it does." He paused and scanned the crowd. "Situation. A hundred aliens drop into this camp and start killing everyone. What do you do?"

There was a silence, then someone said, "Run like hell."

The men chuckled.

"All right," said Wit. "New situation. A hundred Rémeseh charge into camp and begin killing everyone. What do you do?"

"*Send* them to hell," said Deen, to another round of laughter.

Wit smiled. "I'm glad to see we have a plan for the Rémeseh." He paused again, then in a louder voice asked, "What do we train for?"

The man answered in unison. "Every contingency!"

Wit doubled his volume. "What do we train for?"

"EVERY CONTINGENCY!"

"A contingency is a possible event that cannot be predicted with certainty," said Wit. "And we cannot with one hundred percent certainty dismiss the validity of this idea. Is it likely? No. It is possible? Yes. Is it absurd? You may think so, but I would rather be trained for the absurd than dead."

The men said nothing. He had their attention.

"Which militaries in the world are preparing for such an event?" asked Wit. "Answer: none. Which militaries are prepared for tech weapons far beyond our own? Answer: none. Which militaries would be caught with their pants down and completely unprepared for this? Answer: all of them. But not us. What do we train for?"

"EVERY CONTINGENCY!"

"So how do we prepare?" asked Wit.

They answered him with silence.

"You analyze before you act," said Wit. "You have no idea what you're up against. Your previous training and tactics may get you killed the instant you attempt them. You can't assume this enemy will think or fight or react like a human. A terrified human will flee. A terrified pit bull will jump for your jugular. How will an alien respond to fear? Does it experience fear at all? Analyze before you act. Take note of everything. Their movement, weapons, group behavior, anatomy, reactions to the environment, speed, equipment. Even the smallest detail is valuable new intelligence. Analyze before you act." A few of the men were nodding. "And in all cases," said Wit, "without exception, you always presume hostile intent. You must presume they want to kill you. That doesn't mean you shoot first, it just means you never, never, never trust. And when they do show hostility, you do not hesitate to take them down."

He looked at each of the men in turn. "Situation. A hundred aliens drop into camp. What do we do? Deen?"

"Analyze before we act, sir. Presume hostile intent."

"Correct. And what do we do if they prove to be hostile?"

"We send them to hell, sir."

"You bet your ass," said Wit.

CHAPTER 23

Kleopatra

The beeping alert on Lem's desk woke him, and he peeled himself out of his hammock. He drifted to the desk and waved his hand through the holospace. Chubs's head appeared. "The Formics are approaching Kleopatra," said Chubs.

"Have they vented?" asked Lem.

"No. They're decelerating. Fast. We did some additional, long-range scans to see why. It looks like a mass of ships has congregated at Kleopatra and positioned themselves directly in the Formics' path. They've essentially built a blockade."

"How many ships?"

"Twenty-four by our last count. Data from the sky scanner continues to come in, so we may have some more ships pop up as we get closer. We're still quite a distance behind the Formic ship, but we were closing the gap with the Formics decelerating. I went ahead and ordered the flight crew to match their deceleration and maintain our distance until you could get up here."

"I'm on my way."

Lem threw on his uniform and made his way to the helm. He was still buttoning his jacket when he arrived and met Chubs at the holospace. The systems chart had been replaced with a rendering of all the ships positioned in space forming the blockade. There was a bit of distance between each ship, but together they made a giant wall between the Formic ship and Earth.

"Who are they?" asked Lem.

"Corporates and free miners," said Chubs. "We can tell from their shape and design that there are ships from Juke Limited, WU-HU, Mine-Tek, and several clans of free miners."

"Then people know about the Formics," said Lem. "Does everyone know? Does Earth know?"

"Impossible to say," said Chubs. "But I highly doubt it. We're still way too far away for the Formic ship to show up on Earth scopes. The ship's too small and too dim. The only way Earth could know the ship exists is if someone out here told them. And the interference here is as thick as ever. These ships forming the blockade can't communicate with Earth any more than we can. Just because *they* know doesn't mean anyone *else* knows. Plus notice that they're all mining ships. No military ships among them. These aren't ships sent from Earth. They were already out here. My guess is, one of them saw the Formic ship on their sky scanner and alerted the other ships in the immediate vicinity. Transmissions within a few hundred kilometers get through fine, and this is a main flight path. So there's going to be traffic. Plus the interference would cause ships to cluster together anyway to try to figure out what was going on."

"When will the Formics reach them?"

"Within a few hours."

"Those ships have no idea what the Formics are capable of. They'll try to communicate with them like the Italians did. We've got to tell them what we know."

"We can't, Lem. We'd have to get close enough to reach them on the radio. That would put us within range of the Formics' weapons. There's likely to be a battle, and we would be thrown into the middle of it."

"We can't sit back and let them die, Chubs. Some of those ships are our own people."

Chubs lowered his voice. "May I speak to you in private, Lem?"

Lem was surprised by the question but he obliged. They moved into the conference room adjacent to the helm, and Chubs closed the door behind them.

"We can't lose sight of our mission, Lem. We've got intel to get to Earth."

"We're not losing sight of anything," said Lem. "We're saving people's lives. We don't have to join in the fight. We don't even have to slow down.

We fly in fast and transmit a message to the ships as we pass. We tell them to flee. We send them everything we know, and we get out. We've been waiting for the Formics to decelerate so we can pass them and beat them to Earth. This is our chance."

"It's too dangerous, Lem. We can't go anywhere near the Formic ship. It's set to vent at any moment. If we're even remotely close to it when it does, we're ashes. Consider another alternative. We change course now. We get off the ecliptic and move up in a tall parabola, going high over the Formic ship while it's stopped. Then we come back down toward Luna. That way, even if the ship vents, we're too far away to suffer any damage."

"Then everyone on those ships will die," said Lem. "They'll stay and fight and they'll die. Plus we would lose valuable time taking a circuitous route. Look, I've heard your counsel. I appreciate it. I acknowledge that what I'm proposing is a risk. But I'm making the call here. We're not ditching anyone else to save our own necks. I've done that too many damn times already. We're staying the course." He wiped his hand through the holospace over the conference table in a particular sequence, and the navigator's head appeared. "Accelerate back to our previous speed," said Lem.

"Yes, sir." The navigator looked to his left as he reached for his controls.

"Hold that order," said Chubs.

The navigator stopped moving. Lem was shocked. Chubs had just challenged Lem's authority in front of a member of the crew. The navigator didn't move. He was either so stunned by Chubs's insubordination that he was too shocked to fulfill Lem's orders, or he was actually following Chubs's orders over Lem's.

Chubs waved his hand through the holospace, and the navigator disappeared. "You can't do this, Lem."

"I am the captain of this ship. Don't tell me what I can and can't do."

"You don't understand, Lem. I can't *let* you do this."

Chubs's expression was calm and his tone polite, but the implication was clear. He was claiming to have more authority. He was completely undermining Lem's position as captain. It was total insubordination, if not outright mutiny. Lem opened the door and waved two crewmen inside. When they entered, he gestured to Chubs. "This man is removed from office. He is to be confined to quarters for the reminder of this flight. I want him off this helm."

The two crewmen looked sheepish and didn't move.

"Is there something unclear about those orders?" said Lem. "Place this man under house arrest."

There was an awkward silence. The two crewmen glanced at one another and then looked at Chubs, as if waiting for him to give them orders.

Lem suddenly understood. He wasn't actually the person in charge. He had never been in charge. Not for one minute of the expedition. Chubs was the real captain. And everyone knew it but Lem.

"You don't actually have the authority to remove me, Lem," Chubs said kindly. "Your father was afraid that we might get in a tough situation, and he gave me the authority to override any decision that might put you in physical danger. And in my judgment, what you're proposing puts you in danger, so we won't do it."

His tone was polite but final.

Lem turned to the two crewmen, who averted their eyes, embarrassed.

Lem laughed inside. This whole trip had been a charade. His entire assignment: serving as captain, overseeing the field tests, safeguarding the glaser. It was all one of Father's games. Father hadn't given him any authority. Father hadn't trusted him. He had merely allowed Lem to foolishly play pretend. All because Father didn't think Lem intelligent enough to make his own decisions and command his own destiny.

"I've been in danger this whole trip," said Lem. "That never stopped you before."

"You were never in danger during the bump," said Chubs. "And Weigh Station Four caught me off guard. I made a mistake by agreeing to join El Cavador. Had I known then what we know now, I never would have allowed it. Your father will have my head for that. I'm not making that mistake again."

Lem smiled. "Well, I appreciate now knowing the real situation."

"We'll take the parabola route," said Chubs. "And we will issue these orders in your name, so that no one will know that there's been any interference in your authority. This will be treated as if it were your decision."

"Thank you," said Lem, without a hint of sarcasm. "That's very thoughtful." He wasn't going to act like a petulant child. He wasn't even angry with them. They were merely doing their jobs.

"And for what it's worth," said Chubs, "I think your course of action is better than what we're actually doing. We'll burn a lot of fuel changing course like this. We have the fuel, yes, but doing this will deplete nearly all of our reserves. We'll still make it to Luna, but we won't be able to deviate course again. We'll be coasting into home. So if it were up to me, we'd plow ahead and take the risk. But it's not up to me. It's not my ship."

"It's not my ship, either," said Lem.

Chubs nodded. They understood each other.

Lem excused the men and stayed behind in the conference room, standing at the window. Soon the canvas of stars in front of him rotated slightly as the ship changed course. There would be a fight at Kleopatra, Lem knew. Or a slaughter, more likely. Lem didn't believe he could have saved all of the ships, but he was certain he could have saved a few. It would have been a simple matter of convincing them to flee—which wouldn't have been that tough of an argument to make, really. Instead, he was cutting them loose and running away, just as he done to Podolski and El Cavador and his own men.

I am your puppet, Father. Even when you're billions of klicks away.

He realized then that there was no one on the ship he could trust. In fact, as long as he worked for Father, he could never trust anyone else under Father's employ. Father would go to any length and use any person to keep Lem under his control. Ah, Father. Such irony. You probably actually think you're being a loving, protective parent.

Lem looked at his reflection in the glass and straightened his jacket.

This is war, Father. I will never be free of you as long as you own this company and I am under your employ. I am done playing your little life lessons. It's time I taught you a few of my own.

CHAPTER 24

Data Cube

By now, Victor was convinced that everyone in the rehabilitation center thought he was insane. The nurses and orderlies all treated him kindly, but the moment he started talking about hormigas and aliens and the interference in space, they all put on that false smile that said, "Yes, yes. I'm listening to every word you say, Vico, and I *believe* you." Which was a lie. If they believed him, they would *do* something. They would give him back his belongings and send him to someone who could help: a government official, the press, the military, anyone who would take him seriously and help him get a warning to Earth. Instead, the staff all nodded and smiled and treated him like a head case as they wheeled him to his various physical therapy sessions and shot him with meds that were supposed to help rebuild muscle mass.

So when they told him someone from the Lunar Trade Department was coming to speak with him about his case, Victor allowed himself to hope. Finally. Someone with some authority who can actually help.

Then they wheeled him into the room where the woman was waiting, and all of Victor's hope went right out the window. She was way too young. Not much older than him, probably. Either an intern or barely out of college. A nobody in the professional sense.

"Hello, Victor. I'm Imala Bootstamp."

"Who's your boss?" Victor asked.

The question caught her off guard. "My boss?"

"The person you report to. Your superior. It's a simple question."

"Why is that relevant?"

"It's absolutely relevant because that is the person I need to be talking to. Actually, I need to be speaking to your boss's boss's boss's boss. But since you probably don't have access to that person, I'll start with your boss and we'll work our way up."

She smiled, sat back in her chair, and looked around her. "This seems like a nice facility. They're taking good care of you?"

"The bed is comfortable, but I'm a prisoner. The two kind of cancel each other out."

She nodded. "Seems clean at least."

They were sitting alone in a stark white room with a glass wall and ceiling, affording them a view of the city and the ship traffic high overhead.

"Haven't you been here before?" asked Victor "You work with the LTD. You're a caseworker. All injured immigrants come here. Are you telling me you've never actually done this job before?"

"Let's say I'm new," she said.

He could tell he was annoying her. He didn't care.

"Incidentally," Victor said, "do you actually know who your boss is? Because you seemed rather unsure when I asked a second ago."

"I thought I was supposed to be the one asking the questions."

"Are you unsure of that, too?"

She forced a smile. "All right, Victor. If we're going to be perfectly honest with each other, no, I don't know who my boss is. I got this assignment about twenty minutes ago from someone who doesn't even work in Customs. So he's technically not my boss. I haven't even been to the Customs offices yet. I came directly here from my previous job. So I don't even have a computer terminal or a desk or a mail account yet. If the door was locked, I couldn't get in the building because I don't yet have an access ring. Fair enough? That's my résumé."

"Wow," said Victor. "I can't tell you how much confidence that instills in me to know that my assigned caseworker, the person responsible for getting me out of here, is so deeply experienced in the field. Boy am I going to sleep well tonight."

"You're welcome to file an appeal and request a new caseworker, but you should know that there's a three-week turnaround. Don't expect a new person to walk in here tomorrow."

He leaned forward. "Look, Ms. Bootstamp—"

"Call me Imala."

"Fine. Imala. I'm sure you're a nice person. And I'm not normally a jerk, but you are not the answer to my problem. You are so far removed from the answer to my problem that you and I shouldn't even be talking. I wish you well in your new job, but the best way for you to help me is to find out who your boss is and to bring me that person. Make sense?"

She was quiet a moment. Then she smiled again. "You broke the law, Victor. Maybe that hasn't been explained to you clearly enough, but you entered lunar gravity in a manned spacecraft without clearance or authorization. A rather serious offense. You also illegally disrupted a government flight-control frequency. Another serious offense."

"I didn't know it was a restricted frequency. I was trying to—"

"I'm not finished," she said. "You also have no passport, no birth certificate, no proof of identity, no right whatsoever to be on this moon. You may have broken these laws in ignorance, but the law doesn't care. My job is to review the law with you and hear your case to see if your situation warrants legal leniency based on extenuating circumstances beyond your control. These are defined as potential loss of life and potential property damage of a 'significant' value. You may not like the fact that I'm new and inexperienced. But I am the person assigned to your case. This is my job and I'm going to do it. Now, you obviously think I'm stupid. And apparently you have no social skills because you're unable to *conceal* the fact that you think I'm stupid. But here's the thing, I'm not actually stupid. I know how this world works. You don't. I know trade and customs law. You don't. I know what's necessary to get you freed. You don't. So you can make demands until you're purple in the face, but you will never see anyone above me until I say so. And right now I don't say so. As far as I'm concerned, you have two options: You can submit to my questions and possibly let me help you. Or you can sit in your room until your grace period expires and the judge plops you on a shuttle back to wherever it was you came from. Your choice. When I come back tomorrow, you can give me your answer."

She got up. And without waiting for him to respond, she was out the door and gone.

Great, thought Victor. It's not enough that I have a nobody. She has to be a snooty nobody. He sighed. He wasn't helping the situation. And now another precious day was wasted.

He was waiting for her the following day in the same room.

"I obviously can't go above you without going through you," said Victor. "So let's do this your way. And let me preface this by saying, everything I am about to tell you can be proven. I have evidence. It's all on my data cube, which the staff locked away with all my other belongings when I got here. Should you want more evidence, I can tell you exactly where to look to verify its veracity for yourself. Fair enough?"

"Works for me," said Imala.

"You've heard about the interference in space scrambling all transmissions?"

"Every day on the news."

"Well, I know what's causing that interference. And if you can get my data cube, I'll show you."

She was gone for ten minutes. When she returned she had a clear bag with all of Victor's personal items. He took out the data cube, placed it on the table, and turned it on, creating a holospace in the air above it.

"The interference is being caused by a near-lightspeed alien starship on a direct course to Earth."

"An alien ship?"

"That's right."

"Coming to Earth?"

"That's what I said."

"I see."

"I know that sounds insane to you. I know you think *I'm* insane. But my family put me on a quickship from the Kuiper Belt. Eight billion klicks from here. I was on that ship for nearly eight months. There was a very good chance that I wouldn't make it to Luna alive. And if you know anything about free-miner families, you know we simply don't do that. We protect our own. Family first. And if you *don't* know anything about free miners, then why do you have this job?"

"I didn't say you were insane."

"You didn't have to. It was written all over your face. And frankly I can't afford that. I need you to have an open mind and look at this evidence without having dismissed it beforehand. I don't care what you think of me. I only care that the information I have gets to everyone on Luna and Earth. That won't happen if we do this with you trying to disprove it."

"I told you I would listen, Victor."

"Listening isn't enough. You need to have an open mind. If you play bureaucrat and worry about how this will affect your standing with that new boss of yours, you'll only find excuses to bury it."

"Remember, I'm not stupid," said Imala. "I will keep an open mind. You're simply going to have to trust me."

He didn't want to trust her. He wanted to trust the person five or six steps up the org chart, but what choice did he have.

He showed her everything: the charts, the trajectory, wreckage from the Italians, video of him and Father and Toron attacking the pod, the hormigas fiercely fighting back, Toron's death, interviews with the surviving Italians recounting the pod attacking their ships. There was even footage of Victor modifying the quickship and launching it toward Luna. It took nearly two hours to go over it all, and Imala sat in silence the whole time. When Victor finished, Imala remained quiet for a few moments.

"Play back the part where we see the aliens," she said.

Victor found the spot and played it.

"Stop right there," said Imala.

Victor freeze-framed on the hormiga's face.

Imala stared at it for a full two minutes. Finally she looked at Victor. "Is this a hoax?"

"Yes, it's big elaborate hoax, Imala. I went out and invented a near-lightspeed ship just so I could prank you."

"I'm asking, Victor, because it looks completely real to me. Not just the alien, but everything. All the data. The math. The sky scans. It looks authentic, and I believe it."

"You do?"

"Completely. But if this *is* a hoax then you need to tell me now because I am prepared to help you as much as I can. And if I help you, and this turns out not to be real, I will lose my job, and you and I will go to prison for a very long time."

"It's real. If you can get access to a scope powerful enough to see out to that far, you can see it for yourself."

She shook her head. "That will take too long. The only scopes that powerful on Luna belong to Ukko Jukes. And believe me, he won't help us."

"So you'll take this to your boss?"

"Of course I'll take it to my boss. I have to. That's my job. But not the original data cube. I want that to stay with you. I'll take a copy. Today. Right after I leave here. But that can't be *all* we do, Victor. I'm not putting the fate of the world into the hands of a few bureaucrats in Lunar Customs. I don't know those people, and even if I did I wouldn't trust them with something like this. Sad recent experiences have taught me never to trust the people above me. So we'll follow the proper channels, yes. We'll start the ball rolling that way. But we also do our own thing. We get the word out our way. Now. Immediately."

"How? We go to the press?"

"No. Not fast enough. The world isn't watching the Lunar news. I mean right now, Victor. We upload this video of the alien onto the nets. Right now. We get people all over the world watching this video within the hour."

"How do we do that?"

She took her holopad from her pouch, set it on the table, and copied the video from Victor's data cube to her own holospace. Using her stylus, she selected a section of video featuring the alien attacking Victor and his Father and Toron on the pod and set it aside. Then she selected other bits of video to follow. The interior of the Formic pod. The wreckage of the Italian ships. Select, frightening accounts from the Italian survivors. She then created several frames with additional information, including coordinates, trajectory, and other data from Edimar. When she finished, she played it back. It was just over five minutes long.

"We can't make it too long," she said. "Or people won't watch it."

"It's good," said Victor. "It's just the right length."

She was moving her stylus in the holospace, bringing up several different windows. "There are about twenty major sites we can upload this to. They all get a lot of traffic. Other sites will see it and pick it up. It'll go viral."

"How quickly?"

"No telling. My guess is very fast. Once it gets momentum, it will explode. You want to tell the whole world aliens are coming? Here's your chance." She handed him the stylus. The windows in the holospace were all selected. Twenty vid sites on the nets. A large green button in the center of the holo was marked "send." All he had to do was touch it.

He thought of Father and Mother and Concepción and Mono and everyone back on El Cavador praying for him to reach this moment. This is what he had come for and nearly died for. This is what Toron *had* died for. He thought of Janda. He thought of her hand atop his, holding the stylus, too. He thought of the twelve billion people on Earth who were in for the wake-up call of their lives.

"This better work," said Victor. Then he reached out and pushed the button.

AFTERWORD

The story in this novel didn't begin as a novel. It began as backstory to *Ender's Game,* which was first published as a novelette in August 1977, and then later as a full-length novel in 1985. Backstory, by its definition, is everything that happened in the world of the story before the story begins. It's easy to ignore backstory. It's in the past, after all. Yet in the case of *Ender's Game,* I'd argue that without the richly imaginative history that Scott Card gave his universe, the premise of *Ender's Game* would have failed.

Consider how the novel begins. Here you have this six-year-old kid with a medical device on the back of his neck—likely connected to his brain stem—that monitors his every action, thought, and conversation, all to determine if he has what it takes to be the next great military commander. It begs the question: What happened to the human race that led us to allow such an invasion of personal privacy or, for that matter, the use of innocent children for war? The answer, of course, is the Formics. Scott Card created a history for the world filled with alien invasions and do-or-die heroics in which the human race was nearly wiped out. In other words, he created a history on which the circumstances of Ender's story could exist. And yet he only gave us as much of that history as we needed to know. We knew that the two conflicts were called the First and Second Formic Wars, and we heard whispers of pivotal events, such as the Battle of the Belt or "the scouring of China," but the specifics of those wars and events were largely unexplained. Instead, Scott kept our eyes and hearts laser-focused on the story he was telling, the story of Ender Wiggin.

Flash ahead to 2009. Marvel Comics has just published a ten-issue adaptation of *Ender's Game* and a ten-issue adaptation of *Ender's Shadow*. The response from critics and fans was overwhelmingly positive, and the praise was well deserved. The comics were beautifully drawn and extremely well written. Credit goes to Marvel, who showed their respect for and love of the original material by staying faithful to Scott's original stories and by hiring some of the most talented creators in comics today to bring the stories to life. (Christopher Yost, Pasqual Ferry, Mike Carey, Sebastian Fiumara, Frank D'Armata, Giulia Brusco, Jim Cheung, Jake Black, and others.)

Marvel wanted to do more and assembled a team to adapt *Speaker for the Dead* and *Ender in Exile*—both as limited-issue series. In addition, Marvel produced a few one-shot comics in the Ender universe as well. (One shots are stand-alone issues not part of an ongoing or limited series.) One such comic adapted Scott's short story *Mazer in Prison*. Another told how Peter and Valentine initiated and then stopped the League War. Another told a completely original Valentine story. In short, the world of Ender Wiggin was thriving in comics.

But Marvel wasn't finished. They wanted to do more. And it was here that Scott Card made the proposition that would eventually result in the book you're holding now. Scott essentially asked, "What if, instead of another adaptation, Marvel does an original series in the Ender universe? What if we told the story of the first two Formic wars? Why not bring all the backstory from *Ender's Game* to life, with a completely new cast of characters?"

Marvel said yes, and Scott and I agreed to write the series. I had been working with Marvel adapting *Speaker for the Dead* and *Ender in Exile* and writing a few one-shots. Scott had comic experience as well, having written *Ultimate Iron Man* for Marvel some years before. It wasn't the first time Scott and I had worked as a team, either. We had collaborated on the novel *Invasive Procedures* and on a limited-issue comic series for EA Comics based on the award-winning video game *Dragon Age*.

While Marvel began assembling an art team, Scott and I began to develop the story. *Ender's Game* had been on Scott's mind for over thirty years, so many of those early story sessions consisted of Scott sharing what had been stewing in his brain all those years and me furiously taking notes. The early conversations were primarily focused on world-building. Scott had given a lot of thought to the concept of asteroid mining and how the whole industry would work. What was the science of it all? How do the miners get the metals back to Earth? What economic infrastructure must exist to make survival in the Deep possible? Would miners work exclusively in the Asteroid Belt, or would some miners venture farther out? Were there only corporations doing the work or was there room in the economy for independent mining families and clans? And if so, what is the relationship between free miners and corporate? And how do miner families marry and prosper? How do they mix up their gene pool and exist in such an empty and isolated environment?

And what about the military? Scott and I knew that Mazer Rackham had to play a pivotal role in this story. Where was he trained? And more importantly, who trained him? Who showed Mazer how to command?

Once Scott and I had a basic framework of the world, we began populating it with characters. We knew from the get-go that we weren't writing *Ender's Game*. This wouldn't be the story of a single hero; it would be the story of many.

The challenge was, we were writing a comic book. And comic books, in case you've never counted, are generally twenty-two pages long. You can only squeeze so many panels of art onto a page, and the more dialogue you write, the more art you cover up. So it's best to be extremely economical with words. Some of the ideas and characters that Scott and I were developing simply wouldn't fit in the comics.

Around this time Marvel introduced Scott and me to the art of Giancarlo Caracuzzo, who blew us away with his environments and characters and style. The immensely talented Jim Charalampidis joined as colorist, and in no time, beautifully vibrant pages of the comic began popping up in our inboxes.

Creating comics is much like filmmaking in that's it a highly collaborative process. Ideas can come from anywhere, and the contributions of each individual shape the outcome for everyone. The character of Victor Delgado, for example, will always exist in my head exactly as Giancarlo drew him. And the muted earth tones that Jim gave El Cavador are the colors I see whenever I think of the ship.

There were other people involved in the comics, of course, but the person who deserves the most credit and a lifelong standing ovation is Jordan D. White, our editor at Marvel, who had a hand in every aspect of the comics and who may be the nicest person working in the industry today. (You should follow him on Twitter at @cracksh0t. That's a zero, not the letter O.)

Additional thanks go to Jake Black, Billy Tan, Guru-eFX, Cory Petit, Jenny Frison, Salvador Larroca, Aron Lusen, Bryan Hitch, Paul Monts, Arune Singh, John Paretti, Joe Quesada, and everyone else at Marvel.

As Scott and I continued to develop the stories for each issue, we continued to create story elements that simply wouldn't fit in the comics. To give you a sense of what I mean, this novel only includes the story contained in the first three issues of the comics. And not even the complete story of those issues; there are bits of issues two and three that won't exist in novel form until a subsequent book.

So Scott and I had to make some concessions and exclude people and events from the comics that we knew would only exist in the novels. If you've read the comics as well as this book, you've likely noticed some of the changes. Scott and I think of it this way: The comics are an adaptation of the novels even though the comics existed before the novels. Or perhaps it might be more accurate to say: The comics are an expansion of the backstory of *Ender's Game* and an adaptation of the novels that followed them. Hmm. Think about that too much and you might get dizzy. Of course, this practice of evolving a story is nothing new to the Ender universe. Remember, *Ender's Game* began as a novelette.

As for this novel, thanks goes to everyone at Tor, especially our editor, Beth Meacham, whose wise counsel was critical in bringing the novel to life. Additional thanks go to Kathleen Bellamy, Kristine Card, and my wife, Lauren Johnston, for their careful reading of the manuscript and constant encouragement. Thanks also to the children still living in the Card and Johnston homes, for their patience as Scott and I closed ourselves in our respective offices to make this novel happen. Thank you, Zina, Luke, Jake, Layne, and little Meg. We couldn't have done it without you.